MARK COOPER VERSUS AMERICA

PRESCOTT COLLEGE #1

J.A. ROCK

LISA HENRY

CROCOBEAR PRESS

Mark Cooper Versus America (Prescott College #1)

J.A.: To Blake. The sunshine of my life.

Lisa: To Blake. The wind beneath my wings.

CHAPTER 1

R ush week.

Deacon hated it. Working at a bar this close to campus meant that sooner or later some little asshole with a fake ID would saunter up to the bar, trying his best to look casual, and attempt to order a shitload of beers for his buddies—who would be clustered around a table in the darkest corner they could find, also trying to look casual.

Except this guy didn't look casual.

He looked pissed.

He narrowed his eyes at Deacon like Deacon had already personally offended him. Okay, Deacon wasn't one of those now-tell-me-all-your-problems bartenders who existed mostly on TV, but he wasn't used to copping hostile stares like this one. Not this early in the afternoon.

The guy, all five feet eight of him, strode up to the bar, slapped down an ID, and issued a challenging look that fell just short of belligerent. "Can I get a beer?"

Deacon looked at the ID. Mark Cooper. An out-of-town address, but that accent was from farther away than

Bedford. And then he saw the date of birth. Most useless fake ID ever. He slid the ID back to the guy. "Sorry."

"No, look." The guy's forehead creased with a frown. He shoved the ID back. "It's my birthday today."

"Happy birthday," Deacon said. "Come back in three years, and I'll buy you a beer myself."

"Un-fucking-believable," Mark muttered. "In a country where they let embryos drive cars, I have to wait until I'm twenty-one to buy alcohol. What sort of place lets you drive and vote and fuck before it lets you drink a beer?" He glared at Deacon accusingly. "Well?"

Angry little bunny was angry. Deacon folded his arms over his chest and looked back at him. Couldn't help the smile that turned up the corner of his mouth. "Um...happy birthday and welcome to the United States?"

"Fine," Mark said. "Can I buy cigarettes, or do I have to be exactly thirty-eight and a half?"

Deacon ignored the sarcasm. "Sure."

"Can I get a pack of Winfield Blue?"

"There's a gas station down the street."

"I can't get cigarettes in a bar?"

Deacon shook his head. "You can smoke 'em here, though. Be glad for that."

Mark sighed. "Seriously unbelievable." He headed for the door.

Deacon watched him. Nice ass, clad in expensive jeans. A T-shirt that rode up and showed a band of flesh as he dropped a coin and bent to retrieve it. And a pair of shoulders squared rigidly as he shoved his money back in his pocket.

Angry little bunny was *very* angry.

Deacon wiped down the bar. He looked up when he heard Mark's phone ring, blaring out some song Deacon didn't know. Mark stopped a couple of feet from the door, next to the pinball machine, and answered.

"Hi, Mum." He angled himself toward the corner. "Can I call you back later? I'm pretty busy." He dragged the toe of his sneaker across the worn carpet. "Yeah, I got it. Thanks. Yeah, Jackson's been good. He's throwing me a party. Yes, right now."

Liar. Deacon felt a stab of sympathy for the kid.

"It's fun, yeah." In the dancing lights of the pinball machine, his expression was suddenly achingly wistful. "Okay, I'll talk to you later. 'Bye, Mum." His shoulders slumped as he shoved the phone back into his jeans.

"Hey, Mark."

The kid turned.

"Let me buy you a Coke for your birthday," Deacon said.

He saw the moment the refusal was on the kid's lips, but then Mark shrugged and came back and sat at the bar. "Thanks."

Deacon put the Coke on the bar, then reached behind the register and found Bill's pack of Newports. Figured Bill wouldn't mind. Flipped it open and held it out to Mark. Mark withdrew a cigarette, looking slightly less angry. "Thanks," he said again.

Deacon took out his lighter and offered Mark the flame. Mark leaned forward, the cigarette dangling from his lips, his chin inches from Deacon's hand. Then he pulled back, the tip of the cigarette glowing.

"So how come you're not partying with Jackson?"

Mark blew out smoke. "You really want to know?"

"Sure."

Mark stabbed at the ice in his drink with his finger. "Because he's my stepfather's nephew, and I've met him

twice, and he doesn't want to look out for me just because
Jim said he had to."

Deacon slid an ashtray next to the glass. "You don't have
any other friends?"

"Plenty," Mark said. "They're just all at home."

Home. He said the word like it hurt.

"It's hard when you first start at college," Deacon said.
"But it gets easier, once you put yourself out there and meet
people."

"I'm supposed to be rushing this week," Mark said. "I
don't even know what the fuck that is."

Deacon laughed. "Then why are you doing it?"

"It's Jim's old fraternity," Mark said. "Alpha Delta Phi. It's
a *tradition.*" Air quotes. "Jackson says I'll for sure get a bid on
account of him being in the frat, and Jim, but I dunno.
Wouldn't some prick trying to get in on his family name just
make you *not* wanna take him?"

"Worked for George W. Bush, didn't it?"

Mark snorted. "I don't care if I get in or not. Jim's not my
real family—and I don't mean that in a whiny-little-kid way.
Just, it's true. But Mum says I ought to give it a go, as a kind
of peace offering to Jim. I guess I haven't been great to him
lately."

"So, where are you from, Mark Cooper?"

"Australia."

"I guessed that." Deacon poured himself a Coke as well.
"Where in Australia?"

"Place called Bundaberg," Mark said. "It's famous for its
rum, which is another fucking thing you can't get here." He
grimaced. "It's not like I miss it, you know, but I miss my
mates. I'm not usually... This isn't how I imagined my eighteenth, I mean."

"How did you imagine it?"

"We'd go surfing in the morning at Bargara," Mark said. "Me and Baz and Richo. I had the best board—a Rip Curl DHD Pistol Whip." He frowned. "Jim got it for me when he started going out with my mum. I gave it to Baz when I left."

"You probably wouldn't get much use out of it around here," Deacon said.

"No, I wouldn't." Mark showed him a rueful smile.

"Good skiing here, though. And snow tubing."

"Snow tubing?"

"Yeah. You get on a big inner tube, and you slide down a snow-covered mountain."

"I hate snow."

Deacon grinned. "It's not so bad. Hope you have tire chains. Or do you have a car?"

"Not me. Not here. Jim's letting me drive one of his around town." He wrinkled his nose. "I'm not driving in snow, though. No fucking way. You ever see those World's Craziest Drivers? It's *always* snow."

Deacon raised his eyebrows. "Not always, surely. Anyway, who hates snow?"

"Always," Mark said. "And snow, God! We moved here in February, and it was supposed to be all nice and Christmas-cardy, you know? Instead we got that massive fucking blizzard, so I was stuck inside for a week with Mum and Jim, and no power. And then when it finally cleared or melted enough or whatever it does, I went for a walk into town to check the place out, and—" He shivered at the memory. "So there I was in, like, twenty-six layers of clothing, somehow still soaking wet, and my balls were screaming and trying to climb back inside my body."

Deacon laughed, the sound filling the near-empty bar.

"Don't laugh," Mark said, fighting his own smile. "Mate,

I nearly *died*!" Then, losing the battle, he flashed a grin at Deacon. "Fuck my life, right?"

"Sucks to be you," Deacon agreed.

Angry little bunny had needed to vent. And maybe just needed someone to talk to on his birthday to take his mind off his homesickness. Laughing at his own misfortune seemed to be a step in the right direction.

"You want another Coke?"

"Sure." Mark looked down at his glass like he was surprised to find it empty. "My shout this time." He pulled his wallet out of his pocket and set it on the bar, as though he was settling in for a while.

Deacon didn't mind that. The place was empty except for a couple over at one of the corner tables who'd been sitting on a pitcher of beer for ages now, and Bill, who was a part owner in the bar and usually just helped himself anyway. Tuesday afternoons were hardly pumping, and it wasn't every day that someone as cute as Mark Cooper brightened the place up.

Scruffy light brown hair with sun-bleached twists, hazel eyes framed by dark lashes, and a smattering of freckles across the bridge of his nose. A crooked grin, when he showed it, that was utterly free of artifice.

"My advice?" Deacon said, setting the second Coke on the counter. "Don't rush Alpha Delt if you're not really into the idea of fraternity life. They're, like, in it to win it."

"What do you mean?"

"They're the frat boys you see in movies. Parties, girls, Hell Week, the whole deal."

Mark furrowed his brow. "What's Hell Week?"

Deacon braced himself on the bar. "Seriously? You have no idea what you're getting into, do you?"

Mark stared at him, long enough that Deacon's stomach

fluttered. Then Mark's phone rang, a different ringtone this time, and Mark's gaze snapped down as he fished in his pocket.

"Jackson," he said, looking at the screen. "He's gonna meet me here and take me back to the house for some rush thing. The fuck is frozen-turkey bowling?"

"Just what it sounds like."

Mark set his cigarette in the ashtray and began typing. "I don't know what it sounds like."

"It sounds like it'll involve a Slip 'N' Slide, Crisco, ten two-liter-size bottles of pop, and a frozen turkey."

"Great," Mark muttered, finishing the text and putting away the phone.

Deacon took in Mark's jeans and shabby T-shirt. "No offense, but you're not exactly dressed for rush week, are you?"

Mark took a long sip of Coke. "I said I'd rush to make Jim happy. Didn't say I'd put any effort into it." Another sip. "God, have you *seen* all the wankers in polos?"

"I'm told girls can't resist a man in a polo. Especially with the collar popped."

Mark barked out a laugh. "Not really the girls I'm here for, mate."

Deacon tried not to feel too hopeful. Mark could just mean he was here to study. Speaking of which...

"What are you studying?" he asked and immediately regretted it when Mark rolled his eyes. "Sorry, you must've heard that a million times during orientation."

"It's all right. I haven't decided yet. Just signed up for some required courses now. Maybe biology?"

Deacon laughed.

"What? Is it called something else here?"

"No. Just trying to imagine an Alpha Delt bio major."

"Okay, look, all I know about Alpha Delt is Jim liked it, and it's, like, they do community service or something. So maybe it looks good on job applications."

Oh boy. Secretly-not-so-angry misguided little bunny. "How long ago was Jim at Prescott?"

"Uh...I dunno. He's maybe fifty."

"Okay, well. A lot has changed since then. Alpha Delt used to be pretty service oriented, but now it's a lot of rich kids, foam parties, pig roasts, and date-rape cover-ups. And I'm not just saying that because they're Phi Sig's sworn enemy, all right?"

"Is that...?" Mark trailed off as the door swung open and a tall kid in a dark polo and perfectly pressed khakis walked in.

Jackson Phillips. Deacon had seen him around before, but he'd never put a name to the face. Jackson was one of the less offensive Alpha Delts. Maybe because he didn't look like a bro. He had an expression that managed to be chilly and slightly anxious at the same time. His shoulders stooped a little, and he had a long, thin nose and dark circles under his eyes that were noticeable even in the dim light of the bar.

Jackson nodded at Deacon, and Deacon might have been imagining it, but he thought Jackson's eyes narrowed.

"Hey," Jackson said awkwardly to Mark.

"Hey," Mark said.

"You ready?"

"Uh, yeah. Just lemme pay." He opened his wallet and thumbed through the bills. "All your money is the same color, you know."

"Yep," Deacon agreed.

Mark extracted a ten and slid it across the bar. "It's fucked-up."

"Well," Deacon said, ignoring Jackson's stare, "I'm sure we didn't do it *just* to confuse you."

Mark showed him that crooked grin again. "Okay, then. As long as you're sure."

Jackson frowned at Mark's clothes. "You've got to change."

"I know," Mark said. He glanced at Deacon and popped an imaginary collar on his T-shirt.

Deacon laughed. Jackson looked toward the door.

"See you later," Mark said, pocketing his change.

"Good luck."

Mark made a face. "Thanks, um...?"

"Deacon," Deacon said. "Deacon Holt."

"Thanks, Deacon," Mark said and, squaring his shoulders back into angry-bunny stance, walked with Jackson out of the bar.

————

This was bullshit. Of all the bullshit things that had happened since moving to the States, this was absolutely, without doubt, the most bullshitty. Mark was pretty sure he didn't like any of these guys, and he was pretty sure they didn't like him either.

"Don't name-drop," Jackson told him when they arrived at the house.

"G'day," Mark said in his most belligerently laid-back manner to the first guy who approached. "I'm Mark Cooper. My stepfather is Jim Phillips. He was in Alpha Delta Phi. His company makes castors for office chairs, which doesn't sound exciting, but he's really, really wealthy. He's a good friend of the dean's. Oh, and Jackson's my cousin."

Jackson shot him a disgusted look that was completely worth it.

Before coming to Prescott, Mark had only met Jackson twice. Once at the rehearsal dinner, and once at the wedding. And he was pretty sure Jackson thought he was mentally deficient. Which was okay, because he thought Jackson was a tool.

Jackson grabbed him by the elbow and pulled him away. "What the *fuck*, dude?"

"Oh," Mark said. "You said *don't* name-drop. Sorry." He blinked. "*Dude.*"

He hated the word.

Jackson shook his head and turned away.

Mark made a face at him. He was pissed off, and justifiably. It was his eighteenth birthday, and he was stone-cold sober. But...there was a keg on the table over there. And who cared if he helped himself? He wasn't here to win friends and influence people, though most of the other guys appeared to be trying to do that. Well, good luck to them.

Moments later, beer in hand, Mark looked for Jackson again.

"Hey," someone said. Someone so big and broad that Mark wouldn't have been able to get around him if he tried. "You rushing?"

Was he? Fuck knew. Maybe. First there was rush week, then what? Jackson had said something about the fraternities bidding on who they wanted before the pledging took place. Did he mean actual bids? None of it made sense at all to Mark.

"Dunno," Mark said. All right, so between Jim and Jackson, he'd had the whole process explained to him, but he couldn't have been expected to listen.

The big guy stuck out his hand. "I'm Blake."

"Mark."

"Nice to meet you," Blake said and seemed almost genuine about it. "You play?"

"Play what?" Mark asked.

Blake looked slightly offended. "Football, dude!"

Right. As though he couldn't have possibly been referring to anything else. Although, going on his size alone, it made sense.

"Do you mean soccer, or rugby, or league, or AFL, or that other shit?" Mark asked.

Blake looked confused. So footballers were mostly the same the world over.

"Football," Blake said. "Ya know...football?"

That other shit, then. But given Blake's size, probably not the best guy in the room to insult. "I don't play."

Blake nodded and then stared at the ceiling for a while. "Okay. So, nice to meet you and stuff."

"Yeah, you too," Mark said.

Blake ambled off.

Mark sipped his beer, then glowered at it. American beer was shit. Weak as piss, and about as appealing. But at least he was drinking *something*, right? It was his eighteenth birthday, and he was having a beer. So that was finally going right.

Just not the right beer. And just not with his friends or even his family.

Which was only Mum, really, however much Jim had tried to make himself a part of it.

The worst thing was, Jim was a nice guy. Three years ago when Jim had come into Mark's life as Mum's rich American boyfriend, he was great. He didn't treat Mark like an inconvenience. He played Xbox with him, took an interest in what he had to say, and bought him that Rip Curl DHD Pistol Whip board for his sixteenth birthday.

Then, out of the blue, Jim had finished whatever the hell it was he was doing in Australia—Mark had always been sketchy on the details; Australian office chairs already had castors, thanks very much—and decided to move back to America.

He'd asked Clare to marry him.

She'd said yes.

Now here they all were, and it was fucked-up.

Mark should have stayed at home. Mum would have caved, sooner or later, if Mark had applied a little more pressure. Except he'd seen how much she wanted him with her, and he couldn't bear to break her heart like that. Or his own, probably. It'd been just them for so long, and the thought of not seeing her for months at a time, maybe even years, was too depressing.

But he missed home. He missed his friends. He even missed his surfboard.

What had the guy from the bar said earlier? *You probably wouldn't get much use out of it around here.*

Too right.

Mark wasn't a great surfer—it wasn't his life—but he liked sitting on his board with his legs in the water and the sunlight on his shoulders, waiting for the waves. Couldn't do that anymore.

Fucking Pennsylvania.

Mark had told himself that he'd stick it out until he turned eighteen, and then he'd go back home. But it wasn't that simple. He had bugger-all money and nowhere to stay. He couldn't crash on Baz's couch for the rest of his foreseeable future. And that was what stung the most. In the end, it wasn't Jim and Mum keeping him stuck here; it was his own treacherous sense of... Was it responsibility? Mark hadn't been troubled enough by it in the past to recognize it now, but Baz was offering him a couch, and Jim was offering a fully paid ride to Prescott. And Mark wasn't stupid enough to refuse that. Not by a long shot. He just...he just wished he had been. A little dumber, a little more stubborn, and a lot more selfish, and he could have been at home right now instead of here, at Prescott, doing whatever this was. Rushing.

What the everlasting fuck was *rushing?*

Mark sidled up to a guy leaning against the wall who looked like he didn't know either. "Hey."

The guy looked at him gratefully. "Hey."

"I'm Mark."

"Brandon," the guy said. "Are you rushing?"

The question made Mark think he was late for a bus or something. "Yeah, I suppose so."

Brandon looked at him curiously. "You don't seem too sure."

Mark shrugged. "Mate, I have no idea what I'm doing."

Brandon nodded quickly. "Me neither. But you've got to do it. If you're not in a fraternity, you're nothing, you know?"

Mark raised his eyebrows. Coming from anyone else, he would have shot right back with what he was certain he *did* know, but Brandon seemed to truly believe it. Not in the cocky way that some of these self-entitled wankers were sounding off about it. Not *Alpha Delta or death, dudes!* Brandon was kind of quietly earnest.

"You reckon?"

Brandon nodded. "That's what my dad says."

"Oh." Mark had no idea how to respond to that, only that it seemed the wrong moment to share how fucked-up he thought this entire thing was. And how unnecessarily complicated. Didn't you go to university to take classes, pass exams, and get a degree? Not to stand up in front of a room full of guys and be judged on whether or not you were cool enough to be their friend. Uni was supposed to be about growing up, leaving adolescence behind, not reverting to a form of it that would make a fourteen-year-old girl proud.

Oh, sure. Jim had talked a lot about friendship and camaraderie and responsibility, but this was a popularity contest. No question. Luckily Mark didn't give a fuck what any of these guys thought.

"Well, good luck," he told Brandon.

"Thanks," Brandon said, that same earnest look on his face. His expression slipped toward anxious as Mark watched. "It's *fun*, right?"

No. It was absolutely not fun, and they both knew it.

Mark smiled. "Sure," he said. "It's fun."

Then some guy arrived with the frozen turkeys, and shit got really weird.

———

The Phi Sigma Kappa house was lit up when Deacon got back to campus that evening. The old red-brick mansion was warm and welcoming...and the front lawn was littered with beer cans and toilet paper, even though it wasn't even seven p.m. yet. Deacon shook his head at the mess and scowled at the Alpha Delta house next door. The Alpha Delta house was welcoming as well, if you were the kind of drunken douchenozzle who was into that sort of thing. There was at least one guy passed out on their front lawn already, under a layer of foam, the bass was pumping out of the open doors and windows, and—oh, *classy*—an inflatable sex doll had been lashed to the front stair rails, her arms and legs splayed and a beer can shoved into the exaggerated scarlet O of her mouth.

They were an absolute fucking cliché.

He met Tony at the front door. Tony was premed and had his first-aid kit in hand.

"Is the guy still on their lawn?" Tony asked him.

"Yeah. You know, if you keep cleaning up after them, they'll never learn."

"Sure, and letting some freshman choke on his own vomit will teach them what exactly?" Tony headed out the door.

There were guys inside the Phi Sig living room, rushing. Rushing at a much more sedate pace than was happening over at Alpha Delta. Conversation and board games instead of beer and turkey bowling. Which was staid, and maybe even boring, but Phi Sig wasn't a party fraternity. They took their charter seriously: academic honors, community service, and fostering relationships that would last well past graduation and into their professional lives. And unlike Alpha Delta, they didn't just pay lip service to the antihazing laws.

"None of that shit," James had told Deacon three years ago when he'd thought about rushing. *"Absolutely none!"*

James was the president of the chapter now. Deacon could see him in the living room talking to a couple of the rushees. He had paperwork on the table in front of him explaining the fraternity fees and how Phi Sigma could help them out with low-interest loans if they needed it.

Deacon had needed it, and he wasn't alone. Phi Sigma didn't care about your family's money, only about your academic record and, if they were honest, whether or not you could play Risk for sixteen hours straight. Which was usually as wild as things got at Phi Sigma, although some of their arguments about string theory could get pretty heated.

Deacon headed up the stairs, thinking again of Mark Cooper and wondering what the hell someone interested in biology wanted with Alpha Delta. The only biology those guys were interested in was the sort that was parodied in the blow-up doll on their front steps. Still, Mark would figure out soon enough if he was a good fit for the Delts or not. That was the whole point of rush week.

He wondered again if he should have encouraged Mark to rush Phi Sigma. Hearing Mark talk about rushing Alpha Delt had killed any desire on Deacon's part to mention his own affiliation. Not that he had anything to apologize for, or cared what Mark thought of him.

Mark hadn't known anything about Greek life anyway. Maybe he wasn't going to rush any other fraternities. Maybe he was putting all his eggs in Alpha Delt's vomit-splattered basket, and if he didn't get in, it was probably for the best.

Deacon's room was on the west side of the fraternity house, and he could hear the music blaring from Alpha Delta even through his closed window. During a break between songs, he heard snuffling at his door, then a jingle of tags, getting fainter. Anabelle, a very chill yellow Lab James and Tony had brought to the house last year. Anabelle never wanted much to do with Deacon—she was always looking for James.

Deacon changed out of his work clothes and into something that didn't smell like stale beer and cigarettes. Then, resisting the urge to look out the window and see if he could catch a glimpse of Mark, he headed back downstairs to talk to the rushees.

And kind of hoped, foolishly, that Mark would be standing there.

CHAPTER 2

The headache Mark woke with wasn't terribly impressive, but he wondered if it was a good enough excuse to cut class. Bad news, if this was only the second class meeting and he already wanted to cut.

Rush week had been exhausting. How Brandon had managed to rush half the fraternities on campus was beyond Mark. Just rushing one had been enough of a trial. Hours of parties, interviews with the Alpha Delt pledge trainer—whose name was Rob Stowe, but everyone called him Bengal—and through it all Mark was trying to read the first three chapters in his bio textbook, because he was supposed to have them read by the first class, but the shit was so *boring*.

And all week Brandon had insisted they couldn't drink too much. Parties every night. With *beer*. And Brandon said no, that getting drunk during rush week did *not* make a good impression, that no matter how wild the parties got, rushees were expected to remain in control.

So Mark had gotten shit-faced at the first available opportunity. He'd done it the next night as well at the graffiti party and had written *Alpha Delta can kiss my arse* on the paper-covered wall. Which was pretty dumb, in sober hindsight. Because even the Alpha Delts would be smart enough to spot the smoking gun of his spelling.

Brandon hadn't been there for that, and Mark was glad. He didn't want to admit it, but he sort of hated the idea of disappointing Brandon. He'd met few people in his life who were so...sincere. Brandon had been over at a charades night at Delta Delta Pi or Kappa Kappa Gamma or whatever the fuck. Who could keep them all straight?

Anyway, Mark had ended the week fairly sure he wouldn't be getting a bid, but surprise—the night before classes started, Jackson had turned up at his dorm to formally extend the bid. That had been an awkward-as-fuck conversation. Neither Mark nor Jackson had any inclination to pretend to be happy about the situation. It was only when Brandon called to announce he'd gotten a bid from Alpha— and from about eight other frats, but he was gonna accept Alpha's bid—that Mark was able to muster any semblance of enthusiasm.

At least he'd have a pledge buddy.

He hauled himself out of bed, threw on jeans and a T-shirt—fuck a polo—combed his hair, and headed for campus. His dorm was on North Side, and American lit was on South Side. He didn't have the route down yet. A look at his phone showed Blake had texted him about walking to class together. At one point last week, they'd exchanged numbers because they'd been drunk and had discovered they had American lit together, but Mark was at a loss to remember which night that had been, or which party. The text didn't have much going for it in terms of correct spelling, but Mark got the gist.

It had been sent forty-five minutes ago, so Blake was

likely already on South Side. Blake didn't seem to under-stand what was going on in class any more than Mark did, but he claimed he always showed up to classes on time—otherwise he got reported to the athletic center. Mark, on the other hand, was going to be at least five minutes late.

Mark crossed the street he thought he was supposed to cross. It was a gray day, he was in a lousy mood, and tonight he had to go to Alpha Delt for some pledge introductory activity. He most definitely hadn't read Nathaniel Hawthorne's "Young Goodman Brown" for class today. Seri-ously, how had he gotten stuck in the one class that made you do shit the first week?

Oh, right. His adviser had told him to get his English credits out of the way. And this lit class with this let's-jump-right-into-it professor had been the only one still open. And his adviser had seemed to think it would be a brilliant cultural experience for him to take American lit. Um, yeah. It was a class mostly for sophomores and juniors, but something or other Mark had taken in summer school had made him eligible to sign up. Great. He was the worst student in class short of Blake, and people would think he was some kind of show-off freshman whiz kid.

The problem with a title like *Young Goodman Brown* was that it didn't give him a hint as to what it was about. Apart from the Brown guy. And all Mark got when he thought about Nathaniel Hawthorne was the image of a man in a tricorn hat. Who was probably Ben Franklin anyway. Shit, he didn't even have time to Google it.

He slid into a back-row desk at seven minutes past the hour. Blake was sitting a couple of rows away, his earbuds in, staring blankly at the front of the room, where Professor Heyman had some notes up for "Young Goodman Brown."

Mark took out his notebook and pretended to write. Instead, he doodled.

You didn't know what you had until it was gone, right? Mark estimated 88 percent of the days he'd been in Pennsylvania had been overcast. All right, the summer hadn't been that bad, and Jim swore in the fall when the leaves turned, New England was gorgeous. But Bundaberg was sunny nearly all the time. Plus, *beaches.*

And he'd been close with his mates, but he'd kind of taken them for granted, because they'd been hanging out since they were kids, and Mark had figured they'd always hang out.

Here he had Blake, who was currently nodding in time to his music, which was loud enough that Mark could hear it, tinny and muffled, when Professor Heyman stopped talking. And he had Brandon, who was probably in his dorm right now practicing his shoe-polishing skills so he could give the Alpha Delts free shine-ups tonight. And he had Jackson. Or maybe he didn't have Jackson. Jackson certainly didn't want anything to do with him. He didn't think Jackson hated him, necessarily. They just didn't have a damn thing in common.

Baz and Richo would have laughed their arses off if they could have seen Mark in his rush interviews. Interviews, Jesus—like you were applying for a job or something. All Mark could compare it to was that time he and Baz had built a tree house and made Richo apply for membership of their Super Secret Club. They'd been eight. And the Super Secret Club had lasted right up until the first stiff breeze had knocked the tree house, and Baz, out of the tree. Still, the girls liked his rakish scar.

But Mark had sat through the interview with Bengal —*Bengal?* Tool—and almost managed to keep his sarcasm under control, since Jackson was there too, and the last thing Mark wanted was for Jim to find out how not-seriously he was taking all this.

"So tell me, Mark, why do you want to join a fraternity?"

"We don't actually have frats at home, and—"

Bengal had held up a hand. *"Dude, you never shorten it. Don't call a fraternity a frat. You wouldn't call your country a cunt, would you?"*

And he'd smirked proudly, as though he thought Oscar Wilde might have been applauding from beyond the grave at that display of razor-sharp wit.

"No," Mark had answered. *"Not my country."*

Jackson got it. Mark had felt the full force of his glower, but Bengal, still high on the buzz of his own joke, had missed it.

Mark sighed and glanced up again. *Shit.* Those were a *lot* of notes for what was supposed to be a short story. Wait...Goodman Brown's wife did *what?* And it was an allegory for *what?* The professor had underlined the word *Faith.* Seemed like a good starting point, so Mark wrote it down, between his drawing of Baz falling out of the tree house, and his drawing of Bengal getting savaged by a shark.

And realized, without a doubt, that he was going to fail American lit.

———

Mark figured since he'd been late to class, he ought to shoot to arrive early at the Alpha Delt house for pledge introductions.

As he walked up the steps, he could hear shouting.

The door was ajar, but Mark still knocked.

"Dude, you're fucking *wrong*!" someone yelled. "Get your shit straight. Paterno had no *idea* what was going on."

"You're telling me he worked every fucking day with Sandusky, and he had no idea?" someone shouted back.

There was a chorus of "ohhhhs."

"Joe Pa's not the one who put his dick up those boys' asses, okay? So why are people trying to drag his name through the mud, and—"

"Because he's just as bad! He's covering up for his homo buddy, instead of—"

Mark knocked again, loudly.

There was a scuffling of feet, more muttering and swearing, and then the door swung open to reveal a tall kid who looked like he should have graduated a couple of years ago. It took Mark a second to come up with the name: Chris. Mark had had an interview with him last Thursday. He was lean with broad shoulders, a buzzed head, and a sculpted swath of stubble along his jaw. His blue-gray eyes would have made him sort of pretty if it wasn't for his mouth, which was perpetually slack, as though he'd opened it to say something, then forgotten what.

Mark thought a little wistfully of Deacon Holt. Now there was the whole package. Well, Mark hadn't seen the whole package, but he wouldn't have passed up a chance to. Deacon had a sweet face. Intelligent.

"Hey," Chris said, stupid mouth hanging open.

"Hey." Mark nodded, hands in his jeans pockets. He'd caved and put on a polo before coming. Just so Jackson wouldn't yell at him. "Guess I'm a bit early."

"Come on in." Chris opened the door wide, and Mark stepped reluctantly into the house.

It was a big house. It must have been old, properly old. It had polished hardwood floors, architraves, and picture rails.

But whatever old-worldy colonial style the house had going on in its bones, the effect was ruined by the pyramid of empty beer cans stacked in the foyer, the collection of bras tacked to the walls, and the blow-up doll jammed headfirst into the banister rails.

Maybe that was a rush-week thing, Mark thought. Not that he was a clean-living prude, but come on? These guys weren't only dickheads; they were proud of it.

"Well, the football team's got nothing to do with it," said the first voice from the common room. "I'm not gonna punish them for what some sick fuck did."

"We're having a football argument," Chris said, leading Mark inside. "You root for Penn?"

"Is it compulsory?" Mark asked. "I prefer not to think about football at all when I'm rooting."

Chris looked confused.

"Root means fuck," Mark told him.

"No, it doesn't."

"It does." And Mark was totally, belligerently ready to argue the point like he had on his first day of high school back in Bedford when a girl had said, *"Oh, you have to pick a team to root for!"* and then looked at him strangely when he'd said, *"Is it a team sport here?"*

And of course he knew better. He just enjoyed being stubborn about it. Like walking into Deacon's bar the day of his birthday and asking for a beer, knowing full well he wouldn't get one. Fuck it. He'd had a point to make. What that point was, Mark wasn't sure. To feel righteously indignant, maybe. Well, it hadn't exactly worked out that way. Deacon had been a nice guy, the whole package, and Mark was fairly sure he'd been interested.

Okay, so he hadn't been able to buy a beer on his eighteenth, but he might have been able to get a root out of it if only Jackson hadn't interrupted.

Chris tilted his head. "And who the fuck are you again?"

"Jackson's cousin," Mark said.

"You should learn to speak American, dude," Chris said.

"Murica," Mark said, giving the guy two thumbs up.

Which must have been the secret password, because Chris grinned and slapped him on the back. Apparently nobody was fluent in sarcasm around here.

Mark had arrived early, but not as early as Brandon, who was standing in the common room trying not to look too nervous, and kind of failing miserably.

"Hey," he said to Mark, adjusting his collar.

Mark flashed him a smile and, for the first time in months, didn't wish he was on the other side of the planet. Brandon was nice. A little too earnest and a little too anxious, but he just needed to relax and learn not to give a fuck. And Mark could certainly help him with that.

He practiced not giving a fuck at that very moment, as Jackson wandered up to him.

"At least you dressed properly," Jackson said, and there wasn't so much a sneer behind that as a sigh of relief. Like wearing a polo shirt somehow *mattered.*

"G'day, Jacko," Mark drawled in his best nobody-actually-speaks-like-that accent. "How ya goin'?"

One of the other frat—sorry, *fraternity*—brothers roared with laughter, and Mark suddenly understood how he'd been offered a bid. Somehow these guys liked his obnoxiousness. All this time he'd been trying to offend him, they thought he was exotic and interesting with ways strange and different from their own. Like their personal anthropological specimen. Or, most likely, a trained monkey.

Well, bugger.

"What are you doing?" Brandon asked in an undertone as Jackson shook his head and walked away.

"Being friendly," Mark said.

"You're being a dick," Brandon told him. "On *purpose*."

Because yeah, in a room full of dicks it was important to make the distinction.

"Sorry," Mark said, and almost was. "I just..." He gestured at the room. "This whole *thing*, you know? But I'll behave, promise."

Which was what he'd been saying, more or less, ever since he'd arrived in the States. To his mum, to Jim, and now to Brandon.

"Good," Brandon said in a low voice. "Because I *really* don't want to do this on my own."

The pledging ceremony began ten minutes later. Mark had filled out his recruitment information sheet at the beginning of the week and thought he'd been a pretty good sport about it, listing all his information correctly and handing over the forty-dollar pledge fee with minimal muttering. Forty dollars? Really? He'd also been given a handbook so he could look over the fraternity's rules and regulations. He had been curious to see what sort of rules existed within a group that used an inflatable sex doll as its unofficial mascot.

The rules were boring as shit, it happened.

Whenever a member, alumnus, or undergraduate of Alpha Delta Fraternity violates the oath taken at initiation...blah, blah, blah. Expulsion, suspension, fines, and reprimands. And a whole lot of crap about who was in charge of this cluster-fuck, and the ridiculous titles they gave themselves. Presidents, wardens, heralds—un-fucking-believable. Like it was a serious business.

Which it turned out to be.

Mark was surprised by how quiet everyone got when Chris went up to the podium. The guys who'd been arguing about football had reconciled as soon as the pledges had started to arrive. A couple of the pledges who were whispering and snickering when the ceremony began were quickly reprimanded. An air of solemnity descended, and suddenly the blow-up doll seemed completely out of place.

Chris cleared his throat and began:

"Tonight we welcome the Alpha Delta Phi pledge class for fall semester. Pledges, listen up. We are about to place upon you the pledge pin of our fraternity, which is a token of the high esteem in which you are held by the Prescott Chapter of Alpha Delta Phi." He held up what was presumably a pledge pin. "Our crest is a hawk sitting on a gorse branch, which is a symbol of the ideals which you will find within Alpha Delta Phi—inner strength, intelligence, and high ideals."

Mark basically had to tune out there, because this was too much. He'd spent a week watching his fellow rushees staring down the shirts of sorority girls who'd written "*rush Alpha Delt*" on the tops of their breasts in marker. He'd seen a brother throw up what looked like whole spaghetti all over his own pants. He'd been asked whether he'd go down on a girl who wasn't shaved.

High ideals? No fucking way. That Chris could even say that with a straight face was impressive.

Beside him, Brandon was leaning forward, rocking slightly like a sycophantic congregation member hanging on the preacher's every word.

The rest of the speech went along in that vein—they were here to learn, to grow, to serve the community, and to inspire. They were supposed to search within themselves to find the values that formed the basis of brotherhood.

Mark snorted.

He hadn't meant to do it loudly, but since no one in the room except Chris was making any noise, it carried.

A few of the pledges and brothers turned to look at him. Those who hadn't heard him snort turned to see what everyone else was looking at. Chris stopped talking and looked right at him.

For several seconds, no one said or did anything. Then Bengal stood. "You," he said, pointing at Mark. "Cooper. Mark Cooper."

Mark didn't respond.

"Do you have a problem with something?" Bengal asked.

Mark opened his mouth to tell them this was all bullshit. That they were a bunch of hypocrites, and he sure as fuck wasn't going to wear their hawk on a gorse branch. Then he caught Brandon's stricken expression. Remembered the promise he'd made. Thought about Jim, and how he genuinely wanted things to be okay between them again.

He was glad he couldn't see Jackson's face right now. He would be too tempted to forget about Brandon and Jim and be an arsehole.

"No," he said, trying to keep the sarcasm out of his voice. "Just had something in my throat."

Chris was still staring at him. None of the other brothers cracked a smile.

Where were the *dudes* he'd partied with all week?

"Sorry," he added.

Chris continued with his speech, and Mark tried his best to listen. When Chris was done, Bengal took the podium.

"All right," Bengal said. "That was the official speech. Remember it. Carry it in your hearts. Recite it to yourselves each night before you go to bed. It's important." He glanced around the room, making sure he had everyone's attention.

"What's also important is knowing where you stand. So I got a speech to make to you too."

His gaze fell on Brandon, and Mark half expected Brandon to put his hand to his heart, like Bengal was a rock star who'd just singled him out for a wink or a smile.

"You all think you're the shit," Bengal went on. "You got into Prescott. Wow. Congratu-fucking-lations. You must be a genius. Or your parents have money. Mommy and Daddy probably signed you up for an overpriced meal plan. Maybe they gave you a car to celebrate your graduation from teenage day care—sorry, high school. And maybe your friends wrote in your little yearbook that they all knew you'd be successful and wished you luck. And maybe at fucking freshman orientation, some provost told you it was a big accomplishment to get in here, and you ought to be proud of your achievement." He air quoted "achievement."

"Basically, at some point, someone has said something that made you feel like you're the shit. When in fact you're not *the* shit. You're just *shit*."

A couple of pledges smiled uneasily.

"You're laughing?" Bengal demanded. "Don't laugh. Not unless you want one of my brothers here to piss in that open mouth of yours. You're not the shit. I'm the shit. Chris here, he's the shit. Every single man in this room is better than you boys in every way, because we're older. Because we pledged before you did, and our pledgeship was much harder than your pussy-ass pledgeship is gonna be. Make no mistake, we will ride you until you collapse and have to be shot in the head like a lame racehorse. But know that we had it tougher than you, and we handled it better."

The noise level in the room swelled considerably, so Mark figured it was safe to snap his fingers, point at the podium, and say, "There it is!" He spoke just loudly enough for Brandon to hear. "I knew something was missing from when we partied with these guys last week. It's the poorly articulated megalomania and unearned sense of superiority." He turned to Brandon. "What a relief. I was getting scared they actually cared about high ideals."

"No, no, *shh*," Brandon said, waving his hand like Mark needed to calm the fuck down. "It's all part of the process. You have to—"

"Shut up!" Bengal shouted to the room. He slapped the podium. "Here are the rules for the next two weeks." He held up one finger. "You do whatever we tell you to, no questions asked." He held up two fingers. "No pussy complaints." Three fingers. "We will not provide you with alcohol. You will not procure alcohol from another source and drink it on the premises. Alcohol has to be earned, like the right to eat and the right to bathe and the right to clean up dog shit with your bare hands when the Phi Sigs let their bitch shit on our lawn. Once you put your pin on, your pledgeship begins. So if you can't handle this, get your pussy ass out of here now. But first, listen to rule four."

Bengal waited until his audience was completely silent. "No snitching." He paused. "You hear that? We're gonna make you do a lot of shit these next two weeks that you're not gonna want to do. You tell anyone we made you do it— you tell anyone what I'm telling you right now—we have ways you can't even imagine of making you sorry. You can decide not to pledge. You can pledge and then run away crying after day one like the little mama's boy you are. But you don't tell anyone what goes on here. You got it?"

Mark got it, all right. These guys were a bunch of psychopaths, made even more dangerous by the fact that they didn't have a brain among them. But all the loneliness and resentment from the last few months welled up in him, and he knew this was perfect. He could take whatever these fuckers gave him and find a way to give it back to them tenfold, because he was smarter. They'd end up kicking him out long before he ran crying from them.

Bring it on, douche bags.

Bengal waited, but no one left the room. "All right," he said. "If there are no questions, it's time to recite your pledge."

―――――

Secret pledge was secret.

Mark had dutifully held up his hand, solemnly sworn, and now he was an official pledge of Alpha Delta. Yay. He felt in the pocket of his jeans for his cigarettes and decided it was time to go outside for a smoke.

"Hey, pledge!" Blake yelled at him. "We need groceries!"

"Okay," Mark said and wondered if he was supposed to care.

Then they all started shouting stuff at him, and he realized that not only was he supposed to care, he was supposed to find a grocery store that was still open at this hour, and buy everything they wanted. Which was chips, dips, curly fries, some brand of confectionary he'd never heard of, a cowboy hat, a plush pink kitten, and a blue eraser. There wasn't a shop in town that would stock all those things, which was probably the point. Mark tuned out somewhere around lube and strawberry-flavored condoms. Because if they thought they'd embarrass him by making him ask for that stuff, they were wrong.

And anyway, he wasn't going to spend hours on a scavenger hunt for this bunch of pricks.

"And make sure you're back before midnight!" Chris yelled, laughing.

"Sure," Mark said.

Both Jackson and Brandon looked at him suspiciously.

Mark detoured to the kitchen on his way out and helped himself to a six-pack. He lit a cigarette as soon as he was outside, and decided to walk to the nearest bar off campus and spend a few hours there instead. And if the nearest bar happened to be Deacon Holt's, and if Deacon happened to be working?

Sweet.

CHAPTER 3

"So," Deacon said when Mark Cooper sidled up to the bar. "I see you're pledging."

Mark tapped the badge on his polo. "Apparently."

"Want a Coke?"

"I want something a lot stronger, but I'll settle for that," Mark said.

If Deacon wasn't mistaken, Mark was buzzed already. Not totally, but definitely on his way there. "Shouldn't you be running around naked or something by now?"

Mark grinned at him. "If you like."

Well, that was more than a blip on the old gaydar. That was straight to DEFCON One, and man the battle stations. And there was at least one part of Deacon that was standing to attention. He leaned on the bar. "I meant, surely they've got some stupid, humiliating, and possibly dangerous activity lined up for you back on campus."

"Actually," Mark said, placing his wallet on the bar, "they sent me grocery shopping."

Deacon raised his eyebrows. Mark was unencumbered by groceries of any sort.

"And condom shopping, and fuzzy-pink-cat shopping, and some other shit that I've already forgotten." Mark sipped his Coke and shrugged helplessly. "What can you do, hey?"

"Well, you could go shopping," Deacon suggested.

"Yeah, I'm not going to do that."

Deacon laughed. "Aiming to go down in history as the pledge who flunks out the fastest?"

"Oh, sure," Mark said. "I'm a high achiever." He sighed. "Okay, so maybe I don't want to flunk out straightaway, but I'm not going to bend over and let them fuck me every which way to Sunday for the next however long this takes."

There was another image Deacon didn't need. "You know, Alpha Delta is not exactly the right place to express your individuality."

Mar tugged at the collar of his polo shirt. "I noticed that."

Deacon would have laughed, except he had the feeling that Mark really didn't understand what he'd gotten himself into. He was going to get the shit hazed out of him by those assholes. "Just be careful, okay? They're…bullies."

Actually, a couple of them were sadistic fucks who got off on their own sense of entitlement. And turned their pledges into sadistic fucks who picked up a sense of entitlement somewhere along the way. Because they were rich, popular, and they ruled the campus. Deacon liked to think that in a few years, out in the real world, they'd learn a thing or two, but he suspected guys like that never did. Bullies in school, and bullies in the boardroom, what was the difference?

"I can look after myself," Mark said, sounding offended.

Of course he could. He was an angry little bunny, remember? He was also the kid who'd lied to his mother about the great birthday party his gazillion new friends were throwing him. Angry little bunny, Deacon knew, had a very brittle shell. Not brittle enough that he wouldn't be able to land a couple of good punches if he ever found out about the bunny thing, though.

"I didn't say you couldn't look after yourself," Deacon told him. "I just told you to be careful."

"Okay." Mark didn't look at him for a while. Then, when he did, his gaze was more guarded than it had been. "I can, though."

It was like arguing with a three-year-old.

"I'm sure you can."

Mark lit a cigarette and glowered at the floor.

Deacon busied himself around the place, wiping down the bar, serving a woman who came in, tipping out the ashtrays.

"So," Mark said when Deacon found his way down the back to Mark's end of the bar again.

Deacon reached for his empty glass. "Another one?"

"I actually came here to get laid," Mark said. "Wanna help me out with that?"

Deacon almost dropped the glass. He stared at Mark, wondering if this was part of pledge week now. He could just imagine the Alpha Delts sniggering as they came up with something as outrageous as propositioning a *guy*. But there was no hint of a smirk in Mark's face. Was it possibly a straightforward question? Well, not straight, but sure as hell forward.

"I think maybe you've had too much to drink," he said at last.

"I think maybe I've had just the right amount," Mark countered. He showed Deacon his palms. "If you don't want to, it's no biggie. I just thought you might be interested."

"I might be," Deacon said. "But you've had too much to drink."

Mark mulled that over. Then he grinned. "I'd better have another Coke, then, and sober up before you finish work."

Deacon shook his head, smiled, and thought briefly about telling Mark to leave. Then he rethought that and went and got him another Coke.

————

There'd never been any question for Deacon about going to college. He had a couple of friends who'd opted out, who'd gotten blue-collar jobs or continued waiting tables at the restaurants they'd worked at all through high school. Deacon had been accepted everywhere he'd applied, except Columbia, and he'd chosen Prescott because it was close to home.

He'd never seen college the way some people had—as this thrilling opportunity to be independent, to discover who he really was. He'd felt independent for some time now. And he either had a pretty good handle on who he was, or else he was fine with not knowing.

College was a way to get qualified for the jobs he wanted. It was a way to ensure he'd be financially stable in the future. He hadn't thought too much about parties or getting laid, though some part of him secretly hoped he'd be able to relax when he got away from home.

And then he felt guilty for thinking it.

His older brother, Ben, had joined the military at the beginning of Deacon's junior year of high school. Six months before Deacon had graduated, Ben had gone to Afghanistan. He hadn't been stationed in a danger zone. He'd e-mailed now and then and had IM'd a couple of times through his AKO account. But once Ben had gone, there'd begun a long stretch of awkward, mostly silent scenes between Deacon and his mother.

Deacon didn't have to ask what his mother was thinking about when she ate dinner staring out the sliding glass door into the backyard. The bright red-and-yellow swing set was still out there from when Deacon and Ben were kids—their mother's one concession in her quest to rid her home of anything that wasn't immediately useful or necessary. The neighbor's kids, Mayla and Brody, liked to use it. He didn't have to ask why he sometimes heard his mother up at four a.m. in the kitchen, reorganizing the cupboards or watching TV. She wouldn't have wanted to say it anyway; she was afraid Deacon would tell her she was being irrational.

But she was convinced Ben was going to die.

Growing up, her OCD had almost been a joke. She had a good sense of humor about it and didn't mind Deacon and Ben teasing her about the coat hangers that had to go through the dishwasher before clothes could be hung on them, or the fact that there were two bottles of spray disinfectant under the sink—one you were allowed to touch with dirty hands and one you couldn't touch unless you'd washed first.

It wasn't until Deacon was older that he saw how the germ phobia was only a small part of her disorder. It was the catastrophic thinking that really affected her ability to function. She'd be doing fine, and then suddenly she'd become utterly convinced of some pending disaster. It had scared Deacon as a teenager, because her certainty had made it easy to believe she was right, that something terrible was going to happen. Her fear was infectious. When Deacon spent the night at friends' houses as a kid, it wasn't uncommon to be woken in the dead of night by the friend's mother handing him the phone. His mother would be on the other end. She'd sound slightly breathless, her voice thick like she'd been crying. She'd ask if he was okay. She'd say she needed to hear his voice.

She needed to hear her children's voices regularly. Needed to know they weren't dead or hurt.

Which was what had made Ben's choice to join the army so frustrating. It wasn't like Ben had had military aspirations growing up. He'd simply wanted a way to pay for college because his grades kept him out of the running for most scholarships. Sure, Ben needed to live his own life, make his own choices. But he had to have known that getting sent to Afghanistan would destroy their mother. And Deacon couldn't help but feel like he'd been abandoned to deal with the fallout. To endure those long stretches of nothing but his mother's silent fear and the knowledge that if he tried to tell her how his college applications were going, or what activities he was doing for Senior Week, she'd smile, she'd listen, but her mind would be with Ben, picturing him wounded, dead.

It was better when Deacon's father was home, but that was only for a week here and there since his job had transferred him to Michigan, and Deacon's mother had refused to go. Not refused like they'd argued about it and she'd put her foot down. Refused, like she physically couldn't leave the house she'd lived in most of her adult life. She'd stood at the front door, holding a box she was supposed to be packing in the truck, shaking, and couldn't physically move.

So Deacon had been the last one to leave home, and he'd hated himself for being so relieved to get out. He'd gotten a partial scholarship to Prescott, and the rest of his tuition he paid with what he made tending bar. Before he'd turned twenty-one, he'd worked at the campus bookstore, a royal nightmare. He was a junior now, and he still went home pretty much every other weekend.

And Ben was still gone. Not dead, like their mother feared, but far away, where she couldn't see or talk to him. Sometimes Deacon hated him, and sometimes Deacon envied him.

Deacon had been glad to find it was much easier to get laid in college than it had been in high school. That it was easier to be himself here, and that there was always something going on if he was restless, if he couldn't sleep. If he was sick of the Phi Sig house or of his physics textbook. But in truth, he hadn't done much with his first two years of school except study and work. And play Risk, occasionally.

If Mark wanted help getting laid, then shit, Deacon was happy to help him. Something quick, fun, no strings attached. God, sometimes Deacon ached to hold someone he didn't have to worry about hurting. Plus, taking Mark to bed instead of giving him a lift to Walmart would be helping stick it to the Alpha Delts, which was always rewarding on some level.

Why not? Deacon thought as he wiped down the bar. Mark was chewing the straw of his third Coke and seemed sober enough. At least he'd moved on from pronouncing the Alpha Delts a bunch of shitheaded, hypocritical fuckers and was holding a coherent conversation about his lit class. He was good company, cute as hell, and Deacon wanted to do something with his night that wasn't reading pages 123-148 in *Advanced Theories in Electricity and Magnetism.*

The question was where to do it. The Phi Sig house was too crowded. Deacon shared a room with James and Matt, and they'd both be studying. There was the restroom here, but Deacon had never been one for public-restroom sex. The legacy of his mother's germ phobia, probably. Plus he didn't want to risk getting caught fucking a customer on work property. Mark almost certainly had a roommate at his dorm.

Deacon didn't want to talk himself out of this by throwing out reasons why they shouldn't hook up. Instead he kept Mark's Cokes coming, and between bouts of idle conversation, they both watched the clock tick down. By the time the minute hand was inching up toward the hour—*the big hand is on twelve, the little hand is on eight. What time is it? Time for Deacon to get laid!*—and Bill appeared to take over until closing, Deacon was more than looking forward to getting Mark somewhere private, getting him naked, and getting them both off.

"Another drink, kid?" Bill asked Mark gruffly.

"No, thanks, mate," Mark said, shoving his wallet back in his pocket and flashing a grin at Deacon. "I've got plans."

"Five minutes," Deacon told him and hoisted the trash bag from behind the bar. He'd just dump it out the back in the alley, and—

And Mark was right behind him. And then, somehow, Deacon was pressed against the back wall of the bar, with Mark pushing up against him. Deacon dropped the trash bag, decided to save the talk about personal boundaries and appropriate workplace behavior for later, hooked his fingers through the belt loops in Mark's khakis, and bent to kiss him.

Which Mark somehow dodged, pulling back and dropping to his knees. He gazed up at Deacon, his smile cheeky. He lifted his hands to Deacon's belt. "Want me to blow you?"

Yes. Fuck, yes.

That from the part of Deacon's brain that was currently directly connected to his cock and shouldn't be trusted with life decisions.

"Let's go somewhere," Deacon said.

"We are somewhere," Mark said.

His logic was flawless.

"Fuck," Deacon said, hoping to hell nobody wandered into the alley. Or that Bill wouldn't stick his head out the door. Or that the waiters from the restaurant next door didn't decide to hold one of their randomly scheduled smoke-and-talk-shit-about-the-boss meetings.

Mark tugged at Deacon's belt and began to work on his fly. He'd lost his cheeky smile and replaced it with something more intense. Sheer want and determination. Deacon fixed his gaze on Mark's face, a jolt of arousal pulsing through him when Mark wet his lips with his tongue, and tried not to let his rational brain derail this moment.

Because if they went somewhere else, somewhere with facilities, then he could freshen up. And not just his face. He'd been working for four hours straight, and surely he was getting sweaty down there. Not that it seemed to bother Mark in the least—he pulled Deacon's fly down, then leaned forward, pressed his nose to Deacon's briefs, and inhaled deeply. Which was simultaneously the dirtiest and the hottest thing anyone had ever done to Deacon in his life. Mark was just so...visceral.

Deacon groaned as he felt Mark's hot breath through the fabric. His cock tried its best to find a way out of his underwear, and Mark helped it. He pulled Deacon's underwear down, the elastic snagging on the way, and moved in. One of Mark's hands went straight for Deacon's balls, cupping them. The other one gripped Deacon's cock, angled it, and then it was happening: the most phenomenal blowjob Deacon had ever received.

Eighteen. Shit, the guy was eighteen. Where the hell had he learned to suck cock like this? At eighteen Deacon hadn't even kissed another guy, let alone learned how to cup his balls and tease the skin behind them at the same time.

Deacon struggled to stay upright. "Fuck. Where'd you learn that?"

Mark mumbled something, the vibrations multiplying every already-incredible sensation engulfing Deacon's cock.

Right. Dumb time for conversation.

Mark worked his tongue around the head of Deacon's cock, looked up again, did his best to smile, and then shifted forward and swallowed him.

Oh fuck.

Fuck, fuck, fuck.

The last guy who'd tried to deep throat Deacon had choked, which Deacon could have taken as a compliment, except it hadn't been. The guy had just been more ambitious than experienced. And it was hard to feel good about yourself when your date was vomiting on the floor.

Deacon could have come right then—didn't want to make Mark work too hard, didn't want to linger in the alley too long. But he also wanted this to keep going. Preferably forever, but he'd settle for longer than sixty seconds.

He placed a hand on Mark's shoulder as Mark hollowed his cheeks and sucked *hard*, pulling his lips up the length of Deacon's shaft until they caught on the ridge under the head. Mark tongued his slit, and Deacon squeezed his eyes shut, panting and kneading Mark's shoulder. He moved his hand up, pushing his fingers through Mark's thick hair and rocking gently. Mark hummed again, and suddenly both of Deacon's hands were in Mark's hair, and it was all he could do to keep from thrusting.

Mark pulled off his cock, gripped the base, and licked around the head several times. He flicked the slit again with his tongue, and at the same time pumped with his hand.

"God." Deacon tipped his head back, then snapped it forward as Mark swallowed him again.

It happened too fast—Deacon was pumping cum down Mark's throat, and Mark didn't seem to mind at all. Mark sat back and gulped theatrically, then wiped his mouth and grinned at Deacon. "You've got a nice dick," he said.

Deacon was still panting. "Uh, thanks. You've got a nice... You do a nice... That was really good."

Mark got to his feet. "Thanks."

They stood there for a moment, and then Deacon figured he should probably pull his pants up. He fumbled for the waistband, and Mark stooped to help him. Even after Deacon was zipped, Mark left his hand on the front of Deacon's jeans.

"So, uh, what about your grocery run?" Deacon asked.

Mark shrugged. "Guess they'll just have to go one more night without lube and strawberry-flavored condoms." He reached forward and brushed Deacon's bangs back. His fingers were warm, a little damp, and they smelled like Deacon. Deacon wasn't sure he liked that, but he decided to go with it. He definitely liked Mark touching him. Deacon leaned in hesitantly, and Mark met him, crushing his lips to Deacon's.

"Wish you had gone shopping before you showed up here," Deacon murmured.

"Why?" Mark stroked Deacon's softening cock through the denim.

"If we had lube and a condom, I could offer to let you, uh...to return the favor."

Mark cupped Deacon's face, then dragged his fingers down Deacon's throat. Kissed him again. "You'd let me fuck you? Just as a thank-you?"

"I mean I want you to." Deacon sucked in a breath as

Mark kissed the side of his neck. Mark placed a palm between Deacon's shoulder blades and licked the spot he'd just kissed. Deacon glanced around the alley, sighing as Mark's hair tickled his jaw. "Maybe not here, but..."

Mark laughed, sending a rush of air into Deacon's ear. "I'm all right for now. Better than all right." His voice dropped to a whisper. "But I will..." He nipped the edge of Deacon's ear and tugged. Chuckled again at Deacon's whimper. "Take you up on that. Hopefully soon."

"You're all right?"

Mark ground against him. "Yeah, that was hot."

Deacon caught him by the hips. "You don't want to...?"

Mark's breath was warm against his ear. "Mate, I came too."

Without even touching himself? Holy *shit.*

Mark pulled away and ran a hand through his scruffy hair. "So, thanks for tonight. It was fun." He nodded toward the door. "I need the toilet. Can I go back through there?"

Deacon shook his head. "Not before we exchange phone numbers."

"No worries." Mark smiled and reached into the pocket of his jeans. He took out his phone and carefully typed in Deacon's number as Deacon recited it breathlessly. A second later Deacon felt his phone vibrate in his pocket as Mark sent him a text. "I'll see you around?"

"Yes," Deacon said. *Hell, yes.*

Mark flashed him another smile and headed back inside.

Deacon leaned against the wall.

So, that had happened.

He dug his phone out and checked his messages. There was one from a new number. Mark.

BTW, I also bottom.

Deacon laughed.

————

After cleaning himself as best he could in the bathroom of the bar, Mark headed back to campus. He collected his remaining beers from the bush he'd stashed them behind, and drank them underneath the statue of Prescott College's namesake. Who rode a horse and wore a tricorn hat and was possibly the guy Mark had been thinking of this whole time instead of Nathaniel Hawthorne. Or Ben Franklin. He squinted at the brass plaque but couldn't read it in the dark. Prescott had done something heroic in the Revolutionary War. Personally bitch-slapped George III with the star-spangled banner, maybe. Mark's knowledge of American history was definitely lacking, even after all that summer school. There was no way he'd considered taking it at college.

Mark stacked his empty beer cans around the tarnished hooves of Prescott's horse and headed for the Alpha Delt house. It was almost midnight when he approached, already planning what he was going to say.

I couldn't find any of the stuff, so I gave a bartender a blowjob instead.

That'd have to get him kicked out, right?

Kicked out in glorious, glittery, gay-as-all-fuck disgrace.

And then he'd tell Jim why: *I tried, Jim, but they found out I was gay.*

Insert sad face here.

And maybe then Jim would finally stop trying to make Mark *fit in*. He'd been doing it since they arrived. Encouraging Mark to join sporting teams when he had never even played the games. *"Not sports? Well, how about debate? I know you can argue, Mark. I've heard it!"* Not debate? How about the

AV club? How about the chess club? How about the Model UN? *"They'd probably even let you be Australia."*

Fuck that. Mark didn't want to pretend to be Australia. He wanted to go back there, and sitting around with a bunch of smug kids who knew the GDP of Botswana and what NATO actually stood for wasn't going to help him any, was it?

Jesus. Jim had been more desperate to find Mark friends than Mark had been. As though seeing Mark mope around had been a sign of personal failure for Jim, who'd promised him he'd love it here. Promised him he'd have heaps of friends and have fun and be *happy*. Except the harder Jim tried to push him into doing stuff, the more Mark had resisted. The more he'd been determined to show Jim that he was wrong.

The fraternity thing was just the latest idea out of Jim's *Top One Hundred Ways to Get Mark a Friend or Die Trying*. Copyright Jim, 2013.

Mark was perfectly capable of finding his own mates. Like Brandon. Or like Deacon. Who wasn't a mate exactly, but a blowjob was a pretty good start. Mark wouldn't mind spending more time with Deacon at all. And with Deacon's cock.

Mark smiled as he approached the house.

And the sooner he was out of this pledge bullshit, the more free time he'd have to do that.

He reached the front steps.

"Mark!"

He turned to see Brandon lurking behind the bushes. "Brandon?"

"What did you get?" Brandon brushed leaves off his shirt.

"Um," said Mark. "Nothing?"

"I thought you said you were going to take this seriously." Brandon frowned at him. "You're not even trying, are you?"

"No," Mark said honestly.

Brandon shook his head, turned around, and pulled a plastic bag from the bushes. "Here. Chips, dips, curly fries, and Reese's Pieces." He produced a second bag. "And a pink cat, a blue eraser, condoms, and strawberry lube."

"You remembered all that?" Mark asked, astonished. "And you got it for me?"

"It was like ten things," Brandon said. "Plus, I have an eidetic memory. And I *knew* you'd fuck it up." He grabbed a cowboy hat out of the bushes. "Don't forget this."

Guilt bit at Mark. Brandon was a good guy, and he'd obviously been running all over town while Mark had been at the bar. And for what? So Mark wouldn't get thrown out of the frat. Brandon was a better friend than Mark was. "Thanks," he said and meant it. "Really."

Brandon looked at him worriedly.

"Thanks," Mark said again.

He jammed the cowboy hat on his head, picked up the bags, and walked up the steps. With any luck, it would piss Jackson off no end that Mark hadn't failed. Mark was prepared to settle for that, for Brandon's sake.

He was just making friends all over the shop, wasn't he?

Jim would be proud.

CHAPTER 4

Mark looked at the quiz score. A 65. He still had to think for a second about what the hell that was in American grades. Because in Australia, it wasn't half-bad. But here it was, if not failing, close to it.

He tossed his quiz in the bin on the way out the door and yawned as he leaned on the wall outside the classroom, waiting for Blake. Alpha Delt had assigned Blake to be Mark's big, and before Mark had been able to ask big what —adventure? Idea? Pain in the arse?—Chris Wilson had explained all pledges got assigned big brothers. Mark didn't even want to get into how weird that was.

A 65.

Big deal. There were eight of these quizzes throughout the semester, and individually they didn't count for much. He'd do better on the rest of them. Maybe try actually reading the material.

Except when was he going to find time to read with all the pointless tasks he was doing for the Alpha Delts? *"Take a picture of the outside of the chemistry building and send it to Chris Wilson. No, you idiot, there are* two *chemistry buildings—*

go out in the dead of night in your boxers and undershirt and get a picture of the right one. Oh, and put this around your neck." It was a dog collar with I'M AN ALPHA DELTA BITCH written on it. *"Cook three pounds of spaghetti."* What? Didn't they have a chef for that? Turned out they wanted him to eat until he threw up. After his second bowl he'd politely—he thought—declined to have more. So Logan White had shoved his head into the pot and held him there, then eventually let him up, gasping and with his face covered in mushed noodles.

"Go and get us toilet paper." He'd done it. *"Now open it—with your teeth, bitch. And put a roll on the holder. Don't fucking touch it with your hands."*

Bad move refusing that one, because Bengal had tried to shove his head in the toilet. Tried. Mark had elbowed him in the groin, and Bengal had been laid up for about half an hour. Then Mark had been forced to stand on one foot and sing an apology song to Bengal.

He would have laughed in Bengal's face and walked right out of the house, except that he owed Brandon.

Even though Mark would have been fine showing up empty-handed from the "grocery run," he couldn't ignore the fact that Brandon had gone out of his way to make sure Mark didn't fuck up his chances with the Alpha Delts. So Mark was trying to show he was grateful by being on his best—okay, *better*—behavior.

Besides, he didn't want to *walk away* from Alpha Delt. He wanted them to kick him out. Didn't want anyone to be able to say he hadn't had the balls to handle pledging. But if he could prove the brothers didn't have the balls to handle him—that would be something.

It would have been one thing if the brotherhood had kicked him out right away, saying they weren't going to waste time on someone who didn't have the right attitude or whatever. But they'd kept him. Even when he mocked their requests. Even when he nailed Bengal in the balls.

Why?

Could he really be such a novelty?

The pledge who couldn't handle it and ran away was pretty common.

The pledge who obeyed until his body betrayed him and then broke down—also common.

But the pledge who fought back...not so much.

Chris Wilson seemed to like it, at least.

Bengal had been no fan of Mark's after their bathroom scuffle, but he was the pledge trainer, and he took pleasure in breaking pledges.

Maybe he liked a challenge.

The prick.

Mark opened his eyes as a bag knocked against him.

"Sorry," the girl said, lifting it over her shoulder. An attractive girl, serious-looking, with glasses. Her hair pulled back in a messy ponytail. Jeans and a T-shirt.

"No worries," Mark told her.

Her answering smile was hesitant as she moved away, as though she thought he wasn't sincere. As though she thought a frat pledge in a polo and khakis couldn't possibly pass up a chance to say something rude.

He should have made friends like *that*. Well, not that girl specifically, since Mark didn't know her from a bar of soap, but that sort of person. The ones who carried books around and didn't care if they didn't look like they'd stepped out of the pages of a Ralph Lauren catalog before coming to class. The type that hung out at the library and actually talked about what they were supposed to be learning. With a group of friends like that, Mark would never have got a 65 on a quiz, and never got spaghetti stuck up his nose either.

Blake wandered out of the classroom. He beamed when he saw Mark waiting. "Hey, pledge."

Mark grunted at him.

"So you're my bitch for the afternoon," Blake announced.

A couple of other students turned and looked, and Mark sighed. "Apparently."

If he had to be anyone's bitch, he didn't want to be Blake's. Wouldn't mind being Deacon's for a few hours, though. Fucking pledging. He didn't have time to study. He had even less time for hooking up. Apart from a few filthy text messages, he hadn't spoken to Deacon in days. And the filthiness was only on Mark's side. He got the impression from Deacon's carefully neutral responses that Deacon wasn't completely into sexting.

"You can start by coming to practice with me," Blake said and slapped him on the back. Then he wrinkled his nose. "Dude, you're not really my bitch, you know? You're my little brother. I'm gonna look out for you, make sure you make it through pledging."

"Yeah," Mark said, wondering how Blake was supposed to look after anyone. Mark was fairly certain Blake couldn't tie his shoelaces without instructions. But at least he wasn't a prick like Jackson or Bengal or half the other guys at Alpha Delt.

Jackson was Brandon's big brother through the pledge process. And Brandon, for some reason, had seemed delighted by that.

Mark followed Blake to practice.

American football. Seriously. What was that about? Mark hadn't watched enough of it to understand the rules. It seemed to involved lots of shouting of numbers, lots of pointless running and blocking, and enough fucking body armor to sink the *Bismarck*. And why? Most of the guys were already fifteen feet tall and built like brick shit houses.

Mark had played football at home. With nothing but a mouth guard, thanks. He wasn't big enough to be a forward, but he'd made a fairly decent hooker. Not something that he'd mention here. Because, okay, Americans rooted for their teams, but hooker? Even Mark knew how ridiculous that sounded.

When they were nearly to the practice field, Blake cuffed Mark affectionately on the shoulder. "That track over there? You run laps. You run laps until I'm done."

"Uh..." No? "Okay." Mark wasn't in the best shape ever, but he briefly entertained a fantasy where he started running laps every day and wowed Deacon with his hot runner's body the first time Deacon saw Mark naked. Which, if Mark had anything to say about it, would be soon. Like, tonight.

Except there was a party tonight at Alpha Delt. There was a party every night at Alpha Delt. He sighed. He'd figure it out later. Blake cuffed him again. "Go on, pledge. Hit the track." Mark didn't bother to point out that khakis and a polo weren't exactly a practical—or fashionable—running outfit. Had a feeling that was kind of the idea.

Mark started running, occasionally looking over at the field to see what the football players were up to.

They were...prancing. There was no other word for it. They ran back and forth across the field, picking their legs up high. How this country had won a world war was beyond Mark. *How shall we go about becoming the greatest empire on earth? Say, I know. Let's have our manliest sport involve butt-slapping, shoulder pads, and prancing.*

Mark concentrated on running—not too fast; he didn't want to burn out, because he had no idea how long practice might go. But as he thought more about his situation, he ran faster.

This is so stupid. Just tell them you don't want to be an Alpha Delt, and move on with your life. And Jim will understand. He's not a bad guy.

He wasn't a bad guy. Which was precisely what made it so hard to disappoint him. He was friendly and generous, but sometimes that goodwill could be overbearing. Mark was used to a more relaxed relationship with his mum, who kind of let him do his own thing and didn't worry about whether he had friends or an eternal brotherhood. Mark figured Jim felt guilty for uprooting him, and that had something to do with Jim's tour-guide approach to their life in America. If they went grocery shopping and Mark couldn't find something right away, Jim asked what he was looking for—as though it might be some obscure Australian delicacy that Mark would have to be gently told didn't exist in American stores.

Last spring Jim taken them to the Mütter Museum, which was actually pretty cool—wax figures illustrating various pathologies and medical anomalies. But Mark was distracted by his irritation toward Jim, who was determined to make introductions: *Mark, this is America. America, this is Mark. I know you'll get along great, if you give each other a chance.*

Mark was breathing hard now, and suddenly he was thinking about Deacon. Deacon's cock in his mouth—it had been salty with sweat, but so perfect and smooth. The way Deacon had tried not to lose control, had tried not to thrust into Mark's mouth, had braced himself when Mark swallowed him...

Mark glanced at the field. The players were slamming into padded red dummies. *Make that arse-slapping, shoulder pads, prancing, and hurling yourself into inanimate objects. Well done, fellas.*

His legs were tired. He kept sucking in air, but breathing wasn't going so well.

The guidance counselor at his high school had told Mark the first year of college was a confusing time for everyone. But the shit that was bugging him—shouldn't he be over it? New father figure—that was something you freaked out about if you were five or eight or even thirteen, maybe. But once you grew up and got your own life, who cared if your mother married someone new?

He didn't know what to do with his life—big deal. Who did? He was hot for a guy he couldn't see very often—boo hoo. They'd see each other when they saw each other. And then they'd fuck each other. And just the thought of that was gonna give Mark a boner while he was running laps. Great.

Mark needed to stop running, if only for a few seconds. But each time he thought about slowing down, he pictured Blake looking over and seeing him lose this battle. Sometimes the indifferent, I-don't-give-a-shit-what-you-do-to-me angle worked for Mark during pledge activities. But right now he was overcome with a bizarre energy that barreled over his physical exhaustion and lit up his mind. He could handle this. Could handle pledging, could handle Jim, and Jackson, and his mum's perpetually upbeat attitude toward America that always felt like a betrayal. He could handle a fucking 65 on his quiz and Quakers instead of surfers and this goddamn prancing kind of football.

When he came around the track again and looked over, he couldn't see Blake anymore. Granted, the team was a bunch of giant guys in matching gear huddled together, but even when Mark tried to slow down and pick Blake out, he couldn't. He glanced over at the water fountain, but Blake hadn't gone off to get a drink. Mark let his pace drop to a walk. God, his whole body was *shaking*. How long had he been running? He stopped and put his hands on his knees, trying to get the hang of breathing again.

A couple of members of the football team seemed to have noticed Blake's absence. They were shielding their eyes from the sun and looking around. One pointed to the small brick building that housed two Portaloos. Another guy ran over there and banged on the door of one of the stalls. Mark could hear someone on the other side banging back. The football player hauled on the door for a minute; then it popped open, and Blake emerged.

Mark couldn't hear what they were saying, but Blake shook his head, grinning, and the teammate clapped him on the back. They headed to the field.

Seriously?

Had Blake gotten stuck in a Portaloo?

That's my big brother.

He saw Blake look over at the track. And yeah, Mark wasn't running anymore. And yeah, Blake would have to deal with it. Mark felt dizzy and a little sick to his stomach. What he really wanted to do was text Deacon and say something that would get a reaction. Maybe not something dirty. Maybe something...nicer.

Want to have dinner with me?

Where? The dining hall?

And who said Deacon wanted to do shit like have dinner with him? Maybe Deacon only wanted him for a fuck. Mark had never bothered to give him the impression he was interested in anything else. *Was* Mark even interested in anything else?

He didn't fucking know. Maybe he'd fixed on the idea of Deacon because he was hot, he was gay, and he was currently the one guy in Mark's life who wasn't trying to fucking haze him. Still, it would be nice to find out if there was something there.

"Hey, little dude!"

Mark lifted his head and glared at Blake, who was jogging over toward him.

"You okay?"

I'm not the one who got stuck in a toilet. Shame he couldn't actually speak yet. So he continued to glare instead, and gasp for breath, and wait for Blake to tell him he was a useless, weak pussy.

Blake shoved a bottle of water at him, his face full of concern. "Seriously, I meant to tell you to stop a half hour ago, but I got stuck in there."

Mark took the bottle, straightened up, and began to drink.

"Don't drink too much." Blake's eyes widened. "Slow down. Dude, Mark, seriously, don't drink it all at once, or—"

Too late.

The water hit Mark's guts and came right back up again.

He vomited all over Blake's shoes.

———

Deacon knew long before Mark's text that there was a big party at Alpha Delta tonight. Firstly, because it was a day ending in Y. And secondly, because a bunch of delivery guys had already turned up with kegs of beer, tables, and...bales of hay? Fuck, if this was turning into a petting-zoo kegger, then Deacon was calling the dean's office. And the ASPCA. And the cops.

As the day drew on, though, and the only animal that appeared was a mechanical bull, Deacon relaxed. He watched as a bunch of guys erected a marquee on the Alpha Delts' expansive back lawn. From his room, he could see most of the yard, including the pool. Which had seen more action than the hot tub at the Playboy Mansion, Deacon was sure. When the Alpha Delts partied, nobody partied harder. As someone who'd been kept awake too many nights to remember, Deacon could attest to that.

Deacon was studying when Mark's text came through.

Wanna come to a party tonight?

Deacon's first thought was to flat out refuse. No way would he crash an Alpha Delt party, and not just because they were the sworn enemies of Phi Sigma. Because he had *standards*. But then he remembered how lonely Mark had looked on the phone to his mother the first time Deacon had seen him, how he'd lied about his friends throwing him a party, and figured that if Mark needed a friend, Deacon would be an asshole to refuse.

A fraternity party? he sent back.

His phone buzzed a moment later. *You have to come dressed like a cowboy.*

Well, that explained the bales of hay and the mechanical bull.

Are pledges allowed to invite people? he sent back.

Nonfraternity people? He still hadn't let on to Mark he was in Phi Sig. Gay nonfraternity people? Gay nonfraternity people they'd sucked off in alleys? Deacon doubted very much that was the case. The Alpha Delts usually treated their first major party of the year like an NYC nightclub—guest lists, invitations, *bouncers*...

Come as Zorro. Dare you.

Deacon laughed when he read that. Dressing up in a disguise to sneak into a rival fraternity's party? Either Mark had been watching too many dumb college movies, or he really wanted a friend there. Deacon shook his head at his own stupidity as he tapped out a reply.

What time?

Eight, Mark sent back. *I owe you one.*

Actually, if he was keeping tabs, Deacon was fairly certain that he owed Mark one. And he couldn't wait to settle his tab.

I'll see you there.

He closed his textbook and went downstairs to see if there was anyone who could help him out with a Zorro costume.

———

Pledges, it turned out, were exactly like slave labor. While the rest of the fraternity was getting drunk and trying to screw sorority girls, the pledges would be serving drinks. Mark had expected as much and didn't care. Hell, the sooner those arseholes wrote themselves off, the sooner he'd be able to drag Deacon away into a dark corner and do filthy things with him. Mark didn't care at all about what he had to do in the meantime. Not until he turned up at the frat house with the rest of the pledges at seven p.m. and Bengal showed them what they were wearing.

Fuck it. Frilly French-maid outfits, complete with stockings.

A few of the other pledges looked sick. Brandon looked mortified. And Mark really, really wished that he hadn't invited Deacon to the party. *Hey, look at me. I'm wearing a*

French maid's outfit because this bunch of misogynistic homo-phobes thinks that the most humiliating thing you can do to a guy is put him in a skirt and call him a woman. And instead of telling them to fuck off, that if I wanted to wear drag, I'd do it fucking proudly, I'm letting them win.

Bengal leered at Mark as he shoved the costume into his arms.

"I wasn't aware they had French maids in the old west," Mark said, staring right back at him.

"Go and get dressed, pledges," Bengal announced as the brothers laughed and whooped. "And make yourselves look pretty!"

Mark rolled his eyes and followed the other pledges upstairs and into one of the large bathrooms.

"Dude," one of them whispered anxiously. "They can't really do this, can they?"

This. As though everything else had been perfectly sane and rational—the calls at three a.m. to drive drunk Alpha Delt arses all over town, the all-night toilet-scrubbing marathons, being made to run past the sorority houses in their underwear with *free dick* written on their chests in lipstick—but *this* was too much?

Mark pulled his shirt over his head. Bright side? He didn't have to wear a polo.

The guys undressed silently, awkwardly. Mark sat on the edge of the bath and rolled his stockings on the way he'd seen his mother do when he was a kid. Except she'd made it look easy and not immediately put her toe through one. Oh well.

There was also a suspender belt. Mark got that on over the frilly knickers but then couldn't figure out how to attach the little dangly things to the tops of his stockings, until one of the other guys, blushing furiously and muttering under his breath, helped him. The corset thing was tricky too. Suddenly Mark understood why drag queens so often traveled in packs. Because there was no way in hell a guy could get himself into this getup on his own. Still, the obvious gaping space where tits should have gone would give him somewhere to keep his smokes and phone.

There were no shoes, which was a small mercy. Mark jammed his stockinged feet back into his sneakers and stared at himself in the mirror. He didn't look like a girl. He didn't even look like a drag queen. He looked like a guy in a dumb outfit. Masculinity: not undermined at all. Sexuality: no more questionable than before. Not even with the hat.

Mark made a face at himself as the pledges began to file out of the bathroom. He could either try for fabulous, or he could do what he'd promised Brandon and behave himself.

Brandon.

Mark looked around for him. Brandon hadn't filed out like the other guys. He was standing against the wall, looking kind of adorable in his frilly skirt. Except for his visible shaking.

"Hey," Mark said, walking over to him. "You okay?"

Brandon was breathing so hard he had difficulty answering. "I can't...I can't do this." He sounded stricken.

Mark showed him an encouraging smile. "It'll be okay. It's just a stupid outfit."

Brandon shook his head, and Mark saw that his eyes had filled with tears.

Shit.

"It's just clothes," Mark said. "It doesn't *mean* anything, you know?"

"I'm not gay," Brandon said, his voice cracking.

And shit again.

"It's just clothes," Mark repeated. "Mate, clothes don't

make you something you aren't. They can't. You can't catch gay from clothes, or people, or anything."

Not even from guys who hope you'll stay friends with them when you find out.

He would never have picked Brandon as prejudiced.

Except simple prejudice didn't explain Brandon's very real distress.

"Brandon?"

"When I was twelve," Brandon said, "I had this teacher who—" Then he clamped his mouth shut and shook his head again. "He's in jail now."

"Oh fuck, Bran." Mark wanted to reach out and hug him, but he didn't know if Brandon wanted the contact. He put a hand on Brandon's shoulder instead and squeezed gently.

Brandon wiped at his face with the heels of his hands. "And I think my dad thinks I asked for it, you know?"

"I think your dad's an arsehole," Mark said. He looked at his clothes lying on the floor. "You want to get changed and get out of here?"

"No. I can do this."

"You don't have to," Mark said. "If you want, we'll walk right now. We'll get a pizza and go back to my dorm and play *Call of Duty* instead."

"I can do this," Brandon repeated. "I can do it." He sucked in a deep breath. "Thanks, Mark. You won't...um..."

"I won't tell," Mark said.

"Thanks." Brandon wiped his face again and squared his shoulders. "Let's do this."

The rest of the pledges were still clustered anxiously on the stairs, unwilling to head into the common room.

"What's the holdup?" Chris shouted from the hall. "Did someone break a nail? Get your asses in here, pledge bitches!"

The pledges entered the common room to hollering, cheering, and the flashes from what must have been a million camera phones. Which was one good thing about having no friends here, Mark supposed. They could post that shit all over social media, and nobody who mattered to Mark would see it. Besides, the Hazing Secrecy Clause or whatever wouldn't let the Alpha Delts actually identify the people in the pictures.

Not that he cared about wearing a dumb frilly dress that showed off his arse if he bent down. The thing that bothered him the most was the way he'd fallen in line, the way he was letting himself be humiliated because that was the order of things. Because it was the tradition.

It was a stupid fucking tradition.

What Mark didn't understand, and hoped he would never understand, was why you'd let a bunch of dickheads torment you for months in the hope that they'd let you stay in their little club. It had to fall somewhere between kindergarten and Stockholm Syndrome on the What-the-Fuck-Are-You-Thinking scale.

Mark didn't care about the dress, but he cared about Brandon, and about what Brandon was putting himself through just to give these ignorant fuckers a cheap laugh. Just so they wouldn't reject him.

"You've got to rush," Brandon had told him that first time. *"If you're not in a fraternity, you're nothing, you know?"* And then: *"That's what my dad says."*

Brandon had a smile pasted onto his face now, a little brittle, less goofy than the grins the rest of the pledges were wearing as they paraded up and down in the common room while the guys cheered. Mark wanted to grab him by the hand and haul him out of there, and tell him again that his dad was an arsehole, and that Brandon didn't have to *prove* anything, not to anyone.

Mark scowled.

A scowl that was wiped off his face the second a wooden paddle connected with his backside. "What the fuck?" he yelped.

Bengal laughed at him. "Keep moving, princess."

"Fuck you," Mark muttered under his breath.

"I said move, faggot!" Bengal yelled and swatted him with the paddle again.

Faggot? Nice. He resisted the urge to look back at Brandon, who was following him.

Mark shook his head and walked a few steps. Behind the jeering, cheering group of frat brothers, he could see Jackson standing there, staring. Looking as disapproving and pissed off as always, probably because Mark was being singled out as a troublemaker again. Blake was standing beside Jackson, beaming proudly at Mark. As Mark caught his gaze, Blake gave him an enthusiastic two thumbs up.

Mark almost smiled at that. Blake was oblivious to Mark's foul mood.

And to pretty much everything else. Ever.

The pledges did another circuit of the room, until the laughing and whooping had died down.

Then Chris stood in the center of the room, cracked open a can of beer, and held it up over his head. "Let's get this party started, Alpha Delts!"

This time the cheer was loud enough to wake the dead.

CHAPTER 5

When Deacon arrived at the Alpha Delt castle's front gate, the lawn was crammed with shirtless guys in cowboy hats, girls in bandanna-patterned tube tops and cowgirl hats, several people in overalls with no shirts underneath, and a small, flimsy wooden shed painted to look like a red barn with the words Kissin' Shack on the front.

A shirtless guy with a beer belly went by on a "horse" composed of two people—one costumed as the back end, another as the front. He was holding the front end's reins in one hand and singing drunkenly.

This was like a state fair gone horribly wrong.

Country music blared from a huge speaker system, and Deacon winced. He reached up and adjusted his mask. He hadn't been able to come up with anything genius on short notice. Just his black work clothes and a cape James said was a Halloween costume, but that Deacon suspected might be related to Comic-Con. Then a cheap mask he'd picked up at a discount store and a mustache drawn with eyeliner he'd borrowed from Matt's girlfriend.

The mustache helped disguise Deacon better than the

mask. Plus it was dark out, and the party was crowded—he didn't really think he'd be found out. And if he was, well, Phi Sig would have to watch its back for the next couple of days.

There didn't appear to be a bouncer, and the gate was open, so Deacon walked in. From the backyard came a cheer even louder than the few Deacon had heard over the last forty-five minutes. He'd shown up fashionably late to help himself slip in unnoticed, but he'd been able to keep tabs on the party pretty well from next door. From what he gathered, when someone fell off the mechanical bull, you cheered, and when someone stuck a ride for eight seconds, you cheered louder. And if someone fell off and appeared to be in serious pain, you cheered loudest of all.

A guy and a girl stumbled out of the Kissin' Shack together. The guy was leaning on the girl, and when she put her arms up to yell "Whoooo," he fell over. She paused, tucking her hair behind her ears, and yelled down at him, "Are you okaaaayyyy? Are you okaaaayyyy?"

How the hell was he supposed to find Mark in this mess?

On the front porch, a girl in cutoff shorts that barely covered her crotch and a flannel shirt tied just under her breasts was twirling a lasso and trying to snare a blond guy standing in a huddle. Deacon pushed through the crowd and went around to the backyard, where the mechanical bull stood in all its glory. It actually looked like a bull— brown and white with faux fur and wild, glassy eyes. Deacon wondered how much it had cost to have the thing hauled in, and why anyone thought it was a good idea to place a mechanical bull anywhere *near* the pool. There was a thick mat on the ground around it, and when Deacon walked up, a guy was lying flat on his back on the mat, clutching his stomach, either laughing or crying.

"Help him up, bitch!" someone yelled.

A girl in a French-maid outfit crouched next to the guy. Nope, wait...not a girl. Deacon blinked to make sure his eyes weren't playing tricks on him.

It was Mark.

Mark, in a maid's outfit, helping the bull's latest victim to his feet. The guy groaned.

"Are you seriously hurt, Greg?" a girl asked.

Deacon looked at Greg's left ankle, which was swollen.

"I think I..." Greg started, as Mark guided him forward. He tried to put his weight on his left foot and gave a shout.

He was leaning too heavily on Mark, and they were both about to go down. Without thinking, Deacon got on Greg's other side, placing his arm under Greg's and hoisting him up. Deacon saw Mark glance at him, saw an expression of gratitude quickly replaced by one of surprise as he recognized Deacon.

Together they dragged Greg over to a nearby hay bale and sat him down. Deacon knelt to get a better look at the ankle. A few people crowded around, but most of the spectators stayed back, as if they expected Deacon to perform some kind of healing miracle. Or like they were too drunk to understand what was going on. Somebody else had already mounted the bull, and the bull operator started it up.

Greg whimpered as Deacon pressed lightly on the swollen skin.

Deacon turned to Mark, trying not to look up his skirt. "We need some ice," he said.

Mark nodded and left to get some. Deacon addressed Greg. "How bad is it?"

Greg groaned and squeezed his eyes shut. Deacon didn't think his ankle looked broken, but it was a bad sprain. Deacon turned to the bystanders. "He should probably go to the ER," he said. He realized he was looking right at Rob

"Bengal" Stowe and lowered his head, not wanting to be recognized.

"We need a pledge to do an ER run," Bengal called.

"They're all dressed like maids," someone else said.

Bengal muttered something and headed into the house.

Mark returned with ice and someone's discarded shirt, and he and Deacon started to pack the ankle. When they finally stood, the people who hadn't yet wandered away cheered. "Zorro saved Greg!" yelled the girl who'd asked if Greg was really hurt.

"Fuck yeah, Zorro!" yelled someone else.

A chant started up of "Zorr-o, Zorr-o," which caught the attention of the rest of the backyard crowd, most of whom had no idea what had happened. Soon everyone was chanting out of sync.

So much for sneaking into the party, Deacon thought.

Bengal pushed through and announced a sober ride to the ER had been found—some guy named Blake, who wasn't allowed to drink because he was on the football team —and Mark and Deacon helped Greg to the front and into the car. By the time Greg was carted off, most of the party-goers had lost interest in the incident, and Mark and Deacon were left standing in the drive.

"Nice costume," Deacon said.

"Shut up," Mark replied.

"Did they have French maids in the Wild West, or..."

Mark cracked a half grin and elbowed Deacon. "I said shut *up*." Mark was wearing sneakers, at least, not stilettos. His legs looked incredible in those stockings—calf muscles firm and well-defined. "Can't believe you actually dressed as Zorro," Mark muttered. "Can't believe you showed up, and I'm dressed like this."

"You look good. I prefer schoolgirl costumes, but this'll do in a pinch."

Mark snorted with laughter. "I'll keep that in mind."

Deacon had a vision of Mark in a schoolgirl costume—kneesocks and a plaid skirt—that didn't seem at all ridiculous. Well, maybe a little ridiculous. But definitely hot. Deacon blinked to bring himself back to the present before he delved too deep into that particular fantasy. He was into that now? Who knew?

Mark's grin was still embarrassed. "Will you stick around for a while? Maybe help me get out of my stockings at the end of the night?"

"Yeah," Deacon whispered, that image pushing the schoolgirl right out of his head. "Hell, yeah."

"Good," Mark said. "Because I really want—"

"Pledge bitch!" Bengal bellowed from the front stairs of the house. "Get your frilly ass back here and dance for us, bitch!"

Mark rolled his eyes. "Fucker." He shot another look at Deacon. "See you later, then."

Deacon watched as he jogged up the stairs, his frilly skirt bouncing around his lean ass. That was way more distracting than it should have been.

By the time he went around back again, a space had been cleared by the pool, and eight pledges in French-maid costumes were dancing very unenthusiastically to Shania Twain's "Man! I Feel Like a Woman." As Deacon watched, one of the Alpha Delts leaped in with them, grabbed one of the pledges by the hips, and began to gyrate against the kid's ass. The kid looked terrified.

"Hey!" Mark pushed him away from the kid.

The guy, drunk, stumbled and went face-first into a bale of hay.

Everyone cheered. It was that sort of party.

Mark took the other pledge by the wrist and pushed him into the back row of dancers.

Deacon shook his head. Really, he shouldn't hang around. He could slip next door for a few hours and come back when things were winding down a bit. At least that way he wouldn't have to watch this unmitigated display of drunken douchebaggery.

He became aware that the attention had shifted off the dancing pledges and onto a new spectacle. Deacon turned to look and saw two Alpha Delts leading a dog into the party. Anabelle the Lab.

"Phi Sig's bitch was crappin' on our lawn again!" one of them announced. "So we kidnapped it!"

Cheering and whooping, and suddenly Anabelle was getting sprayed with beer. She tugged at her leash to get away, but the guy holding it yanked it back, dragging her across the lawn.

Deacon elbowed his way through the crowd. "What the fuck are you doing?" he demanded. "You don't treat an animal like that!"

"Zorro!" one of the girls shrieked. "Zorro's going to save the puppy!"

"Dude," the drunk with the leash said, "we're not hurting it!"

"Give me the dog," Deacon said. And Anabelle, who had always been standoffish with Deacon, must have recognized a familiar voice. She strained toward him.

"Dude, what's your deal?"

And then Bengal was right there, right in his face. "Who the fuck are you, anyway?"

"He's Zorro!" the same girl shrieked.

Bengal glared at him. "He's fucking Phi Sig!" He knocked Deacon's hat off. "Fucking Phi Sig has crashed our party!"

Deacon shoved his mask up. No point pretending otherwise. "Give me the dog, *Rob*."

"Give him the fucking dog," Bengal said, shoving Deacon in the chest. "And then get the fuck out. It's on now, asshole. It's *on*."

Deacon resisted the urge to punch him in the face. He took Anabelle's leash instead and drew her toward the exit. He cast a look back over at the pledges and saw that Mark was watching. Well, Deacon would find out now how much of an Alpha Delt Mark was, wouldn't he? Rumor had it that the Alpha Delts swore eternal hatred of Phi Sig in their pledges, because that was just how juvenile they were. As though a fraternity actually devoted to study and community service was the North Korea of Greek life. When in reality Phi Sig couldn't give a flying fuck about Alpha Delta, as long as they occasionally turned their music down to a dull roar.

On the front lawn, he met James, who was being restrained by a bunch of Alpha Delts who were not listening at all to his threats to call the dean's office if they didn't give him back his dog. James gaped when he saw Deacon emerging from the party. "Deke?"

"Let's go," Deacon said. "Anabelle needs a bath."

James shrugged the laughing Alpha Delts off him and fell into step beside Deacon. "That's why you wanted my cape? To crash an Alpha Delt party?"

"Yeah," Deacon sighed. "Sorry, but apparently it's now *on*."

"What is?"

"The hell if I know," Deacon said.

James shook his head. "Look, I don't care what you did.

If you hadn't been in there, who knows what they would have done to Anabelle." He looked at his watch. "Is it too late to call a house meeting? We should probably give everyone the heads-up before the Alpha Delts start their shit."

Great. So instead of going to a party and hooking up with a cute guy, Deacon had managed to start a fraternity war instead. It was going to be a long semester.

————

Bengal was pissed off. *Really* pissed off. He was so pissed off that Mark hadn't even volunteered the fact that he'd invited Deacon to the party. He had the impression that if he did, this Wild West party would end with a good old-fashioned lynching. As it was, Bengal was already mad enough at Mark for pushing Logan White over when he'd grabbed Brandon like that. Fucking Logan. Grinding against Brandon's arse like it was the funniest thing in the world.

"And you, pledge bitch, can clean this whole fucking yard up by morning," Bengal told him once the party had wound down. He glared at the other pledges. "The rest of you, fuck off. If I find out anyone helped this piece of shit, you're out."

Brandon looked like he was going to cry, so Mark winked at him to try and cheer him up. Then, once the others had left, Mark took a garbage bag, turned off the stereo, and began to pick up beer cans.

It was three a.m. So much for classes in the morning. He'd be lucky to be finished by noon.

As he worked, Mark looked over at the Phi Sig house. A couple of lights were still on, but mostly it looked quiet and peaceful. Mark didn't know anything about the Phi Sigs, except they were the sworn enemies of Alpha Delta. Because they liked books, or something. Blake, whom Mark had asked, had been sketchy on the details.

And Deacon was in Phi Sig. Rescuing that dog had been pretty cool. Calling out the Alpha Delts on their arsehole behavior was even more cool. Mark hadn't known Deacon was in a fraternity. Mark hadn't known Deacon was even in college, although he'd assumed it when Deacon had told him about frats the day they met. And he'd said something about Phi Sig then, hadn't he? But not that he was in it. And Mark had figured frat boys didn't have jobs. That shit just got in the way of drunken parties, right?

There was a girl passed out in the Kissin' Shack. Mark checked that she was breathing, and took her phone out of her hand. He checked her messages. There was one unsent: *Hey bitch come get meejjidsj*. Mark backspaced through the typo, added *from Alpha Delta*, and hit Send.

Then he went back to collecting beer cans.

Half an hour later, when he was still working his way around the side of the pool, three drunk girls wandered in, collected their friend, and wandered out again. Mark wasn't even sure they'd noticed him.

He found himself glancing more and more at the Phi Sig house. Then he took his phone from his corset and texted Deacon.

Are we like Romeo and Juliet?

He wasn't expecting a reply, but Deacon must have been awake still.

I call dibs on Romeo.

Mark grinned at that.

A light came on in the Phi Sig house, in the corner room on the second floor. Then someone stepped out onto the balcony.

That u, Romeo? Because if ur on the balcony, we're doing it wrong.

The figure raised a hand and waved slowly, the glow of a screen moving back and forth.

But ur the one in a dress.

Mark snorted. He dropped the bag of cans and leaned against the mechanical bull.

Maybe I should take it off then.

Deacon's reply came almost instantly: *What if I like it?*

Oh, now that was interesting. Mark held his phone in his left hand and reached under his ruffled skirt with his right. He rubbed his cock through his frilly knickers and wondered if Deacon was actually getting the hang of sexting.

I am so hard right now. Not even kidding.

Pic?

Oh fuck yeah. Mark stared up at Deacon on the balcony and pushed his knickers down. He pumped his cock a few times, then, holding the skirt out of the way, took a photo of it and hit Send. He was debating whether to pull his knickers back on or just rub one out right there in the back-yard, when Deacon's reply came through.

Wait there, Juliet.

Mark crossed to the pool and washed his hands. Better to smell like chlorine than stale beer. Then he went back and waited by the mechanical bull. Deacon had vanished from his balcony. Any second now, and he'd appear.

Mark's gaze fell on the controls for the bull. Seized with a brilliant idea, he turned it down to its lowest setting and climbed on. It rocked gently, just like the swell of the ocean. Mark closed his eyes.

"You look so fucking hot up there," Deacon said quietly.

Mark's eyes flashed open. "Wanna ride 'em, cowboy?"

Deacon climbed up behind him and settled his hands around Mark's hips. Mark leaned forward, pressing his cock against the hide of the bull and showing his frilly arse off to Deacon at the same time.

"Oh yeah," Deacon whispered. He slid one hand up Mark's skirt and smoothed it over Mark's arse.

Mark didn't speak. He felt like he ought to make some clever comment—he was in a French-maid uniform, riding a mechanical bull with a de-caped, unmasked Zorro. But it didn't feel as funny as it should have. He liked Deacon touching him. He liked that it was quiet now, that the pool glowed, that the night was warm, but every now and then a light breeze came through and rustled the trees, which were black against the dark blue of the sky. In Bundaberg, spring would be starting. Here it was almost autumn.

He was saved from a moment of homesickness by Deacon, who moved his hand to Mark's front and stroked Mark's cock through his knickers. Mark let out a soft breath. Deacon found the waistband and slipped his hand under-neath, and suddenly his palm was on Mark's dick, pushing lightly. The bull rocked them forward, and Mark ground against Deacon's hand. They rocked back, and Deacon made a loose fist around Mark's shaft, fingertips ghosting his balls. Forward, and Deacon's thighs slid more firmly against Mark's. Mark, with his skirt lifted, could feel how hard Deacon was.

Back, and Mark lifted off the bull, sitting down again right on Deacon's crotch. He enjoyed Deacon's little gasp. Forward, and Mark slid off, and Deacon leaned to place a kiss on Mark's shoulder. Then Mark's neck. Then the hand that had been on his hip moved up his side and drifted over the front of his corset. Mark reached back and took ahold of Deacon's arse, pulling Deacon more snugly against him. He gripped the bull with his legs and rocked into Deacon's fist, his breath coming faster and heavier.

Deacon kissed him again, just behind his ear, teasing Mark's earlobe with the tip of his tongue. Mark closed his eyes, feeling the motion of the bull, the heat of Deacon's body against his, the fabric of Deacon's pants as he kneaded Mark's arse. The cool dampness of Deacon's lips. The pleasure of being around someone who didn't have it in for him. Whom he didn't have to fight against or strive to please or look out for. Deacon was quiet, steady. And after weeks of noise and feeling off balance, this was welcome.

"Gonna come?" Deacon whispered against his neck.

Mark gladly would have, just let go and flooded these stupid frilly knickers, except a light went on in the kitchen, and the back door opened.

"Shit!" Deacon hissed.

Mark and Deacon dived off the bull at the same time, landing in a heap on the mat. There was no time to turn the bull off; they raced to the shadows at the side of the house. Mark stopped to look back at the bull, still bucking slowly in the light from the house.

"Hey, pledge bitch!" Bengal shouted.

Mark snickered.

Deacon swatted his side. "You'd better get back there."

"No." Mark turned to him, his grin gone. "No. Absolutely not." Deacon stared back at him, his face younger, softer than it looked in the bar. "I don't come when I'm called."

They both moved forward at the same time, their bodies crushing against each other as they kissed furiously. Mark wrapped his arms around Deacon and squeezed, and Deacon sifted through the layers of tulle in Mark's skirt until he found Mark's arse and cupped it.

"Do you come when you're fucked?" Deacon whispered.

Mark grinned and eased Deacon steadily backward, to the front yard. "Let's find out." He spun Deacon and gave him a little push, then took off toward the Kissin' Shack. Deacon followed him in, laughing.

It was completely dark inside, and once Mark was situated on the straw-covered floor, he reached out and found Deacon, pulling him down.

They kissed for a while, their body heat filling the small space. Deacon kicked off his shoes, and Mark followed suit; then Deacon helped Mark undo the corset. Mark wriggled out of the dress and pushed the knickers off while Deacon removed his pants and shirt.

"If we get caught..." Deacon whispered, settling his body on top of Mark's once more.

"I don't care," Mark whispered back fiercely. He was struck by a feeling he'd had several times since moving to America, like he was strapped too loosely into a roller-coaster cart, like all that kept him from falling were the sagging straps of his bravado. There was no real refuge to be found in a perpetual fuck-you to the world. In keeping himself aloof from and above the Alpha Delts and the other pledges and the students who actually did the readings in his lit class, and tight-arsed Jackson and overly optimistic Jim.

But he wasn't looking for a refuge; he was just looking for a way to live without having to think too hard about what he wanted. If he stripped away any negative memories of his home, he was left with a flat, idyllic image of a place where he'd been happy. Surfing and hanging out and having a good time. He could long for it because it wasn't this place —wasn't real and immediate and demanding that he know what he wanted to do with his life, what he planned to make of himself.

He wrapped his legs around Deacon and pulled him down for another kiss. Pushed Deacon onto the floor and straddled him so he could learn Deacon's body even though he couldn't see a damned thing. He used his lips, his tongue, his hands to trace the muscles, to find the places where Deacon had a little bit of hair—between his pecs, around his nipples, and under his navel—and to make Deacon gasp, or tense suddenly, or sigh. Each time part of him brushed Deacon's cock, he was filled with a wild need. Finally he couldn't take it anymore. He scooted down and kissed the head of Deacon's dick, licking up some of the fluid leaking from it. Then he stretched out on the straw beside Deacon, hoping Deacon would take the hint and fuck him.

"Mm. Shit. My dress didn't have pockets. You got a condom?"

"Grabbed one on the way out," Deacon murmured.

"Good thinking, Romeo." Mark rolled his shoulders, enjoying the scratch of the straw against his back. "It's going on you, by the way."

Deacon laughed quietly.

Mark heard the rip of foil, and his cock got harder in anticipation.

"Do you prefer to bottom?"

"Sometimes," Mark said. "I do tonight. Must be the stockings."

Deacon reached for him in the darkness, running a hand up his leg. "Fuck. You're still wearing them."

"Want me to take them off?"

"No." Deacon's voice was low and strained.

"Wish we were still on the bull," Mark whispered to him.

"You like having something to ride?"

Mark groaned as Deacon pulled him closer, Deacon's cock leaking all over the frilly material of his suspender belt.

Okay, so Deacon was pretty bad at sexting, but he could sure as hell talk dirty when it counted. "Yeah, I do."

"Come on, then." Deacon got onto his back, and Mark straddled him again. Deacon's cock pressed against his arse, and Mark shifted so that he could feel his balls dragging across it. Back and forth, just like on the bull. Then Deacon gripped his arse and tugged his cheeks apart. His fingers were slick. He'd grabbed a condom *and* lube. Those Phi Sig guys really were smart.

Deacon's slick fingers pushed at his hole, and Mark shuddered.

Mark reached behind him and grabbed Deacon's cock. He angled it as he rose onto his knees, then sank back down slowly. *Fuck.* That burn. He loved that burn. Knew guys who wouldn't let a cock near them unless they'd done the whole one-two-three-fingers thing first, but Mark wasn't one of them. The problem with getting fingered like that was it made him come so hard he lost all interest in the main event.

Deacon's breath shuddered out of him as Mark lowered himself. "Oh fuck."

Mark stayed seated for a moment, closing his eyes as his arse adjusted to Deacon's cock. Then he started to ride. Gently at first, like on the bull. Rocking himself on Deacon's cock. Deacon's hands slid to his waist, to the frilly belt that Mark had thought was ludicrous when he'd first put it on, but now didn't seem so stupid. Deacon's thumbs glided over the fabric in small, tight circles. Then he shifted his hands to Mark's thighs, running them along the stockings. His breath hitched.

Mark should have left the corset on too. Hell, he should have left the fucking skirt on too. Would have, if he'd known Deacon would be so hot for it.

Mark began to move faster, his thighs burning. Deacon moved with him, thrusting his hips up every time Mark pushed back down, working in counterpoint. Mark's balls were already tight, and his cock was aching for release. He resisted the urge to grab it. Instead, he put his hands over Deacon's and laced their fingers together.

"Fuck me, Deacon," he groaned, squeezing his eyes shut. "Fuck me."

"I'm gonna come," Deacon said, his voice straining. He pulled his right hand free from Mark's and reached for Mark's cock.

One firm stroke was all it took, and Mark was shooting everywhere. Like, *everywhere*. It was too dark to be sure, but he was fairly certain he'd hit himself in the chin, and he bet he'd made a mess all over Deacon as well.

Except Deacon, who was jerking his hips quickly as he came, probably hadn't noticed.

Mark gasped for breath, leaning forward and resting his forehead on Deacon's shoulder. Fuck, his legs would be like jelly in the morning. After running all those laps for Blake, and then a very different kind of marathon with Deacon. Which had turned out to be a sprint in the end.

Deacon stroked Mark's back. "Oh...wow." He tugged at Mark's suspender belt.

"Kinky fucker." Mark grinned into his shoulder.

"You or me?"

"Both of us," Mark said.

Deacon laughed. "Yeah, probably."

"We have *got* to do this again sometime," Mark said, rolling off Deacon. Which should have been his cue to get dressed and leave, but he wasn't sure his legs would hold him at the moment.

"We do," Deacon agreed. He leaned over Mark and kissed him.

That was unexpected. And nice. Not at all the sort of kiss you used to get the blood pounding. Something much softer. Sort of sweet.

Mark liked it.

He liked Deacon a lot.

Kinky fucker on one hand, and sort of sweet on the other. He could get used to that.

Suddenly college life was looking up.

CHAPTER 6

"What's that smell?" Deacon asked.

"Dunno." James didn't look up from his textbook.

"Seriously. It smells like shit in this house."

"Matt probably took a dump. Vegetarian shits are the worst."

"But it's been here since last night." Deacon moved around the common room, trying to pinpoint where the smell was the strongest.

"Maybe you stepped in Anabelle poo. Did you check your shoes?"

"It's not my shoes." Deacon stopped next to the AC vent. "It's coming from here. Fuck. It's the fucking Alpha Delts. Gotta be."

"They shit in our AC?"

"I'll go check the outside unit."

Sure enough, when Deacon got outside, there was dog shit smeared on the unit. Anabelle had wandered out after him and now stood, panting and staring at the back lawn, tail waving. He looked at her. "Did you leave an Anabelle pie somewhere the Alpha Delts could find it?"

She ignored him.

He sighed. The shit was inside the unit too. And he was supposed to drive home this afternoon. Well, maybe he could get a start on cleaning it, and the other guys could finish it. He felt it was at least partly his responsibility, since he'd been the one to crash the Alpha Delt party.

And I fucked Mark in their goddamn Kissin' Shack.

Which would have been the most epic fuck-you ever against the Alpha Delts and all their homophobic bullshit, except Deacon would never tell anyone about it. Mark was probably having a hard enough time pledging as it was with his abrasive attitude, without being outed. Why the hell he was bothering, Deacon didn't know. He'd said it was a family tradition, but Mark didn't seem like the sort of guy who cared about stuff like that.

Deacon headed inside to the kitchen and dug around under the sinks for cleaning supplies. Unlike most fraternities on campus, Phi Sig didn't have a house mom. They used a laundry service and had a cleaner come in once a week, but most of the household chores were divided up and taped to the roster on the fridge. Cleaning dog shit out of the AC wasn't on the list, but someone had to do it.

Deacon looked around as a guy wandered into the kitchen.

Kevin. That was his name. One of the pledges.

"Deacon, right?" Kevin asked him.

Deacon nodded.

"Can I ask you something?"

"Sure."

Kevin shoved his glasses back onto the bridge of his

nose. "It's about the fee structure for the fraternity. I mean, what happens if you can't pay it?"

Deacon shoved rubber gloves and a bottle of cleaning fluid into a bucket and stood. "If you fall more than three months behind, you're out. But James talked to you about the loans, right? The interest is really low. I've got one. I pay what I can now, but if you need to talk about delaying it until after graduation because of special circumstances, that's fine."

"Okay," Kevin said. "It's just...I think I might have special circumstances."

Deacon leaned back against the sinks.

"My dad's in chemo," Kevin blurted out. "And he doesn't have insurance, so...you know. Does that count?"

"I'm sure it does," Deacon said.

Kevin scrunched up his nose. "I don't want to be a problem or anything."

"It's not going to be a problem," Deacon assured him. "Look, obviously you're a good student, we like you, and we want you here. We wouldn't have asked you to pledge if we didn't. If you're having financial problems, we'll help you out with that. James is the guy to talk to about all that stuff. And if you're having any other problems, you can talk to any of us."

"Thanks, Deacon." Kevin smiled hesitantly and looked at the bucket of cleaning supplies. "Do you, um, do you need help with something?"

Deacon smiled despite himself. "I am currently on my way to clean dog shit out of the AC, courtesy of the Alpha Delts. If you want to help, feel free."

Kevin made a face. "Um, sure. This isn't some kind of hazing thing like in other fraternities, is it? Like cover the pledges in shit or something?"

Deacon laughed. "No, it isn't. Tell you what, I'll do the cleaning, and you hold the bucket. Deal?"

"Deal."

Halfway through the cleaning process, Matt stormed out of the house and over to where Deacon and Kevin were working. "Did they seriously put shit in the AC?" Matt demanded.

Deacon looked up. "They seriously did." He went back to work with the toothbrush and the dish scrubber. "We turned the AC off, so at least the smell shouldn't spread anymore."

"No. This is fucking too much."

Deacon glanced up again. Matt's face was red, and he looked more than ready to punch someone. He was definitely the most temperamental of the Phi Sig brothers.

"We gotta get them back," Matt said.

Deacon dipped the sponge in the bucket. "I don't think we gotta."

"We can't let them keep getting away with shit like this! No pun fucking intended."

"James says if they do anything worse, we'll take it up with the school."

"No." Matt shook his head. "Back when my dad was here, you didn't go tattling when fights like this started. You handled it among yourselves. You *won*."

All right, so *some* Phi Sigs hated the Alpha Delts as much as the Alphas hated the Phi Sigs. The last thing Deacon wanted was to get involved in an actual war with the Alpha Delts. But he knew Matt and a couple of the other guys were probably willing to go there. "Well, this is a different time," Deacon said. "And the school's gonna hold us liable for any property damage caused by dumbass pranks. So I say we don't escalate this."

"So we're just supposed to turn the other cheek?" Matt muttered. "Great. This is why they hate us, you know? This is why they walk all over us—because we don't fight back. This is a house full of nerds afraid to stand up to the jocks."

"So basically this fraternity thing is gonna be like high school all over again?" Kevin asked tentatively.

Deacon chuckled. "Basically. But you get better food."

Matt watched Deacon scrape the last of the shit off the slats of the unit. "I don't get what you crashed their party for."

"To see a friend," Deacon replied calmly. He tossed the sponge in the bucket and took the bucket from Kevin.

Inside the house, he picked up his phone and saw he had a text from Mark. *You working tonight?*

He sighed. He would have loved to see Mark again tonight. But it wasn't gonna happen. *Driving home for the weekend.*

He hit Send, hesitated, then typed, *You have until Sunday night to find us a place to fuck.*

Too forward? He had a feeling Mark would like it. He hit Send.

A few seconds later, he got back: *Got about 5 ideas right now. When do u have to leave?*

Deacon stared at the phone. It was too tempting to put off the drive and find out what Mark had in mind. He'd already spent way too much time today thinking about Mark's body, hard and hot on top of his. About the costume, and how Mark had still looked like *Mark*, frills and tiny apron and all. Like he could put on anything—a snowsuit, a candy striper uniform, a Green Bay Packers Cheesehead— and still be completely himself.

Now, he typed. *Sorry, Jules. I really want to see you.*

Mark didn't respond right away, and Deacon tried not to

worry that he was angry or offended or just didn't give a shit that Deacon wanted to see him. But as he went upstairs to pack, his phone buzzed. *Guess we'll just have to have phone sex.*

Deacon grinned. *Never had phone sex in my life.*

Me either. Let's try it.

Okay.

Deacon hadn't known he liked guys in garter belts. How did he know he wouldn't like phone sex?

When? Mark texted.

Call me in half an hour.

Deacon hurried the rest of the way upstairs and began throwing stuff in his backpack.

———

"Jackson's not a bad big," Brandon said.

He and Mark had gone for a pizza at a place near campus. Mark wasn't sure how what they were eating could be called pizza by any stretch of the imagination, but it beat dining hall food. He actually liked the meals at the Alpha Delt house—the chef was good. But he'd been invited to partake in few enough of those. It always depended on whether or not Bengal felt like letting the pledges eat.

Denying pledges dinner seemed kind of pointless, since Bengal had to know they all went and stuffed themselves with fast food as soon as they left the house each night. But there were nights when Bengal ordered them not to eat at all, not even when they went home. And the next day, Bengal usually pulled aside one or two pledges and took them to the "confessional" down in the basement to find out whether or not they'd obeyed. Mark had never been to the confessional, and the pledges who had refused to talk about it. All Mark knew was that any pledge who had defied an order not to eat didn't do it again after a trip to the Alpha Delt basement.

"He's kinda uptight," Brandon went on. "But he's not, like, a dick."

Mark begged to differ.

"The shit they're doing to us?" Brandon continued. "You can tell some of them like it—Bengal, and Logan. But Jackson seems like he's just doing his job."

His job is fucked-up. Mark was trying to pay attention to his conversation with Brandon, except he kept checking his phone. They needed to get out of here in fifteen minutes if Mark was gonna be on time calling Deacon. "Yeah, Blake's not a bad guy either," he said. "Except I saw him get stuck in a Portaloo, and now I can't take him seriously."

"A *Portaloo*?"

"Yeah. You know, one of those disgusting toilet stalls you can set up anywhere."

"You mean a Porta-Potty?"

"No," Mark said. "I mean a Portaloo. Why the hell does nobody here speak English?"

Brandon grinned. "You cannot be serious."

"Mate, I am deadly serious," Mark said but couldn't stop smiling. "You should have seen me the first time I heard someone use the term 'fanny pack.'"

"Because that means…?"

"Vagina," Mark said, loudly enough for the woman at the next booth to stare.

"Oh!" For a second it looked like Brandon didn't know whether to laugh or be horrified. Then he snorted. "Why'd you have to say it so loud? You're such a jerk-off sometimes."

"Wanker," Mark corrected him with a grin. "I'm such a wanker sometimes."

Brandon laughed louder.

Mark liked to make Brandon laugh. It felt like a challenge but the good sort. Not the sort where you pledged to Alpha Delta just to see if you could out-bastard them. Mark got the impression that Brandon didn't really have any friends at Prescott. Not that Mark did either, but he didn't give a shit. The difference was that Brandon *deserved* friends, because he was nice and smart and cute enough that the girl from their geology class had been giving him the eye for weeks, and shy enough that he hadn't noticed. Brandon was pledging because he thought being an Alpha Delt would make him like them—loud, brash, and inexplicably popular —without realizing he was already pretty bloody awesome on his own.

"You want to study tonight?" Brandon asked.

"Sorry, I can't," Mark said, letting him take the last piece of pizza. "I'm kind of hooking up with someone."

Brandon raised his eyebrows. "Kind of?"

"We're going to try it by phone," Mark said.

"Oh." Brandon wrinkled his nose. "A girl from home?"

"No," Mark said. God, he hated this. Here was the perfect time for him to correct Brandon on both counts— not a girl, and not from home—but he wasn't going to do it. And not because he thought Brandon might freak out, but because Mark was too selfish to risk losing the closest thing he had to a real friend at Prescott. Actually, on the entire continent. No, wait, the entire *hemisphere*. Fuck, he was pathetic. "Not from home."

"Okay," Brandon said. "But you really ought to study, you know, while you get the chance."

The chance? The chance was Buckley's and none. Mark was sure the Alpha Delts had put a tracking device in his head or something, because it seemed like as soon as he veered anywhere toward the library, they called him to invoke their rights as arseholes. Sorry, brothers. *Drive me here. Fetch me that. Do something incredibly demeaning and/or repetitive, just so we can all point at you and laugh.*

"I know I should," Mark sighed, pulling some bills out of his wallet. "Jesus, all your money is the same color, and I never know what to tip."

"Fifteen percent usually covers it," Brandon said.

Mark rolled his eyes. "Bran. I just ate half a pizza and a whole garlic bread. The only thing stopping me from curling up and falling asleep like a happy fat puppy is the fact that I have to have smoking-hot phone sex in a minute." He smiled at the lady in the next booth. "I cannot be expected to do maths at a time like this."

"Nobody's expecting you to do maths. *Math*, maybe."

"Oh, come on."

"Why would you add an *s* to math?"

"Because that's how you say it."

Brandon picked up one of the bills and passed it back to him. "You are the weirdest person I know."

"I get that a lot," Mark agreed.

He liked it when Brandon laughed.

———

Deacon was an hour from Chambersburg when Mark finally called. He'd figured Mark had forgotten, or got a case of nerves or something, but when he hit the speaker on his phone, Mark sounded as cocky as ever.

"So, Romeo, wanna tell me what you're wearing?"

Deacon smiled. This was fantasy territory, right? No need to tell Mark about his track pants with a rip in the knee. "Just jeans and a tee. What about you?"

"Hang on." A rustling noise. "Nothing, now."

"Seriously?"

"Yeah." Mark's voice lifted with a smile. "My roommate has gone to some Occupy Someshit—they're still doing that, right? He's protesting something, anyway, so I've wedged the door, and I'm lying on my bed. Naked."

"Shit. Wish I could see that." Deacon fixed his eyes on the road and wondered exactly how distracting this was going to be.

"What sort of car do you have?" Mark asked.

"What? That's not sexy."

"It would be if you had a Ferrari or something," Mark said. "But it's an automatic, right?"

"Yeah," Deacon said.

"Awesome." Mark breathed heavily into his phone. "Because you are going to need a hand free for this, Romeo."

For someone who claimed never to have had phone sex, Mark seemed very confident in the power of the spoken word. Although, to be fair, he was sex on legs. A fucking firecracker, with way fewer inhibitions at eighteen than Deacon had now. "Okay," he said but kept both hands on the wheel. "So how do we do this?"

"Dunno." Mark was silent for a moment, then: "Maybe I should tell you I've got my hand on my cock."

"Wow. Straight for that, hmmm?" Deacon asked him, a jolt of surprise traveling through him. They were really doing this.

"You think I should do something else first?"

"Maybe." Deacon braked to allow a truck the space to change lanes, and racked his brain for something. "What about your nipples? What does it feel like when you pinch them?"

Mark didn't say anything for a while.

Shit. It was the word "nipples." Maybe he should have called them tits. Although that might be worse. Deacon would have preferred to be with Mark, licking his nipples and pinching them and not calling them anything at all.

"I like it," came Mark's breathy reply at last, and Deacon relaxed. "What else should I do?"

Deacon's cock hardened.

For a moment he thought about turning the car around and heading straight back to Prescott. But his mom, who was probably watching the clock with a growing sense of dread, certain that every minute he didn't arrive meant he was dead in a crash on the highway, wouldn't cope with that. It was bad enough with Ben and their dad away. Somebody needed to be there, to make sure she took her antianxiety meds and try and get her on a more even keel by Sunday night so she could manage a new week on her own.

Mark was like every fantasy Deacon hadn't known he had. Mark was reckless, he was uninhibited, and he did whatever the hell he wanted. He was fun and full of life, and if Deacon hadn't seen the look on his face that first day in the bar, he would have thought Mark was completely carefree.

But everyone had something, right?

"Put your fingers in your mouth," Deacon said, dropping one hand to his cock and feeling it swell. "Suck them."

"Mmm."

"They're my fingers," Deacon told him, wondering if he was finally getting the hang of this. "Gonna touch you with them. Gonna put them in your ass."

There was a long pause. "Arse."

"What?"

"I have an arse," Mark said. "Not an *ass*. Say it right."

"Wow. Way to kill the mood," Deacon said but laughed. "Whatever it is, it's asking for a spanking."

"Huh," Mark said. "I've never done that either."

There was a thickness in Mark's tone, and Deacon swallowed. "Wanna try it?"

"Yeah," Mark said. "Yeah, I do. You ever done it?"

"No." But somehow the idea of spanking Mark's ass was appealing on a lot of different levels.

"Do I get to spank you?" Mark asked. "Or does it only go one way?"

"Uhhh..." Deacon shifted, trying to relieve some of the pressure in his groin. This was definitely new territory.

"Maybe I shouldn't ask," Mark continued. "Maybe I should bend you over someday when you're so hard you'd blow if I breathed on your dick. And just give it to you."

"I..." Deacon had a feeling phone sex ought to involve less stammering. "I might be better at spanking than being spanked," he admitted. Was he supposed to be giving honest answers? This was fantasy. He should just go with it. But maybe these actually were negotiations for future encounters. In which case Deacon really wasn't sure about being spanked. Probably unfair of him to expect Mark to take it, then.

But Mark didn't seem to mind. "That's all right. We want to play to your strengths. Now tell me, are you touching your cock?"

Deacon made a decision. He was on a straight road with little traffic. He unzipped his pants and stuck his hand down the front of them, cupping the warm bulge in his underwear. "Yes." He stroked lightly, trying to ignore the voice that told him if he wasn't careful, he'd end up in a scene from one of his mother's prophesies—his car in a ditch, on fire, and his body bloody and broken in the front seat, his fly down…

"Are you hard?"

Deacon banished the image from his mind. "So fucking hard." He pushed his hips forward and bit his lip.

"You wanna listen to me finger my arse while you wank yourself?"

Deacon breathed out. "Yeah." He fumbled for his cock through the slit in his underwear, keeping his eyes on the road.

"How should I do it?"

Deacon felt amazing, powerful, as though Mark really was spread out in front of him, waiting for Deacon to tell him what to do. "Suck on your fingers again."

"Okay," Mark said softly.

Deacon could hear the wet sounds of Mark working his fingers in and out of his mouth. Occasionally Mark gave a quiet moan, and Deacon answered by huffing out a breath as he awkwardly stroked his half-exposed cock.

A car was passing Deacon on the left. Shit. No way they could see what he was doing, right? As long as he faced forward and didn't pump too obviously…

"Take them out of your mouth," Deacon said. The sucking noises stopped. "What position are you in?"

"What position do you want me in?"

Deacon ran a thumb around the head of his cock. "On your back. Legs up. Put your fingers at your…arsehole?"

"Arsehole," Mark confirmed. "Okay."

"Now slide them in."

"All of them?"

"Two," Deacon said. Fuck, he was close. He took his hand off his cock for a few seconds. "Can you handle two at the same time?"

"Can handle anything you give me."

Deacon's cock flooded with heat at Mark's barely stifled groan as he pushed his fingers in. Deacon wondered if Mark was really doing it. "Are you fucking yourself?"

"Yeah." Mark's voice was tight. "Listen."

Deacon didn't hear anything at first. Then, very faintly, a slick, rhythmic noise. Deacon stroked himself again, then moved his fingers down to touch his balls. "Faster," Deacon said hoarsely. Then he realized Mark probably couldn't hear him.

"Faster?" Mark's voice sounded farther away, but the rhythm picked up.

"Are you touching your dick?"

"Now I am. What are you doing?"

"I'm..." How had Mark phrased it? "...wanking myself."

Mark chuckled. "How's it feel?"

"Good. I'm close." He was too. "Harder. Fuck yourself as hard as you can. Use three fingers."

Mark grunted, and the slick noises were coming faster, louder. Deacon wondered where Mark's phone was if Mark could hear and be heard, but Deacon could also hear Mark working his ass with his fingers. Deacon hoped to God he wasn't on speakerphone.

"Gonna come, Deke," Mark murmured. "Unless you stop me."

Deacon could have come too, just from the way Mark said it. His voice was still low, a little breathless, a little strained. And that accent was so fucking hot, and Mark had called him Deke, which filled Deacon with a whole new kind of warmth. Deacon gave his cock two hard pulls and arched out of his seat. The car veered slightly, and Deacon corrected. "It's all right," he said between gasps. "I want you to come. I want you to fucking come all over yourself."

From the other end of the phone there was a harsh mix of grunting, sharp breaths, and a short whimper that ended in a sigh. Deacon jerked on his cock until it was raw, holding his breath and then letting it go as he came over his hand. Mark's panting fueled his orgasm, and by the time he was done, he could barely speak. "You still there?" he asked finally, shaking his sticky hand onto the floor mat. He found a fast-food napkin wedged between the seat and the door, and he used that to wipe off.

"Yeah." Mark's voice was gravelly, like they were having a late-night conversation and he was about to drift off. "I'm still here."

Deacon wasn't sure what to say now. *Was it good for you?*

Mark groaned. "Christ, Romeo. I'm a mess."

"Wish I was there to..." *Lick it up? Clean you off?* "See. I wish I could see what you look like."

"Look me up when you're back in town. I may have a repeat performance in me." Mark paused. "Did you get off?"

"Uh, yeah. Gonna have to air the car out when I get home.

"Why? Bet it smells good."

Deacon laughed. "Gross." He passed a sign for Chambersburg. Twenty-five miles.

Mark was quiet. "You know, that really wasn't bad. Never knew I'd be so into phone sex."

Deacon zipped his fly. "I agree."

"We ought to try more stuff we're not sure about. Like that spanking."

Deacon grinned. "I *definitely* agree."

"All right. It's a date. When you get back."

"When I get back," Deacon echoed. He felt strange, sort of buoyed and relaxed, like he wasn't driving but drifting. Like his brain was moving slower than his body. "I like you pretty well, Juliet," he said before he could stop himself.

"Was just thinking the same about you, Romeo."

Deacon floated a little higher. "So I'll see you Sunday. And tell those brothers of yours no more dog shit in our AC unit."

"What?" Mark sounded fully alert now. Deacon immediately wished he hadn't mentioned it.

"We've started a war, you know. You've got the arse that launched a thousand ships, or something."

"That's mixing your classics a bit, yeah?"

"Maybe so," Deacon said.

"They really put dog shit in your AC?"

"Yep. Had to hold Matt back when he found out." Deacon passed a billboard advertising an adult video store. *No, thanks. I'm good.* "So," he said, only half teasing. "You willing to risk your pledgeship to fool around with a Phi Sig?"

"Don't be stupid. I'm not risking anything. They can take me no matter whose cock is up my arse, or not at all."

Deacon grinned again. "Well, then. It's gonna be my cock up your arse Sunday. Right after that arse has been spanked."

"I like the way you say 'arse.'"

"Arse," Deacon repeated.

"You could stand to put a bit more *oomph* behind it. But it's cute."

"See how cute you think I am Sunday, pledge."

He could hear Mark's grin. "Can't wait."

———

Phone sex was the shit.

Phone sex with Deacon, anyway. But everything with Deacon was pretty much the shit. Mark couldn't wait until Deacon got back. Spanking, fuck. Would Deacon really be up for that? And would Mark really like it? Maybe it was one of those things that sounded awesome in theory, and people raved about it, but in reality turned out to be kind of meh, and you couldn't see what all the fuss was about.

Like s'mores.

But you had to try everything once, right?

Even s'mores.

Not even the fact that Deacon wouldn't be back until Sunday night was taking the shine off that phone call. On Friday night when Mark should have known better than to think he'd get any studying done, and maybe finally figure out who Nathaniel Hawthorne was, he found himself summoned to Alpha Delta House to serve as their beer bitch for the night. At least this time he didn't have to dress up for them.

"Hey, little dude," Blake greeted him at the door. "You're looking happy tonight. You get laid or something?"

Sometimes Blake was shockingly perceptive. And other times he got himself locked in Portaloos.

"Uh…" Mark hesitated, stepping inside. "Yeah, actually."

"Up top, bro!" Blake held out his hand, and Mark slapped it. "She hot?"

It was once again on the tip of Mark's tongue to make the correction. *He. I like cock. Whenever you guys talk about a girl's tits, I picture a giant, fat, throbbing, leaking cock. I think about sucking it, I think about it hitting the back of my throat, and I think about swallowing cum.* What had he told Deacon? *"They can take me no matter whose cock is up my arse, or not at all."* And yet all he could make himself say was, "Oh yeah."

"Score!" Blake gave him a noogie. "So are American chicks as hot as Australian chicks?"

Mark wrenched away. He hadn't paid a lot of attention to American chicks. Or Australian chicks. "'Bout the same, really."

Blake followed him into the common room. "Where was she from?"

"Uh, Chambersburg."

"No, c'mon, little dude. What sorority was she from?"

"She wasn't from a sorority."

Blake nodded. "That's all right. Sometimes it's hard for pledges to get with sorostitutes right away, you know what I'm sayin'? I think it's the polos. But hey, when you do start makin' it with the Greek girls, you make sure you know where they're from, okay?"

"Sure," Mark said uncertainly.

"I'm serious. Alpha Delts don't date Phi Moos, Jamma Vibratas, or Chi Hos. Easy DZs are fine, though. Just check with me if you got your eye on someone, all right?"

I have no idea what you're saying to me right now. "You bet."

Blake shook his head. "Bro, I was checkin' out this hottie Wednesday night—banging bod, okay? This ass like... whew! So I'm thinkin', okay, I gotta go for it. I go up to her and say hey. She turns around—total butterface."

"Uh-oh?" Mark tried.

"I'm talking my mama could've made an apple pie out of that face. It was bad, bro."

"Well, better luck next time."

"Yeah." Blake gazed into the distance for a moment. Then he turned back to Mark. "Hey, lemme show you what you're doin' tonight, all right?"

They headed to the kitchen, where Mark was disappointed to see Bengal leaning against the counter, eating chips and picante dip. Oh well. Not even Bengal could ruin his mood. Mark nodded at the pledge trainer, who stared at him. "Pledge bitch. Where you been?"

"My little brother's been out getting *laid*!" Blake announced, heading for the fridge.

"Oh yeah?" Bengal said. "What's her name?"

Mark didn't answer right away. He was furious with himself for pretending there was some hot chick he was banging, yet the last thing he wanted was to be forced into an impromptu coming-out and then have to listen to Bengal's opinion of faggots. Mark wasn't afraid to fight, if it came to that. He'd just rather it didn't come to that.

"Did she have a name?" Bengal prompted. "Or did you make her up?"

"That's not really your business, mate," Mark said.

Bengal's eyebrows went up. "It's not?" He straightened, rolling the bag of chips shut. "Everything you do is my business, pledge bitch."

"Aw, Bengal, you're just jealous because you haven't gotten any in, like, a year," Blake said, pulling a case of beer out of the fridge and setting it on the counter.

Bengal didn't look away from Mark. "Come on, bitch. What's her name?"

"Maybe I don't remember," Mark said evenly.

"Maybe you're a liar."

"Maybe I'm not in the habit of sharing details of my sex life with arseholes who'd put dog shit in someone else's AC unit because of some pointless rivalry that—"

"Whoa. Whoa, whoa, whoa," Bengal said. "First of all, what we do to the Phi Sigs is none of your business. This is between brothers. Second, who the fuck do you think you are, talking back to me?" Bengal raised his voice and gave Mark a light shove. "Huh? Who do you think you are?"

"Bengal," Blake said.

"Who told you about the dog shit, huh? You friends with the Phi Sigs? Maybe with that asshole who crashed the party?" Bengal was trying to back Mark against the counter, but Mark refused to move. As a result, Bengal's face was now inches from his. "You two looked pretty cozy when you were helping Greg. And Chris saw you talking in the driveway afterward."

"Are you trying to make out with me or threaten me?" Mark asked.

Bengal stepped back. He turned and picked up the bag of chips and picante sauce. "Come on down to the basement, pledge bitch. I wanna show you something."

"Going somewhere more private for the make-out session?" Mark couldn't stop himself. "I have to warn you, mate, you're really not my type."

Bengal grabbed his arm. "Get down here, you little freak." He threw open the basement door and pulled Mark down the stairs.

―――

Ben's room was straight ahead at the top of the stairs. Deacon always poked his head in. It looked just like it always did—tidier than Ben had ever kept it, thanks to their mother. Nothing on the walls except a framed poster of some football player Ben had had since he was fourteen, and a bulletin board above his desk where he'd pinned family photos, a couple of to-do lists, and an army-recruitment flyer. The air was a little stale; it reminded Deacon of a dead person's room. Which maybe made sense, since their mother didn't believe Ben would make it home alive, no matter how many e-mails Ben sent saying he was fine, that he was in good hands, that where he was, the biggest danger was the chow hall's chicken stew.

The to-do lists were telling, Deacon thought. Ben had never been terribly organized or motivated. But he had tried. When they were younger, if Ben ever had a problem on his mind or a tricky decision to make, he'd sit down and write out a pros-and-cons list. If he had an appointment, he scrawled it on a calendar—even though he never remembered to check the calendar. If he turned eighteen and had no idea what to do with his life, he didn't bum around waiting for his destiny to be revealed. He signed up for the army.

It was Ben's uncertainty, the superficiality of his planning ability, that had perhaps motivated Deacon to be so sure about his own future. *This* college, *this* major, *this* fraternity, *this* career path... Deacon had it all figured out. Deacon's mother didn't have to fear losing him. He would always be home for the holidays, and he would always be close by if he was needed. He would have steady work and a good salary. He wasn't going to die when some land mine exploded under his feet just because he hadn't had the GPA to get into a decent school.

So why did he suddenly feel he wasn't any more sure of what he was "supposed" to do than Ben had been? Yes, he would leave Prescott with a solid educational base to build on. He'd go on to grad school, and then he'd be qualified for the jobs he wanted to be qualified for. And then what? He'd get one of those jobs and do it for the next forty years? Was that it?

He tried not to let himself think like this. Tried to focus on all the cool shit that was happening in his life. Phi Sig had an awesome new pledge class. They were probably going to be able to score the Jameson Historical Home for their semiformal. After this semester, he'd never have to take a statistics course again. And he had Mark.

Was it stupid to consider Mark part of his life already?

Deacon shut the door to Ben's room and moved down the hall to his own room. He set his backpack by his bed and was about to head to the bathroom for a shower when he heard his mother downstairs.

"God*damn* it! This piece of *shit*."

He smiled. She'd been getting her cross-stitching out when he'd left her to come up here. He hung his towel back on the door, then returned downstairs. He entered the living room to a hiss and a, "Fuck. I give up."

"Mom, sailors everywhere are cringing. What's wrong?"

She sighed and waved her sampler at him. "I don't know why I took this up. I really don't. I just needed something to do that wasn't work or watching the true-crime network, and I picked this because the girls who knit over in that courtyard at the cultural center always look so cute. But this is not knitting. And it's not cute. And I'm too old to do something so old personish."

"So maybe you should give it up." He sat next to her on the couch. "Try something else."

"I already promised the Farmers I'd do a little ornament thing for the new baby."

The Farmers were the next-door neighbors. They had Mayla and Brody, the kids who came over to use the swing set, and they were expecting a baby in the spring.

"Well, maybe it'll get easier, once you get the hang of it."

His mother set the sampler aside. "I don't want to think about it while you're here. I just want to enjoy your visit." She leaned back. "Tell me what's new at the house."

"Uh...hmm. James is planning a meeting to discuss some community-service thing. We're gonna try to provide some materials to kids at local schools who want to enter the regional science fair. And, um..." *I crashed a party at a rival house, fucked one of their pledges on the front lawn, and now we're in an all-out war.* "Tony's being an idiot about the fall semiformal. He broke up with his girlfriend over the summer, and now he's obsessed with finding a date."

"Do you have a date?"

Deacon tried to glare at her but ended up grinning. "You know I don't care about having a date."

She shrugged. "There's free food. I'm sure plenty of boys would be willing to go with you just for that."

"Maybe what I ought to do is say I'm bringing a date on the form, then pretend my date canceled at the last minute and see if I can get two dinners out of this."

"Sounds like a plan."

"All right. That's what I'm doing."

"How was the bar this week?" she asked.

"Same old. Made crazy tips the night of the grad-school symposium. I think eighty percent of the grad students skipped it and went out drinking instead. Or at least pregamed."

They sat in silence for a few minutes, Deacon's mother flexing her fingers as though the attempt to cross-stitch had done irreparable damage to them. She was tall and thin, her short hair darker than Deacon's—almost black. Sometimes she seemed to take up hardly any room, like her spirit and her sense of humor had all been condensed in an effort to avoid being noticed. Like she was trying to make herself a smaller target for her illness. Other times, when her anxiety wasn't so bad, she seemed strong and sure, and Deacon wanted permission to be a kid again, to ask her for advice, let her drive when they went somewhere, and let her pay when they ate out.

Deacon sometimes wondered if that feeling of disjointedness in his family was what had led him to seek a fraternity like Phi Sig. He liked the idea of a found brotherhood. A big family with no blood ties, no real obligations to one another, just a shared sense of purpose. He liked the forced proximity to his brothers too. He never had to worry about the Phi Sig house feeling as lonely as this one.

"Your brother's coming home," his mother said eventually.

Deacon looked at her.

"For good," she added.

"I thought..." Deacon didn't know what he'd thought. Ben had never said anything about coming home.

His mother flexed her fingers again. "Just before Christmas. I was hoping sooner, but doesn't sound like that will happen."

"When did you find out?" *Why didn't you tell me?*

No, why didn't he tell me?

"A couple of days ago. Ben didn't want to say anything until he knew the date. But he should find that out by the end of next week. It's great, isn't it?"

"You don't sound like you think it's great," he said.

She blinked. "I know. I just... Now that we know he's coming home, wouldn't it just figure if...?"

"Mom," Deacon said. No matter how many times he found himself in this position, he still didn't know what to say. *Nothing bad will happen to Ben.* He didn't know that. And she knew there was no way he could know that. "It's really unlikely anything will happen to him."

"In *Afghanistan?* He could die any second."

"He could die any second here too." Maybe not the best response.

She nodded. "But here I feel closer to him. Here, if something happened, I could help."

Deacon was silent a moment. "Whatever's gonna happen will happen. And he'll probably make it back fine. So just try to be happy he's coming home, all right?" Deacon was trying to get used to the idea of having Ben home. Would Ben stay here, in Chambersburg?

She patted her thighs. "You want coffee? I'm going to make coffee."

"Nah. I'm gonna go shower. Make it an early night."

"You're good to come visit," she said. She said it every week. "I'm sure there are things you'd rather be doing."

Deacon thought of Mark. Thought of lying around watching TV with James and Matt while Anabelle sniffed around the couch for chip crumbs.

He shook his head. "Glad to be here."

This was his real family. His college life came second to this.

Deacon lingered on the couch and listened to his mother in the kitchen.

All the family's last best hope wanted to do right now was fuck Mark Cooper and forget anything else existed except Mark's gorgeous ass.

Arse.

But he could hardly tell his mother that.

So he went upstairs to shower.

CHAPTER 7

F amilies.
    Wrecking Mark's life since forever.

Because Jim and Mum had decided to drive all the way in from Bedford for some reason—Mark had missed the details, concentrating more on picking his jaw up from the floor when he'd opened the door to them—and now they were taking Mark out for an early dinner. With Jackson.

"More salsa?" Jackson asked. "You like it hot, right?"

Fucker. He knew exactly how much picante sauce Mark had swallowed in the basement confessional of the Alpha Delta house the other night. And exactly how it had all come up again straightaway while Bengal roared with laughter.

And the whole time, all Mark could think was, what the hell was he doing? Why was he letting Bengal do this to him? At what point did the hazing cross a line? Maybe it already had, and Mark was just too stubborn to realize it. *They're not humiliating me, right, if I agree to it? It's all a joke still, right? I'm not a victim yet.* Because if he'd complained about it, if he'd told, then it would be proof he was weak, proof he couldn't handle it. So he handled it. He drank the fucking sauce, even though it burned. He drank it.

"Yeah, whatever," Mark said, dragging his potato skins out of Jackson's reach.

His mum shot him a look. It was her why-aren't-you-even-trying-Mark? look. She'd been wearing it on and off since the turn of the millennium. Which wasn't even fair, because he wasn't being a dick to Jackson just because. There was *context*.

"So, Jackson," she said, "it was good of you to come to dinner on such short notice. You must be busy."

Whereas Mark had nothing better to do. He stuck his finger in his sour cream and tasted it.

Jackson smiled that charming smile that seemed to fool pretty much everyone. "It's no problem, Clare. It's actually great to catch up and get away from the books sometimes."

The books, right. Because it was the books Jackson was spending all his time with. Not the chicks or the beer or all those pledges who wouldn't bastardize themselves.

Jim chuckled. "And you're keeping an eye out for Mark, aren't you?"

"Of course, Uncle Jim," Jackson said.

Uh-huh. Right. Sure. Of course.

Mark pushed his chair back. "I'm going outside for a smoke."

Clare sighed. "Mark...?"

"I'm quitting," he said and showed her his palms. "It's on my to-do list."

It was. Pennsylvania was way too fucking cold for him to keep going outside to smoke. He needed to quit by winter. If those early blizzard weeks had taught Mark anything, it was that trading death in the future from lung cancer for dying immediately of hypothermia was probably not a much better option.

Outside the restaurant, Mark leaned on a potted shrub and lit a cigarette. Through the window he could see Jim and Clare and Jackson all sitting around the table, talking and laughing. He watched Clare. She looked as at home here, with them, as with anyone. Mark was standing on the outside looking in, like a sad little matchstick girl. Except with cigarettes and a bad attitude.

But it felt good to resent Clare for excluding him, even though he'd been the one to walk away. When he tried to put his finger on what bothered him about this arrangement, he couldn't. He wasn't some sulky kid from a Disney movie, angry about the dissolution of the family he'd known. Jim wasn't some evil stepfather, and Mark's real father hadn't exactly been a prize. So what was the problem?

Maybe it had something to do with how easily Clare had adapted. How little she spoke about her marriage to Mark's father, as though this had all been scripted. She'd always known that she would get divorced, meet Jim in due time, and move to America. That she'd end up with chains on her tires in winter and a little fuckwad like Jackson for a step-nephew, and that she'd learn to root for Philadelphia even though she'd never given a shit about sports in her life.

A few times, though, Mark had caught her looking sad or lost or like she didn't quite get Jim's sense of humor or like she wanted to personally take a blowtorch to every snowflake in the state of Pennsylvania. But for the most part, she looked just like she did now. At home. And her seem-ingly placid acceptance of their new life turned it into a bit of a competition for Best Adjusted. If she didn't need to complain about the snow or the cloud cover, neither did he. If she could make new friends, so could he. If she thought Jim was an acceptable replacement for her husband, Mark thought he was an acceptable replacement for his father.

Except he didn't think that, and it was totally pointless to try and make new friends at a place like Prescott, and the weather here did pretty much fucking blow.

He did have friends, though. Didn't he? Deacon, and Brandon, and... Okay, Deacon and Brandon. And Jim *was* a good stepdad. Just...

Didn't it ever rattle Clare? That they were somewhere completely different? That she'd traded in their life to do what Jim wanted to do? What about feminism and all that? Clare had had a job back in Bundaberg, but as soon as Jim was transferred, it was, *Okay, I'll resign*, and off to Pennsylvania.

What rankled the most about this whole situation was the fact that Mark had never been one of those kids. One of those date-my-mother-and-I'll-make-your-life-hell kids. His dad had been out of the picture for so long that he was barely even a memory, so it wasn't like Mark was on some weird Freudian quest to protect his territory or anything. He'd been nice to Jim, damn it. All, "Hi, nice to meet you" and "Yes, let's do that small-talk thing." He'd been grown-up all the way through—pointedly not thinking about his mother's sex life with this American bloke, thanks very much—when suddenly he wasn't allowed to be an adult anymore. Suddenly they were getting married, and he was moving halfway around the world with them, and nobody gave him a choice. Two years of good work down the drain; Mark had been turned instantly into a stereotypical whining teenager.

He smoked quickly and angrily, only making it through

half the cigarette before he coughed, decided fuck this, and went back inside.

He took his seat across from Jackson again.

"And how are you enjoying Greek life?" Jim asked him.

Mark badly wanted to ask him if that was a euphemism, but Clare still looked disappointed in him. That rankled as well. They'd been on the same side once. "It's...it's different," he said at last. That was certainly the truth.

Mark couldn't resist looking at Jackson as Jim waxed lyrical about the benefits of fraternity life. Brotherhood. Honor. Some other stuff that Mark had tried to reflect on whilst swallowing picante sauce and half his throat lining. Jackson didn't even have the decency to look guilty. He just stared at Mark like he knew exactly what Mark was thinking, and thought Mark had brought it on himself.

Jim said something about brotherhood again.

"...and you boys," he finished up.

What?

Jim smiled at him encouragingly. "You're family now," he said. "Not only cousins, but brothers, and I know you'll look out for each other."

Guilt stirred in Mark's guts. Guilt that he wasn't trying. God, it was impossible to hate Jim. Mark had *tried* to hate him, but sooner or later his earnest fucking goodwill just crept up on your anger and smothered it. Didn't even give it a fighting chance.

So Mark smiled at Jim, promised his mother he was doing his best in his classes, and hit them up for money before they left.

"You can't have gone through your allowance already," Clare said, giving him a suspicious hug. The sort that might turn into a pat-down any second.

Allowance. She was calling it that now? Such an American word.

"I spent it all on drugs and prostitutes," Mark told her. He'd been telling her the same thing since he was fourteen. He'd said it the first time to see if he could shock her.

"Fine," she said. "As long as you're not wasting it."

Which had been her answer then as well. She had always been unshockable.

Jim laughed and pulled out his wallet.

Money for Mark, and a few bills for Jackson. Then more hugs, and an offer to drop them both back at Prescott.

"Nah, I'll walk," Mark said. After everything he'd eaten, it would do him good. Deacon was due back in a couple of hours, and Mark suddenly wanted to stay toned. And limber.

"I'll walk with you," Jackson said.

They waved Clare and Jim off.

"So," Jackson said. "Your mom is kind of cool."

"Fuck off," Mark said. "You don't need to pretend to be my friend now they're gone. I can find my own way back to campus just fine, you know."

"I wasn't..." Jackson trailed off, then sneered. "Later, pledge bitch."

Mark showed him his middle finger and made sure he picked another route back to campus.

————

I have cash for a hotel.

Deacon looked at his phone and spent a moment wondering how he felt about Mark's text. Being Mark's fuck buddy...fair enough. Absolutely no argument there. But having some eighteen-year-old rich kid pay for a hotel so they could meet up and have sex in a bed like adults? It left Deacon feeling like one of them was taking advantage, but he wouldn't be sure which one until he saw the Movie of the Week dramatization. Either Deacon was the older guy stringing along the pretty younger naive boy just because he had money, or Mark was slumming it, and Deacon was his good-hearted, rough-around-the-edges poor boy. Either way it would end in tears, melodrama, and running mascara.

Deacon dropped his bag on the floor of his room and read the text again.

I have cash for a hotel.

Fuck. On one hand, Mark might be everything Deacon wanted: fun, spontaneous, and with a sex drive that would put a bonobo to shame. On the other hand, there was a reason Deacon hadn't made room for those things in his life. Because someone had to be reliable. Because when everything else fell through, when everyone else had abandoned her for Afghanistan or Michigan, someone had to stay for his mom. Someone had to be her one piece of solid ground when everything else was crumbling.

He needed Mark to understand that. And Mark might. Someone as spontaneous as Mark probably didn't do boyfriends. And that would work out just fine for Deacon. Except for the part where he wanted Mark to stick around.

He texted back, *Where are u?*

Dorm.

Deacon glanced around. Matt was gone for the night, and James was in the basement playing table tennis.

Can you come to the Phi Sig house?

Might be unfair to ask Mark to do that. If the Alpha Delts found out, they'd be furious with Mark. Still, Deacon didn't want to go to a hotel. He wanted Mark in his bed. He could always do the old tie on the door. God knew the Phi Sigs had plenty of ties.

Romeo, Mark texted back. *Thou art as daring as thou art smoking hot.*

Deacon grinned. *Is that a yes?*

Give me 15 min.

Come around the side away from Alpha Delt. I'll let you in.

Do I look crazy enough to go in the front?

Deacon snorted. *Yes.*

Ok. Side door. See u soon.

James came upstairs while Deacon was waiting. Deacon almost groaned with disappointment.

"Hey, Deke," James said as he entered the bedroom. "How was home?"

"Same as usual."

"Your mom doing all right?"

"Yeah, she's pretty good." *Just convinced we should go casket shopping for my perfectly healthy brother.*

James grabbed a sweatshirt from his wardrobe. "Some of us are gonna go grab second dinner. You wanna come?"

"No, thanks. I ate. Um, and I hate to do this, but...would you be able to stay gone for a few hours?"

James looked at him curiously. "What's up, Deke? You havin' someone over?"

"Yeah. And, I mean, you don't have to stay gone, but just, if I could have the room for, like, an hour or so..." Not nearly enough time with Mark. Maybe Deacon should have agreed to the hotel. He wouldn't be able to invite Mark to stay over. Couldn't even invite him to *linger.*

"Dude." James shut the wardrobe. "Matt's at A Phi for the night. And I can crash on the couch if you want the room."

Deacon knew he ought to be polite and refuse, but fuck,

he wanted to take James up on the offer. "You don't have to do that."

"I owe you one anyway," James added. "You took the couch when I had Mclissa over last month."

"Seriously, James, thanks."

"No problem. Just stay off my bed, okay?"

Last year Matt had fucked his then-girlfriend in James's bed. James had yet to let it go.

"We'll stick to my bed, I promise."

"Sweet. Have fun, Deke. It's been a while."

Deacon almost protested that for all James knew, Deacon got laid all the time. But it wasn't true, and Deacon kept his mouth shut.

Fifteen minutes later, Deacon let Mark in through the side door and ushered him past a group of guys watching TV in the common room. As soon as they were in Deacon's room with the door locked, Deacon put his arms around Mark and kissed him awkwardly. It was only awkward for a second. Then Mark kissed back, and Deacon lost track of how long they made out.

When they parted, Mark said, "Is this gonna be some kind of five-door farce? Where you're trying to sneak your mistress out a window as your roommate's coming up the stairs?"

"We have the room all night, if we want it."

"Well, in that case, I'll make myself at home." Mark shrugged off his hoodie.

"Thank you for coming," Deacon said.

Mark grinned. "I haven't come yet, mate. But I'd damn well better, after the weekend I've had."

"What happened?"

"My mum and stepdad dropped by. Unexpectedly. Took me and cousin Jackson out to dinner. Jackson was an epic wanker; Jim was far too kind. And my mum was my mum."

"Do you get along with your mum?"

Mark nodded. "And sometimes that's the problem. I never really know what she's thinking. She rarely says anything revealing around me, so I never say much about my life around her. We just...get along."

"Oh."

"It's all right, though."

"My mum—mom, I mean." Deacon flushed at Mark's grin. "She's got OCD."

"So she washes her hands a lot?"

"And thinks people are dead when they're totally fine."

"That's rough."

"She's funny. And we're really close. Just, she needs a little looking after sometimes."

"Don't we all?" Mark wasn't grinning when he said it, but he drawled the way he did when he said something sarcastic.

"Anyway, we don't have to talk about that," Deacon said.

"Yes. Let's forget our families and get down to this business of sucking, fucking, and, ah...arse spanking."

Deacon felt a jumble of nerves in his stomach. They were actually gonna do this, then.

Mark looked around the room. "You're cleaner than my possible future brothers."

"It's early in the year yet," Deacon said. "Give us time. After all..." He wound his arms around Mark from behind and kissed his neck. "I can be pretty dirty." He slid his hands down to Mark's belly so he could feel the muscles move as Mark laughed and gave a low hum. Mark turned his head to brush his lips against Deacon's cheek.

Deacon nudged Mark forward, and they both collapsed

on the bed. Mark rolled onto his back and kissed Deacon hungrily. Deacon ran his hands up and down the front of Mark's shirt, feeling Mark's nipples harden under the fabric.

"That stuff you said on the phone," Deacon whispered. "Were you really doing it?"

"Fuck, yeah, I was." Mark gasped as Deacon brushed his left nipple again.

Deacon slipped his hand under Mark's shirt, skimmed it over warm, damp skin, and pinched the nipple. Mark straightened his legs, lifting his hips off the bed. "You did this?" Deacon asked, tugging.

"Not quite that hard." Mark's voice was strained. "But yeah."

Deacon pinched his other nipple and gave it a twist. Smiled. Then he pulled Mark's shirt up as high as it would go and yanked it over his head. Took a moment to trace the grooves between and under Mark's pecs. He sat back on his heels and pulled his own shirt off, then reached down and undid Mark's pants, yanking them partway down his thighs. Mark's cock was already pushing out the slit in his briefs. Deacon rubbed the bulge lightly with his palm. "When you came? That was real?"

"Yeah." The word was barely more than a breath.

"You're gonna come again," Deacon promised, loving Mark's groan as he trailed his fingertips down Mark's inner thighs. "And this time, I'm gonna watch." He peeled Mark's underwear down and bent to take Mark in his mouth.

Mark gave a long sigh that seemed to fill the room, and every second it went on made it possible for Deacon to take Mark deeper. Deacon knew he wasn't as skilled as Mark at this, but Mark didn't seem to have any complaints. Mark fisted the sheets and grunted, twisting his hips in an effort to keep himself from thrusting into Deacon's throat. Deacon laughed around his cock. Mark placed a hand on Deacon's hair, petting him in quick strokes that matched the bobbing of Deacon's head. "Oh God…shit… Okay, we have all night, remember, and I'm not…gonna…last…" Mark's knees came up, his thighs tensed and quivered, but he somehow held off from coming.

Deacon released Mark's cock. "Roll over," he said.

Mark obliged. Deacon stared at his ass. This was the first time he'd actually seen it. It was pale with a little bit of gold hair, and slight dimples on the sides of his cheeks. He ran a hand over it, his cock hardening as he watched the muscles tighten and release in response to his touch. "Mark?" Deacon said softly.

"Yeah?"

"You've got a nice arse."

"Thanks. You gonna sit there talking about it, or are you gonna do something to it?"

Deacon took a deep breath. He was grown-up enough to say the words without blushing, wasn't he? "Gonna spank it if you're not careful."

"Then why the hell would I ever want to be careful?"

Deacon grinned and raised his hand. There was a moment's hesitation, a few seconds where Deacon wasn't sure whether he could really do it. Then he brought his hand down, smacking the center of Mark's ass. Mark's breath hitched, but other than that, nothing much happened. The spot Deacon had slapped was barely pink. "Was that okay?" Deacon asked.

"Was what okay?" Mark asked, lifting his head.

"Uh, the way I did that?"

"Did you do something?"

"What do you mean?"

"I might be wrong, mate, but isn't a spanking supposed

to hurt a bit? You've got arm muscles; why don't you use th—"

The crack of Deacon's palm against Mark's flesh made Deacon cringe—not out of sympathy for Mark so much as fear that the entire house had heard it. Mark bucked, and the pink patch that appeared on his right cheek was quite satisfying. "Better?" Deacon asked.

"God. Fuck. Yes. Better," Mark said into the pillow.

Deacon spanked him again. Then again, fascinated by the way Mark's ass quivered on each impact.

They heard footsteps pounding up the stairs, and the door to the room next to Deacon's opened, then shut.

"We're so loud," Deacon said, rubbing Mark's flushed skin. "You think they can hear?"

"Fuck 'em," Mark said. "Keep going."

Deacon swatted him again, but he couldn't make himself do it very hard. He was worried about the noise. "Maybe if we get under the covers?" Deacon suggested, removing his pants. Mark kicked out of his jeans as well, and they climbed under the bedspread. "Maybe this'll muffle it a little."

"Not much swing room," Mark replied.

Deacon tried spanking him again, but Mark was right— Deacon couldn't raise his hand without it getting caught in the bedspread, and if he tried to hold the comforter up with this free hand, it was just awkward. Deacon called it quits after a couple of light swats and crawled on top of Mark, kissing across Mark's shoulders. Deacon's cock was hard, and he loved the sensation of rubbing it against the swell of Mark's backside.

"Fuck yeah, that's good," Mark murmured.

Deacon repositioned himself so his cock was in Mark's ass crack. Then he supported himself with his hands on either side of Mark's shoulders and slid his dick up and down Mark's crack.

"Yeahhhh." Mark let out a long breath.

Deacon whimpered as Mark clenched his cheeks, creating hard mounds of muscle on either side of Deacon's cock. Deacon licked the outline of Mark's shoulder blade, then nipped the soft skin right above it. Mark began squirming, moving his hips in time with Deacon's thrusts. They were both sweating, and finally Deacon threw the comforter off them, relieved to feel cool, fresh air. Mark wriggled onto his back under Deacon, and they continued rutting, rubbing their cocks together and panting in each other's faces. Deacon felt his balls draw tight, and he leaned down so that he could be kissing Mark when he came.

Suddenly there was shouting outside. Deacon wanted to ignore it, wanted so badly to come, to watch Mark come too. But he recognized Matt's voice, and Matt sounded furious. There was a loud thud. A couple of unfamiliar voices were shouting too. Deacon froze. Mark tensed under him.

"Shit," Deacon said. "I don't want to... But it's Matt yelling."

"Go see what it is," Mark said. "Like I said, we've got all night."

Deacon clambered off Mark and went to the window. In the front yard, Matt was facing off with two Alpha Delts. A small crowd had gathered, Alphas on one side, Phi Sigs on the other, along with random passersby strewn about. Riley, a sophomore Phi Sig, was trying to hold Matt back.

"Shit. Fuck. Balls. I gotta go down there." Deacon yanked on his pants and stepped into his shoes. Mark was scrambling for his clothes as well. "I'll be back, I promise."

Deacon ran out the front door just as one of the Alpha Delts threw the first punch. It grazed Matt, who turned and nailed the second Alpha in the jaw. Then all Deacon saw was a blur of bodies, heard Riley yelling his name as he raced for the three fighters. The first Alpha Delt pulled Matt off his friend and threw him to the ground, but Matt was right back up, yelling, "Fuckers! You retarded, pansy-ass fuckers!"

"Matt!" Deacon shouted.

But it was too late. Matt drew back and punched the first Alpha full in the face. The guy staggered back, hands over his nose, blood pouring from between his fingers.

Deacon grabbed Matt and yanked him away. He could see that Matt's cheekbone was bruised, and Matt was still screaming at the Alphas, who were screaming back at him. Moments later, a campus police car rolled up the Phi Sig driveway.

Fuck. Fuck, fuck, fuck.

"*Matt*. Calm down," Deacon snapped.

"They started it!" Matt yelled at him. "Shoulda heard what they said."

"Matt." Deacon caught him by the shoulders. "Matt, it doesn't matter what they said. You're better than them!"

Jesus. Matt was easily the most volatile of the Phi Sigs. Too bad this shit had kicked off before he'd left for A Phi, because Matt was not the sort of guy who turned the other cheek. As he said before when things flared up with the Alpha Delts, he'd put up with asshole popular kids the whole way through high school. He wasn't going to do it here as well.

"Fuckers." Matt glared at the Alpha Delts. He raked a hand through his hair. "They put shit in our AC!" he yelled at the campus police officer.

"Shut up, Matt," Deacon said. He turned his head as James came hurrying down the steps. "Let James sort it out."

So much for his night in with Mark. Why, of all nights, did the Alpha Delts have to start their shit tonight when Mark was currently lying bare-ass naked between Deacon's sheets? A bare ass that Deacon hadn't had nearly enough time to explore. Deacon resisted the urge to look at his watch as the campus police began to ask questions.

He dug his phone out of his pocket and texted Mark: *This could take a while.*

CHAPTER 8

Good or bad protocol to rub one out in your date's bed while he was sorting out some blue downstairs that your soon-to-be frat brothers had most likely started? Mark decided it was bad form and put his hands behind his head for a while. Then he got tired of lying there, waiting, and got out of bed and pulled his clothes back on.

He tried to feel like a spy in enemy territory, here in the heart of Phi Sig, like the Mata Hari in a hoodie. But really, three beds, three desks, and three shelves stacked with books—actually, every free surface was stacked with books —didn't make an exciting investigation, and Mark had no desire to dig deeper into the private lives of Phi Sig. Given that their reading matter included textbooks on electrical engineering, heat and thermodynamics, and "delicious" vegan and vegetarian recipes, Mark figured that what you saw was what you got with Phi Sig.

Mark checked his phone when it buzzed. A message from Deacon: *This could take a while.* And then, a moment later: *A plague on both our houses, Juliet.*

Mark grinned. Yeah, they were getting that star-cross'd

thing right, at least. He typed out a reply: *Get back up here, Romeo. I wanna suck your dick.*

Mark lay on Deacon's bed and slid a hand down his waistband, waiting for a hopefully filthy reply. He got: *Little bro, get over here now. Shit's kicking off with the Phi Sigs.*

Fuck. Blake. Although, was that correct apostrophe use in a text? Must be a fluke.

Mark made a face at the screen. *Stop cock blocking me, Blake.*

Srsly bro. Get here NOW. House meeting.

Mark groaned in frustration. He was this close to getting off. This close to getting something up his arse. Something that was connected to Deacon: either his very nice thick cock, or his fingers. Mark wasn't fussy. Either would be good.

And maybe even this close to a bit of reciprocation. Because if Deacon offered him his arse in return, Mark would be in like Flynn.

He heard the front door open, and too many voices for him to be able to distinguish who was talking. He got a text from Deacon: *Matt's inside. Delaying him in the kitchen but u better go. Fuck I'm sorry.*

Mark sighed. Texted back: *Yeah I'm being called to a house meeting. Just remember where we left off, ok?*

He slipped out of the room and into the empty second-floor hall. He heard raised voices on the first floor—what sounded like a good deal of Alpha Delt slandering. There were a couple of guys standing near the side door, but they were too excited about whatever had just transpired to notice Mark. He went out the door and crossed the lawn, which was mostly empty now. Passed through Alpha Delt's iron gates.

Inside Alpha Delt, people were even more riled than they were at Phi Sig. It took Chris a few minutes to get everyone to calm down enough to listen. Then he made a speech that Mark thought sounded bizarrely akin to Roosevelt's "A Day That Will Live in Infamy" speech, which he'd had to listen to in media studies last week. From what Mark could gather, two brothers had been out in the yard when Matt walked by. Matt had yelled at them about the dog shit, they'd yelled back, and things had escalated steadily until Matt asserted he could beat either of them in a fight, and the brothers had taken up the gauntlet.

"What's embarrassing," Chris said, "is that we got GDIs involved."

A week ago, Mark hadn't known what GDI meant. Now he knew it stood for God Damn Independent—someone outside of the Greek system. More like God Damn Intelligent, he thought.

He glanced around, noticing that Brandon wasn't here. What the fuck? Had he not gotten the memo?

"Not just GDIs, but the cops," Chris continued. "And now we gotta attend this Interfraternity Council meeting." Chris gazed at everybody in turn, looking extremely disappointed. "Feuds like this are supposed to stay between houses. We're not putting on a public performance here, all right? Yes, we wanna fuck with the Phi Sigs. No, we do not want the fucking campus cops involved. Got it?" He stared at the two brothers who had been involved in the fight. One of them nodded tersely. The one with the swollen nose kept his face in his hand, a rejected ice pack on the floor by his chair.

Mark made it through the rest of the combination warmongering/you-ought-to-be-ashamed-of-yourselves speech by thinking about Deacon's hands on him. Deacon twisting his nipples, spanking his ass—which, why exactly had *that* been so hot, by the way? He wished Deacon had gotten even more into it, had hit him harder, and for longer. He could have taken it. He indulged in a detailed fantasy in which Deacon fingered his ass slowly while spanking Mark with his free hand.

Everyone was getting up. House meeting over, apparently. Would it be wrong to text Deacon and see if he was interested in that hotel room?

Mark saw Jackson crossing the room and called, "Hey, Jacko. Where's Brandon?"

Jackson turned and stared at him, coldly furious. Then he walked on.

"Brandon's not feeling well," a brother named Ray said, walking backward as he passed Mark. He had a sly smile Mark didn't like. Brandon wasn't feeling well? Brandon would have come to an Alpha Delt house meeting if he'd had the bubonic plague.

Mark started for the door.

"Li'l bro!"

Oh boy. Blake incoming.

"I got a coupla questions to ask you."

As long as Blake asked him here, and not in the basement with a jar of picante salsa in hand, Mark could handle that. "Fire away."

"First of all..." Blake lowered his voice. "Where's your pin?"

Mark looked down at his defiantly nonpolo shirt. The pin, which he'd attached earlier, was no longer there. But it had been there when he'd arrived at the Phi Sig house, because he remembered pulling his hoodie over to cover it when he'd entered the house—just in case someone saw it. "It's at my dorm. I forgot it."

"Dude. Do *not* let Bengal see, okay? Like, get out of here before he notices."

"Okay." Gladly. Mark headed for the door.

"No, no, no, don't go yet," Blake said. "I gotta ask you if you have a date to semiformal."

"The whatter huh?"

"Semiformal. In December? Where you been, bro? Hot girls, a fuck ton of booze, suits and ties, and we rent out the country club."

"Ooh," Mark said. "All of my favorite things."

"Sometimes it's stupid as shit," Blake said. "But it's fun if you know how to make it fun. Last year was nuts. I got locked in the bathroom for like an hour."

"Does that happen a lot, mate?" Mark asked.

"I was askin' if you had a date, because I might have found someone for you."

"What?" Mark was genuinely startled.

"I know you're, like, a pussy magnet, so if you wanna take one of your hoochies, that's cool. But this one you might wanna keep around long-term, you know what I'm saying?"

"Not really," Mark replied.

"Dude, she's Zeta Tau." He stared at Mark like that was supposed to mean something. "I told her about you, and she's totally into you. And she's hot. Not drunk hot —actual hot."

Mark opened his mouth, but for once he couldn't think of anything to say.

"It's a good match. I know you don't know a lot about Greek shit yet, but trust me. Lotta Alpha Delts marry Zeta Taus."

"*Marry*?"

"Not tryin' to freak you out. Just sayin'."

"Blake," Mark said, trying to keep his voice gentle. "I don't need help finding a date to an event I'm not even going to attend. And I definitely don't need you to find me someone to *marry*."

"Of course you're gonna attend! It happens right after induction. It'll be your first event as a brother."

Mark sighed. "Even if I do go, I don't need a matchmaker."

"You already got someone you're seeing."

"Yes!"

"Is she hot? You can tell me, little bro. Tits medium-large, large, larger, or astronomical?"

Mark felt the rush of wild anger that sometimes presaged his saying something mean or unfair to Jim. The realization that the world was never gonna unfold and be the tidy picnic he was supposed to want it to be, and the *pleasure* he took in understanding that. He didn't want to be here; he'd never wanted to be here; he had *nothing* in common with these guys. And it was time to end this farce right now.

"*He* is incredibly hot," Mark said. "Great pecs, gorgeous face, lovely round arse. Hung like Prescott's stallion. I like him quite a lot." Mark turned and stalked away from Blake. Left the house and headed down the street toward campus.

So that was that, then. Without the pin, it was mighty hard to behave like a good pledge. Maybe it had been cursed, warping Mark's brain every time he wore it. That was the only explanation for why he'd stayed with the Alpha Delts as long as he had.

He kept his shoulders hunched even though it wasn't cold.

He didn't care what anyone thought. Especially not a bunch of pathetic frat guys. That didn't mean it wasn't hard to tell people something that would make them look at him funny. Something he actually cared about. It was fine to be mocked or disliked on his own terms. But his sexual orientation was such a naked target, unfortified by nonchalance and lacking the benefit of being a persona he'd constructed. Gay Mark wasn't sheddable like Smart-Ass Mark or Bitter-About-the-Move Mark.

Gay Mark *was* Mark, and 98 percent of the time he was fine with that. Except when he had to think about what fifty testosterone-laden, overcompensating, perpetually drunk arseholes would say to him now that they knew.

Because he had a feeling Blake wasn't going to keep this a secret.

He pulled out his phone and texted Deacon. *You wanna meet me by the statue of Ben Franklin?*

He had to walk a few minutes before he got a reply. *What statue of Ben Franklin?*

Sorry. Nathaniel Hawthorne.

What did they slip in ur drink at the meeting?

Who's the charming fellow in the tricorn hat on horseback outside the library?

Wolford Prescott. Reason you're here. Show some respect.

How did Wolford know my mother?

Sigh.

Mark laughed.

And yes, Deacon's next text said. *I want to meet you there.*

———

Mark wasn't by the statue of Wolford Prescott when Deacon arrived. He was on it. Straddling the horse, with his arms around Prescott's waist, reminding Deacon of exactly what they'd gotten up to on the mechanical bull. Except Wolford Prescott was nowhere near as cute as Mark, and his stockings weren't as sexy.

"So," Mark said, scrambling down. "I might have just come out to the frat. To Blake, anyway."

"Huh," said Deacon. "And how do you feel about that?"

Mark regarded him silently for a moment. "You always know the right thing to say, you know?"

"I do?"

Mark nodded. "Most people would have asked me what the hell I was thinking, or if I was sure I knew what I was doing, but you didn't."

Deacon smiled. He was pretty sure he was just the latest in a very long line of people who had no idea what Mark Cooper was thinking. "And how did the fraternity take it?"

"I only told Blake so far," Mark said. "But I reckon sooner or later I'll get a summons to the basement confessional where I'll be held accountable for all my big gay sins. But I never came here to lie, you know. And people always say, why do you have to shove it in people's faces, but I'm not, am I? They're shoving it in mine. Asking who this chick is, how big her tits are, and trying to set me up with girls. Fuck, you have to draw a line in the sand, right?"

"Yeah," Deacon said. "Wait, there's really a basement confessional?"

"It's fucked-up," Mark said. "I had to drink a whole bottle of picante salsa just because I wouldn't tell Bengal which chick I was fucking."

"Really?" Deacon reached out for Mark and caught him by the belt loops. He pulled him closer, aligning their hips. Mark, a few inches shorter, lined up against Deacon's body nicely. "That...that just sucks, Mark."

"I threw it up," Mark said. He sighed and, for a moment, looked as lost and alone as he had the night Deacon had first seen him in the bar. "I've been a prick, I know. Why join the game if you're going to refuse to play it, right? But I just don't *get* the rules. I never got the rules."

Deacon tugged him closer. Mark was clearly more rattled than he wanted to admit by coming out to Blake. "I think you did the right thing, for what it matters. And I think you're tough as hell for doing it as an Alpha Delta pledge."

Mark scowled at the ground. "Brandon's gonna be upset with me."

"For pissing off the fraternity?"

Mark shrugged. "Yeah. And he's got some other stuff going on."

"Mark?"

"Hmm."

"If you really want to be in a fraternity, there are ones that aren't like Alpha Delt. None of this hazing shit."

"I don't want to be in a fraternity. First I did it to make my stepfather happy, and now I'm doing it because fuck the Alpha Delts for thinking they control me."

Deacon kissed him gently. Mark hesitated a second, then yielded, placing the fingers of his left hand against Deacon's cheek and letting his forehead rest against Deacon's when they parting. "You can't stop fighting, can you?" Deacon asked.

"I don't know." The fact that Mark didn't have some smart-ass quip saddened Deacon, but it brought out something protective in him as well. "I don't know what I'm doing." Mark wrapped his arms suddenly around Deacon and squeezed, burying his face in Deacon's shoulder.

Deacon slid his hand up to Mark's hair and tangled his fingers in it. "Anything I can do to help?"

"You're doing it," Mark mumbled.

After a few minutes, Deacon said, "So maybe you tell Alpha Delt you're done. Maybe that's how you win this one."

"And what does that leave Jim thinking?" Mark raised his head. "His pussy queer stepson couldn't handle the pressure?"

"Whoa." The statement was so at odds with Deacon's image of Mark—someone who didn't care what others thought, who was himself no matter what—that Deacon felt a familiar sinking fear. It was the feeling he got when his mother said something that reminded him just how serious her disorder was. They could joke about her needing to run pens through the dishwasher before using them, or disinfecting the covers of library books before she read them, but her fears about Ben weren't funny.

"Forget it," Mark muttered, stepping back. "It's not really about that. Jim's not like that. He's the opposite of that. He's too fucking nice."

"What's it about, do you think?"

"I don't know." Mark leaned against the base of the statue, jamming his hands in his pockets. He looked away from Deacon. "It's like, if I don't have these guys, what do I have here?" He glanced Deacon's way, then turned his gaze to the quad again. "Pathetic, yeah, I know. But I'm not exactly racking up friends."

"To be fair, you've been at Prescott, what, less than a month?"

"You're out, aren't you?" Mark still didn't look at him. "At Phi Sig?"

"Yeah. The guys have all been cool. I know the atmosphere's different at Alpha Delt, but maybe more of them'll be cool with it than you think."

Mark shook his head, still tense. The lights in front of the library cast an eerie, greenish-gold glow on Wolford

Prescott and his horse. Across the quad, three girls were chalking the walkway. "I don't care whether they're cool with it. I don't know why I'm even talking about this. Can we change the subject?"

"If you'll let me say one more thing."

"What?"

Deacon stepped forward and leaned on the statue too. He rolled his head toward Mark, reached out, and tugged Mark's hand from his pocket. "They're not all you've got here. Okay?"

Mark looked at their entwined fingers and nodded. "Good," he said softly. "I'm glad. Because I like you better than I like them."

"Good."

"Come to the library," Mark said suddenly.

"What?" Deacon let Mark draw him across toward the entrance. "Why?"

"They've still got a microfiche section," Mark said.

"Really? How do you even know that?"

"Brandon made me come to the library with him once," Mark said. "He's got an eidetic memory. I'm not sure what that means, except the Dewey decimal system is his bitch. He can tell you where to find anything. Even old copies of the *Prescott Literary Review* from 1823, which is all on microfiche because nobody's got around to converting it yet."

Deacon shook his head as he followed Mark inside the building. "Why would I want copies of the *Prescott Literary Review* from 1823? Why would anyone?"

"Exactly," Mark said. "A whole room of microfiche readers, and nobody ever goes in there."

"Not even the drug dealers?" Deacon asked, only half sarcastically.

"Everyone knows they use the second-floor toilets," Mark shot back with a reckless grin. "Come on!"

"Wait," Deacon said as Mark led the way down toward the back of the library, past the study rooms and into the stacks. "Mark, wait."

Mark leaned against the stacks. Section 291. Comparative religions. "What?"

Deacon drew a breath. "First of all, you're hot. You are so fucking hot."

"You don't want to do this?" Mark's smile vanished. He narrowed his eyes.

"No." Deacon reached out, but Mark flinched away. Angry bunny was back. "I *really* want to do this, I do. But if we're going to keep hooking up like this, I want to know where we stand. You and me, are we an item? Because I think you're hot, and sexy, and Jesus, the things you can do in lace, but if we're fucking because you want to prove to yourself how you're not like the rest of the Alpha Delts, well..."

Mark scowled at the floor.

"You just came out to your fraternity," Deacon said. "Maybe you need a friend right now, not a fuck."

"Why can't I get both?" Mark asked him, lifting his gaze and jutting his chin out.

Deacon didn't know how to explain himself, not without pushing Mark away. But he thought he recognized something unhealthy in Mark's behavior, something that skirted very close to self-destructive. And Deacon figured the last thing Mark needed was another audience to play the Mark-doesn't-give-a-fuck song for. What Mark needed was a break. From his family, from his fraternity, from his homesickness and his carefully cultivated bad attitude. What Mark needed was a break from the Mark Cooper circus.

"You can," Deacon promised him. "Just...just take a breath sometimes, okay?"

Mark nodded.

"Come on," Deacon said. "Show me this microfiche room."

Mark flashed him a smile, a little less manic than usual, a little less confident, and led the way through the stacks.

The microfiche room was hidden away behind the anthropology shelves. It was a narrow, windowless room with one long desk set up against the wall. The desk was divided into four booths. In each booth was a microfiche reader, which Deacon wouldn't have had a clue how to work. He wondered if anyone did.

Mark flicked the lock on the door. "And now we're all alone."

Deacon looked at the stained carpet dubiously. "Maybe I should have taken you up on that offer of a hotel, Juliet."

Mark raised his eyebrows. "You had your chance, Romeo. Now finish what you started back in your room. Ravish me."

"Ravish you?" Deacon laughed.

"It sounded Shakespearean," Mark said.

Deacon was struck by the image of something truly Shakespearean: a boy in a dress. Shit. Before Mark, he'd never even guessed he was into that. But the thought of seeing Mark in a dress, again was sending some serious signals straight to his dick.

Deacon took a chair and wedged it under the door handle. Better safe than sorry. "Get over here, then, Juliet."

Mark's smile was back. That reckless, cheeky smile that Deacon knew was only skin-deep. Mark dropped his hands to his fly. "You want me to get out of these, Deke? Or you wanna do the honors?"

"Strip for me," Deacon said. He'd never had the courage to say that to anyone before, but he'd never been with anyone so...shameless. He leaned against the wall and watched as Mark swayed his hips, his hands framing the bulge in his jeans.

Mark unsnapped his fly and teased the zipper down. He toed out of his shoes and kicked them under the desk. His movements got quicker, less graceful as he pushed his jeans to his ankles and stepped out of them. But he slowed as he straightened, and he stood in front of Deacon in his gray briefs and T-shirt, chest moving in and out. He crossed his arms, grabbed the hem of his tee, and pulled it up and over his head. Deacon admired the shadows of his ribs, his tight nipples—a little bit of light hair around them, which Deacon remembered feeling that night in the Kissin' Shack when he'd explored Mark's body in the dark.

Mark grinned again when he saw Deacon staring, and he tossed the T-shirt so that it landed over Deacon's face. Deacon swiped it off, static crackling in his hair. He didn't want to miss a second of this show. He turned his focus to Mark's hip bones, beautifully defined even in the god-awful lighting of the microfiche room. Mark hooked his thumbs in the elastic of his briefs, easing them down, freeing his hard cock. He stepped out of his underwear and spread his hands.

"Well? How do you want me?"

"Would you...?" It took Deacon a minute to find his voice. And he was almost too shy to finish the question. "Would you strip me?"

Mark's smiled was genuine this time. He stepped toward Deacon. "What are you blushing for?" he asked.

Deacon wasn't blushing. Was he? "The lights, I guess. They're really bright. I feel like I'm on a stage."

Mark trailed a finger down the front of Deacon's shirt. "Too bad. You got away with fucking me in the dark once. Now I want to see you."

He took hold of Deacon's shirt and tugged Deacon toward him. He bunched fistfuls of the fabric, squeezing Deacon's pecs as he did. Deacon felt a jolt in his dick as Mark's hand brushed his nipple. Mark let go with one hand and traced the side of Deacon's neck with two fingertips, sending warmth through Deacon's body. He placed his chest against Deacon's so that their hearts thudded against each other. His eyes were hazy as he met Deacon's gaze, and then he leaned in and kissed Deacon, still holding onto Deacon's shirt, as though afraid Deacon might escape if he let go.

Deacon closed his eyes, concentrating on Mark's lips on his. A friend and a fuck. Mark could definitely have both. He could have anything and everything Deacon could give him.

Mark stepped back and pulled Deacon's shirt off. Ran his hands over Deacon's chest, down his sides, and pushed them around to the small of Deacon's back. He hooked his fingers in Deacon's back belt loop and forced Deacon's hips against his, rubbing his cock against the front of Deacon's jeans. Deacon kissed Mark again, mostly out of a panicked need to distract himself from how badly he wanted to come.

The way Mark thrust his tongue into Deacon's mouth didn't help, though. Deacon thought he could feel his whole body pulsing, hot and frantic. He wanted to grab Mark and pin him against one of the cubicle walls and fuck him until Mark was shouting. He wanted to come with Mark's ass gripping his dick, milking it. Mark undid Deacon's fly, and Deacon twisted, desperate to get out of his jeans.

"You could stand to take a breath yourself, Deke," Mark whispered, laughing. He stroked the front of Deacon's underwear, cupping Deacon's balls through the fabric and then squeezing gently. Deacon moaned. He suddenly didn't remember words.

"Want you," he said finally, sucking in a breath and going up on his toes as Mark continued to squeeze.

"Yeah?"

Deacon whimpered and nodded. He let out his breath in a rush. "Yeah. Mark! Mark, wait, wait…" Mark was tracing the outline of Deacon's cock. Deacon caught his wrist.

Mark's voice was so soft. "I want to see you lose control."

"Not yet." Deacon managed a smile, though his thighs were still tense and his balls were dangerously tight. Looking down, he saw that the head of his cock was peeking over the top of his underwear, slick with precum.

Jesus. In the past it had always taken him a pretty decent amount of time to come. One guy he'd slept with had told him he took longer to get off than the guy's ex-girlfriend. Pleasant memory. But with Mark, Deacon could have shot in seconds.

Deacon herded Mark toward the back wall. Spun Mark around and pressed himself against Mark's naked ass. Rubbed slowly up and down until he got his underwear down around his balls. Mark braced his hands against the wall and groaned. He turned suddenly and shoved Deacon's underwear the rest of the way down, supporting Deacon as Deacon stepped out of them.

They both, as though by some unspoken agreement, staggered toward the center of the room and went to their knees. Deacon cupped Mark's ass and pulled him almost onto his lap. Their chests bumped, and Deacon drew back a hand and slapped Mark's ass. He kept his hand there and clutched at the hard muscle, digging his fingertips in. Mark's breath hitched, and he leaned into Deacon. Deacon repeated the gesture with the other hand on the other cheek. Mark shifted forward, straddling Deacon with his knees on either side of Deacon's hips, his torso flush with Deacon's. He wound his arms around Deacon and held on tight as Deacon spanked him several more times, stopping after each blow to knead the flesh he'd struck, to grip it and claw at it. Mark made soft noises into his shoulder. Then his teeth latched on Deacon's throat, nibbling and sucking, and Deacon paused, unable to concentrate on anything else.

Mark rolled his hips, trying to get his cock in contact with Deacon's. Deacon slapped him one more time, skated his palm briskly over the entire surface of Mark's ass, then eased Mark back. They ended up with Mark lying diagonally against Deacon's left hip, facedown. One of his legs was draped over Deacon's thighs; the other was on the floor. The damp head of his cock nudged Deacon's hip.

Mark folded his arms on the floor and rested his chin on them. Deacon stroked his ass. "On the phone," Deacon whispered, "you used your fingers…and you came…" He slid his fingers down Mark's crack, brushing his hole. Mark jerked, toes curling against the carpet. "I wanted to be there. Wanted it to be my fingers."

"Please," Mark murmured.

"You want to?"

"I'll come fast if you use your fingers," Mark warned.

Deacon smiled. "We'll take it slow, then."

Deacon leaned down, spread Mark's cheeks, and spit. Ran his pinky through the saliva, circled Mark's hole, then pushed inward. Mark lifted his head and moaned softly. Deacon moved his finger inside Mark for a moment, just enough to get Mark squirming, then withdrew.

"Deke, *please.*"

Deacon almost snickered. This was perfect. He was no longer in immediate danger of coming, but his cock was still hard and eager, and now he had Mark at his mercy. He circled Mark's hole again, occasionally tapping it or pressing the pad of his finger against it. Mark was chanting the word "please," shifting restlessly. Deacon worked both his pinky and his ring finger in together.

"Mhhnn," Mark said, tensing, then relaxing. Not just his ass—his whole body went limp, and he lay still as Deacon thrust slowly inside him. He gave a nearly inaudible murmur of contentment. His calf muscles flexed, and he squirmed a little, but other than that, he seemed completely at peace.

"What if I put all four fingers inside you?" Deacon whispered, reluctant to speak and risk breaking Mark's trance.

"Do it," Mark whispered back.

A few minutes later, Deacon had four fingers buried in Mark to the second knuckles. Mark was breathing deeply, clenching and releasing around Deacon. Deacon waited another minute, then slid his fingers in farther. He didn't move, just left them in place, feeling the heat that engulfed them. He stroked his free hand down Mark's back, keeping him relaxed.

Deacon pushed toward Mark's prostate. Mark arched, encouraging him with a whimper. Deacon brushed a spot that made Mark gasp, then pulled partially out, falling still once more.

Deacon didn't know how long they played the game. He lost himself in the silence of the small room, in the thrill of being able to make Mark jerk or moan with the slightest movement. He used his other hand to touch Mark's ass and thighs, to scrape his nails lightly over the backs of Mark's knees and make him kick and clench around his fingers. After a while Deacon felt as much in a trance as Mark seemed to be. He was rubbing Mark's shoulders, crooking his fingers every now and then. His legs prickled from kneeling so long and from Mark's weight over his left thigh, but he didn't mind.

Eventually he began to worry they might be pushing their luck staying here too long. He thrust harder and more frequently, making Mark grunt and rub against him. "Gonna come," Mark mumbled after a minute. Deacon tapped Mark's prostate in answer.

Mark's whole body tightened, and he rose off Deacon, but amazingly, he didn't come. "Your cock. Please?" Mark's voice was strained, and his legs were rigid, trembling.

Deacon withdrew his fingers. Rolled Mark gently off him and onto his back on the stained carpet. Mark raised his legs, and Deacon entered him, not thinking, just acting. He closed his eyes and sighed at the sensation of Mark's heat around his cock. He started thrusting, a nice, easy rhythm, his earlier desperation replaced by a wonderful sense of drifting, of a deep pleasure that he wanted to sustain as long as possible.

Mark wrapped his hand around his cock and stroked in time with Deacon's thrusts.

Mark came first, arching as his cock emptied onto his belly.

Deacon pulled out at the last second, coming on Mark's balls and between Mark's cheeks, sliding the tip of his dick through the cum as he leaned down to kiss Mark.

"Shit," Deacon whispered.

"God." Mark's eyes fluttered.

Deacon tensed a little. "Sorry about— I shouldn't have, without a condom. But I'm clean, Mark. I swear. Got tested at the start of the semester."

Mark grinned lazily. "It's all right. I told you to. I figured Phi Sigs keep up with that shit."

"I do, but not everyone would," Deacon said, suddenly in protective mode again.

Mark's grin remained. "Well, as I'm hoping not to fuck anyone else anytime soon, maybe it's okay?"

Deacon fought a smile. "Hmm."

"Besides. It's college. I'm supposed to do stupid shit while I'm here, right?"

"Within reason," Deacon grumbled, stroking back and forth between Mark's nipples, pausing to flick one.

"You can't be stupid within reason, can you? Bit of an oxymoron."

"You absolutely can be stupid within reason. But I'm gonna have to supervise you twenty-four-seven if you can't promise me you'll be reasonably stupid."

Mark reached up and touched his cheek. "Promise, Deke."

Deacon felt a flash of fear, as though his mother's anxiety had somehow transferred to him. He didn't want to spoil the moment, but he couldn't shake the feeling that promises like that invited something to go wrong. He helped Mark up. "This is Shakespeare without the tragic ending, okay?"

Mark laughed and groped for his underwear. "If we get caught naked in here, there's definitely gonna be a tragic ending."

They dressed and left the microfiche room cautiously. No one seemed to be using this floor, let alone waiting to look at old copies of the *Prescott Literary Review* under a microscope. Deacon checked his phone. It was well after midnight.

Mark walked him back to the Phi Sig house.

"If I'm kicked out of Alpha Delt," Mark said, "I might take you up on the twenty-four-seven supervision thing. But if by some miracle they decide to keep my queer arse around, we'll have to settle for you supervising me whenever I'm not being force-fed salsa in the basement. Or being force-fed Nathaniel Hawthorne in American lit."

"Sounds good," Deacon said.

They kissed. Deacon noticed Mark cast a glance over at the Alpha Delt house as they parted. Then he looked back at Deacon and smiled. "Good night, Romeo."

"'Night, Juliet."

They kissed again. "Uh-oh. Are we gonna say good night until it be morrow or some shit?"

Another kiss. "It's already morrow," Deacon said. "So we might as well keep going."

They ended up saying good night for quite a while.

CHAPTER 9

Michael Danes was a senior from Theta Chi, and the current head of the Prescott College Interfraternity Council. He was a high achiever, the captain of the lacrosse team, was aiming to pursue postgraduate studies in linguistics, and the look on his face as he sat across from the representatives of Alpha Delta and Phi Sigma clearly said he did not have enough time for this shit.

Deacon privately agreed. He'd rather be having teeth pulled than trying to mediate some sort of truce with Chris and Bengal.

"Okay," Michael said, lacing his fingers together. "This is how it is. In half an hour, the dean is gonna walk in this door and ask me what the hell is going on between your houses."

Deacon tried to keep his face impassive as he thought of Romeo and Juliet again. This was the part where someone was banished, right? And someone died, and then there was a plague on both their houses.

"Because if this goes any higher up the chain," Michael

continued, "and it gets official, then getting dragged in front of me is the least of your worries."

James looked worried, pissed, and righteous all at once. Not an easy look to accomplish.

"Mike, c'mon," Bengal said, spreading his hands. "Dude. We didn't even do anything."

"You put *shit* in our AC," James said through his teeth.

Bengal rolled his eyes. "You can't prove that."

"Shut up," Chris told him. "Look, Michael, we can sort something out."

"I've heard that before," Michael said. He leaned back in his chair. "So who started it?"

That was an interesting question, and one that Deacon didn't exactly want to answer.

"They did," Bengal said. He pointed at Deacon. "When he crashed our party."

Michael actually looked surprised. He'd confided to James and Deacon before the meeting started—they were early, while Chris and Bengal were late—that this was a formality, that the Alpha Delts were out of control, and the only thing the Phi Sigs were guilty of was living next door to bad neighbors.

"That's not relevant," Deacon said. "You wouldn't have even known I was there if your guys hadn't stolen our dog." He looked at Michael. "I had to step in to get her back."

"You stole their dog?" Michael asked Chris.

"It was harmless," Chris told him, a hand on Bengal's arm to stop him from speaking. "She wasn't hurt, and we would have taken her back."

"And then they put shit in our AC," James said. "And some of their guys came and started a fight on our lawn."

Well, that was murky territory. Deacon still wasn't sure what had happened there. Matt was volatile when he was riled, and after the dog-shit incident, it wasn't hard to imagine he'd called the Alpha Delt guys out.

"Come on," Bengal said, shaking his head. "The fight was no big thing."

"No big thing?" Michael said. "When campus police get involved, it's already gone too far."

Bengal slumped in his chair and sighed.

Deacon exchanged a look with James. At least it wasn't hard to come across as responsible and serious when Bengal was the competition. He could make a toddler in the candy aisle of the supermarket look good. And Chris, who must have realized he'd made a tactical error in bringing him, elbowed Bengal to sit up straight.

"So right here is where we draw a line in the sand," Michael said. "Right now. No more bullshit. No escalation." He pointed a finger at Chris. "The dean's already caught a whisper about some of your pledge activities, so you need to keep that shit legal."

Chris was smart enough to keep his mouth shut. He nodded.

Was it legal, Deacon wondered, to humiliate your pledges by making them dress up in frilly skirts? Was it legal to force them to drink a bottle of picante sauce because they wouldn't tell you who they were seeing? Such a wide fucking chasm between what was legal and what were the actions of a decent human being, and Bengal exploited every inch of it.

Deacon wasn't sure if any of Mark's future brothers had been smart enough to put it together yet. Mark's admission to Blake that he was gay, and Deacon's reason for being at their party. But why would they? The Alpha Delts probably deluded themselves into thinking their parties were so epic that everyone wanted to attend, and that Deacon was no exception. When in reality, if Mark hadn't wanted him there, Deacon would have gone to the library instead just to get away from the noise.

"So here's what I think," Michael said at last. "You guys need to demonstrate to the IFC, and to the dean, that you can work together. And James, weren't you saying last week that the place you booked for your semiformal had fallen through?"

James nodded warily. "That's right."

Michael raised his eyebrows at Chris at Bengal. "Lot of room at the country club, right?"

"You want us to share our venue with Phi Sig?" Chris blinked.

Deacon groaned inwardly. He couldn't think of anything worse than sharing a semiformal with Alpha Delta. It'd be keg stands, vomit, and topless sorority girls as far as the eye could see.

"I want you to share the venue, the planning, the costs, and the whole thing. I think that would show the dean that you've fostered a spirit of cooperation," Michael said. "Problem?"

Bengal opened his mouth, and Chris elbowed him again.

"Problem?" Michael repeated.

"No," Chris said. "No problem."

Deacon and James shook their heads.

"Okay," Michael said. "Then we're done here. You guys can learn to play nice, and I can tell the dean he won't be getting any more complaints from the campus police."

They shook on it. Bengal looked as though he'd rather swim through raw sewage than shake hands with a Phi Sig, but Chris was at least half-decent about it. He was smarter than Bengal, after all, and must have known they were skating on thin ice when it came to both the IFC and the dean.

"Jesus," Michael said when Chris and Bengal had left. "You really crashed an Alpha Delta party, Deacon?"

The Phi Sigs and the Theta Chis had a good relationship. There was a long history of friendly academic rivalry between their fraternities. And Risk tournaments.

"I was invited," Deacon admitted. "And okay, it was stupid to go, but if I hadn't been there, who knows what would have happened to Anabelle?"

James nodded. "Those assholes." Then he made a face. "Wait, we're done with the interview part, right?"

Michael showed him his palms. "Absolutely. And I agree with your assessment, as it happens." He looked at Deacon. "Are you serious? You were invited? What kind of idiot invites a Phi Sig to an Alpha Delt party?"

Deacon's kind of idiot.

"He's a pledge," Deacon said. "He didn't know any better."

And wouldn't have cared if he did. But Deacon kept that to himself.

"A pledge," Michael said thoughtfully. "He tell you what's going on over there? Rumor has it their pledge activities are crossing the line into hazing now that Bengal's in charge."

Yeah, that would be about right.

"I haven't heard much." Deacon wasn't going to break Mark's confidence. "But if he wants to make a complaint, I'll send him to you."

He figured Michael could tell he knew more than he was saying. And the stuff with the picante sauce crossed a line. Not just because it was sadistic and dangerous, but because Bengal had no right to demand to know who his pledges were hooking up with. No right at all. But it wasn't Deacon's place to tell Mark's secrets. And he knew Mark would never forgive him for making Mark out to be a victim, whether it was true or not.

"Okay," Michael said at last. He looked at his watch. "So, I'll tell the dean it's sorted out. And you guys let me know if the Alpha Delts cause you any more trouble."

"Thanks, Michael," James said.

A few minutes later, crossing the quad, Deacon said cautiously, "Well, that went okay."

James snorted. "Yeah. I'm just wondering how to break it to everyone that we're now sharing a semiformal with the biggest assholes on campus."

"At least we can split the costs," Deacon said.

"Which is about the only good thing to come out of it."

Deacon nodded and tried not to imagine how disastrously this could turn out. They were in for interesting times.

———

Mark was definitely going to fail American lit. *Young Goodman Brown* had made no sense even on his second read-through. Mark couldn't tell if the whole incident in the woods had been a feverish delusion or a hazing ritual gone horribly wrong, and neither could young Goodman Brown, apparently. Well, shit. When people on the Internet couldn't agree on what had happened in the story, how the hell was Mark supposed to figure it out?

He shoved the book under his pillow and pulled his comforter over his head. He listened to his roommate snore and snuffle for a while; then, figuring he wouldn't get any sleep anyway, Mark checked his text messages in the ghostly light of his phone screen. Nothing new from Deacon, which was no surprise. After the shit Deacon had been doing with his fingers the other night, he probably wasn't able to text yet. He probably had his fingers in splints. Because Jesus, just thinking about Deacon's fingers inside him made Mark half-hard.

Mark had always loved arse play. He was sixteen the first time he'd topped another boy—a fake ID, a few beers, and a lot of bravado—and sixteen and a half the first time he'd bottomed. Two years of sexual experience wasn't enough for Mark to pick a preference. Twenty years wouldn't be, since Mark liked it all. But he loved arse play and loved how Deacon indulged him in it.

Shit. Mark slid a hand down his abdomen, under the elastic of his boxers. He rubbed his palm against his dick. Four fingers. Deacon had put four fingers inside him, and Mark had wanted more.

At what point in your life did you decide you were the sort of guy who wanted to be fisted?

Um. No. The shiver that ran through him was not all good. So maybe put that idea on the back burner for a while. A decade or so.

Well, maybe not a *decade*. Because that shiver wasn't all bad either.

But Mark wasn't ready to look the idea in the face yet.

And Deacon thought Mark was reckless. Mark saw the edge there and took a step back instead of flinging himself off it, thanks very much. He could be responsible. Okay, there was the unsafe-sex thing in the microfiche room of the library. And that was dumb. Really fucking dumb. *Embarrassing* dumb, and even now Mark couldn't help imagining himself months down the track having to explain to his mum how he'd just made a mistake that one time...just that one time. And there was no way she'd get that. Because Clare had never let the fact that Mark didn't have a father in his life get in the way of sex education. She'd been showing Mark how to roll condoms onto bananas long before he'd known it was other bananas he was interested in.

But Deacon had said he was clean, and Mark trusted that. Deacon didn't do dumb things. Not usually anyway. Deacon wasn't Mark.

Deacon was...

Mark frowned. What was that in the library anyway? That talk that came before the awesome—and stupid—fucking. What Deacon had said: *"But if we're going to keep hooking up like this, I want to know where we stand. You and me, are we an item?"* What was *that*?

Mark took his hand off his dick. Figured he needed the blood for thinking right now. Because Mark was happy to play star-cross'd lovers with Deacon and everything—it would be a shame not to put the balcony to use, after all—but a relationship? What was a relationship anyhow? Friends with benefits was a relationship, wasn't it? Everything was a relationship, from a philosophical point of view. Even hooking up with a stranger in a pub toilet was a relationship. Shortest relationship known to mankind, maybe, but still a relationship. Human interaction, a bit of conversation, and a mutual exchange of bodily fluids. It still counted.

Fuck's sake, Mark was eighteen. He was *supposed* to be a slut. Then at twenty-five he was supposed to regret it. Then at thirty he was supposed to settle down. And then from forty through to the grave he was supposed to get nostalgic for his slutty salad days. That was the pattern.

Mark sighed and closed his eyes. Although...a relationship with Deacon would be nice. Mark would fuck it up somehow, but it would be nice while it lasted.

His phone buzzed, and he felt a wild surge of hope that it was Deacon. He pulled his phone out. It was still buzzing, and the caller ID said Jackson.

Great. Fucking great. Jackson calling him to ream him out for being a queer and bringing his big-gay-arse-queer-cock love into the Alpha Delt house. Now all the couches had gay on them. The bowl of nuts on the coffee table—of course Mark had gone for the nuts. Blake, who had patted Mark fraternally on the back the day Mark had gotten sick running laps—Blake was probably gay now too.

Okay, he needed to quit feeling sorry for himself and answer the damned phone. Better to get this over with now. Then he could spend tomorrow working out how to tell Jim he'd been kicked out of Alpha Delt. His roommate grunted as the phone kept buzzing. Mark steeled himself and answered it. "H'llo?" he muttered.

"Mark." Jackson's voice was curt, as it always was when they spoke. "I need you to come to the house, please."

"It's three in the fucking morning."

"I know that. But it's an emergency."

Interesting that this was a call from Jackson, and not Bengal barking, *Get your sorry ass over here for some push-ups, bitch!* or Blake's cheerful *Hey, little bro, rise and shine. We've got plans for you.*

But then Jackson had a family stake in this one.

The kind of emergency where you all beat my ass for trying to change the tenets of Alpha Delt to service, leadership, and cum-guzzling? Or are you worried I'd like an arse beating too much?

"Look, if you're gonna kick me out, can we just do it over the phone?"

"Christ, Mark, just come over," Jackson snapped. "We think you can help."

"With what?"

"With Brandon."

———

Mark made it to Alpha Delt in record time. He did knock, but as soon as he determined the door was open, he pushed inside. Jackson and Bengal were in the kitchen. Brandon was seated at the table, his head in his hands. Blake stood next to him and was urging him to breathe into a paper bag. "This always helps me, bro. When I exercise over my VO_2 max."

Brandon took the bag. His hand shook so bad the paper rattled.

Jackson looked up and saw Mark. "There you are."

"What the fuck did you do to him?" Mark demanded, moving toward Brandon. "Jackson? What the fuck did you *do*?

"Same thing we did to five other pledges," Bengal said. "Except he was the only one who couldn't take a damn joke."

Mark pushed Blake aside and sat in the chair next to Brandon. "Hey, mate. What's wrong?"

Brandon wouldn't look at him. Just dropped the paper bag on the table and buried his face in his hands again. He was breathing almost asthmatically. Mark felt an icy fear that maybe Brandon wasn't speaking to him because he knew.

Mark looked at Blake. "What happened?"

Blake glanced at Jackson.

Mark turned to Jackson as well. "What. *Happened*?" he asked, enunciating each word.

"He was in the middle of a pledge activity, and he freaked." Jackson looked uncomfortable. "We knew you guys were friends, so—"

"What pledge activity?"

Jackson didn't respond, and Mark looked back at Brandon. "Hey, Bran?"

"Get him out of here," Bengal said flatly. "He's dropped out of Alpha Delt. Help him get home, all right?"

"I'm out too," Mark said immediately. "Assuming you weren't going to tell me that anyway."

"No," Jackson said sharply.

Mark turned, startled.

"Just..." Jackson closed his eyes and sighed. "We'd like you to stay in."

"And I've got no fucking interest."

"We'll talk about it later, okay? Tomorrow, lunch?"

"I have class." Mark reached out, wanting to put a hand on Brandon's shoulder but afraid of how it might look, how Brandon might take it. "Brandon? Let's get you home, all right?"

Brandon froze. God, what had these freaks *done* to him?

"Can you get up?"

To Mark's relief, Brandon got slowly to his feet. His eyes were red and he looked a little unsteady, but there didn't appear to be any serious physical damage.

"Mark?" Jackson said. "I know you don't have class all afternoon. Will you meet with me?"

Mark glared at him. "Two o' clock."

"The coffee shop on High Street?"

"Whatever," Mark muttered.

Jackson stepped toward them, his expression less cold, more sincere. He held out his hand to Brandon. "I'm sorry," he said softly.

Brandon stared at his hand for a moment, then shook it. Mark guided Brandon gently toward the door, trying not to rush him, as much as he wanted to get out of there. As they left, he heard Bengal say, "What're you apologizing for? We've been doing this shit since the beginning of time."

"Shut the fuck up," Jackson responded.

Once they were out on the street and away from the house, Mark stopped. "Bran? What's the matter, mate? You need to go to the health center?"

Brandon shook his head and sucked in a breath. He let it out shakily. "Sorry, Mark. I'll be fine. Seriously."

"What happened back there?"

"I don't, um... I overreacted."

"Fuck that!" Mark exploded. "I don't know what they did, but I'm sure you didn't overreact. They're fucking twisted, and I'm glad as shit to be out of there."

"No, no. Mark." Brandon grabbed his sleeve. "Don't quit."

"What are you talking about? *You* quit."

"But you shouldn't." Brandon scrubbed his eyes with the heel of his hand. "This is a personal thing."

Mark nodded. "Look. I don't think I'm getting any sleep tonight. You wanna go get greasy pub food?"

Brandon managed a slight smile. "Bar food. We have bars, not pubs."

"Christ," Mark muttered, grinning. "And next you're gonna tell me we get fries there, not chips. Come on."

Over a basket of fries, Mark got more of the story from Brandon. The Alphas had set the basement up as a "gay room," where six pledges were stripped to their underwear, doused with cold water, and forced to stand in front of a fan. After that, three of the pledges were asked to put on tight spandex shorts, and the other three were blindfolded and forced to rub their faces against the fronts of the other guys' shorts.

"Fucking shit," Mark said.

"I wasn't doing...what I was supposed to do," Brandon said, dunking a fry repeatedly in ketchup but not eating it. "So, uh, Bengal, he started asking me if it was because of you."

Mark's stomach flipped. "Me?"

Brandon glanced at him, then looked quickly back down. "Like, if you were my boyfriend, and if I didn't wanna put my face...because it would be cheating on you or whatever. He said you were gay, that you'd told Blake you were, and they asked if we'd ever fucked. What kind of shit we did. Tried to make me say you'd..." Brandon stopped. "Shit. *Fuck*. It shouldn't be a big deal. It's just a joke."

"Listen to me," Mark said, trying for the moment to ignore the fear rising in him. Brandon hadn't said he hated Mark. Hadn't told Mark to stay the fuck away from him. That was a good sign. "It *is* a big deal. If it's a joke, it's not fucking funny."

"I know. I just... Now what do I do?"

"You have a good, frat-free first semester. And you pledge somewhere else in the spring, if you really want to."

"I could have made it through," Brandon said quietly. "I could have. I don't know what happened. I lost it."

"They're creeps," Mark said. "You can find better friends than that. I'd like to murder my fucking cousin, personally."

"Jackson was all right. He's... He wasn't a bad big. It was mostly Bengal who thought up, uh, fucked-up stuff, you know?"

"Except it's *all* fucked-up, Bran," Mark said. "Not just the shitty stuff they make guys do, the whole thing. It's like they'll push and they'll push and they'll push, but the second you push back, suddenly you're the arsehole because you can't take a joke. That's what's fucked-up. You can't win.

The whole system is rigged so that you can't win. Fuck 'em. I'm out."

"Don't," Brandon said. "Please don't quit because of me."

"I don't want to be in their club."

"Don't quit," Brandon said. "Then they'll blame me for it, won't they? You've gotta be in a fraternity, Mark, or you're nobody."

Mark stared at him. "That's what your dad says, Bran, not you."

"Well, I'm a nobody, aren't I?" Brandon squashed a fry on the table. "I couldn't even make it through some dumbass pledge game."

"There is so much wrong with what you just said that I don't even know where to start," Mark said. "Seriously, mate, I have no idea."

Brandon shrugged and hunched over.

"You," Mark said, pointing a fry at him, "are the smartest bloke I know. You don't need some bullshit frat to tell you that. Also, you're funny, and you have a magic brain." There was a small container of individually wrapped toothpicks on the table. Mark picked up the container, which was inexplicably shaped like a cactus, and upended it. Toothpicks spilled all over the floor.

"What'd you do that for?" Brandon asked.

"For your magic brain," Mark said. "Count them!"

"I have an eidetic memory. I'm not Rain Man," Brandon said.

Mark looked at the toothpicks on the floor. "Shit. I'll pick them up," he said to the glaring bouncer. He dropped onto the floor. "I'm picking them up."

Classic Mark. Make a dick of yourself to take the heat off someone else.

The first time he remembered, he was in grade two, and

Baz had called their teacher, Mr. Frankston, "Dad" by accident. The other kids had laughed, and Baz had started to cry. Then Mark had got his head stuck in the class guinea pig cage—something he'd discovered was possible the day before much to Mr. Frankston's consternation, and put the knowledge to good use when he needed to create a diversion. Then, when the kids were laughing at Mark instead, and Mr. Frankston was trying to pry the cage off Mark's head so he could send Mark to the principal's office, all Mark could see was Baz's shy smile.

It looked a lot like Brandon's did now, which was worth getting thrown out of the bar for.

"You won't quit the fraternity, will you?" Brandon asked him earnestly as they headed back to campus.

Mark didn't answer.

"Don't," Brandon said. "I don't want you to quit just because I couldn't handle it."

Mark bit back what he really wanted to say.

His mum said there was no arguing with some people. Usually she was talking about her brother Steve and his habit of voting conservative, but the point was valid. All the logic in the world couldn't change some people's fixed opinions. And Brandon had one. Brandon thought that you had to be in a fraternity, that there was something inherently worthy about being in one, and if experience couldn't show him the truth, neither could Mark.

And if Mark ditched the frat now, Brandon would blame himself.

"I'll stick with it," Mark said. "Until they throw me out, right?"

Which would probably be tomorrow anyway.

———

Mark forswore his usual battle of wills with the barista at the coffee shop on High Street. Their feud had started the day Mark had tried to order a flat white, and the guy thought he was making it up. Mark's insistence that a flat white was different to a café latte didn't unmuddy the waters at all. And his refusal to put his change in the tip jar after their first run-in had only deepened their mutual animosity. Mark would have stopped going there weeks ago, except for his stubbornness.

Today he didn't have the time or the energy to restart the war, so he ordered a Coke and slunk into a booth to wait for Jackson.

Jackson arrived right on time, nodding at Mark and going to order a coffee before sliding into the booth across from him. "Thanks for coming."

Mark didn't know how to respond to that, so he didn't. He slurped his Coke loudly instead.

Jackson chewed his lip for a moment. "How's Brandon?"

"What do you even care?" Mark asked.

A guilty look flashed across Jackson's face. So maybe he did care. Mark didn't know if it was because he felt responsible, or because he was worried he might be in trouble. Because hazing was bad, m'kay? Not bad enough to stop doing it, obviously, but bad enough to panic that you might be in the shit when it went wrong.

"He's a nice kid," Jackson said at last, stirring his coffee furiously. "I wouldn't have let him go down there if I'd known..."

"Known what?" Mark asked. "Known what they'd do, or known he'd freak out?"

Jackson's silence spoke for itself.

"Question." Mark folded his arms over his chest. "There were only six pledges there last night. Why?"

Jackson didn't meet his gaze. "Dude, c'mon…"

Mark snorted. "Right. Because you chose the ones you knew wouldn't complain. And I wasn't invited because I'd already told Blake I'm gay, right? Because you put me in your little 'gay room' in the basement, and I'd probably fucking like it, is that it? Get a hard-on instead of humiliated, yeah? Well, guess what, Jackson? The only time I like rubbing my face up against a guy's dick is when we're both into it. You arseholes don't even know the difference. You know what your hazing game is called in real life? Sexual assault."

"Dude," Jackson said quietly. "Mark, please."

Mark stabbed at his ice with his straw. "And that's what they'd call it all the way from the dean's office to the local courthouse too, am I right?"

"The room wasn't my idea," Jackson said.

"You were supposed to look out for him," Mark said. "You were his big bro."

"I didn't know he'd freak out."

"It still would have been sexual assault if he hadn't," Mark said.

Jackson opened his mouth to answer, then clamped it shut again.

Ding. Mark could see the lightbulb moment. So there was a human being inside that popped collar after all. Who would have guessed it?

"Well, go on," he said.

Jackson raised his eyebrows. "What?"

"I take it you're here to throw my extraordinarily gay arse out of the frat," Mark said. "Now that you've had the chance to think about it overnight, right?"

"No," said Jackson. "We don't want you out. Out of the fraternity, I mean. *Out* out is okay."

"Mmmm," said Mark. "Because Alpha Delta is all about tolerance and inclusiveness. It's purely an accident that you're all white, straight, and rich."

"Oh, fuck you," Jackson muttered. "I put my reputation on the line to get you in as a pledge, and you throw it back in my face every single day. I don't know why you pledged, since you obviously don't want to be there."

"Me neither," Mark said. "But knowing how much you want me there just warms my heart."

"What the hell do you want from me, Mark? I don't even know you, and suddenly Uncle Jim's calling every few days making me promise to be your friend!" Jackson flushed. "I wasn't...um, I wasn't meant to mention that."

Ouch.

Mark stirred his straw through his Coke, making bubbling eddies. So he was so unlikable that Jim had to keep reminding Jackson to play nice. That was how it was, was it? It should have stung, but it didn't. Mark felt a sinking sensation in his stomach instead. Not a revelation so much as confirmation of a suspicion he'd held for a long time. He really was that unlikable.

Jackson bit his lip. "But, um, but we want you in Alpha Delta. We want you to be a brother."

"Right," Mark said. "You might, because you're doing Jim a favor, but the rest of them? Don't bullshit me. None of them even like me."

"Blake does," Jackson said.

"Blake likes everyone. He's like a dog. With no brain."

Jackson almost smiled.

"And I'll bet Bengal and Logan and Chris are just desperate to get me to stay as well, aren't they?"

"Chris is okay," Jackson said, his tone defensive. "Anyway, with all this shit with Phi Sig, now the dean's getting involved, and if it gets out about the hazing..."

"Ah," Mark said. "How handy for you to have your own tame fag in the frat just when you're about to be accused of being homophobic frat-boy arseholes, right? Any other minority groups you need to get on board in a hurry? Because I think I met a Latino guy in a wheelchair at the last Minority Meeting. If he's gay as well, you've hit the trifecta. The holy fucking trinity of diversity."

"The..." Jackson frowned. "The Minority Meeting? Are you being sarcastic?"

"If you have to ask," Mark said, "then yes, of course I'm being sarcastic. I didn't go to the Minority Meeting the other night because firstly there is no such thing, and secondly I was busy getting fucked by an extremely hot guy from Phi Sig in the library."

"Mark," Jackson said, looking horrified. "Dude."

"Sorry," Mark said. "Sometimes even us tame fags have claws, am I right?"

"I don't know what you're talking about," Jackson said. "I came here to see how Brandon was, and to make sure you're staying in the fraternity. All this shit about tame fags and stuff... Where the hell is that coming from?"

Mark wasn't sure himself. "Forget it," he muttered. "You want me out, you're gonna have to throw me out. You want me in, it better not be just because you think I'm gonna throw some big gay fit about discrimination."

Jackson shook his head. "Fine. You do what you want, Mark. I really couldn't care less. Word of advice, though? Maybe stop seeing how many enemies you can make? We're not all idiot assholes."

Prove it. "Think I'll stay in just for a shot at living in the house. I love that fireplace. Once you take the blow-up doll out of the chimney, it's gonna be real cozy in the winter, huh?"

He didn't know why it gave him so much pleasure to see Jackson trying not to punch him.

"If you're determined to hate me, there's nothing I can do about it," Jackson said stiffly.

"I don't hate you," Mark said, surprising himself. "But this hazing shit is fucked-up. You know that, right? You ought to try a little harder not to scar people for life."

Jackson nodded, not looking at Mark. "Bengal gets out of control sometimes."

"And *you* go along with it," Mark said, scowling. "Don't blame it on him."

"Okay. Fine. We're definitely not gonna let it get to the level it did with Brandon again, though."

"And this whole thing with Phi Sig is stupid," Mark went on. "What's the point?"

Jackson shrugged. "Used to be a friendly rivalry, I'm told." He sipped his coffee. "And anyway, we'll be spending enough time with them in the next two months. Maybe we'll *bond*."

"What do you mean?"

"Interfraternity Council weighed in on the fight. Apparently we're supposed to extend the olive branch."

"And you're gonna do it?"

"We already have. We're having our fall semiformal in conjunction with theirs."

Mark snorted. "You asked them to your prom?"

Jackson flushed a little. "The IFC's idea, not ours. And it's not a fucking prom."

"They turned you down, right? I mean, they're probably having theirs in a planetarium or something."

"They didn't have much choice. Their venue didn't pan

out. It was supposed to be at the Jameson Historical Home. Now they'll be joining us at the country club."

Mark tried to imagine Deacon's reaction to that. Though for all he knew, Deacon adored country clubs. There was a shit ton he didn't know about Deacon. Mark recalled with some embarrassment spilling that stuff about his mum and Jim to Deacon yesterday. And then Deacon had mentioned his mother's OCD, and all Mark had said was, *"That's rough,"* and then they'd fucked.

"Maybe you need a friend right now, not a fuck," Deacon had said.

Could he have both? Deacon had said he could. Could he *be* both? He'd never really tried. Mark supposed being friends—being an *item*—would mean eventually they'd have to do more than fuck. They'd probably have to talk.

"And now the whole thing's a joint effort," Jackson was saying. "The planning committee, the catering selection..." He sighed. "Fuck."

"Maybe you'll make new friends."

"Maybe you'll make *a* friend," Jackson muttered, raising his cup.

"Touché."

Mark clinked his glass against Jackson's cup and drank.

"Next chapter meeting, we'll be discussing plans for the semiformal," Jackson said. "So if you have any ideas, bring 'em." He glanced warily at Mark as though expecting Mark to say something obnoxious. "We'll talk about the pledge retreat too."

Fuck. They'd mentioned that last week, and Mark had been horrified. Some kind of weekend bonding thing some fraternities did with their pledges.

Mark nodded. "Okay." He drank more of his Coke and wondered if he ought to make an excuse about needing to get to a class or turn in a form at Student Affairs or do *anything* besides keep having this awkward conversation with Jackson.

"So...I guess it's a lot different here from Australia?" Jackson offered tentatively.

Oh hell no. Jackson was not gonna try this lame let's-kind-of-be-friends shit. Except last time Jackson had actually tried to make conversation, Mark had told him to fuck off. And exactly what had that attitude got him? A stepfather who had to find his friends for him. So he said, "Yeah. It's taken some getting used to."

"You think you'll go back there when you're done with school?"

"I don't know." Mark felt the ache in his throat he sometimes did when he talked about home. The one he tried to cover up with a hundred different shades of sarcasm because...because fuck it, he didn't need anyone to feel sorry for him.

And again, what had that attitude got him?

"Well..." Jackson's voice was quiet, and he spoke to the table rather than to Mark. "There's actually some cool stuff to do around here. Especially in winter. So maybe sometime we can hang out or something."

Mark wasn't sure whether to be touched or suspicious. Jackson seemed sincere enough—or at least, sincerely awkward enough—that the invitation might be genuine, and not a trap or a favor to Uncle Jim. As little as Mark wanted to hang out with Jackson, he appreciated the effort it must have taken to offer. "Yeah," he said. "That'd be cool."

"Okay. Well." Jackson shifted and stood. "I'd better get going. Thanks for, uh, meeting with me. And I'm glad you'll be staying in Alpha Delt."

"Sure." *Thanks for the dubious honor of being allowed to remain?*

"Keep an eye on Brandon for me, okay?" Jackson shoved his hands in his pockets. "He's got my cell, but I don't know if he wants to talk to me."

"Yeah, I can't imagine why."

Jackson left, and Mark drank the rest of his Coke. He wondered if compromising his integrity, obnoxious as it was, to stay in the frat was the act of a guy who was finally deciding to make the best of things, or that of a spineless dickhead who'd given up the good fight. In the end, unable to decide, Mark cheered himself up by ordering a flat white.

CHAPTER 10

"Ricketts Glen? That's awesome," Deacon said, looking over the brochure Mark had handed him. "Maybe you'll see a bear."

"A bear?" Mark said.

"Yeah, there's lots of wildlife there. Great nature trails."

"A *bear*?" Mark repeated.

Deacon glanced up, setting the brochure aside. Mark looked horrified, though Deacon wasn't sure why. His own pledge retreat hadn't been anywhere near as cool as Ricketts Glen. The Phi Sigs had taken a bus to Hagerstown, which had had fuck all in the way of places to eat or things to do, and stayed in a motel. "You have a problem with bears?"

"Yes, I have a problem with bears! Bears *eat people*."

Deacon laughed. "Hardly ever."

"Bullshit. I've read about grizzlies. They crush your skull, and you're still alive to feel it."

"You won't see grizzlies at Ricketts Glen. Black bears. They'll just gnaw your leg." He reached out and snagged a handful of Mark's khakis.

"Don't!" Mark yelped as Deacon tugged him forward and onto his lap. They were in Deacon's room, since Deacon's roommates were out for a while at some club meeting, and Deacon was sitting at his desk. Mark couldn't stop sneaking wistful glances at Deacon's bed. He perched on Deacon's thigh, and Deacon wound an arm around him.

"You look seriously pale. Are you actually scared of bears?"

"*Yes.*"

"Bears are adorable. You have way more terrifying shit in Australia, don't you? Sharks, crocodiles...wombats."

"Wombats are not terrifying."

"What am I thinking of? Wolverines?"

"Probably."

"Do you have wolverines in Australia? Or am I just thinking that because Hugh Jackman's Australian and he's Wolverine?"

"We don't have wolverines."

"Tasmanian devils?"

"That's us."

"See? And you have giant snakes and rabid bugs..."

"Okay, it's not the set of *Tremors*, Deke. Sharks and salt-water crocs can get you if you go in the water. Bears can get you anywhere."

"Climb a tree if you see one," Deacon suggested. "No, wait, black bears can climb."

"Stop!" Mark struck his shoulder, and Deacon laughed.

"Grizzlies can climb too, for that matter. Just not as well as black bears."

"Not funny." Mark was now smacking Deacon hard enough to qualify as assault.

Deacon snickered as he flinched away from the blows. "What?" he asked mock-innocently. "I'm only trying to help."

"Fat lot of help you are. I do *not* want to spend two days at a state park with a bunch of pledges, and I definitely don't want to do it if there's even a five percent chance I'll get eaten by a bear."

"It'll be good for you." Now that Mark had stopped trying to brutalize him, Deacon was able to pull Mark closer against him. "You'll get to know your fellow pledges, get to know the Pennsylvania wilderness... Plus it'll be gorgeous this time of year, with the leaves. "

Mark grumbled, resting his head on Deacon's shoulder. "Where are you taking your pledge group?"

"Phi Sig stopped doing pledge retreats last year. Don't really have the money."

"Oh."

"Which is why we can only afford modest venues for our semiformals, like the Jameson House, unless some other kindly, deep-pocketed fraternity invites us to share their country club."

Mark grinned. "It'll be like we're going to prom together, Deke."

"Except the air will be thick with resentment on both sides. And the pool will be crowded. And please don't call it a prom. I like to think what we do is classier than that."

"Sorry. Prom is my favorite American thing I learned about from movies. That, and your hills are infested with rednecks who like to kill kids with axes." He bit his lip. "Oh, and that all supervillains, and most Nazis, speak with British accents. And all your telephone numbers start with 555."

Deacon laughed and tugged Mark's hair gently. "Nothing else?"

"Just that I want Bruce Willis on my side if shit starts

exploding." Mark rocked back and forth on Deacon's thigh. His breath quickened.

Deacon slid his hands down Mark's back, following the curve of his spine through his thin T-shirt. Mark went from zero to sixty in seconds flat, and Deacon relished the challenge of keeping up with him. "You're so hot."

Mark leaned back suddenly. "How's your mum going?"

"What?" Deacon dropped his hands from Mark's hips. "So, speaking of *non sequiturs*..."

"Non what?"

"Um," Deacon said. "I said you were hot, and you asked about my mom. I'm not seeing the connection."

"I'm being invested. In you."

Deacon looked at him for a moment. Cocky grin notwithstanding, it was obviously the truth. "You really are, aren't you?"

Mark's smile faded at Deacon's serious tone. He chewed his lip and dropped his gaze. Shrugged. "Yeah, so?"

So you should be able to have a serious talk without making it a joke or running away from it.

"So I think that's your way of saying we're an item now," Deacon said. He put his fingers under Mark's chin and lifted it. "Feel free to correct me if I'm wrong, of course. But I like that you're invested in me. I want to be invested in you too."

"Do you?"

"Are you still failing American lit?"

"Way to kill the mood," Mark said, rolling his eyes. Then he scrambled off Deacon's lap and dived halfway under Matt's bed. "What's this?" He drew out a fuzzy pink sweater. "You been seeing a girl behind my back?"

Deacon laughed. "That's Matt's girlfriend's."

Mark climbed to his feet again, holding the sweater up against him. "I think it would fit me."

Deacon stopped laughing and swallowed. He didn't want to appear too eager, in case Mark was joking. But with a glance at Deacon, Mark dropped the sweater on the floor and peeled his T-shirt off. Smooth skin slid over the bones of his spine as he bent to pick up the sweater. He sucked his stomach in, his ribs protruding as he pulled the pink sweater on. He tugged it down and smoothed it, then looked at Deacon, his grin belying a hint of anxiety in his expression.

Deacon stared at him. Deacon had known some gay guys in high school who'd tried dating girls to pretend, either to themselves or to others, that they were straight. Deacon had come out early enough to avoid the need for pretense. He'd always liked the way girls looked—thought a lot of them were pretty, liked the variety in their clothes and shoes and lingerie that didn't seem to exist for men. But he'd never so much as pretended to have sexual feelings for a girl.

But something about the combination of girls' clothes on someone he *was* attracted to made Deacon so hard he couldn't think of anything to say, couldn't think about anything except wanting to fuck Mark while Mark was wearing that sweater. His skin heated and prickled. He sat down on the bed and watched Mark. The sweater hugged Mark, but not too tightly. It looked soft and comfortable. The V-neck exposed Mark's collarbone, and the sleeves were just a little too short for his arms, showing the defined bones of his wrists.

"Well?" Mark asked. He sounded uncertain.

Deacon forced himself to smile. "It fits," he said. It was the best he could come up with. There was so much more he wanted to say, but he didn't know how to say it without sounding stupid.

"I'll take it off," Mark said quickly, grabbing for the hemline.

"No!" Deacon stood, arm out as though ready to physically stop Mark from taking the sweater off, if necessary.

Mark froze and looked at Deacon. This time there wasn't anything cocky in his expression. He looked bewildered as Deacon stepped toward him.

"You look good," Deacon said quietly, reaching out to touch the fabric. "God, Mark."

"Were you seriously into it?" Mark asked. "That night at the party, when I had the stockings on and all that?"

"Yeah," Deacon said. "You think that's weird?"

"Well, considering I was the one *in* the stockings and lacy knickers, no, I don't think it's weird. I just...didn't know if you were kidding around when you said it was hot."

Deacon shook his head.

"Good." Mark caught Deacon's hand and shoved his fingers between Deacon's. Brought their joined hands down to his hip. "Because I like the way you were looking at me just now."

Deacon extended his fingers around Mark's and stroked Mark's hip bone, gently teasing the hem of the sweater. "Like a drooling maniac?"

"It's, um, awesome. That there's something so simple I can do to make you happy."

Deacon squeezed Mark's hand, then released it. He put his arms around Mark and drew him close, running his hands over Mark's back, feeling the fuzzy material, smelling the hint of Kate's perfume that lingered on the fabric. Mark pressed his face against the side of Deacon's neck, his body rigid, then relaxing against Deacon. Mark sucked lightly at Deacon's throat while Deacon continued to stroke his back.

Deacon slid one hand down Mark's jeans and squeezed

his ass through his underwear. Mark gave a soft moan; his knees buckled slightly, and his whole body met Deacon's. Deacon could feel how hard Mark was, how hard they both were. Mark's teeth closed on the spot on Deacon's throat he'd been sucking. Deacon shut his eyes and tipped his head back, giving Mark easier access. He gave a sharp gasp as Mark rubbed the bulge in his pants against Deacon's.

Deacon kneaded Mark's ass again, trying to see how far down Mark's pants he could get his hand. He brushed Mark's balls, the fabric encasing them warm and damp. He pushed his other hand up Mark's sweater, using his nails in broad circles all over Mark's back. Mark shivered and let his head drop against Deacon's shoulder once more. He gripped Deacon tightly, shifting his hips forward.

Deacon withdrew his hand from Mark's pants and thrust both his hands up the front of Mark's sweater, easing Mark back just enough that he had room to explore, and that Mark drew his head up to kiss Deacon. Deacon found Mark's nipples and rolled them, tugged on them. He loved the way Mark inhaled, held his breath, and then took in more air a little at a time, like he was gearing up to sneeze, until Deacon stopped pinching him. Then his breath came out in a rush against Deacon's lips. Deacon smiled and dipped a hand under Mark's waistband again, this time in the front. Wedged his fingers under the elastic of Mark's underwear and played with his cock, spreading precum down his shaft. Mark tensed and pushed against Deacon's hand.

Deacon rubbed harder, faster, and Mark dug his fingertips into Deacon's back. "Deke, can I come?" Mark asked, breathless. "Please? I need— Can I come?"

Mark asked the question so sincerely, so desperately, and all Deacon could think was that he'd never heard Mark ask permission to do *anything*. Yet it made Deacon giddy, almost light-headed, that Mark had asked.

"Come for me," Deacon whispered. "Right now."

Mark rocked his hips once more, and then Deacon's hand was covered in Mark's cum, hot and sharp smelling. Deacon left his hand there for several minutes, wanting to feel Mark's cock as it softened. Mark's heart was still pounding against Deacon's chest even as his breathing slowed.

Eventually Deacon withdrew his hand. He wiped it on his pants and leaned forward to kiss Mark's jaw. "You," he said, "are so. Fucking. Beautiful."

Mark murmured something Deacon didn't catch—it might not even have been words—and slid to his knees in front of Deacon. He undid Deacon's fly and sucked Deacon as expertly as he had that time in the alley. Deacon kept his hands on Mark's shoulders, hooking his fingers in the neckline of the sweater and gradually stretching it to expose as much of Mark's lightly freckled skin as possible. He came quickly, and Mark swallowed, then pressed his forehead against Deacon's thigh. Deacon stroked his hair.

"Thank you," Deacon whispered.

Mark sighed. He was clutching Deacon's pant leg like a little kid.

Deacon stooped and urged him up. Guided him onto the bed and helped him out of his pants, then the sweater.

"I should wash that," Mark murmured as Deacon folded it and put it aside. "I sweated in it."

"We can do laundry a little later," Deacon said. He climbed into bed beside Mark and curled around him. Mark stroked Deacon's forearm. "We've never been able to do this before. The other times we've fucked, we've had to leave right after because we were somewhere we weren't supposed to be."

Mark didn't answer right away. Deacon wondered if he'd fallen asleep. But then he said, "Now we're somewhere we're supposed to be?"

Deacon grinned and tightened his arms around Mark, dropping a kiss on his shoulder. "I think so."

————

The leaves will be nice, everyone always said, as though leaves were magical things that only existed in Pennsylvania, and Mark would never have seen one before in his life. But in the spirit of trying to be more...*flexible*, Mark dutifully looked at the leaves when the pledges got to Ricketts Glen. He didn't touch them, though, because they were probably poison ivy. And maybe even concealing bears.

It was not dumb to be scared of bears. Fear of a large, fast predator with razor-sharp teeth and claws was in fact totally rational. It was an evolutionary edge. The caveman who saw the saber-tooth tiger and said, "Aw, nice kitty," didn't get to spread his genetic material far and wide throughout the tribe, did he? No, that honor belonged to Og, who'd started running the second the cat appeared. What was dumb was to come and set up camp in predators' territory and then expect them not to try and eat you.

Still, at least there was beer on this trip, courtesy of the big bros who had loaded up the pledges before they left. Mark cracked his first one open as he climbed out of the car at Ricketts Glen. The cabin was nice, and presumably bear-proof, so Mark relaxed a little. By beer number three he was actually enjoying being with the other pledges, who all knew his name, and not just because he was strange and foreign and stuck out like a sore thumb.

"Mark, you give it to Bengal," one of them—Dan—said. "You're, like, the only one who doesn't care about talking back to him."

Dan said it like there was something brave about that, or admirable, but there wasn't, was there? Who the hell pledged to a fraternity in the expectation that he'd get thrown out in a heartbeat anyway? It wasn't rebellious. It wasn't proving anything. It was just a colossal waste of time. Time that could have been better spent studying, going by Mark's latest results, or, better still, with Deacon's cock up his arse.

Mark hauled his bag into the room he was sharing with Dan and flung it on the bed. He'd packed light and was worried now that the night would be cold, and Dan would probably not believe any "let's share body warmth" story he came up with. He pulled on his hoodie and hoped that would be enough and then went back out into the den.

So. A fireplace. How did those work exactly? And this was one of those open numbers too, not a safely-behind-glass job. It seemed sort of dangerous. And Mark had the feeling his previous experience with building fires, which usually consisted of driftwood on the beach, was not going to be much help here.

"Does anyone know how to work this?" he asked.

"You're kidding, right?" Blond Pledge asked. Shit, he really had to get on top of names by the end of the weekend.

"Nope," Mark said, trying his hardest not to take offense. "At home when it gets cold, I put on socks. This is a whole other level."

"It's not even cold."

"That is entirely relative," Mark said.

"Relative to what?" Blond Pledge asked.

Mark stared glumly at the fireplace. "I dunno. History? Experience? The fact that I didn't pack a jacket?"

Blond Pledge laughed. "You can borrow mine if you want."

"Thanks," Mark said.

The point of this weekend was ostensibly for the pledges to get to know one another better, but the brothers had assured them that the real purpose was to get shit-canned. They'd spent four weeks being brutalized and humiliated together, which was supposed to have been a catalyst for the bonding process, and now they had two days in the forest to drink and bitch about their tormentors.

Mark was unsurprised to learn that nobody liked Bengal. "The brothers hate his ass too!" Dan declared. "My big says they all want to get rid of him, especially after that shit with Brandon."

Mark felt a sudden stab of guilt. Brandon should have been here with him, not holed up in his dorm back on campus.

"Yeah, the thing is," a pledge named Fraser said, "Alpha Delt's reputation is kind of a new thing. Like, yeah, they've always had the biggest house and thrown the biggest parties, but it's only in the last few years it's become known as Prescott's big dumb party frat."

"Didn't you used to have to keep a 3.2 to stay in?" a red-haired kid asked. Mark didn't know his name, remembered him from a night when the brothers had taken turns dumping red stuff into the kid's hair—ketchup, chili powder, sprinkles, and something Bengal said was blood but that had smelled more like corn syrup and food coloring.

"Yep," Fraser said. "And the hazing shit wasn't as bad. Chris and Bengal and them make this big deal about how every brother before us had it worse than us, but really, once they started letting people like Bengal in, it got way worse for pledges. My dad's friend was an Alpha Delt, like, forty years ago. Worst that happened was they got paddled some and got dropped off in the woods and had to walk like twelve miles back to campus."

"Paddling is the gayest shit ever," muttered the redhead. Mark tried not to take it personally.

"Traditioooooonnnnn!" sang another pledge, who was approaching with more beer. He slung the case down, and everyone attacked it. "Paddling is tradition."

"Yeah, you like it too much, fag," Dan said, popping open his can. A couple of guys laughed.

"I only like it when my boyfriend does it," the pledge— Mark thought his name was Sean—said, sitting down with their group. More laughter.

"Dude, when's Ellis coming to visit?" Dan asked. "I wanna serve him Joe Pa's head on a plate."

"Penn Staters don't come visit lowly little Prescott," Probably Sean said. "He's making me go there for fall break. And he's got us tickets for a game."

Mark was confused. Was Ellis real? And was he actually Probably Sean's boyfriend? Impossible.

Fraser glanced over at Mark and grinned. "You gotten hooked on football yet?"

"Uh, no," Mark said. "I mean, I like football okay. *Real* football."

"What, like soccer?"

"Rugby League."

"I saw a rugby match when I went to Peru," Dan said. "It was pretty badass."

"It's, um, it's different," Mark said. "Rugby Union and League. They're different."

Dan shrugged.

Fraser addressed Mark. "Okay, all you gotta know is that most sensible Prescott people root for Penn State. They're our closest neighbor with any football team to speak of. Prescott's got a football team, but it's like—like what would you say, Sean?"

"Like steaming turds in jerseys," Definitely Sean said.

"Like they put hobos in uniforms and made them play for free bananas," the red-haired kid said.

"Do *not* tell Blake we're saying this," Sean said to Mark.

"Stop!" Dan said. "Prescott won the national title!"

"In 1893," Fraser said. "In D-III."

"So? I'd rather spend my energy rooting for my school than rooting for a fucking empire that cares more about its team than about a bunch of kids who—"

"Uh-uh," Red Hair said. "This is not about the scandal. It's about the team's ability to play football."

Mark tuned them out for a few minutes. He couldn't believe he was here, hanging out with these guys, and he didn't want to kill himself. In fact, it was kind of...fun. Even though he had no idea what they were talking about.

Blond Pledge came back over. He'd been put in charge of the retreat. "So," he said, consulting a form. "It says here we're supposed to play some game involving M and Ms to learn shit about each other. But I was talking to some of the other guys, and we were thinking maybe we'd just eat all the M and Ms and get drunker?"

A cheer went up from Mark's group, and even Mark grinned.

"Sounds like a plan," Fraser said.

"And, uh..." Blond Pledge looked at the paper again. "Do any of you guys wanna go on a nature walk?"

Dan and Red Hair snickered, but Sean said, "I do." He sounded sincere. "But tomorrow. We're too cozy right now."

"Cool," Blond Pledge said.

He walked away, and everyone proceeded to get drunker. From other areas of the cabin, Mark could hear cheers, whoops, and, somewhere, singing.

At one point, Mark found himself mumbling along with a "Down with Bengal" chant and nodding enthusiastically when several pledges suggested they ought to try to get Bengal thrown out.

"At least, like, get revenge," Blond Pledge said. "Do something to totally humiliate him. Mark could help us figure something out."

"Yeah," Dan said, tilting his fifth beer precariously toward Mark. "Wha'shuddwedo, Mark?"

Mark was surprised to find the pledges looking to him as a leader as they discussed possible fates for Bengal. "I'll think about it," Mark said eventually. Revenge plotting while drunk was probably not the best idea. And Deacon had made him promise to be reasonably stupid.

Soon it was dark, and they were telling ghost stories—or slurring ghost stories—many of which featured girls from Zeta Tau as the main characters and situations that involved irreparable damage to the girls' shirts. Mark found himself in the middle of a story with only the foggiest notion of what he'd been saying for the last ten minutes. A few of his audience members were passed out, but a couple of them looked invested.

"There was a scratch...scratch...scratch... It seemed to be coming from the alcove. Then Jason pulled back the...uh... curtain." Was it Mark's head that was bobbing, or the room? "And found himself face-to-face with a hideous bear."

"A bear?" Fraser interrupted woozily. "Not a ghost?"

"Bears are scarier than ghosts," Mark explained.

"But if it's a bear, Jason could just shoot it. You can't shoot ghosts."

In the moment, it seemed to Mark a blindingly good point. "A *ghost bear*," he amended. "Had t'fight a hideous ghost bear. And the kidzzwere...were still...gone...out in the bush...I mean the woods with the...shovel." Mark glanced around the room. Brothers. These guys were going to be his brothers. And some of them sucked, and some of them were morons, but some of them were okay, and it was kind of cool that they were all out here, hanging out. Maybe between all of them, they could take a bear.

"Is that it?" Fraser asked.

"Um." Mark looked at the empty can he was holding. "I think I need more bear. Beer. I need more beer."

"Are you sure, dude?" Blond Pledge asked.

"I am sure," Mark said, enunciating carefully. He tapped his chest. "Because I am eighteen, and technically not...not underage because I am lee-legally allowed to drink at home."

"That's not how it works!" Blond Pledge said.

"It is so." Mark slung an arm around Fraser's shoulders. "Fraser!"

He and Fraser staggered to the kitchen, where they found more beer and talked awhile longer. Mark didn't remember going to sleep, but he woke around four a.m. to make a trip to the toilet to puke. He had a text from Deacon: *Hope you're having fun.*

Mark was in no state to text back, but he tried anyway. He wanted Deacon to know he wasn't having a bad time. He wanted Deacon to know that he was never drinking again. He wanted Deacon to know he missed him, that when he got home, he was going to go shopping at Victoria's Secret just for him, and that the leaves *were* pretty fucking nice here, and that maybe being an Alpha Delt wasn't the worst fate you could wish on somebody.

————

"So you had a good time," Deacon said.

"I wouldn't call it a *good* time." Mark passed Deacon the bread. They were eating at Mama Luna's, a cheap, student-friendly knockoff of Italian fine dining. And Deacon had ordered wine. Like this was a date. Which Mark was okay with. Good. Dates. Yes. Bring them on.

"Mark."

"It was pretty fun. And I didn't get eaten by a bear. So, you know, yay."

"The bears have all started hibernating by now anyway."

"Are you serious? You let me spend a whole weekend in terror, and the bears aren't even *awake*?"

Deacon grinned. "I didn't want to spoil your fun."

Mark threw a piece of bread crust at him. It landed in Deacon's wineglass. Deacon picked it out, then ate it. "Gross," Mark said. "Anyway, yeah, I was too hungover to worry about bears on the nature walk. I drank a lot, Deke. A *lot*."

Deacon didn't say anything. Just raised his eyebrows.

"Which was really stupid," Mark said. "I mean, what sort of dickheads load up a bunch of pledges with alcohol and send them off with no supervision? How is that ever a good idea?"

"Wait. You're blaming them for you guys drinking too much?" A smile tugged at the corner of Deacon's mouth.

"Well, I can't be trusted to do the right thing. You know that." Mark rolled his eyes. "But mostly, you know, it was pathetic. A few of the guys went to bed early, and the rest of us were on their case and everything. But it turned out that was the smart group. You know, the ones not stopping to throw up on the walk the next day. Why am I never in the smart group, Deke?" He screwed up his nose. "No, don't answer that."

Deacon was good enough not to.

"Anyway. The nature walk was hellish, but it turns out the guys aren't so bad. And I had no *fucking* idea I wasn't the only gay guy in Alpha Delt." On the nature walk, Sean had shown Mark a picture of Ellis, his Penn State boyfriend. Mark had still half thought the whole Ellis thing had been fabricated by the other pledges to fuck with Mark. That maybe Ellis was actually Sean's brother or something. But then Sean had shown Mark another photo of him and Ellis kissing in front of Beaver Stadium.

"You sound angry."

"I'm not. Why would I be angry? I just don't know why any homo in his right mind would pledge Alpha Delt."

"Um..." Deacon said.

"I don't count. I'm obviously not in my right mind."

"Fair enough."

"And, like, the guys joke about Sean, but they're not awful to him. No one took him out to the woods and clubbed him with the fire poker or anything. I'm just... surprised. I don't know why it bothers me. It *doesn't* bother me."

Deacon grinned. "Maybe you're a little jealous someone stole your gay Alpha Delt thunder."

Mark felt a flash of annoyance. "This is not about thunder. It's about how Bengal and a couple of the other guys are totally homophobic, and Sean's just, what, hanging out enjoying the party? And the other pledges are just casually asking him when his boyfriend's gonna visit? It doesn't make sense."

"Well, for what it's worth, I still think you were brave to come out."

Mark sighed. "Please, Deke. I'm not looking for a Victoria Cross here. I just... Whatever. Moving on. How was your weekend?"

Deacon rolled his spaghetti carefully around his fork and didn't look at Mark, though his eyebrows had gone up a bit, presumably at Mark's tone. Mark gritted his teeth. He didn't know why he felt so irritated. He'd had a pretty good weekend, and now he was with Deacon again, on a rather datish excursion, and everything should have been perfect.

"Not bad," Deacon said.

"Your mum's okay?"

Deacon nodded, sticking a forkful of spaghetti in his mouth and chewing. "She's all right. My—" He took a moment to finish chewing and swallow. "My brother's coming home soon."

"Did I know you had a brother?"

"He's been in Afghanistan the last four years. I don't talk about him much."

"Do you not get along?"

"We get along fine. Just, he's been gone, and I don't know much about what's going on with him. Anyway, I would have thought that'd be great news for my mom. Ben's death is number one on her list of worries. But now I guess she thinks if she gets her hopes up, Ben will definitely die, like, the day before he goes home."

Mark pushed some gnocchi around on his plate. "Gotta be rough, isn't it? To have her always be so worried?"

"Yeah, it can get a little stressful. It's just sad because she *knows* it's irrational, but she can't change how she thinks. It was easier when Ben was around, since she's better when she can keep an eye on us. Once we get a certain number of miles away, we might as well be dead."

"So maybe once Ben's home and she sees he's in one piece, she'll start relaxing?"

"I hope so."

Mark wasn't sure what to say next. His impulse was to make a joke. But maybe what he ought to do was what Deacon had had the balls to do for him—let him know he was here for him. That Deacon had a friend if he needed one. Mark just wasn't good at saying shit like that. And to be honest, someone like Deacon, who drove home to check on his mother every weekend, probably didn't need help from someone like Mark, who was skilled at lamenting his own difficulties but less than brilliant at supporting other people through theirs.

Deacon went on. "I'm hoping if Ben's around, maybe I can skip a few home visits toward the end of the semester. Things are gonna get crazy when we've got semiformal *and* finals to worry about."

Mark had to grin. "Especially with planning for the semiformal going so well."

Neither of them was part of the planning process, but apparently the joint committee had met earlier in the week, and it hadn't been pretty.

Deacon laughed. "I'm blaming it on your house."

"Um, excuse me? I think the problem was the Phi Sigs' theme ideas. Murder Mystery? Really?"

"Better than Winter Wonderland or whatever your guys were pushing for."

"From what I understand, we're only pushing for that because Chris's girlfriend suggested it. And he owes her for getting drunk a couple of weeks ago and grinding with

Allison Somebody from the Asian sorority." Mark finished his wine. "I hate snow, so Winter Wonderland seems like a fitting theme for an event I don't want to attend."

Deacon nudged Mark under the table. "You're gonna like snow this year. I promise."

"Highly doubt it."

"First snow, we'll do something fun."

If you still want to be anywhere near me by the time that happens. "Can the fun thing be staying inside and closing the curtains so I don't get cold just looking at it?"

"Nope."

They ate for a few minutes in silence. "I guess Murder Mystery would be a good theme if I decide to fake my own death to stop our houses from feuding, huh, Romeo?" Deacon gave him a look he couldn't read, so Mark dropped his gaze and tore off another hunk of bread. "Or if I want the perfect opportunity to murder Bengal and not have anyone notice right away." He swirled the bread in what little olive oil remained on his plate. "I'm not letting him get away with what he did to Brandon, you know. It doesn't matter that he didn't know about his history—" He caught the look on Deacon's face. "Shit. *Shit.* I wasn't supposed to say that."

"It's okay," Deacon said. He shrugged. "I figured there was a reason he freaked out. And it doesn't go any further."

Mark sighed. "Anyway, the other guys agreed Bengal needs to get kicked the fuck out of Alpha Delt. Even the other brothers hate him, which I didn't know."

He felt stupid admitting it. Maybe Sean *had* stolen his gay thunder. And maybe the rest of the pledges had stolen his Bengal-is-a-wanker thunder. Mark had been holding on to all that anger, and it hadn't been misplaced exactly, but it hadn't been righteous either. Not when Mark was so in love with the idea of being martyred by the frat for his attitude, his sexuality, and his nationality that he hadn't noticed the other pledges weren't all falling into line like good little pod people. Mark wasn't the lone individual in a sea of conformity and douchebaggery after all.

And he'd been so enamored with the idea of being distracted from his self-indulgent misery by being fucked by a hot guy that he'd never thought about all the shit that Deacon might have going on in his life.

"Your stars are wrong," he said later as they walked back to campus hand in hand.

"Do you mean we're star-cross'd?" Deacon teased him.

"No. I mean, you spend your entire life looking up at the pattern of the stars, and then you change hemispheres and it's suddenly different. There are whole constellations you can't name anymore. When I was a kid, my Uncle Steve used to take me camping. I was six when I picked the Southern Cross for the first time. When I saw it, I mean, and not just some random pattern. When I was older, I used to sit on my board at night and watch it. And it was no big thing, until it wasn't there anymore. Until I went outside here one night for a smoke and a think, and I looked and saw your stars were wrong."

Deacon squeezed his hand. "We should go camping one night. I can at least show you the Big Dipper."

"I've seen your Big Dipper," Mark said with a leer and then snorted. "Actually, let's not call it that. That sounds weird."

"Yeah, we were never going to call it that," Deacon said, rolling his eyes.

Mark grinned, and then his attention was caught by a display in a shopwindow. "Shit. Check that out." He tugged on Deacon's hand, pulling him to a stop.

There were girlie clothes, and then there were girlie

clothes. And this was proper stuff. Not saucy French-maid stuff, but proper stuff: lace and silk and pretty ribbons and catches. And Deacon had that strange look on his face that was kind of horrified, but mostly turned on. As though he liked it but was ashamed to admit that he liked it.

"I want that," Mark said, pointing to a soft blue satin set of things: knickers, a camisole, and a suspender belt. He leaned so close to the window that his breath fogged it up. "I want you to fuck me when I'm wearing it."

He turned his head to watch Deacon's expression, because this was a big step. This wasn't unplanned like the French-maid thing. And it wasn't coincidental, like the pink fuzzy sweater lying on the floor. This was actually acknowledging that maybe Deacon had a thing for seeing Mark in girl's underwear, and maybe Mark had a thing for seeing Deacon so turned on by that, and taking control of it. Because Deacon might freak out about this, might laugh it off and back away, when it wasn't a joke. It was a long way from a joke.

Mark wanted to wear the lingerie. He wanted to feel the slide of the fabric over his skin as Deacon touched him. He wanted to be shameless, and he wanted Deacon to see it.

"Let's go in," Mark said.

They went into the shop, Deacon glancing around nervously, as though Mark had suggested they try to score some cocaine off the woman behind the counter. The woman greeted them and gave no indication she thought it was strange for two men to have come into a lingerie shop together. Mark went straight for the blue satin set. Flinched at the price tag—how they could charge so much for so little material was beyond him—but he picked it up anyway. The fabric felt as slippery cool and delicate as he'd imagined, and he could picture Deacon running his palm over the ruffles, yanking the knickers to one side so he could thrust a finger into Mark's arse…

"What do you think?" he asked Deacon, holding it up.

"Do you actually like wearing this stuff?" Deacon asked uncertainly.

"Yeah," Mark said. "I really do."

"But is it…?" Deacon paused. "Would you like it even if I didn't?"

Mark nodded, looking at the cashier, who didn't appear to be paying them any mind. "Might not have figured out I liked it for a while, without you. Not saying I have a burning need to put on girls' knickers. But damn, it's hot to wear them when you're fucking me."

Deacon studied the lingerie set again. The longing in his expression was so blatant it was almost funny.

"So I'll get it, then," Mark said. "Unless you want to make a case for another set. I like the blue, personally."

"You really don't have to. That's a lot of money."

Okay, he'd been hoping Deacon would be 100 percent on board with this. Because the longer he stood here holding the lacy underwear, the more foolish he felt. "I know I don't have to," he said, trying not to sound impatient. Wasn't like Mark had never felt shame over his infatuation with arse play. He'd covered it up by being more brazen, by talking dirtier. Now it didn't bother him at all. Maybe Deacon just needed time to come to terms with his interest. Time and practice. "I *want* to."

"I'll pay for half."

"Nope." Mark started for the counter, then stopped at the rack of stockings. "It's called a gift, Deke." He selected a pair of gray stockings with lace detail. "Besides, I'm not interested in sharing custody. Imagine: it's Friday night, and all I want to do is dress up and sprawl on the common room couch, sipping champagne and puffing on one of those cigarette holders, but I can't because it's your weekend with the knickers." Mark didn't bother keeping his voice down.

"Hey."

Mark turned.

Deacon was grinning, his eyes full of hope and wonder. "If it's Friday night, I'm gonna be right there with you, watching you put on those knickers."

Mark grinned too. "That's what I like to hear."

"Holy fuck," Deacon whispered, nodding at the ensemble in Mark's arms. "You're gonna look so hot in that. Mark, I... Seriously, thank you."

"One night soon, we *are* gonna get that hotel."

Deacon followed Mark to the counter. "What's wrong with tonight?" he asked casually, stepping beside Mark as Mark handed his stuff to the cashier.

Mark nearly shivered.

What was wrong with tonight was that tomorrow was Monday, and Mark had a quiz in American lit.

"I want to," he said. "I want to so much, but I've got a quiz tomorrow. Which, you know, I'm gonna fail anyway, so I s'pose—"

"No." Deacon raised his eyebrows. "Study first, and play later. You pass that test, and later in the week we'll get that hotel room."

Mark pulled his credit card out of his wallet and handed it to the cashier. He wondered fleetingly if Jim actually read the bills or just paid them. Because this might make for an interesting topic of conversation. *Say, Mark, I couldn't help but notice you spent two hundred dollars at a lingerie store. Did your card get stolen, champ?*

"Okay," he said. "Study first, says the Phi Sig nerd."

Deacon flashed him a smile. "That's the spirit. You're getting the hang of this fraternity-rivalry thing after all."

Mark hugged his wrapped lingerie to his chest as they headed back out onto the street. "Yay me."

CHAPTER 11

M ark failed his test.

Deacon knew it the moment Mark slunk through the front door of the bar, pulled up a stool, slapped his cigarettes on the bar, and sat there in a slouch. So no lingerie tonight. Not that Mark wouldn't be up for it, Deacon was sure, but not everything had to be about getting off. Sometimes, when you'd failed an exam, you wanted to eat chips and dip and watch bad sci-fi movies instead. At least that was how things went in Phi Sig.

"I thought you were quitting," Deacon said, nodding at the cigarettes.

"I'm quitting tomorrow," Mark muttered.

Deacon got Mark a Coke and counted down the minutes until the end of his shift. Walking back to campus, Mark was quiet. Then, underneath the statue of Prescott, he suddenly turned to Deacon. "Does it matter if I'm not smart?"

"What?"

"Hot won't last," Mark said. "Smart gets smarter, but hot just turns into pathetic, right?"

"You're not pathetic," Deacon said, trying to figure out where Mark was going with this, and then just admitting defeat. "You're also not stupid. And when does hot turn pathetic? Two weeks down the track, or two years, or twenty?"

"I don't know," Mark said in a low voice.

"You'll be hot even when you're eighty," Deacon said. "With a neck like a turkey's."

"Phi Sigs go for smart," Mark said. "That's what Blake said today. *'You need to lift your game, little bro. Phi Sigs only go for smart.'* Fuck, Deke, Blake got more questions right than me. *Blake!*"

"You're smart enough," Deacon said. "But you've never read American lit in your life before, right? There's a whole lot of cultural baggage and history and context and stuff that of course you don't get, but it's not because you're dumb; it's because you haven't been exposed to it."

Smart or hot. He wondered if Mark really thought those were his only options, and if they were mutually exclusive. Deacon thought Mark was both. Not that his grades reflected his smartness, but grades never told the whole story. Even Phi Sig knew that. Okay, so a guy had to maintain a decent GPA, but they weren't Mensa. And a student like Mark would probably do a whole lot better in Phi Sig, where studying wasn't seen as a mortal sin, than in Alpha Delta, where nobody cared what your major was as long as you could do a keg stand.

Deacon took Mark back to his room. Matt was working tonight, and James was at the library, so they had the place to themselves. Deacon turned on his laptop, and they watched a dumb shoot-'em-up movie, curled up on the bed together.

Mark fell asleep somewhere before the ending.

Deacon smoothed Mark's hair back from his forehead. Asleep, with all his attitude stripped away, there was no trace of angry bunny at all. Just tired bunny. Sweet bunny. Maybe lost bunny, who had looked up at the stars only to discover that they were wrong, that he didn't recognize them anymore.

Mark snorted once or twice and drooled a bit against Deacon's chest. Deacon didn't mind.

As the credits of the movie rolled, Deacon's phone buzzed. He tried to keep the sigh out of his voice as he answered. "Hi, Mom."

"Deacon." She sounded breathless. "Are you okay?"

"I'm fine," he said, stroking Mark's hair. "What's wrong?"

"It's only six more days to go," she said, and Deacon knew she wasn't talking about when Ben arrived home. She was talking about when Ben died, because there was no way in hell her brain would let her believe, even for a moment, that it could turn out any other way. As though entertaining the thought that Ben might just be okay would jinx it.

The worst part was, a lot could happen in six days. And if, God forbid, something actually did happen to Ben, for the rest of her life their mom would live with every single irrational fear totally validated. She would be unmanageable then.

"It's like any other thing, Mom," Deacon said. There was a fine line between humoring her and pandering to her. "A day at a time, remember?"

That was what every therapist ever had said to her.

"Yes," she said. "Oh God, Deacon. Don't come and visit me this weekend. I couldn't bear it if you were in an accident."

Because in his mom's world, nothing could ever be

allowed to go right. If Ben didn't die, then Deacon absolutely would, on his way to the family reunion.

He hadn't heard her this bad in a while. Usually she was embarrassed by the way her brain worked, and covered up her embarrassment by either joking about her fears or getting angry at herself and swearing a lot. But right now, she just sounded scared.

"You know I drive safe," he said, trying to forget the whole phone-sex thing with Mark.

"I don't think I should leave the house tomorrow," she said.

"Okay." All this time he'd been telling himself she'd be better once Ben was home, but maybe he was as delusional as his mom. He didn't know that she'd improve. Wasn't it more likely that she'd find some other thing to obsess over? Once, when Deacon was thirteen, she'd refused to drive the car for a month because she'd seen some program about a sinkhole that had opened up and swallowed a lane of traffic. It wasn't enough to be scared of traffic crashes or stuff that actually happened every day to people. No, his mom had to pick something as completely improbable as a sinkhole.

Deacon closed his eyes as she began to talk. The same old litany of fear and worry and shame.

"I know," he said whenever she paused. "I know, Mom."

Mark stirred against his chest. He opened his eyes and peered up at Deacon blearily. Deacon averted his gaze.

"Mom, he'll be okay," he said. "He *will*."

Please, please, please, God, don't make me a liar.

Mark shifted slightly. He slid his right hand up Deacon's shirt. He pressed his palm lightly over Deacon's heart and splayed his fingers. He caught Deacon's gaze and held it solemnly.

Deacon wasn't sure what Mark meant by the gesture, but he was comforted by it.

"It would just figure. If after all this time…"

"I know, Mom," Deacon told her, his throat aching. "It'll be okay."

"Honey," she said, and there was pity in her tone. Real pity, as though she knew Deacon's ignorance would wound him terribly when Ben inevitably came home in a flag-draped box, but he just wouldn't listen. "You can't know that!"

Mark rubbed his palm across Deacon's chest and snuggled closer. He was so warm and so solid.

"I know I can't know for sure, but it's what I believe," Deacon told his mother.

Please, please, please, God, make it true.

His mother took a deep breath. "I'm sorry. I'm bothering you."

"It's all right," he said. "You can always call me if you're worried."

She was silent for a while.

"Mom?"

"I just wanted to check in," she said quietly. "Make sure you…you're okay."

"I'm okay. And Ben's gonna be too. All right?"

"All right."

Deacon knew she wasn't convinced, but it was the best he could do.

"I'll be there this weekend," Deacon promised. "I wanna see you and Ben."

"Okay." Her voice was small.

"I love you, Mom."

"Love you too."

They hung up. Deacon didn't say anything for a few minutes. Mark kept his hand on Deacon's chest.

"She okay?" Mark asked finally.

Deacon nodded slowly. "She will be. Once Ben's home."

"Are you nervous about seeing Ben?"

Deacon peered down at him. "Why would I be?"

"Dunno." Mark paused. "When my mum and Jim first got together, he took her with him on a trip to Europe for like a month. Not that long, I know, but I remember when it got close to time for her to come home, I got nervous. Like maybe I thought she'd be different after spending all that time with him, or I worried I'd act like an arsehole because I kind of resented her going in the first place." He met Deacon's gaze briefly, then looked away, running a hand over Deacon's chest again. "Sorry. Not the same thing."

"No." Deacon shifted, staring at the ceiling. "I get what you're saying. I guess I hadn't really thought about it. When I think about Ben coming home, I only think about how it will affect my mom."

But it would be strange to see Ben. Spend time with him —not just a couple of days while Ben was on leave. Deacon wondered if Ben would be different. If they'd still have anything in common. If they ever had.

Mark traced a wrinkle in Deacon's T-shirt. "You ever get tired of being good?"

"Good?"

"Yeah. You're a good student and you belong to a good fraternity and you take care of your mother. And you refuse to serve alcohol to minors even if everywhere else in the bloody world, they're not minors. Do you ever want to be just totally selfish and awful?"

Deacon tried to laugh. He'd never seen himself the way

Mark described him. His GPA wasn't as good as James's. He'd used Phi Sig mainly as a way to ensure he belonged somewhere without having to go through all the effort of actually making friends. And his thoughts about his mother were often far from selfless. He'd told her to call him anytime she felt worried. What he'd meant was *Please don't* need *to call. Please just be okay.*

He wanted her to be able to fix herself, which wasn't any more rational than her fears about Ben.

"I can be pretty selfish and awful."

"I doubt that," Mark said. "I'd recognize my own kind."

"You're not—"

"Hey," Mark said. "I'm not fishing for reassurance. I know who I am. I'm like the Good Samaritan's bum of a younger brother who's always asking to borrow money and putting it up his nose and never paying it back. And everyone's like, 'Why can't you be more like Henry?'"

"Henry?"

"That's the Good Samaritan's name. I've just decided."

"I don't think you're like that." Deacon really didn't. He remembered how Mark had looked sleeping. Remembered Mark picking out the lingerie. *"It's called a gift, Deke."* Mark was sweet. And Deacon could only imagine how Mark would react to hearing that. Which was maybe why Deacon said it: he was curious. "I think you're sweet."

Deacon braced himself for Mark to laugh at him, or to tell him to fuck off. He felt Mark tense, and he tensed as well. But Mark didn't respond, except, after a while, to ask, "What's the worst thing you've ever thought?"

"The worst thing I've ever thought?"

"Yeah."

"Something I've thought about doing, or, like, if I were directing the next *Saw* movie, here's a scene I think would be great?"

"The thought that most makes you feel like a horrible human being."

"I don't know."

"Come on, Deke."

Part of Deacon wanted to refuse to have this conversation. But he was interested in the question, and its answer. And for some reason, he felt safe talking to Mark. "Uh… Okay. When Ben first left, sometimes I'd imagine that he did get killed. I guess because sometimes, when my mom freaks out about stuff, I get freaked out too. Like these are things I *should* be worried about, but because I don't worry about them, they're gonna sneak up on me and happen. So I thought if something did happen to Ben, it would be almost a relief. Because then we could stop *worrying* about it. And I'd know how it felt to deal with something that bad— whether or not I could handle it. That's pretty shitty, huh?"

"Oh, come on. I wished loads of times Jim would fall into the ocean and get eaten by a shark. Or roll down a flight of stairs testing one of his castor sets on an office chair. And if you knew Jim, you'd know that's like saying you want to drop-kick a baby otter. Jim's so fucking *nice*."

"But he was an outsider. And he married your mom. So I can see where there'd be some resentment. And besides, you didn't really want him to die."

"I don't know, Deke. Sometimes I did. Or thought I did."

"Thought you did. That's the important part."

"Did you really want Ben to die?"

Deacon thought. Of course he hadn't. It was just that imagining it had come more naturally than he'd expected. "No."

They were silent a moment.

"So, uh…" Mark swallowed. "I can't promise you much. I'm not a hopeless romantic, and sometimes I forget that people generally like it when you do nice things for them. I've never been anyone's boyfriend. And I probably could, in my own way, out-douche a lot of the Alpha Delts." He turned his head slightly and pressed his face against Deacon's chest. "But I..." He turned again so he wasn't speaking into Deacon's T-shirt. "But you don't have to be afraid to tell me anything. Because I won't judge you for it. And you don't have to worry about not seeming like a good guy in front of me. Because I guarantee I've been a worse guy. And if you need anything from me, just ask. I'm not the best at figuring out what people need on my own. But if you tell me, I'll try to give it. That's what I can promise you."

Deacon's throat tightened. He ran a hand once more through Mark's hair, making a fist around a hank of it and tugging gently. "Thanks," he whispered. "That's a better offer than I've ever gotten before."

Mark tilted his head up, and Deacon could see the cocky grin was back. "Maybe I'm a better guy than you've ever gotten before."

Deacon laughed. "Maybe." He combed his fingers through Mark's hair. "What's the worst thing you've ever thought about?"

Mark's expression grew sober. "I don't know."

"Come on. I answered."

"There's seriously too many bad thoughts to sort through. If I think of a really juicy one, I'll let you know."

Deacon snorted. "Not fair."

"Hey, I didn't make you answer. I just asked. And then prodded a bit."

Deacon wound his arms around Mark and rolled sideways, crushing Mark to him. "All right," he murmured. "I'm going to assume your refusal to answer is because you've never really had a bad thought in your life."

Mark squeezed Deacon back, throwing his leg over Deacon's hip. "Delusional," he muttered. But he sounded pleased.

Deacon's heart still pounded from Mark's promise. *"If you tell me, I'll try to give it."*

"Mark?"

"Yeah?"

"I think I might need you to stay the night. And wake up with me tomorrow."

"Good. Because I'm so comfortable I wouldn't leave this bed if you paid me."

"Even when I do this?" Deacon squeezed tighter. Mark grunted.

"Especially when you do that."

Deacon smiled.

"What if your roommates come in?" Mark asked.

"We'll keep our clothes on."

"I already told you what I could promise. Did you hear keeping my clothes on anywhere in there?"

Deacon snickered and buried his face in Mark's hair, easing his grip on Mark's body. "No."

"Then it's anyone's guess what state your roommates will find me in."

"Pennsylvania," Deacon murmured, then snickered some more. He really did feel good now. Warm beside Mark, and safe.

Mark laughed. "You sound like you need to go to sleep."

Deacon nodded into his hair.

"All right," Mark said softly, running his fingertips down Deacon's spine. "Clothes on, lights out." He reached out and switched off the lamp on Deacon's desk. Settled back next to Deacon, pulling him close. "I'll see you in the morning."

The smile wouldn't leave Deacon's face, even as his eyes fell closed. "Okay. See you."

He probably fell asleep with that dopey smile on. And he didn't care.

————

Deacon was about the one thing going right in Mark's life at the moment. Classes sucked. Quizzes sucked. Bengal sucked. Quitting smoking sucked. And Brandon was unhappy, which completely sucked. He pretended it didn't matter that he'd quit pledging, but Mark saw the way his gaze was drawn to Mark's stupid pledge badge—apparently Matt had not been happy to find that on the floor of the bedroom in Phi Sig. Deacon and James had barely managed to talk him down from mounting a counterattack, since Matt was so convinced the Alpha Delts had sent their pledges into the house to cause damage. Mark had offered to swear solemnly he'd only ever sneaked in to suck cock, but Deacon seemed to think that wouldn't help.

"So, you're pretty serious with this guy from Phi Sig," Brandon said, stirring sugar into his coffee.

The barista at the place on High Street had refused to serve Mark, so they'd found a place a few blocks away that at first seemed like a seventies-themed diner, but turned out to be the real deal. Sticky linoleum floors included. The coffee was bad, but it was cheap.

"I don't know," Mark said and hated that he didn't. "I s'pose."

"What's his major?" Brandon asked curiously.

"Um," Mark said. "Engineering? Something brainy. I can't even understand the titles on half his textbooks."

"You're going out with someone, and you don't even know what his major is?" Brandon raised his eyebrows.

"For starters," Mark said, "we never officially started going out. We're a one-night stand that went horribly wrong. And I might not know exactly what he's studying, but I know some other stuff. His mum lives in Chambersburg, and his brother is coming home from Afghanistan at the end of the week." *And I know what he thinks is the worst thought he's ever had. I know he likes seeing me in ladies' underwear. And that he actually makes cuddling fun.*

Brandon smiled and set his spoon aside. "That's good."

"Yeah, that's good." Mark tapped the napkin dispenser. "What about you, Bran?"

Brandon started. "What about me?"

"Well, you've canceled on me twice this week for coffee," Mark said. "And usually I'm the one who forgot he had a class or a quiz or a dental appointment or something. You don't double book, Bran. You have a magic brain."

"I don't have a magic brain," Brandon mumbled.

"You totally do. So are you avoiding me? Or are you avoiding everyone? Or are you ditching me for a better offer, because I would completely understand that."

"Apart from classes, I haven't really been leaving my dorm," Brandon admitted.

That was what Mark was afraid of.

When Mark had started at Prescott, someone from the students' union gave him what he thought was a show bag, except it had condoms and dental dams in it instead of fairy floss and plush animals made in China. And somewhere in among all the pamphlets that warned him not to have unprotected sex and share needles, Mark remembered there had been one about mental health services for students.

Had Brandon got the same bag of stuff when he'd started? And had he read it or just thrown it out like Mark had?

"I think that..." Mark began. *I think you're in more trouble than you're saying, and I think you would never admit it in a million years.* "I think that maybe I need your help to pass American lit."

Brandon frowned. "You do?"

"Yeah." Mark forced a sheepish grin. "I'm flunking. Seriously flunking. Can you tutor me?"

Brandon straightened up, squaring his shoulders. "Maybe. I'm not that great at lit."

"I need all the help I can get," Mark told him, back on the truth now. "Will you do it?"

Brandon sipped his coffee. "If you think it will help."

It will at least help one of us.

"I know it will," Mark said. "I'll try too, I promise. If you tutor me, I won't slack off."

"All right." Brandon sort of smiled.

"But you've got to do me a favor too," Mark said.

"Aren't I already doing you a favor?" Brandon asked. "Tutoring you?"

"Shit. Okay, I meant I'm gonna offer to do you a favor. Because you can't stay in your dorm and avoid the world. Alpha Delt isn't everything. It isn't even most things."

"Try telling my dad that."

"I will. Better yet, you tell him."

"Yeah, that'll go over well."

Mark didn't know Brandon's dad, but he did know that at eighteen years old, it was time to stop caring what went over well and start living your life the way you wanted to live it. At some point, life had to stop being about making your parents happy.

Which is why you're pledging the fraternity your stepdad told you to?

That was different. He'd pledged Alpha Delt so that he could get kicked out and rub it in Jim's face.

And okay, maybe a little bit to make Jim happy.

Jim was, after all, part of his mum's life now, and Mark couldn't help being terrified of whose side his mum would be on if Mark managed to alienate Jim completely.

And Mark did think Jim had more to offer than overly enthusiastic recommendations of museums. There was some stuff that was even easier to talk about with Jim than with his mother. He couldn't think of an example off the top of his head, but he was sure there was something.

"Anyway," Mark said. "We need to do something fun."

"Like?"

Mark thought for a minute. What was everyone always going on about that was fun around here? "We should go to the zoo."

Brandon snorted.

"I'm serious! I've heard at least three people tell me to go to the Norristown Zoo. You like zoos?"

Brandon hesitated. "They're kind of sad." A thoughtful expression came over his face. "But not if you're high."

Mark raised his eyebrows. "Brandon. Is there something you're not telling me?"

"I've got some pot in my dorm. I've been smoking sometimes to help me relax. Don't tell anyone."

Mark decided to save his lecture on dubious methods of self-medication, because the idea of going to the zoo high sounded perfect.

"And, uh," Brandon went on, "I went to the zoo stoned once in high school. It was pretty fun."

Mark set down his cup. "It's settled. We're getting high and going to the zoo. Do you have money for the tip?"

"We're going *now*?"

"When better?"

"Don't you have lit tomorrow? Maybe we ought to get started on your tutoring."

Mark waved his hand. "We can do that this weekend. Come on." He stood as Brandon fished out some quarters for a tip.

"Okay," Brandon said. "But you know you're crazy, right?"

"Most definitely."

Brandon grinned as he set down the money. He looked happier than Mark had seen him in a while.

They were about to head out the door when Mark's phone buzzed. Bengal. *All pledge bitchezz at the house in one hour.*

"Shit," Mark said.

"What is it?"

Mark glanced at him. "Uh, Bengal. Wants the pledges over at the house." And *bitchezz* meant it was gonna be a pledge torture session, not a house meeting.

Shit, shit, shit. Any other time, Mark would have blown Alpha Delt off and suffered the consequences later. But he was absolutely determined now to defeat Bengal, and to do that, he needed to attend the hazing sessions. Needed to push Bengal to take the game too far with someone who'd fight back. Like himself.

Brandon nodded, his smile gone. "You'd better go."

"I really don't want to. But I..." Probably not wise to tell Brandon about his plan to annihilate Bengal. He had a feeling Brandon would disapprove.

"But you can't just blow them off," Brandon said.

"We're going to the zoo stoned tomorrow, though. I promise. Soon as American lit's done."

"Don't you have another class in the afternoon?"

Damn Brandon and his magic memory. "It's canceled," he lied.

"Okay," Brandon said suspiciously. "Tomorrow."

"I'm really sorry, Bran."

"No problem."

It definitely was a problem. Fuck Bengal.

They left the coffee shop and headed back to campus.

CHAPTER 12

"It's pregnant. Not fat." Brandon snickered.

"How do you know?" Mark asked.

"Because the sign says Susie's Pregnant!" Brandon pointed to a cardboard sign taped to the side of the pen.

"Yeah, but maybe the zoo's just embarrassed because she ate all the other meerkats. So they made up a bogus pregnancy." Mark stared at the potbellied meerkat, who stared right back at him, her tiny front paws resting on her bulge. "Seriously, where are the others?"

"Do you have meerkats in Australia?" Brandon whispered.

"That's Africa, mate," Mark whispered back. He wasn't sure why they were whispering. "We're in the Africa exhibit, remember?"

Brandon tried to stop snickering as a man with two children joined them at the pen.

"Look, girls," the father said.

"Ooh," said the older girl, who was maybe seven. "He's *fat!*"

"That's what I said!" Mark exclaimed.

The little girl looked at him.

"*She's* pregnant," the father said. "That makes her tummy big. Soon she'll have babies."

"How many babies?" the girl asked.

"I'm not sure," her father said.

"Between three and four pups," Brandon supplied. "She'll gestate for about ten weeks, then give birth, most likely at night, in a burrow she's created. However, infanticides are bound to occur at the hands of other female meerkats, who want to increase chances of survival for their own young. Which is probably why the zoo has removed other females from the pen."

The family looked at him in amazement.

"You know a lot about meerkats," the younger daughter said.

"I studied them for a while. In Africa," Brandon replied. His shoulders jerked as he stifled a laugh.

The father wanted to know more about Brandon's studies, so Brandon said he'd studied a clan of thirty meerkats over a period of six months when he'd worked as an intern for NatGeo.

"Well, that was a load of bullshit," Mark said when the family had gone. "You didn't even know meerkats lived in Africa until five minutes ago! Did you just make all that up about the babies and stuff?"

Brandon grinned. "I memorized the sign outside the exhibit."

Mark laughed and whacked him on the arm. "You bastard."

They said good-bye to Susie and wandered on. Doing the zoo stoned really was fun. Mark had never been more impressed by the array of animals that existed in the world, or by the logistics of re-creating their habitats in a hundred-acre chunk of east Pennsylvania. Brandon was in a good mood, and Mark was still preening from what felt like a victory over Bengal yesterday.

When he'd arrived at the Alpha Delt house, Bengal had announced that each pledge was responsible for going to sorority row and locating one sorority girl who would admit to finding him so unattractive she'd never have sex with him. He was then to bring her back to the house. Mark had gone along with that part, since he didn't care whether girls wanted to sleep with him, and since the time didn't seem right to defy Bengal yet.

He'd met up with Dan and Fraser on the way to sorority row. Dan, who wasn't terribly attractive, declared the activity bullshit. Fraser, on the other hand, believed he'd be hard-pressed to find a girl who didn't want to sleep with him, though he agreed the activity was bullshit.

Only Logan White had been present when Bengal explained the task, which made Mark wonder if any of the other brothers knew about it. If they'd approved it.

"So let's not play the game," Mark had suggested.

"What do you mean?" Dan had asked.

Things had gone better than Mark had expected when, at the Phi Mu house, he recognized the girl from his lit class, the one he'd noticed early in the semester and had thought would make a better friend than fifty Alpha Delts. Her name, he'd learned weeks ago, was Chelsea, and she loved Mark Twain.

Which probably meant she had a sense of humor.

When prompted, she'd declared a lack of sexual interest in Mark, and had found a couple of her friends to hail Dan and Fraser complete gargoyles. Fraser looked put out, despite the fact that the girls were kidding. Or pretending to be kidding. Mark didn't know.

On the way back to Alpha Delt, Mark, Dan, and Fraser had explained to the girls about Bengal. Two of them had already heard rumors about him.

"We don't know what he's gonna have us do when we get back," Mark had told them. *"But we need to make him look like an arse."*

When they'd arrived back at the house, six pledges were there with the girls they'd found. Bengal had had the pledges strip to their underwear and line up against the wall. The girls had been given markers and been told to mark the parts of the pledges' bodies they found unattractive—places the pledges needed to lose weight, tone up, or as one girl had written on Blond Pledge's nose, *get plastic surgery!!*

Only four of the girls were participating. They were giggling and seemed to be enjoying themselves. The pledges were trying to laugh it off, but they all looked uncomfortable. The other two girls hung back uneasily.

Bengal spotted Mark and Fraser and Dan and ordered them up to the wall. Mark wasn't sure what the hell to do. He could refuse, but then what? Then he and Bengal would get into a shouting match, and what would that help? It might alert some of the other brothers, but the house sounded oddly quiet, and besides, Mark didn't know that any of the other Alpha Delts would actually tell Bengal to stop.

He stripped off his shirt slowly, stalling for time.

He needn't have worried.

Chelsea had walked right up to Bengal. *"Ooh, girls, I found one even worse,"* she'd said. She circled Bengal, and her friends joined her.

"Oh my God," one of the other girls said. *"I'd fuck any of these pledges before I'd fuck this guy."*

Bengal looked confused. Like Blake stumbling out of a Portaloo.

"And it's not the way he looks," the third girl said. *"It's his personality."*

"Yeah." Chelsea picked up a permanent marker, uncapped it, and circled the area on one side of Bengal's mouth before Bengal could step back. *"He's got all these scowl lines."*

"And his eyes look mean," the third girl said.

"And he's being a complete asshole to his pledges in a way that's not fun. Or legal," the second girl added.

The other sorority girls had stopped marking on their pledges and were all watching the scene unfold and whispering. *"Oh my* God," one said.

In the end, Bengal stalked out of the room without a word. He didn't come downstairs all evening, though eventually fifteen more pledges showed up with girls who didn't find them attractive, and some of the brothers came home from class or work, so Mark broke out the beer, and it turned into one of Alpha Delt's better mixers.

Mark knew Bengal was furious. That he blamed Mark, and that he'd be looking for revenge. But maybe that was what needed to happen. If Mark could get Bengal to do something irrefutably illegal—in front of witnesses—he'd be set.

"Look."

Mark looked where Brandon was pointing.

"There's the Australia exhibit." Bran looked at Mark. "You wanna check it out?"

The first part of the exhibit was indoors.

"Holy crap," Brandon said. "Look at all these tree frogs." He tapped on the glass. "Did you ever see them in the wild, where you lived?"

"One used to live in my toilet," Mark said, shaking his head fondly.

"You can go back and visit sometime, can't you?"

"For sure."

"It's cool that you've gotten to live in different countries. I'm jealous."

"I guess." Mark didn't say any more than that.

They stayed at the zoo until almost closing, sitting on various benches, watching the animals, and eating shaved ice and something called an elephant ear, which Mark thought was a bit insensitive to the elephants. Mark tried to hurry past the bear exhibit, but Brandon wanted to stop.

"Look how cute they are," Brandon said wistfully.

"Yeah, see how cute you think they are when they're crushing your skull," Mark muttered. He tried to attract the attention of a passing zoo worker. "Excuse me, how strong are these bars?"

When they got back to campus, Mark said good-bye to Brandon, and they made plans to meet up for tutoring the next day. Mark headed to the Phi Sig house to see Deacon. Matt and James had gotten good at making themselves scarce when Mark came over, and tonight the only one in Deacon's room besides Deacon was Anabelle, whom Deacon gently shooed out when Mark arrived.

Deacon closed his scary-titled textbook and smiled at Mark. "How's it going?"

"Awesome," Mark said.

"Yeah?"

"Yeah." He plopped on Deacon's lap. "How was your day?"

Deacon kissed his neck. "Okay. Talked to Mom a little bit. She sounded better."

"That's good." Mark arched as Deacon's stubble brushed his throat.

"What'd you get up to?"

"Got stoned and went to the zoo with Brandon."

Deacon laughed. "Okay. Not the answer I was expecting."

"He needs to do something fun! He'd gotten all reclusive since quitting Alpha Delt. I was hoping tutoring me in lit would give him a sense of purpose. But he needs fun too."

"So you got stoned and went to the zoo?"

"Oh my God, Deke, camels are so funny when you're high."

Deacon had wrapped one arm around Mark and was stroking his chest, circling his nipples through his shirt. Mark sighed and sank back against him, his cock hardening.

Deacon was so hot, and so grown-up, and so *good*, and camels were fucking hilarious, and Brandon was a good friend, and maybe Mark really was lucky to get to live in two different countries. Maybe life was kind of pretty okay.

"How was lit today?" Deacon asked.

"Okay. We're on Walt Whitman. Sweet beard." That was actually what Mark had written in answer to the question *What was Walt Whitman known for?* on his last quiz, but he didn't need to tell Deacon that. He reached out and rolled the pen on Deacon's desk. Deacon had been chewing the end of it. Deacon was a pen chewer.

"And biology?"

How did Deacon have his schedule memorized when Mark barely knew it himself, even after a month and a half? "I skipped."

Mark accidentally knocked the pen to the floor. He leaned forward off Deacon's lap to retrieve it.

And felt Deacon's hand connect with his arse. Reasonably hard.

"Hey!" Mark jerked up and looked at Deacon. "What was that for?" The sting had registered, and heat flooded Mark's arse and groin at the same time.

Deacon looked..."impish" was probably the right word here. His eyes were wide, and he was biting his lip to hold a smile back. "For skipping class to get stoned and go to the zoo. What happened to concentrating more on your studies?"

Mark rubbed his arse. "I'm going to start concentrating tomorrow."

"Mm," Deacon said, catching Mark's wrist and pulling him closer.

"And since when do I answer to you?" Mark asked. The question started off strong but faded at the end as Mark found himself lost in a fantasy of Deacon rolling up his sleeves and giving Mark a proper spanking for missing class.

"I guess since right now," Deacon said.

Deacon was still holding his wrist. "You gonna do it?" Mark asked quietly.

"Want me to?"

Mark nodded, and Deacon tugged him over his knee. Slapped the seat of Mark's pants once. Then again.

It didn't hurt enough. Wasn't wild enough, real enough. Mark didn't want it to hurt too much, but he wanted the rush of walking the line between too much and just right.

Deacon smacked him again, and Mark grunted, bracing the toes of his sneakers against the carpet. "Deke?" he asked.

"Yeah?" Deacon rested his hand on Mark's arse.

"You got a paddle in your house?"

He didn't breathe while he waited for Deacon to answer. He wasn't sure if the antihazing Phi Sigs would keep one around.

"In the basement," Deacon said. "Forged in the seventies and kept around for posterity."

Mark laughed. "For posteriority, you mean?"

Deacon laughed too. "Why do you ask?"

"You wanna do this proper?"

They headed down to the basement, which, unlike Alpha Delt's combination torture chamber/den of sin, was tidy. Board games were stacked on one shelf, and there was a ping-pong table that didn't look like it had seen much use.

"No one's down here," Mark said.

"They're all upstairs studying. Or at the semiformal planning meeting. Or the Science Week lecture series."

"Oh God. You *nerds*."

"Careful," Deacon warned, pulling an old paddle down from the wall. It was made of blond wood and had the Phi Sig letters carved into it. It had also been signed by a slew of people. "Don't want to get in more trouble, do you?"

"Dunno," Mark said, his heart thudding. "I might."

Deacon had locked the basement door when they'd come down. He pointed at the ping-pong table with the paddle. "Bend over there."

"Don't waste any time, do you?" Mark asked, suddenly more than a little nervous. Yeah, he'd wanted Deacon to hit harder when he'd been over Deacon's knee, his cock nearly hard, his neck still prickly from Deacon's kisses. But now that he'd had a few minutes to cool down, this was starting to seem like a foolish idea.

"What do you want me to waste time with?" Deacon stepped behind Mark and blew softly on the back of his neck. Placed his paddleless hand on Mark's hip and slid it around to Mark's groin, cupping the bulge there and tonguing Mark's earlobe until the bulge grew.

"Shit, yes," Mark whispered.

Deacon nipped his earlobe, and Mark yelped. "Bend over that table," Deacon said firmly.

Yes, okay, it was back again, the fantasy of Deacon, strong and sure and telling Mark exactly how things were going to be.

Mark walked over to the table and bent over it, trying to find a good place for his now uncomfortably hard cock. He almost jumped when Deacon rested the paddle against his arse. "Let's start with five," Deacon said.

That didn't seem like very many, but when Deacon drew back and landed the first blow, it drove every thought from Mark's mind except, *Christfuckholyballs, how about we stop at one?*

The sting gave way quickly to a tingling that covered his entire arse. He forced himself to breathe out.

The second blow hurt just as much, except instead of jumping up and yelling at Deacon to put the bloody paddle down, Mark let his hips move forward, let his cock press into the edge of the table, and moaned at the rush of sensation. He let his knees go slack, then straightened up again so his cock slid against the table through his jeans.

The third swat made Mark moan aloud. Deacon stopped and rubbed the paddle against Mark's arse for a moment. "No more putting off your studies, okay?"

Jesus, a year ago, Mark had thought there was nothing more exciting to sex than a blowjob with a stranger in an alley. He'd never thought about stockings or paddles or mechanical bulls or nerdy older boys who looked unbelievably hot hunched over their textbooks. Okay, maybe the last one. Richo's older brother had been a bookworm, but Mark hadn't—

Good God. Mark wasn't going to have an arse left for Deacon to fuck if Deacon kept on like this. But now the pain hardly bothered him at all; it got all caught up in something else. Spoke directly to his dick, which was so swollen it ached. Deacon ran the paddle briefly between his legs. Mark clamped his thighs around the paddle, grabbing a sharp breath and arching his back. Then he spread his legs as wide as they'd go.

He'd lost what number they were on, and he didn't care.

Deacon rubbed his arse with the paddle again, then drew back and hit him. Mark curled his fingers into his palms and pressed his forehead against the cool surface of the table. He wanted Deacon to keep going until he came.

"Drop your pants," Deacon said quietly.

Mark obeyed without hesitation, fumbling with his fly. Deacon helped him tug his jeans down, and then Deacon's hand was moving gently over Mark's underwear. He hooked his fingers in Mark's waistband, pulled on it, then snapped it against Mark's sore arse.

Mark moaned. Deacon yanked his underwear down the rest of the way and stood behind him. Deacon set the paddle alongside Mark's torso on the table. Mark felt the denim of Deacon's pants against his thighs, Deacon's shirt against his back as Deacon bent over him, dragging his palms down Mark's sides. "Learned your lesson?" he whispered.

"Maybe not quite?" Mark said uncertainly. His cock pressed against his belly, wetting the skin there. "Brandon, um, wanted to tutor me today, and I said no, we should go to the zoo."

"Hmm," Deacon said, straightening. "Two more, then."

He picked up the paddle and laid the cool wood against Mark's bare arse. Mark flinched and squeezed his eyes shut.

The impact was louder and more painful without the barrier of his jeans. Mark pressed his knees together and rocked against the table, slapping one palm against the surface.

Deacon stroked Mark's arse with his palm, using his fingertips lightly on the blazing skin. Mark got control of his breathing and lay there in the stillness, his right cheek resting against the table. He stared over at the shelf that had two different versions of Risk, a deluxe edition of Scrabble, Scattergories, and Scruples. Wondered idly if it was difficult for the Phi Sigs to play Scruples together—if they all just gave precisely the same morally commendable answers to the questions.

Deacon's fingers ghosted down Mark's crack and between his legs, rolling his balls. Mark hitched a breath and tried to move his cock into Deacon's hand. "One more," Deacon whispered, stepping back.

Mark didn't bother bracing himself. He lay there, the tension gone from his body, and accepted the final blow as easily as he'd accepted Deacon's touch.

Deacon dropped the paddle and rubbed Mark's back. "All right?" he asked.

Mark nodded. "Yeah. Fuck yeah, Deke."

"Shit, Mark. So hot. Your arse is so hot."

No kidding.

Mark arched into Deacon's touch, trying to shrug Deacon's hand lower until it was between his legs again. He felt delirious with arousal and was glad that this time Deacon had condoms and lube in his pocket. Mark had brought some too, but his jeans were all the way down around his ankles, and he didn't want to get up, just wanted Deacon to stick his cock inside him and fuck him brainless over the Phi Sigs' ping-pong table.

Deacon seemed only too happy to oblige.

"Come on," Mark said, spreading his legs. "Come on, please."

He heard the rasp of Deacon's zip and then felt the warmth of Deacon's body as Deacon leaned over him. Deacon's breath was hot against his ear. "You are shameless."

"Yeah," Mark said, closing his eyes as Deacon guided his cock into him. He loved that sting, and that pressure that gave way so slowly into fullness. "Wasn't always."

"No?" Deacon rubbed a hand over the small of Mark's back.

Mark rocked against the ping-pong table. "No. I'm at least fifty percent more obnoxious here. Can't—*Oh, shit.*" His breath whooshed out of him as Deacon bottomed out. "Can't be a total whore in a town where the gay scene is so small your high school science teacher warns most blokes off."

Fake ID or not, Mr. Gallin was not prepared to let anyone take Mark home. He'd given Mark a serious talk about how he had to look out for himself, and picking up guys in the street outside the pub was not a sensible or safe choice, and he should be sticking with boys his own age. Mr. Gallin had promised that once he was at university, he'd be able to have more fun. Mark wondered if he should send Mr. Gallin an e-mail telling him he was right about university broadening his horizons.

Mark knew Deacon thought he was the experienced one, the one willing to experiment. He suddenly wanted Deacon to know that he'd never felt that need before, not with anyone else.

"God, Deke," he panted, pushing back into Deacon's thrusts. "It's *you.*"

Anything remotely coherent was lost as Mark struggled

to match Deacon's pace. The need to tell Deacon vanished, and Mark was instead flooded with the need to come. His breath came in gasps, and he was overwhelmed, off-kilter, afraid of *something*. Something he didn't understand, something that made no sense, except Deacon's hand was on his spine now, anchoring him, and he didn't have to do anything except fuck. And he knew how to fuck, didn't he?

Mark didn't want to peel the layers off this relationship. Fuck that. Mark didn't have layers, or any vast undiscovered depths. And if he did, now was not the time to go mentally spelunking in them.

"Fuck me, Deke," he urged instead.

Coming all over a ping-pong table? That was the Mark Cooper everyone knew and loved.

———

Mark didn't stick around. Deacon was sure something was wrong, but Mark insisted he was okay; he just had to take off and get some laundry done before morning. Later that night, watching a movie with the guys in the common room, Deacon checked his phone when it buzzed. A text from Mark.

Sorry.

Deacon typed out a reply. *What are you sorry for?*

I'm a crap boyfriend.

Deacon stared at the screen for a moment, wondering if this was a general statement or if there was something specific on Mark's mind. They'd never talked about being exclusive, but Deacon had assumed they were. Was that a mistake? God, he hoped not.

I think you're a good boyfriend.

Deacon held his breath waiting for the reply.

It scares me how much I like you, Deke.

God. Deacon wanted to smile and couldn't. Not when Mark was hurting. And for no reason at all. Deacon left the common room and went outside, dialing Mark's number.

"Hey, Deke," Mark said in a low voice.

Deacon leaned against the back wall of the Phi Sig house and looked up at the stars that were still unfamiliar to Mark. "Hey, Mark. What're you doing?"

"My laundry."

"Really?"

"No. I'm sitting in my dorm cutting my toenails."

Deacon smiled. "Okay." He exhaled slowly, wondering why Mark couldn't have this conversation face-to-face. "Want to tell me what happened tonight?"

"I freaked out," Mark said. "The things I want to say, I don't know if I can. The things I want you to do to me...I think maybe they'll freak you out too."

"Nothing we've done so far freaks me out," Deacon said. He looked at the stars. "Surprises me, maybe, but not in a bad way."

Mark's breath hitched. "I want you to fist me."

Fuck. Deacon swallowed. "Um..."

"I push," Mark said suddenly. "I always fucking push."

"Mark," Deacon said, before he realized Mark had disconnected the call. "Shit."

So Mark wasn't as shameless as he pretended. Maybe he was nothing more than a homesick kid who was trying to fake it until he could make it. And maybe it wasn't Mark leading Deacon along the path of sexual experience after all. Maybe they were finding their way together. Mark was so brash, so angry, so fearless...except where it counted. Joining a fraternity just to hate and be hated. Demanding a beer on his birthday. Angry little bunny liked to have something to fight, even when it was as pointless as smacking his head against a brick wall, but he couldn't have an open and frank discussion about the things he wanted. The things he was afraid to admit he wanted.

And fisting. Deacon had never considered it. It was the sort of thing he'd seen on porn sites and thought that he'd never let someone's fist near his ass, not for love or money. But Mark loved ass play. And while Deacon didn't like the idea of being fisted, the idea of fisting someone...? The idea of fisting *Mark?* What would he look like, pushed to his limits like that? What would it feel like? The resistance. The pressure. The *trust.*

Deacon's chest tightened, and his cock hardened. He raised his phone.

Pick up. Pick up. Pick up.

"Hey, Deke." Mark's voice was flat.

"You can ask me anything," Deacon said. "And I'm not freaked out."

"You're not?" Mark sounded like he didn't believe that.

"I'm not," Deacon said. He closed his eyes. "And if you want me to fist you, Mark, if you trust me enough to try that with me, then I want to do it too."

Mark breathed heavily into Deacon's ear. "I...I think I do."

"Fuck." Deacon frowned. "We should not be talking about this on the phone." He needed to see the expression on Mark's face. Needed to be able to hold him. "Don't run away from me again, okay? Not from the stuff you want to say to me."

"Okay, Deke."

Deacon thought that was a smile he heard in Mark's voice.

CHAPTER 13

Ben had lost weight. Deacon had seen some portrait project online a few months ago, where a photographer had taken pictures of soldiers before they left for active duty, midway through their service, and when they came home. Almost all the soldiers were thinner in the final picture. There was something in their eyes too. A hauntedness—it sounded like a cliché, but it was true. They looked a little bit colder.

Ben didn't have the haunted look. He looked good. The leaner frame suited him—he'd always been heavy—and he looked tan and fit and...older. It was striking to see him standing in a room where his senior picture hung on the wall. Deacon could see how mature and defined his face had gotten in the past four years.

He'd last seen Ben eight months ago, when Ben was on leave. The changes in his brother hadn't really registered with Deacon then, maybe because he was always aware Ben's visits were temporary, and so he kept himself somewhat at a distance. Maybe too, on some level, he'd believed what his mother had believed—that Ben would never come home for good.

But here he was, sitting on the living room couch. He gestured more with his hands now, Deacon noticed. Like he was giving signals to members of his platoon or something. Deacon had a very cinematic image of Ben in a place full of red dust, his back against a mud wall, rifle clutched to him, bombs exploding nearby, motioning to the other guys to hold...hold...*now!* Probably totally inaccurate. Deacon felt a stab of guilt for never showing any real interest in what Ben's day-to-day life in the army was like.

"I was thinking tomorrow we could go to Do or Dine," Deacon's mother was saying. "My treat." Do or Dine was a local diner Deacon had never cared for, but that Ben had always loved. Their mother was in a good mood, glad to see Ben, trying slightly too hard to keep conversation going.

Deacon felt something suspiciously like resentment. *I was here. All these years, I was here, and Ben was gone. You lost how many nights of sleep worrying about him? And now he's here, and everything's fine. We'll go to his favorite fucking restaurant.*

Deacon was instantly mortified. Ben was *home*. From *war*. Why shouldn't they eat where Ben wanted to eat? Why shouldn't their mother be happy, relaxed? Why shouldn't Deacon, for that matter? He couldn't believe he was stupid enough, selfish enough, to care that his mother's attention was now focused on someone else. But for so long, the situation had been the same: Deacon's mother needed Deacon. Ben was far away, the name and face she put to a broader spectrum of anxieties, but it was Deacon whose presence comforted her. Deacon whose job it was to be around. And as many times as Deacon had wished over the years that it was someone else's job too, he found himself suddenly territorial.

"That sounds good," Ben said.

"Deacon?"

Deacon forced a laugh. "Well, you know it's never been my favorite place, but sure."

He winced inwardly. What was his problem? Did he have to say it like that?

"You still liking Prescott, Deke?"

It took Deacon a second to realize Ben was talking to him.

"Yeah. It's been a good fit."

Ben grinned. "Gotta be close to midterms, right? Phi Sig having wild study sessions?"

"Yep. Everyone's got their nose in their books. Except Matt."

"Why not Matt?"

"He's been seeing some girl, and he thinks he's in love."

"So he's got his nose in something else, then." Ben laughed.

Deacon was taken aback.

"Ben!" their mother said, in the tone she used when she was pretending to be appalled by something one of them had said or done. Then she laughed.

Deacon actually was appalled.

Ben and their mother went on to talk about something else, and Deacon finally excused himself and went upstairs, where he flopped on his bed and texted Mark.

Is it weird if the guys in your fraternity feel more like your brothers than your real brother?

He had to wait almost ten minutes for a response, and in that period he managed to convince himself no less than three times that it was idiotic to go asking for attention like this from Mark. But he wanted to know what Mark would say.

Maybe this was the touch-and-go part of the relationship. The part where he tested Mark to see if Mark could handle being a boyfriend. If it was safe to tell Mark what was on his mind and know Mark would support him.

Or maybe it was too early for that.

Way too early for that, Deacon panicked. He and Mark should focus on having fun and having sex, and Deacon should keep his self-pity and his family drama to himself. Mark was going to start thinking Deacon was a drag otherwise.

Except what had he told Mark the other night? *"Don't run away. Not from the stuff you want to say to me."*

He hadn't just meant about sex. He wanted Mark to tell him what was on his mind. So Mark should want the same thing from Deacon, right?

Deacon's phone buzzed. He sat up and looked at the screen.

I feel that way about the ADs, but only because I don't have a real brother.

Deacon smiled, but part of him was disappointed. Of course Mark would make a joke, and now Deacon felt extra stupid for sending the text.

The phone buzzed again. It wasn't a text. Mark was calling him. Deacon picked up.

"Hey," Deacon said.

"Hey. How's the reunion going?"

"Um, okay."

"Really?"

"It is fine. Just a little weird, having him home." Deacon paused. "I think I might be... I don't know. Maybe I have a thing for being needed." It was a strange thing to say to Mark when Deacon hadn't even said it to himself yet.

"Like your thing for ladies' unmentionables?"

Deacon laughed. "Yeah. Sort of. Ben says he's gonna stick around here for a few weeks. So he and my mom'll spend lots of time together, and maybe she'll be all right without me. Which is great. I'd love to not come home every weekend. And it's not like she *needs* me around in order to function. A lot of the time she's fine; I just like being around because I always thought it helped her. But maybe it doesn't. Maybe it's some weird thing where seeing me so often makes her even more aware of my absence when I'm not there. And now I'm burdening you with all this, and I can't shut up."

Mark was silent. "Have you tried asking her?"

"If she wants me around?"

"I'm sure she wants you around. Knowing you, I can attest that life is considerably more enjoyable when you're around. I mean asking her how she feels about not having you home every weekend. If she feels like she can manage on her own, or with just Ben, or..."

"I'm not sure what I want the answer to be," Deacon admitted. "Is that sick? Are we codependent?"

"I'm no psych major, thank God—can you imagine?—but it sounds like you care about each other. And you're used to being around for her, and even though it's stressful, it probably makes you feel good to be able to help somebody. Gives you a, uh...a sense of purpose, maybe? Not that you don't— I mean, I'm sure you have other purposes."

Deacon smiled. "No, you're right. I guess I get kind of used to patterns. Uh, studying, and going to class, and going home each weekend. 'If you do this, you get this result.' I like when things always work the same way."

"Probably a good way for engineers to feel. Otherwise we'd have all kinds of fucked-up bridges. Roads made of Freddo Frogs, actual stairways to heaven, that sort of thing."

Deacon snorted. "I guess. Sorry to bug you with this. I could have called James."

"Then I'd have to wonder if you had James dressing up like Loretta Young for you the nights I'm not there and bending over your ping-pong table." Mark cleared his throat. "I wanna do this part too, Deke. The part where I'm your boyfriend even when we're not fucking."

"Thank you," Deacon said quietly.

"What time are you getting back tomorrow?"

"Maybe six? We're going out to lunch and then maybe a movie or something."

"How about meeting me at that hotel on Larmott? The one with the fancy door?"

Holy shit. Deacon's dick was immediately interested. "Um, it's a little expensive, don't you think?"

"Discount rates for Prescott students. I checked. And don't worry about it."

"I have to worry about it. We're college students. We're supposed to barely be able to afford instant noodles."

"Well, it's my allowance, and if I decide I want an Oompa Loompa *now*, or to buy us a hotel room, I will."

"You're really hard to argue with, you know?"

"I do know. So I'll see you tomorrow night, at the hotel. Whenever you get in."

"Yes," Deacon said, suddenly way too excited about this.

"And in the meantime, have fun with your family. This is only day one of Ben being home. Yeah?"

"Yeah."

They hung up. Deacon lay on his bed, trying to imagine

what a whole night with Mark, free from the fear of inter-
ruption, would be like.

––––––

"Come on, Mark. You can do this."

Brandon was looking at him with an odd combination of
hope and nervousness Mark remembered from the early
days of his mother dating Jim, when she'd tried to "include"
Mark. *"Jim and I would love to take you to dinner." "Jim thinks
it's a nice day to go for a drive, if you want to join us."* Knowing
that Mark would blow her off, or respond sarcastically, but
giving it a go in case *this time* was different.

"What is the effect of hearing narrative perspectives
from outside the Bundren family?"

Mark slumped in his chair and closed his eyes. "I
don't *know.*"

"Did you read the book?"

"God, Bran. I tried. It was awful. *As I Lay Dying* is exactly
how I felt while I was reading it."

"Mark, your midterm is Wednesday."

"You've said that five times already."

"You've got to know this stuff."

Mark checked his phone. "Actually, I have to run.
Deacon's getting here in an hour."

"No." Brandon slammed his hand on the table, and
Mark jumped. "You are not leaving until you answer this
question. Think about the part on page one thirty-three,
where they take Addie's body..." Brandon launched into a
detailed account of precisely what happened on page 133.

"Well, yeah, if I had a magic brain, I'd be able to answer
the question no problem," Mark muttered.

"This isn't a memorization issue. You can look in the

book anytime you need to remember details. This is a broader question about narrative style. I'm just giving you an example."

Mark sighed. "Please, Bran? I promise I'll study tomorrow night. Deke and I have big plans." Mark specifically had plans involving the lingerie he'd bought—though he hadn't told Deacon that. "He'll worry if I'm late."

"Give me your phone."

Mark looked at Brandon suspiciously, then handed it over. The phone beeped as Brandon fiddled with it. "I'll just shoot Deacon a text... *Hi, Deacon, it's Mark's friend Brandon,*" Brandon read as he typed. "*Mark might be a bit late tonight, as he still has to answer a question about Faulkner.*" He paused to let his fingers catch up. "*It shouldn't take long, if Mark focuses, but just wanted to let you know. Thanks.*" He hit Send and set the phone down.

"You're a jerk."

Brandon ignored him and shoved the study guide and a pencil toward him. Mark gave another heavy sigh and took them up. A moment later the phone beeped. Mark perked up, praying Deacon would tell Brandon they really did have important plans that couldn't be delayed.

"Look at that," Brandon said, showing Mark the screen.

That's fine, Brandon. Keep him as long as necessary.

The traitor! Mark glowered from Bran to the book to the study guide, then picked up the pencil and began writing furiously. See if he ever bought Deacon a nice hotel room and wore fancy satin knickers for him again.

And Faulkner? Well, fuck Faulkner. And his stupid mustache.

Unless that was Hemingway.

Definitely not Whitman, though, because his facial hair wasn't stupid. Whitman had rocked his beard. Also,

Whitman would never get in the way of a boy trying to get off with another boy. Bros before prose.

Unfortunately, Brandon wasn't as cool as Whitman, and he made Mark work for the answer before he let him leave —something about the subjective nature of the narrative. And Mark had used the word "multifaceted" too, which had to be unprecedented. Maybe bullshit like that would be enough to see him pass a quiz or turn in a half-decent paper. Nobody had to know that his first reaction to *As I Lay Dying* would always be *just shut the fuck up and die, then.*

Mark raced back to his dorm, collected the bag he'd packed earlier, and headed into town. He checked his watch on the way. He might still beat Deacon to the hotel on Larmott. It was only a short walk from Prescott, which was why Mark had chosen it. Mark could drive, but this part of town was a rabbit's warren of one-way streets, and confusing enough before you even factored in that whole "Let's All Drive on the Wrong Side of the Road" thing. And what with the parking situation on campus, the car Jim had given him to use while he was at Prescott was probably parked closer to the hotel than his dorm anyway.

Huh. Mark wondered if he should check on the car at some point, just to make sure it hadn't been stolen.

Maybe tomorrow. Or maybe in the new year.

The hotel on Larmott was nice. Small and exclusive, if you went for that sort of thing. Which Mark did, courtesy of Jim's credit card. He booked in at reception, afraid that he'd turn around and see Deacon coming in before he had the chance to get ready.

Bloody Brandon and bloody Faulkner.

He went upstairs.

The room was nice. Not that Mark paid attention to the details. He figured he didn't have much time before Deacon arrived, and he'd run the last three blocks. He pulled the neck of his shirt out and sniffed it. He wasn't sweaty exactly —Mark was pretty sure nobody sweat in Pennsylvania—but he didn't smell clean and fresh. He stripped off and showered quickly, keeping the door open so he could hear Deacon coming in. Worst-case scenario: he'd step out of the shower wearing nothing but a smile. But best-case scenario? Well, he had to hurry.

He dried himself, wrapped a towel around his waist, and shoved his dirty clothes in his backpack. Then he laid the lingerie out on the bed. The blue camisole and knickers. The suspender belt. The gray stockings. Mark wished he had time to savor dressing in them, but he didn't want Deacon to find him half-dressed. He put on the camisole, adjusting the thin straps so that the front didn't gape too much. The fabric was soft and whispered against his skin. Then the knickers, and how weird was it to get turned on by the way the satin clung to his erection? Pretty weird, Mark supposed, resisting the urge to palm his cock as he tugged the suspender belt on. He liked the way it sat higher than the knickers. Together they framed a narrow band of skin, one that Mark imagined Deacon touching, licking. His erection pressed against the knickers.

Mark sat on the bed and rolled the stockings on carefully, clipping them to the suspender belt. He padded into the bathroom to look at himself in the mirror. He thought that maybe he wouldn't recognize himself, that maybe he *shouldn't*, but there he was. The same Mark as always, only wrapped in lace. He combed his fingers through his unruly damp hair and returned to the main room. He lay on the bed, first on his back, and then rolled over onto his stomach and rested his chin on his folded arms. His cock throbbed underneath him, and he closed his eyes and tried to ignore it. He counted his breaths.

He might have dozed, because he didn't hear the door. The first thing he heard was Deacon's voice, low, almost worshipful: "Holy fuck."

Mark stretched. "Hey, Deke."

Deacon stood beside the bed. He ran his hand down Mark's spine, and Mark shivered. Not just from the contact. Deacon's hand was cold. Fucking Pennsylvania. "You look amazing."

Mark shifted, rubbing his crotch against the comforter. "What are you gonna do to me?"

"Gonna take my time with you." Deacon's voice was thick. He slid his hand down Mark's right thigh, tugging gently on the suspender. "Did you bring lube?"

"Backpack," Mark murmured. "I brought lots."

"Okay." Deacon inhaled, his breath shaking. "Roll over."

Satin whispered as Mark obeyed, and the sound made him shiver. His cock throbbed inside the knickers, pushing against the constricting fabric. Wet too. He was already so fucking wet. Deacon climbed onto the bed, still wearing his jeans and his jacket and his boots. Made it seem hotter, somehow, like he couldn't spare the thirty seconds he needed to get naked. He knelt between Mark's stockinged legs and pushed them apart. Then he leaned down and covered Mark's cock with his mouth, breathing through the damp satin. Hot. Wet. Mark almost came from that alone.

"Deke…" He groaned, thrusting his hips forward.

Deacon gripped them, fingers catching in the suspender belt, and pushed him back down onto the mattress. "Not yet. Got the whole night, remember?"

Mark huffed out a strangled laugh. "I'm pretty sure I'm good to go more than once."

"Maybe I like making you wait," Deacon said. He mouthed the wet fabric again. "You're so hard for me." He straightened up, his face suddenly serious. "If it doesn't feel good, you'll tell me to stop, won't you?"

"Yeah." Shit. Deacon was really going to do it. A frisson of fear, laced with excitement, ran down his spine. "Um, so you know what you're doing, right?"

Deacon smiled. "Internet."

"Right," Mark said, drawing a deep breath. He tried for a cocky smile. "Where would we be without it?"

Deacon left the bed. He crossed to the bathroom and returned with a towel, shrugging off his jacket on the way. He pushed his sleeves up, and for some reason Mark was struck with the image of a farmer getting ready to put his hand inside a cow. Which was possibly the worst thing he could have thought of at this moment.

Deacon must have noticed his expression. "Are you having second thoughts?"

"No. I'm having random thoughts. Quick, distract me."

Deacon knelt between his legs again and fiddled around with his suspenders. Mark lifted his head but couldn't be sure what Deacon was doing until he pulled Mark's blue knickers down, freeing his aching erection, and slid them down his thighs. Oh. He'd refastened the suspenders so that the knickers would come off. Mark wriggled to assist, and soon the knickers were hanging from his left ankle. He would have shaken them off, but Deacon closed his fingers around Mark's ankle and held them there.

Mark dropped his head back onto the pillow. He could feel the cool air on his cock, and on his exposed ass. Somehow he felt more naked with the stockings and suspender belt than he would have entirely exposed. This was...dirtier.

Deacon held Mark's ankles, positioning his feet on the mattress so that his legs were spread and his knees were bent. Then he ran his hands up the insides of Mark's thighs.

"You're so hot," Deacon said. "So hot like this. In stockings and lace."

"Put your fingers in me," Mark said, afraid he wouldn't last. "Don't touch my dick, or I'll blow."

Jesus. The sound of Deacon snapping open the lube could almost send him over. Mark closed his eyes as Deacon's slick fingers circled his hole. Circled and teased and finally pushed in. Two. That was definitely two. Mark shuddered at the burn, even as he accepted it and willed his muscles to relax. Two fingers was nothing.

Deacon teased him with those fingers, pushing them inside, drawing them out, pushing inside again. Mark rocked with the gentle rhythm, his hard cock bouncing against his abdomen and leaving wet trails across his skin.

"I'm serious, Deke. I'll blow."

"If you blow, we'll try again later," Deacon said, his voice low. "Or maybe I'll keep going anyway. See if you can reload while I'm fingering you."

Mark squeezed around Deacon's fingers. "Bet I could."

Deacon chuckled. "I'll bet you could too."

But Mark didn't want that. He wanted to hold off until Deacon was all the way inside him. He took a breath and let it out slowly. He opened his eyes and watched Deacon. Deacon was staring at Mark's arse, a look of utter concentration on his face. He was even biting his lip.

Three fingers, and then four, and Mark took it all. They'd been this far before, without this much care and lube, in the library. Maybe not so deep, though, because this stretch was bigger than any Mark could remember. He bore down, his breath catching in his throat as Deacon hit his prostate. He pressed his shoulders back into the mattress, his hips arching off the bed.

"Okay," Deacon said, a little breathless. He caught Mark's gaze. "It's tight. I don't know..."

"Do it," Mark said. He could hardly hear Deacon over the blood pounding in his skull. "Put your fist in me, Deke, please."

Deacon nodded, swallowed, and began to push.

Oh fuck. Fuck, fuck, fuck. That was pain. Real, honest-to-God, no-gammin, losing-your-virginity-in-a-pub-toilet-to-some-guy-called-Mad-Dog pain. Mark's breath whooshed out of him. He couldn't even swear. He made some strange high-pitched sound that was almost a whine.

"Mark?" Deacon froze, looking stricken.

"Don't move," Mark gasped, blinking away tears. "Don't move." It hurt. *Fuck, fuck, fuck*, it hurt. And then Mark realized he wasn't just thinking that. He was saying it, over and over again, and Deacon looked like he was going to panic. Mark squeezed his eyes shut. "Need a minute. Gimme a minute."

"Tell me what to do, Mark," Deacon said, his voice shaking.

"You in me, Deke?" Mark asked, opening his eyes again.

"No."

Really? Because holy fuck, it felt like it Deacon's fist was shoved up his arse, along with something roughly the same size as a 1982 Datsun Bluebird.

"Keep going," Mark said, gritting his teeth.

"No." Deacon shook his head.

"Come on, I can take it." Mark didn't know why he was saying that when it hurt like all fuck. He wasn't this brave. This stupid maybe, but not this brave. "Fuck you, I can take it!"

"No." Deacon eased back. "What are you trying to prove?"

"I dunno." Mark closed his eyes again. Reached down to stroke his flagging dick back into life, now that the pain had faded. "I never know."

"Okay," Deacon said. "You're so tight. We'll try another time if you still want to."

Mark wondered if he should have been angry at himself for failing, or angry at Deacon for being a patronizing dick, but he wasn't. Not when he was so relieved that it had stopped hurting. And especially not when Deacon still had two fingers inside him and was slowly stroking his prostate. All in all, it was pretty difficult to try and be angry at a bloke who'd do that for you. "We'll try again?"

"Yeah," Deacon said, his voice low. "Jesus, Mark. You're amazing."

Mark rocked his hips a little and tried not to snort. What was amazing about getting off by being fingered? In other breaking news, water was apparently wet. He opened his eyes again and blinked in the light. "Wanted your hand in me. Wanted you to feel my heartbeat."

Deacon smiled and leaned forward over Mark. He slid his free hand up along the silky fabric of the camisole and laid it over Mark's heart. "There it is."

Romantic fucking idiot. Romeo.

"Can you come from this?" Deacon asked him, hitting Mark's prostate again.

"Yeah," Mark said. "More. Please."

Deacon obliged. Once, twice, and Mark cried out and arched as he came in spurts up his chest. He fell back onto the bed panting. He was oversensitive now he'd come, over-stimulated, and over-fucking-whelmed. He tried to speak but couldn't get the words out. His eyes were stinging and his cheeks were wet, and he didn't know when that had happened. He was embarrassed it might not have come from the pain, but from the moment Deacon had put his hand over Mark's heart.

So Deacon wasn't the only romantic fucking idiot in the room. Who knew?

Deacon wiped Mark clean with the towel. Then he went and washed his hands and came back to bundle Mark up in the comforter.

"I'm okay," Mark murmured, wrung out, and was surprised to find he was shaking. "You didn't come yet."

"We've got all night," Deacon said and put his arms around him. "You okay?"

"Snug as a bug," Mark mumbled, burrowing into Deacon's chest.

Deacon kissed him on the top of the head. "You're incredible."

Mark smiled and drifted off to sleep.

CHAPTER 14

Mark went home for fall break and was on his absolute best behavior for his mum and Jim. Jim hardly grilled him about Alpha Delt, except to ask if he was getting excited about his upcoming initiation. "I'm excited for pledging to end," Mark said truthfully.

Jim laughed. "It seems rough in the moment. But once you're through it, you'll really feel a bond with those boys. And you'll do the same initiation rituals to next year's class."

Somehow Mark doubted he'd be pouring hot sauce down some freshman's throat next fall. But he let it go.

He called Deacon a couple of times to find out how Deacon's break was going, and it seemed like Deacon was having fun with his mother and Ben, but Mark wasn't sure. He got the feeling there was still a lot Deacon didn't tell him.

Mark tried to make a start on the research paper for his lit class that was due at the end of the semester, but he just couldn't make himself care enough to do it. He'd gotten a sixty-eight on his lit midterm, which wasn't bad, he'd thought—though Brandon seemed a bit discouraged. Mark had promised Brandon he'd at least settle on a topic over break.

When he got back to Prescott, things went fairly smoothly for a few weeks. He didn't take Deacon to Alpha Delta's Halloween party, even though theoretically Deacon could have dressed as Chewbacca or something and gone unnoticed. But the Alpha Delts had already unmasked Zorro; Mark didn't want them to de-head Chewbacca and discover Deacon in their midst once more.

Instead, Mark put in an appearance at Alpha Delt, and then he and Deacon both went to the Halloween at the Morgue party at Phi Mu, Chelsea's sorority. Brandon dropped in too, and he and Deacon finally met and hit it off. Mark actually got so tired of hearing Deacon praise Brandon's eidetic memory that he tripped and "accidentally" sloshed some punch on Deacon's Westley costume.

That night, Mark changed out of his Mad Max costume and put on the knickers and suspender belt for Deacon. Deacon fucked Mark with Mark's legs in the air, the belt tugging on his stockings until one of the suspender loops snapped.

He and Deacon continued their arse play. Deacon worked on stretching Mark, and Mark made Deacon blush by suggesting a trip to a sex shop to pick up some butt plugs and a douche kit. Mark was serious, though. He thought about getting Deacon in the car and telling him they were going to the half-priced textbook store, then pulling into Midnight Fantasy instead. But he wanted Deacon to come shopping of his own accord. He had a feeling Deacon still felt guilty that the fisting hadn't worked—that he worried he'd hurt Mark. Mark wasn't sure how to get him the hell over that, especially since Mark sometimes felt, inexplicably, like a failure for not being able to take Deacon's whole hand. Would it really have hurt so much to keep going?

Then he remembered how bad the pain had been. Remembered what he'd read online, that sometimes it took guys weeks, months—even years—of prep before they could take a fist up their arses. Mark didn't want to give up on the idea, not by a long shot.

He and Deacon tried going on a double date one night with Matt and his girlfriend, Kate. Mark was completely bored; they went to a shitty restaurant, and Matt acted like a lug and Kate was overly peppy. She kept commenting on how she was the only girl in their party. Ordering drinks: *"I guess since I'm the only girl here, I'll order a Cosmo."* Getting up to use the restroom: *"Guess I'll be the first girl in history to go to the bathroom alone. Since I don't have any other girls here to ask."* Then she'd laugh. Matt would give her a snort out of solidarity, but Mark could tell he didn't think she was funny either.

On the way home, Mark told Deacon he never wanted to go on a double date again, unless the definition of "double date" was Mark getting to go out with both Deacon and the hot guy from Tau Kappa Mark shared an intro-to-bio class with, and subsequently they had their first fight—because who knew sweet, stoic Deacon had a jealous streak?

Mark loved learning that kind of shit about Deacon. And Mark apologized first, so look who was getting better at not being a total prick.

Mark was surprised to find he was starting to enjoy his independence. He hadn't thought much about it, since he'd felt enslaved to the Alpha Delts his first few weeks at Prescott. But it was finally occurring to him that he was an adult. If he wanted to get stoned and go look at pregnant meerkats or stay out fucking Deacon all night, he didn't have to worry about having to tell his mum where he'd been when he got home.

The only thing that was strange was Mark's standing with the Alpha Delts. Bengal's idea of revenge, apparently, was to exclude Mark from pledge activities. At first Mark was pleased that Bengal's definition of retribution seemed to precisely match Mark's definition of reward, but after a while, Mark could kind of see what the objective was. Once again, Mark felt like an outsider. He had no way of keeping an eye on Bengal, and he rarely knew what the other pledges were going through. If he asked Dan or Fraser, they didn't say much. Mark figured Bengal had them scared.

Mark hadn't thought he wanted the kind of brothers you had to pay for, but sometimes he felt envious when he saw Deacon hanging out with James or Matt. Wondered how many friends he'd cheated himself out of by keeping his fellow pledges at arm's length. Wondered what it was going to mean to live the next three years in a house with a group of guys who didn't really like him.

Making your bed and lying in it, he supposed.

"What are you doing for Thanksgiving?" Deacon asked him in early November. They were walking toward the library, where Deacon swore they'd find some good resources for Mark's research paper, and where Mark swore there was a microfiche room just begging for two star-cross'd lovers to fuck in it. Deacon said resources before fucking.

"Uh, to be honest, I don't really get Thanksgiving. But Jim's cooking, and—fuck—Jackson's gonna be home. Jim's family's coming over."

Deacon grinned. "You'll have a good time. Food'll be good, at least."

"Ever since frozen-turkey bowling, I've been kind of

turned off by turkey," Mark said. He shivered and glanced up at the gray sky. "Getting cold. I don't like it, Deke."

Deacon took his hand. It still gave Mark a thrill, a gesture that simple. Deacon pulled him close so that Mark could feel his body heat—even if he couldn't walk without tripping over Deacon's feet. "I was thinking," Deacon said. "If it doesn't snow before the semester ends, maybe we could take a weekend and go to the ski lodge up in Tannersville. They've got a snow machine for when they don't have enough real snow."

"A snow *machine*?"

Deacon glanced at him. "Yeah."

"Why the hell would they *make* something no one wants around in the first place?"

Deacon laughed. "Because some people like snow, believe it or not. And they need it to ski."

"They're crazy."

Deacon squeezed his hand. "Mark." Deacon looked at him imploringly. "It's fun. The lodge is nice, and there are fireplaces in the rooms." He nudged Mark with his shoulder. "We could come back from skiing and fuck in front of the fire."

"Why don't we skip skiing and just fuck in front of the fire?"

"You're impossible."

"I'm worried about legitimate things. Like frostbite on my balls. And snow bears."

"Snow bears? Do you mean polar bears? Because we don't have those."

"No, I mean snow bears. Like, bears that forgot to hibernate or woke up early and aren't afraid of snow."

"Jesus Christ," Deacon said. "You're taking biology, and you don't know how nature works."

Mark muttered something about preferring to study Deacon's biology, but Deacon didn't take the bait. They checked out some books instead.

"I'd rather check out..." Mark began loudly at the counter, and Deacon's laugh turned into a cough, and he almost choked. Then, because he was still red and breathless, he made Mark carry all the books.

So college life was okay. Sometimes it was better than okay. And the cold wasn't so bad, not once Deacon showed Mark how to stuff so many marshmallows into a cup of hot chocolate that it was pure diabetes in a mug. Mark liked being inside when it was cold, with Deacon and movies and hot chocolates, but *outside?* Outside it was wrong. Just plain wrong.

All those layers of clothing that had to be put on before he even opened the door, and then painstakingly taken off again minutes later when he stepped into a lecture hall or coffee shop. The cold necessitated so many accessories it wasn't funny. How did people remember them all? Mark could hardly remember his wallet and his keys on a good day. Add to that gloves, a beanie, and a scarf, and he was constantly dropping things, misplacing them, or, in the case of his scarf, trying not to strangle himself.

And then there was Thanksgiving, which American TV had promised Mark would turn into a drunken family drama full of bitter recriminations and feuds that dated back three generations. Sadly, all of the extended Phillips family seemed to have been cut from the same cloth as Jim and were so full of goodwill and bonhomie that Mark wasn't entertained at all. Even Jackson was decent. Mark wasn't sure if that was because Jackson had warmed to him slowly or, more likely, if Mark himself was being less hostile. Jackson even took him out into the woods behind Jim's house to show him the tree house he'd made as a kid. It was a bunch of sticks more or less on ground level.

"Well, I *was* six," Jackson said. "And I built it on my own."

"It shows," Mark told him.

Jackson snorted. Not quite a laugh, but almost.

Mark missed Deacon over Thanksgiving and called him. Deacon said he was having a good time, but he missed Mark too. For once Mark wasn't homesick for a place; he was homesick for a person. He thought about telling Deacon that but then realized how lame it sounded. He'd show him instead, back at Prescott.

He phoned Brandon as well and cheered him up by complaining about the cold, the possibility of bear attacks, and what the hell was the obsession with cranberry sauce anyway? Jackson's mother had been horrified when Mark had eaten his turkey with tomato sauce instead. Although she'd called it ketchup. She'd asked him if they had a Thanksgiving at home.

"Given that our first European settlers turned up in chains and leg irons, they probably weren't feeling very thankful," Mark told her.

"They got the last laugh, though, right?" Jackson said. "Sentenced to prison on what's basically one big beach?"

"It beats snow," Mark agreed.

Snow. Shit. A flake or two was kind of pretty, but then it just stayed on the ground. Just stayed there, building up. Not nice like a dusting of icing sugar on a cupcake. It only looked pretty from the inside. The second you had to go out in it, wearing a gazillion layers of clothing, it was hard work. Like trudging through sand dunes, without the reward of the beach at the end. Just more snow.

Jackson saw him texting Brandon after dinner.

"He doing okay?" he asked quietly.

"Yeah," Mark said.

"Good." Jackson looked relieved.

"Bengal's a fucking prick, you know," Mark said.

"Yeah," Jackson said. "I know. I guess we all do."

"So why don't you do something about it?" Mark asked.

"He's..." Jackson stared out the window at the gently falling snow. "He's still our brother, Mark."

Mark wasn't sure there was any way he could respond to that. Not without losing his temper and punching something, anyway. He walked away instead. Took the high road for once, and there wasn't even anyone there to congratulate him on it.

In the end, Mark kept out of the weather as much as he could. He passed the time by being civil to Jackson, playing computer games, checking out lingerie online, and counting down the hours until he was back at Prescott. Who'd have thought it in a million years?

———

Deacon still felt terrible about his attempt to fist Mark. He tried not to show it—tried to put his effort into learning as much as he could about fisting, into helping Mark prepare. But sometimes he'd have his fingers buried in Mark, and Mark would beg him to push a little farther, and Deacon would freeze, remembering Mark's face when Deacon had tried to go past this point at the hotel. Mark had been completely white, his eyes watering, his mouth open but without any sound coming out.

Deacon had hurt Mark so bad Mark hadn't been able to *speak*. How fucked-up was that?

It seemed like anyone with any sense would have known

to stop before it got to that point. Would have known you didn't just jam your hand inside someone when they felt that tight, when you'd barely given them a warm-up. There was more to fisting than Deacon had thought. The fistee had to train those muscles to relax and expand. Had to learn to relax his mind as well. Had to be cleaned out inside.

But he'd been so excited by how readily Mark took his fingers, how much Mark loved arse play. And Mark had said keep going, so... God, it was so wrong to feel even a twinge of resentment toward Mark over this. But Mark had said it himself—he *pushed*. He was always trying to prove something. Was everything he did always going to be some weird competition with himself that Deacon would have to watch from the sidelines?

Or was Deacon being too sensitive? He used to worry that he wasn't doing a very good job of being gay. Weren't gay guys supposed to go to clubs and bars wearing ridiculously tight jeans and have lots of anonymous sex and never give a fuck about anything but getting their dicks sucked? Or else settle down with their longtime partners and adopt a kid and show the hetero world how "normal" they could be? As he got older, he realized there was no point worrying about fitting a stereotype. He was who he was—sex always meant something to him; he couldn't just fuck some guy in a restroom stall and leave it at that. He liked intimacy even when it scared him. Liked the connection that went beyond sex.

And he had a feeling Mark liked that too, though he pretended his MO was quick, dirty sex, and that he was a "crap boyfriend." Mark had proved anything but a crap boyfriend.

He was thinking about all this over Thanksgiving dinner, when he ought to have been savoring the time with his family. His dad was home on a break from his job, and he and Ben had been glued to the Penn State game most of the afternoon.

Deacon didn't notice Ben was talking to him until Ben waved his hand by Deacon's face and said, "Yo, Deke!"

"Huh? Sorry."

"I said you should come by and see the apartment later."

Ben had rented a one-bedroom downtown, but Deacon hadn't had a chance to see it yet.

"I stopped by on my way in last night," Deacon's father said, cramming a bite of turkey into his mouth. Looked pretty good. No rats."

"I'll come by," Deacon promised.

He let the conversation wash around him once more as he responded to a text from Mark:

Ate my turkey with ketchup and Jackson's mum is acting like I might as well have covered it in snot.

Deacon typed, *That's what the gravy's for, Jules.*

Jim didn't mix the gravy well. Full of cornstarch lumps. Prefer ketchup.

Wish you were here.

Deacon set the phone aside, and his heart pounded the way it always did when he told Mark he missed him or wanted to see him. Because what if Mark didn't respond, or what if this time he was like *Look, Deke, I think we're moving too fast?*

But a minute later he got, *Me too. What're you wearing?*

"So who's the guy?" Deacon's mother asked when she ended up behind him at the kitchen sink, waiting to rinse her plate.

And then scrub it with soap, then maybe spray it with disinfectant.

Then put it in the dishwasher.

"The guy?" Deacon said.

"The one you've been texting whenever you're home."

"Oh, uh... He's a guy I've been seeing from school."

"Uh-huh." His mother smiled slyly. "How long have you been seeing him?"

"I don't really know. We've been hanging out since the beginning of the semester."

"And you didn't say anything?" She nudged him out of the way and rinsed her plate.

"I didn't know for a while if it was serious or not." Deacon set his plate in the dishwasher. He could hear his dad and Ben laughing in the dining room and wondered why he felt so disconnected from everything. He straightened. "And there are some things I don't tell you, you know. Even though I'm home every single weekend."

Shit. He could hear the sharpness in his voice and hated it. His mom was only teasing him, and he was... He was dreading the conversation he'd known he needed to have with his mother for weeks. And he'd just picked the worst possible way to start it.

His mother turned off the faucet and looked at him. She didn't seem mad—maybe a little hurt. She nodded. "It's not fair to you," she said quietly.

"No. That's not what I..." He closed his eyes briefly. "This isn't how I wanted to have this talk." He glanced in the direction of the dining room. "I'm sorry."

"Let's go out to the porch," his mother suggested.

Deacon followed her to the screened back porch. They watched the birds at the feeder for a few minutes, and Deacon felt foolish, like they were in a movie and the director had told them to pause for dramatic effect before beginning their Serious Conversation. Deacon knew if he had something to say, he ought to just say it.

But his mother spoke first. "Deacon, if you want to spend your weekends at school, you should. I've always said that."

"But you don't mean it," Deacon said. "Do you?"

She hesitated. "I do mean it. I'm not an invalid. As long as I take my medications, I'm all right most of the time."

"And what about when you're not?"

"I have friends I can call. My therapist." She placed a hand on the back of Deacon's head and ran her fingers through his hair. "I found ways to cope before you and Ben were born."

"But Dad was around all the time then." Deacon felt a lump in his throat and angrily told himself to knock it off. "And you were..." She'd been better. The disorder had gotten worse slowly. "It helps you to have someone around. Doesn't it?"

"It would help me more to know you were enjoying being young and being in college. That you were spending weekends with your boyfriend, not here. Unless you want to bring him here to meet your mother."

Deacon snorted, then shook his head. "You say that. But what happens next time you start panicking that I'm dead in a ditch somewhere?"

She grinned. "Then I'll call you. And make you tell me you're not."

"I don't want Ben to be a replacement for me." He looked at her. "You know? If you need my help, I want to be around for you."

"Deacon." She was completely serious now. "I'm the parent. It's my job to look after you, not the other way around. I know 'stop worrying' is hard advice to take, especially from me. But stop worrying. Try staying at Prescott next weekend. We'll take it one weekend at a time."

Deacon swallowed. "Okay. But, um, call me if you need

me." He felt simultaneously relieved and like he'd just been fired from a job he needed.

She nodded. "You're very sweet, Deacon."

Would have been nice to be something besides sweet once in a while. To be more like Mark, who was sweet when it suited him, but who was also fun. Exciting. It was never the sweet guys you waited on to get the party started. "Not always," he mumbled.

She laughed.

"Christmas break," he said suddenly. He knew she had said they'd take it one weekend at a time, but he needed to bring this up. "I want to take Mark—that's the guy—up to the ski lodge in Tannersville for a few days. After school lets out. So I might not be home right away." He looked at her questioningly.

Her expression was sad, and for a moment he panicked that he'd hurt her feelings, that she couldn't stand the thought of him not coming home as soon as school was done. "I'm so sorry, Deacon. I didn't realize how trapped you felt."

"I don't feel trapped, just—"

"Please go with Mark to Tannersville. And don't you dare feel guilty about it." She cupped his cheek. "I want you to live your own life. That's what would help me more than anything. That's what would make me feel better."

"Okay," Deacon murmured. Those should have been the words he needed to hear. And they were. So maybe he did function better when he felt someone needed him. Maybe he'd never be the guy who got the party started. That was what Mark was for. And maybe Deacon was good for Mark for exactly that reason. Deacon could look out for him. Could make sure angry bunny didn't get too out of control.

Could make sure he studied for his lit final. Could make sure he had a good time at the ski lodge and didn't get frostbite, or eaten by a rogue bear.

Yeah, Deacon wasn't out of a job. Not by a long shot.

CHAPTER 15

"I hear the hall looks really nice," Deacon said.

Mark turned to look at him over his shoulder. "Are you making fun of me?"

"What are you talking about? James was over at the country club today, and he said it looked good."

They were lying on Deacon's bed. Mark was facedown, his arms folded under his head, and Deacon was on his side next to him, one leg slung over Mark's, the fingers of one hand buried deep in Mark's arse, his other hand rubbing Mark's shoulders. Mark was naked, Deacon shirtless but wearing sweatpants. They did this a lot now—just lay together with Deacon's fingers or a thick plug up Mark's arse, talking occasionally. Every now and then, Deacon would spread his fingers inside Mark or, if they were using a plug, slowly work it in and out of Mark's arse. It was a weird little ritual, but Mark liked it.

He'd never been fingered without the intention of getting off, and these long stretching sessions might have felt pointless if he hadn't kept reminding himself that one day Deacon's whole fucking hand was gonna be inside him.

Well, that and the fact that he liked being near Deacon. Liked Deacon rubbing his back, liked that they could stay still for so long without any expectations or urgency. He didn't tell Deacon that, since *I wanna spoon with you all night while you whisper in my ear how incredible I am* didn't have the same effect in a dirty phone conversation as *I want you to ram your fingers up my arse until I scream your name and flood your sheets with cum.* But Deacon seemed to pick up on it anyway.

Mark liked the way their relationship progressed without them having to talk too much about it. Like when they'd gone to Midnight Fantasy to get the plugs and what looked to Mark like an unnecessarily large anal douche— but hey, it was the only one they had. The first time Mark had used the enema, he'd excused himself to the bathroom to do it himself. He'd been embarrassed to think Deacon could probably hear him expelling it; then he'd reminded himself he didn't get embarrassed, and then he'd thought, no, that was stupid, of course he did.

The second time he'd opened up the kit, Deacon had calmly taken the bulb from Mark, filled it, and told Mark to lie down on the bed. Deacon had administered the enema, then stayed with Mark while Mark was on the toilet, stroking Mark's neck and acting like there was nothing strange about this at all—the tension in his body the only indication that he was unsure of himself. Mark was so bizarrely grateful to him for staying—douching didn't hurt; it was just uncomfortable as fuck—that instead of insisting he could take a shit by himself, he'd leaned into Deacon's touch.

If they weren't the weirdest couple at this school, Mark's hat was off to whoever could claim that honor. If not him and Deacon, Mark would put in a vote for Chelsea and

Blake, who had started dating right before Thanksgiving. Maybe Chelsea accompanied Blake to the bathroom as well, to prevent him getting locked in.

"You know it was all done with slave labor, don't you?" Mark said now. "None of the brothers lifted a finger except to add to our misery."

The committee had been so desperate for decorators— and not to have to do the work themselves—that Bengal had insisted on even Mark coming along to help decorate. And when Mark deliberately put all the glittery cardboard snowflakes in a straight line across the archway, instead of staggering them as he'd been instructed, then stapled white tulle in ugly clumps to the poles, it had been like the old days. Bengal had forced Mark to wear a makeshift tulle skirt, with two snowflakes stapled to his shirt right where his nipples would be, and then redo the decorations like that. Mark had slipped away and taken pics of the outfit on his phone to send to Deacon.

Deacon laughed and trailed his finger in a zigzag pattern between Mark's shoulder blades. "I figured. Was it wrong for me to enjoy your snowflake pasties, then?" He scissored his fingers in Mark's arse, and Mark gasped, then slowly exhaled.

"I wanted you to enjoy them."

"I really hate Bengal," Deacon said after a minute.

"You and everyone who knows him."

"I mean, he's not just a dick. I think he's dangerous. What he did to you with the hot sauce, and now trying to humiliate you somewhere public..."

"Deke. I don't need a white knight, okay? If I'd wanted to leave either of those times, I would have. I can take care of myself."

"And what happened to Brandon," Deacon said.

Mark winced. He knew he didn't have any right to share Brandon's history with Deacon. But he'd been so stressed in the weeks after he'd found Brandon in midbreakdown at Alpha Delt, and Deacon was good at knowing what to do, and Mark had already let it slip accidentally that there was *something*, that Mark had finally caved and told him what little he knew.

But Deacon was right. What Bengal had done to Brandon went way beyond just being an arsehole.

"Let's drop it, okay?" Mark said. "I've had enough of this stretching shit." He tried to grin. "Either stick your whole hand in there or use your cock."

When Deacon didn't respond, Mark shifted, twisting so Deacon's fingers slid out of him.

"What are you waiting for?" Mark asked. He really didn't want to lie here and have a conversation about Bengal. Aside from the topic being a major boner killer, Mark didn't enjoy being reminded that Bengal had sexually assaulted Brandon and all Mark had done about it was take Brandon out afterward for chips. He was freaked out enough that in five days he was going to be officially initiated into the Alpha Delta brotherhood. No more pretending it wasn't real. No more telling himself he was a pledge and could quit anytime. After Friday, he'd be stuck with these guys as his brothers. Including Bengal.

"Would you fuck me?" Deacon asked.

"Huh?" He hadn't been expecting that. But Deacon was staring at him hungrily, a determination in his expression Mark recognized from when Deacon was hunched over a textbook.

"I want you to fuck me. But, like, dirtily."

"Dirtily," Mark repeated, not sure if that was even a word.

Deacon propped himself on his elbows. "I never feel very, um, adventurous. When I have sex."

Mark wondered where this was coming from. "You dress me up in suspenders and lace. You let me blow you in an alley right behind where you work. You sneaked onto enemy territory to fuck me in the Kissin' Shack. You took me down to your basement and paddled me. You're learning how to fist me. Jesus, Deke, what do you have to do to feel adventurous, fuck me on top of Everest during an avalanche?"

Deacon flushed and smiled. "I guess you're right. I just want to feel, like...used. I want you to fuck me like I'm...like I'm—"

"A cheap whore?" Mark supplied. He was familiar with the feeling.

"Yes!" Deacon looked relieved. Then nervous again. "Only don't..."

Mark wound an arm around him and kissed his cheek. "Spit it out. If I can clean my bowels out in front of you, you can tell me how you want to be fucked."

Deacon hesitated. "Just don't be mean about it, okay? I want you to be dirty but not mean. Does that make sense?"

"Completely."

"You've, um, you've topped before, right?"

"Absolutely," Mark said and then wondered what it was about the word "absolutely" that made it sound like bullshit. "I have, promise. Not since you, though. You, like, turned me into your prison bitch." He grinned at Deacon's look of surprise and raised a hand to forestall what he suspected was an apology. "And I fucking *loved* it."

Deacon opened his mouth to say something and closed it again.

Mark pushed him down onto the mattress and straddled

his thighs. "And you'll love it too, right? Being my bitch for a change?"

Too dirtily? Maybe. Deacon was wearing the same look he did when he cleaned out the lint filter on the dryer. Mark regrouped and attacked from a different angle.

"I want to fuck you so bad," he said, running his fingers down Deacon's chest.

Deacon frowned. "Wait. You want to fuck me so bad, as in so *much*, or you want to do a terrible job?"

"Shut up, nerd," Mark said and leaned down to kiss him. It was his own fault for hooking up with someone who knew grammar and shit. "You know exactly what I mean."

He reached down Deacon's sweatpants, enjoying Deacon's gasp as he wrapped his hand around Deacon's cock. Mark stroked lightly, using his thumb to swipe precum off the head and rub it over the shaft. Deacon lifted his knees, arching his back.

"Fuck," Deacon whispered, thrusting his hips in an effort to get more friction. Mark tugged on his balls, then yanked Deacon's sweats down to his knees. Deacon had gone commando, which seemed to be happening more and more often lately. Mark kissed across Deacon's chest, pausing to lick and suck each nipple to a hard peak. Deacon wrapped his legs around Mark, and Mark nudged his knee between Deacon's thighs, giving Deacon something to hump against.

He licked the hollow of Deacon's collarbone, moving his tongue in circles, then dragging it up Deacon's throat to his chin, where he tapped it against the dimple there. Deacon laughed, placing his hands on either side of his head.

Mark grinned, grabbing Deacon's wrists. "Something funny about being my bitch?"

Deacon just smiled, and Mark could see the tension

leave him. Mark was pleased with himself. If Deacon had been nervous about bottoming, he wasn't anymore. And Mark was gonna make him feel so fucking good.

He let go of Deacon's wrists and kissed him slowly, giving Deacon time to open up for him. He ran his hands down Deacon's sides, digging his thumbs into Deacon's hip bones. Then he moved his hands to the backs of Deacon's thighs, using his nails lightly on the creases of Deacon's knees. Deacon tightened his legs around Mark, his stomach muscles fluttering.

"Get these off," Mark whispered, tugging at Deacon's sweats.

Deacon dropped his legs, and Mark pulled the pants the rest of the way off, then tossed them on the floor. Mark scooted down and blew on Deacon's thick cock. He took it in his mouth, sucking until Deacon was begging. Then he released it and stretched over Deacon. Took a fistful of Deacon's hair and twisted it—not quite hard enough to hurt. "We're doing this at my pace," he said, biting the side of Deacon's neck until Deacon whimpered. "Roll over."

Deacon obeyed eagerly, writhing under Mark until he was on his stomach. He shivered when Mark stroked his back. Mark reached between the mattress and the bed frame for a condom and put it on. Grabbed the lube and squirted some on his fingers, then prepped Deacon. His balls tightened at the sounds Deacon made as Mark thrust a coated finger into him. Small moans of what Mark was 98 percent convinced was pleasure, though he asked, "Good?" just to be sure. Deacon nodded into the pillow. Mark withdrew his finger and lowered himself to position his cock. Deacon raised his hips, pulling his knees under him.

Mark started to push in, heard Deacon's breath catch. He bent and kissed Deacon's spine. "Easy, Deke," he whispered against the wet spot his lips had left on the skin. He waited for Deacon's exhale and slid in deeper.

"Good," Deacon whispered, voice strained. Mark wasn't sure whether to believe him. He reached under Deacon and pumped his cock, and Deacon's breathing evened out. Mark pushed the rest of the way in.

Deacon groaned at Mark's first real thrust and jerked his head up. "Yeah," Mark murmured. "That's good. Gonna fuck you now."

"Please," Deacon agreed, fingers curling against the sheets.

Mark thrust faster. Massaged and squeezed the muscles of Deacon's back until Deacon was moaning steadily.

"Now I want to try something," Mark said quietly. He sat back on his heels and hooked his arms around Deacon's thighs. "Straighten your legs." Deacon hesitated, then obeyed, letting Mark's arms take the weight of his legs. Mark slowly raised his ass off his heels, lifting Deacon with him. He held Deacon's legs like the traces of a wheelbarrow and continued to fuck him.

Deacon dropped his head, his chest and forearms rubbing against the sheets with each thrust. He clenched around Mark's cock, and Mark threw back his head and groaned. "Fuck, yes. Let me...fucking...plow you."

Deacon made a sound that was half laugh, half moan. "Faster."

Mark pounded into Deacon as fast as he could go, his arms straining as he held Deacon's legs, sweat beading on his chest and gathering under his palms, making it harder to hold on to Deacon's legs. The bed creaked, and Deacon bent his knees, his heels resting against Mark's shoulders.

"Come on," he murmured suddenly, bumping Mark with his heels. He sounded breathless, desperate. "Faster."

Mark panted. "I don't know...if I can go...any faster."

Deacon started pushing back against Mark's thrusts, and Mark would have prayed the guys had the TV on loud downstairs, except part of him liked the idea of everyone being able to hear what he was doing to Deacon.

Mark withdrew slightly, then yanked back on Deacon, pulling Deacon down the length of his shaft. He did that twice more, and then he came, accidentally dropping one of Deacon's legs as he doubled over, Deacon's ass milking him into the condom.

Mark gave himself a few seconds to recover, then flipped Deacon over and wanked him with one hand while fucking him with two fingers of the other hand. Deacon seized his lip with his teeth and came hard, streaking his chest. Mark tugged Deacon's cock down so that some of it hit his own chest too. Then he collapsed onto Deacon, kissing him as their legs tangled, resting his head on Deacon's chest when he didn't have the energy to kiss anymore.

"Dirty enough for you?" he mumbled, lips damp with Deacon's sweat.

Deacon wrapped his arms around him. "Hell, yeah."

Mark fell asleep with his head on Deacon's chest.

———

Deacon checked his watch. Mark was taking an exam on American lit right now. He should have been about fifteen minutes into the hour-long exam, so Deacon was half expecting him to turn up at any moment now, claiming he'd finished the whole thing and the questions were stupid and he was stupid, and what the fuck did it matter anyway? Just like last time.

When someone sidled into the common room, Deacon sighed and looked up.

Huh. Not Mark. Kevin, the pledge who'd helped Deacon clean the air-conditioning unit. He looked like he was on the verge of tears. "Is, um, is James here?"

"He's in class," Deacon said, hoping Kevin's expression didn't mean what he thought it did. "Are you okay?"

Kevin started to nod, then shook his head.

"Sit down, Kevin." Deacon made space on the couch. "What's happened?"

"My dad," Kevin said, his voice catching.

Shit.

"He's, um, he's not doing great," Kevin said, and Deacon was so overwhelmed with relief that Kevin wasn't telling him his dad was dead that he almost missed the rest. "I, um, I've got to go home for a while."

"Home?"

Kevin put his shaking hands on his knees. "Yeah. My mom isn't coping really well. Kind of falling apart, really, and there's no money for school, so I'm going home. Maybe, um, maybe I'll come back next year if I can save enough."

"Shit," Deacon said. "Have you looked into financial aid?"

Kevin jerked his head. "If it was just me, it'd be okay. But it's my mom too, you know?"

Yeah, Deacon knew.

"And my little sisters," Kevin said. "I'm gonna have to be the breadwinner for a while, I guess. Because Dad won't be able to work for ages, even if he...if he..."

"Okay," said Deacon. He squeezed Kevin's shoulder. "But you're deferring, right, not quitting?"

"Yeah," Kevin said, and Deacon hoped he meant it. "So I

needed to talk to James and tell him I won't be in Phi Sig after all. And you guys have been great, really."

"You're deferring," Deacon reminded him. "There will be a place here for you when you come back to Prescott."

"Yeah?" Kevin looked almost hopeful.

"Yep," Deacon assured him. "I told you before, Kevin. We like you. You're a good fit for Phi Sig. Also, you helped me clean shit out of an air conditioner. You think we'll let you go that easily?"

Kevin's laugh sounded like a sob, and he stared fixedly at the floor. "Thanks, Deacon."

"I'm sorry about your dad. I hope he gets better."

"I just...wanted to tell you and James." He stood. "I'd better go now, I guess."

"Keep us posted if you can." Deacon stood too and gave Kevin a hug. Kevin clung to him briefly, then let go and walked out of the house.

Deacon felt a pang of sympathy. He worried about his mom a lot, and about her quality of life, but he couldn't imagine actually losing her. The thought made him panic for a second—that horrible things happened to people all the time, and there was nothing he could do about it. He made himself take a deep breath. Nothing he could do about it but keep living life and try to help other people when he could.

That was one of the things that had appealed to him about Phi Sig when he'd been rushing. *Service to others.* It seemed so stupid, so naive, to believe that crap. All fraternities had something like that in their mission statement, and while they might pay lip service to the idea of helping the community, they were mostly about socialization and status.

But when you felt as useless as Deacon had in the months after Ben left, watching his mother's downward spiral, you didn't laugh at the idea of joining a group that claimed to dedicate itself to being useful. You signed up and hoped it was true.

He checked his watch again. He wanted Mark to get here. No, he wanted Mark to take his time on his final. But he also wanted Mark to get here. He'd booked them a room for late next week at the Snow Trails Lodge in Tannersville. Mark wouldn't be thrilled with the name, probably, but Deacon hoped he'd be excited about the trip. They'd stay Thursday through Sunday, and Deacon didn't want to admit it, but he was a little nervous. He'd never had that much uninterrupted time with Mark.

What if they couldn't stand each other after four days?

Unlikely.

Four days alone with Mark didn't sound anything but perfect.

He leaned back. He really ought to do something productive while he waited for Mark. He hoped Mark didn't bomb the exam. Mark definitely wasn't stupid, but he was sort of unmotivated. Would that become a problem if he and Deacon tried to do this thing long-term? Mark was also eighteen. Maybe he'd buckle down next year.

And maybe that was the sort of condescending shit Deacon should be careful never to say aloud to Mark.

Deacon didn't think Mark would fail the exam. Not after all the help Brandon had given him. Brandon. Deacon felt sick every time he thought about what had happened to Brandon. Fucking Alpha Delts and their fucking homophobic hazing rituals. Shit like that wasn't a game.

And even sadder somehow was Brandon's belief that you had to be in a fraternity to be someone. That was dumber and more naive than joining a fraternity for the community-service aspect. Still, Deacon didn't blame him. He'd wanted to be part of a group too. Had wanted a label more specific and stabilizing than devoted son or honors student or faggot nerd. He was Phi Sig. What was wrong with wanting that?

He'd have to talk to James, but a plan was starting to take shape in his mind. They were now short a member, which meant they could take an extra person in the spring pledge class. Why not extend a bid to Brandon? He could pledge with the spring group, and by the end of the school year, he'd be in a fraternity. And maybe by that time he'd discover there was more to college life than being a brother, so he'd be able to relax a little during Phi Sig's decidedly stress-free pledging process.

He felt better. He'd thought of something nice to do for Brandon. It wouldn't make up for what Brandon had suffered, but might help him in some small way. He stretched out on the couch and watched a premium cable show Matt had DVRed last night. Spent most of the time thinking about the semiformal tomorrow and wondering if there was any chance Mark would dance with him. Probably not. Probably they'd spend the whole night pretending to be no more than acquaintances.

But who knew? Mark was being officially inducted into Alpha Delt tonight, and he'd be finished with the last of his finals in half an hour. Maybe he'd be feeling daring enough tomorrow to risk dancing with his Phi Sig boyfriend instead of a bunch of tanked sorority girls.

The door opened, and Deacon sat up. It was James. They talked for a while, and James said they'd have to check with some people to see if it was okay to let Brandon know they'd be extending him a bid, or if they had to wait and tell him at the end of spring rush.

"Well, we can tell him now and ask him to keep his

mouth shut about it, then announce it at spring rush. Right?" Deacon said.

James said he guessed, and went upstairs to call Kevin and ask if there was anything Phi Sig could do to help. About twenty minutes later, the door opened again. "Mark!" Deacon called, peering over the back of the couch as Mark shut the door. Hard.

"How'd the test go?"

Mark turned around.

And that was when Deacon saw his face.

CHAPTER 16

So fuck everything, basically. Fuck even being here at Phi Sig, because the last thing Mark wanted right now was Deacon looking at him with that expression of stricken concern, or maybe it was what he wanted most; he didn't fucking know. But he'd come here because he'd promised Deacon he would after the test, and he didn't know where else to go anyway.

"What the hell happened, Mark?" Deacon asked.

Mark glared at him. Was Deacon planning to make that his whole fucking life? *What happened? What's wrong? Do you need anything? You're beautiful; you're incredible; you're amazing; you're gonna be fine.*

What about you, Deacon? Who tells you you're incredible? Who asks you what's wrong, or tells you things will turn out all right? Because I'm pretty sure I do a shitty job with that kind of stuff.

"Went to Alpha Delt after the exam," Mark muttered. "Got in a fight with Bengal."

"Mark."

"What?" Mark snapped. "It was good. I told him he was a

piece of trash, and that what he did to Brandon would rot on his conscience forever, and that I hoped he'd get run down by the campus shuttle. And he punched me in the face."

"Why'd you go over there?" Deacon was off the couch and standing in front of Mark now. He reached out to touch the swelling, but Mark jerked away. "Just to tell him off?"

"I went because he fucking told me to. Then I got there, and he wasn't saying anything, so just to make conversation, I mentioned something about the ceremony tonight. And he said, *'Oh, you're not going.'*"

"What?"

"He said, *'You haven't attended enough of the required pledge activities to be inducted.'*" Mark looked at Deacon again. "He doesn't *invite* me to the pledge activities anymore. He doesn't even tell me they're going on. He planned this."

"Have you talked to the other guys? Chris? Blake?"

"You think I care?" Mark exploded. "So I'm not gonna be an Alpha Delt after all. Can't say it's a fucking tragedy."

"You've got to report him," Deacon said firmly.

"Why would I report him?"

"He hit you."

"Yeah, he's also paddled me and dressed me in a frilly uniform and poured salsa down my throat. I don't care what he does to me; I just want to be rid of him."

"What about other people? What about Brandon? This is going too far. You're gonna report him because it's the right thing to do."

Fuck Deacon for bringing up Brandon. If Mark could have done anything about that, he would have. "Christ, Deacon. Not all of us operate like that, okay?"

"Operate like what?"

"We can't all get straight bloody As and foster fucking

growth in the community and still have time to take care of our sick mums on the weekend, okay? I'm not *you*."

"I'm not asking you to be!"

Of course. Because who would? Nobody in their right fucking mind would ever mistake Mark as someone capable of developing those qualities. He was selfish and immature, and stupid. He felt more stupid now than he had in any exam he'd taken at Prescott. Mark thought back to every time he'd found out Bengal hadn't invited him to some pledge activity, and how he'd laughed about it. How he'd actually thought it was a reward and not guessed that Bengal was setting him up so he could throw him out. Stupid.

God. It wasn't that long ago that Mark had been planning on something like this. Planning on getting hated and thrown out so he could show his sad face to Jim and lie that he'd tried his hardest. Except now that it had happened, it didn't feel like a victory. It felt like another punch in the face. And Mark had the horrible feeling that Deacon could tell exactly how close to tears he was.

"I'm going back to my dorm," Mark said.

"Mark."

Mark didn't look at him. "Call me tomorrow or something, if you want."

"No." Deacon put a hand on his shoulder before he could flinch away. "If you don't want to talk about it, that's fine, but don't run off, okay? Stay here for a while."

Mark didn't want to do that. Because sooner or later he'd spill his guts to Deacon about how dumb he felt, about how embarrassed, and he didn't want to be that guy. The one always needing reassurance. The one fishing for it. *You're beautiful; you're incredible; you're amazing; you're gonna be fine...*

He wanted to go and get some beer and drink it underneath Prescott's statue, and fuck what the campus police thought. Who, if they were real police, wouldn't drive around in golf carts. Mark was quite looking forward to pointing that out to them.

Except somehow Deacon's hand on his shoulder became Deacon's arms around him, and suddenly Mark didn't want to leave so much. Deacon smelled good, and Mark had never been in the habit of caring how guys smelled, but it was never too late to start, right? He took a deep breath and let some of the tension in his muscles go. Swallowed as Deacon nuzzled the side of his neck.

It hurt to be made a fool of. But Deacon never seemed to think he was stupid. Mark tentatively placed one palm on Deacon's back and splayed his fingers. "Fuck them," he murmured, but it didn't come out sounding very forceful. He started to shake, and he squeezed his eyes shut. No fucking way was he going to cry. Because this was even worse than the night Deacon had tried to fist him. At least then he'd had the pain as an excuse.

He curled his fingers, digging them into Deacon's back. "I never wanted it anyway," he continued, trying to will his voice steady. "So if they think this is some kind of big deal, they're..." He stopped. Stood in that instant of total stillness before misery overtook him entirely, and he knew he was going to lose. His eyes prickled, and he clenched his quivering jaw. Not over those fuckers. He was never going to cry over those fuckers. This was about something else. This was about how Deacon stood there without moving or saying anything and held him. Didn't make jokes the way Baz and Richo had the day Mark had found out he was going to Pennsylvania and had been so pissed off he'd kicked a dent in his bedroom wall. Normally he appreciated jokes, liked to avoid the touchy-feely stuff. But that day he'd wanted some acknowledgment that he mattered, that his friends needed him to stay.

He held on to Deacon and thought about all the times he'd shut his mum out or refused to interact with Jim on anything more than a superficial level. If he'd been willing to have real conversations with Jim, maybe Jim could have explained all this fraternity stuff better, and Mark could have told him it didn't sound like his thing, but that he still appreciated Jim sending him to Prescott and hoped they'd find other things to bond over.

He thought about Alpha Delt and how he'd stayed for more than the chance to stick it to Bengal. Some part of him was drawn to the possibility of brothers. Knew he had to start making a life for himself here, and that life needed to be more than Deacon and Brandon and the statue of Wolford Prescott. He needed friends. He needed classes that interested him. He needed to feel like he was *doing* something, working toward something.

He concentrated on drawing a few quick, shaky breaths. "I don't know what to do," he whispered.

And don't say everything'll be fine. You don't know what a mess I've made.

Deacon moved one hand slowly up and down his back. "Mm-hm," Deacon said.

"I don't think I want to be in a fraternity."

"Then Mark? Don't be in one."

Was it really that simple?

There were footsteps on the stairs, and Mark saw James coming down. He didn't pull away from Deacon. Fuck James if he had a problem with it. But James just glanced at them, then said quietly, "I'm going out to get toilet paper," and left.

"I did kind of want to go to that dance," Mark muttered

when the house was silent again. "But only because you'd be there."

Deacon brushed his lips against Mark's hair. "Will you go as my date?"

Mark snorted. "Like the guys don't already have enough reason to hate me. Then I show up at their dance. With you."

"As fuck-yous go, it's a pretty good one."

Mark pulled back and looked at Deacon. "You don't want a date who looks like this."

"I don't?"

Mark shook his head.

Deacon placed his fingers on Mark's cheek, under the worst of the swelling. "Please, will you go to semiformal with me? Otherwise I'll just shuffle awkwardly on the dance floor with other guys' dates. And I'd rather shuffle awkwardly with you."

It'd be dumb to say yes. He ought to sever all ties with the Alpha Delts immediately. He was tired of fighting, tired of fuck-yous. And he did look like shit, probably even more so now that his face had had time to swell. He still felt a flash of pride, though, looking at Deacon through one eye swollen almost shut. It had been good to tell Bengal off.

"I'll go," Mark said. "But not as a fuck-you."

Deacon nodded, though he looked a little unsure. "Okay."

"Because when I picture you shuffling on a dance floor with some sorority girl, you look like such a nerd it breaks my heart."

Deacon grinned. "I know, right?"

Mark pulled the sides of Deacon's hoodie together and held them there a few seconds, like he was adjusting the lapels of a tux. He looked at Deacon's throat, since he wasn't brave enough to say shit like this gazing into Deacon's eyes or whatever. "And because I like you so much, sometimes I'm not sure what to do with all that...you know? That feeling?"

"I know that feeling. Now. I didn't for a long time."

"Yeah, well." Mark had to stop to swallow. "You'll tell me if it goes away, won't you? I don't like feeling stupid, so if there's some hint I'm not getting, tell me."

"The only hint you're not getting right now is that you ought to be kissing me."

Mark had a feeling that if he acted on that hint as many times per day as he imagined he was getting it, Deacon would have taken out a restraining order by now.

Mark leaned forward and took the hint.

"What time are you picking me up, Romeo?" he asked during a pause in a series of short, soft kisses.

"Be outside your dorm at five thirty tomorrow," Deacon replied, tugging Mark by the shirt so Mark's lips bumped Deacon's again. "And Juliet?"

"Yeah?"

"Wear that underwear I like. Because after prom, we're gonna lose our virginity in the back of my car."

Mark kissed him again. "Bad news, Romeo. That ship sailed a long time ago."

"Mmm."

"Made her maiden voyage, then a whole bunch more after that. I'm surprised she's still afloat."

Deacon laughed. "Zack Weirman. I was eighteen. We were in his bedroom. It smelled weird, and he wanted to play video games after."

"Hmm. Mad Dog. Pub toilet. I was sixteen. It hurt. He used a condom from, like, the early eighties." Mark arched his back as Deacon stroked down it. *What if I can't figure out how to be reasonably stupid, Deke?*

"So we won't lose our virginity. Will you still wear the underwear?"

"If you promise to fuck me."

"Duh."

"Done."

"Five thirty. Don't be late."

"Deke?"

Deacon was kissing him again. "Hmm?"

"I don't have an initiation ceremony to go to tonight."

"Oh."

"And I don't have any more finals."

"And?"

"And James is gone."

"So?"

"I think there's a hint you're not getting."

"You want something?"

"Shove things up my arse."

Deacon cupped his arse. "Could you be more specific?"

"Your fingers. Plugs. Um, your couch." Mark laughed against Deacon's lips.

"The banister pole?"

"My copy of *As I Lay Dying*."

"A bear."

"The portrait of that guy who founded Phi Sig. Nerd Weston."

"It's Ned."

"My bad."

Deacon thrust his tongue into Mark's mouth on the next kiss. Mark slowly put his arms up and draped them around Deacon's neck. His cheek hurt when he kissed. But he didn't mind. Liked the sudden throb of it.

"Well, let's get upstairs," Deacon said when they paused for breath. "That arse isn't going to fill itself."

Deacon started to turn, but Mark caught his wrist. Wasn't this the way all their serious moments ended? With sex? With both of them relieved they'd found a common language that still let them avoid what they were really trying to say. "Wait," Mark said. He looked Deacon in the eye. "When I said I liked you, I maybe meant more than that. I think. Maybe you don't feel the same way, and maybe I don't know what I'm talking about. And maybe I'm about to ruin everything."

"I don't think you are."

"I've never been in love before."

"Me either."

"So how do we know if we're...?"

"You could say it and see how it feels."

"I love you?"

"Yeah."

"No, that was me saying it."

"And that was me saying yeah, it sounded good. How did it feel?"

"Like I was asking a question. Hold on." Mark held a finger up. Took a breath. "I love you."

"I love you too."

"And that's it?"

"What else is there supposed to be?"

Mark shrugged. "I thought maybe music would swell, or the plane you were supposed to be on would take off in the distance. Or that I'd feel like an idiot."

"Do you?"

Mark shook his head. "Nope."

"Well, good, Mark. It's about time you realized how often you call it completely right."

"I wrote on my lit exam that Flannery O'Connor founded a chain of popular Irish pubs."

Deacon rolled his eyes. "I said often. Not always."

"I might fail lit."

"You can retake it."

"I'm not in Alpha Delt anymore."

"Their loss."

But I am in love. And that seems way more important.

"Can we do the arse filling now?" Mark asked.

"Absolutely."

They headed upstairs.

————

Mark looked good. Put a suit on a guy, and it could work miracles, and Mark hadn't been anything near ugly to begin with. But that suit. Even his black eye and swollen cheek couldn't take away what that suit was doing for him. Deacon's suit was from the rental place on High Street, off the rack. He had the feeling that Mark's was the sort where some guy felt you up with a tape measure and made the whole thing from scratch.

They'd hired a limo. That had been Matt's idea. Or, most likely, Kate's. They'd split costs with James and Tony too, so with dates included, eight of them piled out at the country club for the Alpha Delta and Phi Sigma Winter Wonderland Formal.

Mark was nervous. He curled his fingers through Deacon's when they got out of the limo and walked in together.

"We'll have fun tonight," Deacon assured Mark as they passed through the curtain of shimmering tinsel snowflakes at the entrance.

Which was probably a lie.

The moment they arrived, they were accosted by Blake.

"Hey, little bro," he said enthusiastically to Mark and slapped him on the shoulder. "We missed you at the initiation last night. Bengal said you quit, but I was like, bullshit, he—" Blake did a double take. An actual cartoonish double take. "What happened to your face, dude? You guys like the rough stuff, hey?" And leered at Deacon. Possibly approvingly. It was hard to tell.

"Got in a fight," Mark said.

"Did you win?" Blake asked, his gaze dropping to Mark's lapel. "Bro, where's your pledge pin? Bengal will have a fit if you forgot it. You've got to give them back tonight."

Mark mumbled something.

A flurry of people arriving pushed them toward an alcove.

"What?" Blake asked. "What'd you say?" He tugged on the sleeve of a guy in a suit standing near them. "Jackson, hey, your idiot cousin forgot his pin."

Jackson turned, eyes rolling. Then he frowned. "What happened to your face?"

They didn't know. Deacon hadn't expected that. And neither had Mark, from the look on his face.

"I got in a fight," he said, his voice wooden.

Deacon reached out and took his hand and squeezed it.

"It doesn't look too bad," Jackson said. "But you need to go back to campus and get your pin. Seriously. We need those back. And we need to talk about doing a private initiation for you before you leave for break."

Mark jutted out his chin. "I'm not in your stupid fucking frat anymore, okay? I'm only here as Deke's date."

Jackson stared at him. "So you really did quit?" he said coolly. "Because I didn't believe Bengal for a second."

Mark didn't say anything.

Blake's face fell. "Are you serious, Mark? Why didn't you tell me you wanted out?"

"I didn't want out," Mark said. Deacon heard the waver in his voice. "Bengal kicked me out, okay? Because I didn't go to enough pledge activities that he didn't tell me about. So fuck him, and fuck the rest of you."

"Mark," Jackson said. "What do you mean he didn't tell you?"

"He's supposed to tell you," Blake confirmed.

"Well, he didn't," Mark said. "And then he punched me in the face and told me to go fuck myself. So thanks for everything, Alpha Delts. It's been a fucking pleasure. Next time you extend a bid to a pledge, you might want to warn him it'll be about as much fun as masturbating vigorously with sandpaper." He glared at Deacon. "You want to dance now?"

"Sure," Deacon said. It would take a braver man than him to refuse the angry bunny.

Mark hauled him onto the dance floor.

It had been a mistake to leave the Alpha Delts in charge of hiring the DJ. The guy played a lot of shit Deacon had never heard. Although Deacon wasn't exactly up with what the kids were listening to. And now he felt like he was forty-one instead of twenty-one. Shades of his father: *That's not music. That's just noise.*

But it was noise with a beat, and Mark's arms were around his neck, and it was a lot less pitiful than swaying awkwardly with some sorority girl. Deacon wanted to tell Mark how incredibly brave it had been for him to come here tonight, but a part of him knew that Mark didn't want to hear it. To tell him he was brave was to remind him he was scared, and Mark wouldn't want that. Not here. Deacon would save it for later, for when they were alone and Mark only had to expose himself to one person, not a hall full of them.

I'm starting to get you now, Mark Cooper.

"What are you smiling about?" Mark asked him, still frowning.

Deacon's smile grew. "I'm dancing with the boy I love. What's not to smile about?"

Angry bunny beat a swift retreat.

"Shut up," Mark said, his face turning red and his own smile appearing. "You're just glad I didn't cause a scene."

"That wasn't a scene?" Deacon teased him.

Mark leaned in closer, his breath warm against Deacon's cheek. "Oh, Deke, that was fucking *nothing*."

"I bet it wasn't."

"I can go off," Mark promised. "Like a frog in a sock."

Deacon stopped. "That's a thing?"

Mark tilted his head. "It's a *saying*. I don't know if it's a thing. I've never literally put a frog in a sock. I don't think frogs would stand for that sort of treatment."

"If you did, I'd have to call the ASPCA," Deacon said.

Mark punched him lightly in the shoulder. "RSPCA."

"Close enough," Deacon said.

Mark smiled again. "Yeah. Close enough."

Deacon drew him into the dance again. Okay, so the DJ was playing hip-hop and Deacon and Mark were...well, swaying, but that was what you got with Mark. He marched to the beat of his own drum, and you fell into step with him. And that was okay. Deacon had always wanted to be one of those people—the ones who didn't give a fuck what anyone thought—but he wasn't. And neither was Mark, exactly. They were a good fit. Mark could be fun and reckless, and Deacon could make sure he didn't go too far. In every relationship, someone had to remember to pay taxes and put fuel in the car, right? And someone had to remember that they were twenty-one and eighteen, and life was supposed to be fun.

Mark leaned in again. "I think, without you, this year would have sucked."

"I know this year would have sucked," Deacon said. "It would have been like every other year at Prescott for me. Except I wouldn't have realized it sucked, because I didn't know it until you were there." He shook his head. "I don't think I'm making sense."

"I think you are," Mark said and tugged his head down for a kiss.

And there it was. That moment Deacon had been secretly dreaming of since high school. Kissing a boy in the middle of a dance, in a room full of mostly straight people who never needed to worry about making a scene. Deacon didn't care if anyone was watching. Deacon wasn't doing this because he was out and proud and didn't care who knew it. He was doing this because it was Mark, and he loved him.

And it was one of those moments that could have lasted forever, if not for the sudden crash and screams from the other end of the ballroom. The music was shut off.

Deacon and Mark pulled apart and craned their necks to see.

They saw Blake, standing over the collapsed table. And Bengal, on the floor, drenched in punch.

"Because you're a fucking asshole," Blake shouted, pointing a beefy finger in Bengal's direction. "Because you always go too fucking far, and because he was my little bro!"

"Holy fuck," Mark squeaked.

Chris and Jackson swept in out of nowhere. Chris took

Blake by the shoulder and led him away, talking to him in a low voice.

Bengal reached for Jackson to help him up.

Jackson shoved his hands in his pockets and turned away.

"Holy *fuck*," Mark said again.

A bunch of girls in glittery dresses and heels descended to help Bengal to his feet, twittering sympathetically. But not a single guy. None of the Phi Sigs, who knew it was none of their business. None of the waiters, who weren't paid enough for that shit. And none of the Alpha Delts, who had maybe discovered there was a line after all.

Jackson crossed the dance floor. He nodded at Deacon and looked at Mark. "You're pledging again next semester."

"I don't think I am," Mark said.

"You are," Jackson told him. "For Blake."

"Um," said Mark. He looked at Deacon worriedly. "Maybe?"

"Bengal will be out," Jackson said. "The process will be a lot different. I gotta go see if we'll get our security deposit back. You need a ride home for Christmas?"

"Sure," Mark said, his eyes too big for his face. "I'm, um... Deke and I are going to Tannersville. But if you're still around when we get back, okay. Thanks."

Jackson walked away.

"Deke," Mark said, "I think I'm back in."

"You don't have to be," Deacon reminded him.

"Blake just punched Bengal in the face," Mark said. "I think that maybe I kind of do. I think that maybe I kind of want to."

"Okay," Deacon said. He wrapped an arm around Mark's waist. "I'm sort of relieved."

"Are you?"

Deacon nodded. "Sure. How could we be Romeo and Juliet if we didn't belong to two feuding houses?"

"Both alike in dignity," Mark added.

"Well, I wouldn't go that far," Deacon said, raising his eyebrows.

"Nerd," Mark said.

"Angry bunny."

"What?"

Deacon pulled him closer. "Nothing."

Mark eyed him suspiciously.

Then the DJ hit the music again, so they danced.

CHAPTER 17

"N o."

"Mark."

"I'm not going out in that. You saw those people—they were up to their *knees*."

"I'm convinced Mother Nature did this just for you," Deacon said, pulling on his boots.

"To torture me."

"To *help* you. You need to get over your fear of snow."

"It's not a fear. It's a totally justified hatred." Mark sat on the bed in their cabin, hoping that if he refused to budge, Deacon would fuck him, in here, where it was warm, instead of forcing him to walk through a fucking *blizzard*.

Okay, so it wasn't a blizzard. It wasn't even snowing anymore. But the snow was high enough that Mark had seen people *trudging*.

"Come on," Deacon said firmly. "We're going to walk to the lodge and look at what it costs to rent skis."

Extra not fair, because that tone made Mark's cock harden, but the words made his balls shrivel. Why couldn't they call the fucking lodge? And ask that the skis be delivered? Or better yet, rent snowshoes, and instead of walking in them, Deacon could spank him with one.

"Why aren't you getting ready?" Deacon asked, straightening.

Mark muttered something intentionally unintelligible.

Deacon walked over and sat on the bed beside him. Mark immediately leaned against him.

"I'm wearing thermal underwear, Deke. What does that even mean?" He plucked at the waffle-weave fabric.

Deacon turned and kissed his head. "It means put on your snow pants and jacket, and let's go. We'll get hot chocolate while we're at the lodge."

"The pants are too puffy."

Deacon ran his hand down Mark's chest and slipped it into the front of Mark's long underwear. Mark let his head drop back and moaned. This was more like it.

Deacon gave Mark's cock a few pumps, just enough to get Mark nearly hard, then withdrew and patted his thigh. "Come on. Up."

Mark rolled his eyes and sighed. "I almost was." He stood and looked for his dumbarse, puffy snow pants.

So yeah, okay, the lodge was nice. Except for the white stuff all around it. And the cabin was incredibly rustic and private and had a fireplace. And Mark had talked to his mum and Jim last night. Jim had said he was proud of him, and that they'd go out to celebrate Mark's initiation into Alpha Delt when Mark got home. Mark still wasn't sure agreeing to be affiliated with that house of freaks was anything to celebrate, but he'd gone out with Blake and Dan and Fraser over the weekend, and it had been pretty fun. Blake knew a place where you didn't get carded, and the barmaid had tits like...like... He'd done something with his hands. Like she was bobbing in the ocean, holding on to a particularly bulky life jacket, apparently. Blake had only got locked in the toilet once, and Mark had woken up the next morning in his own bed with one boot off, the other one tangled around his ankle by the laces, and no memory of how he'd gotten home. Later that day Chris Wilson had offered him a formal apology for what Bengal had done and welcomed him back to Alpha Delta.

The college had gotten wind of some of Alpha Delt's less than savory pledge activities. There wasn't any proof of hazing, not unless former pledges were willing to come forward and testify in an IFC hearing, but the fraternity was going to be monitored closely next semester.

Mark had still been half-convinced that they only wanted him in the fraternity to be their tame fag, their proof that they were being inclusive and diverse, but the night out with the guys had shaken that belief. Maybe they actually *liked* him. And shit, at least he'd be able to move out of his dorm, right? And stop rooming with the Last Legitimate Hippie on Earth, who thought that crystals worked as an alternative to deodorant.

And Brandon was going to be right next door at Phi Sig.

So next year might be all right, if Mark survived the winter.

He grumbled as he fastened his snow pants, then his boots, then his jacket, then looked around for his gloves, his scarf, and his hat. Too much fucking clothing. Okay, the hat was cute. It was white and fuzzy and had pointy animal ears. Mark had asked Deacon to buy it for him, and they'd argued all the way on the drive from Prescott to Tannersville about whether it was a cat or a wolf, and not mentioned the fact that it had most likely been made with a girl in mind. And Mark had not freaked out once about driving on a road covered in ice. Well, maybe that one time, but Deacon had been cool about it.

"If I can drive while you're talking me off, I can drive on a bit of ice."

"Yeah, but I wasn't in the car when I was talking you off."

Which Mark had felt, logically, made all the difference.

"Come on, kitty," Deacon said now.

"Fuck you. I'm a wolf." Mark put his gloves on. Then took them off again and put them on the right way. He pulled his hat down as far as it would go, leaving only a narrow gap between it and his scarf, and shuffled over to the door, trying not to hear the noise his snow pants made as his thighs rubbed.

Fuck. Why couldn't he just stay in the cabin and be naked and sexy in front of the fire? Wearing nothing but his wolf-kitty hat.

"Mark, you'll love this," Deacon promised and opened the door.

Holy mother of God.

Cold.

So fucking cold.

How had people settled here? Seriously, when the country had other perfectly viable states like California and Hawaii, how had Pennsylvania ever seemed like a good idea? But before Mark could step back and slam the door in Deacon's face, Deacon grabbed him by the hand and pulled him outside. Across the porch, down the steps, and into the snow.

The snow.

"The lodge is just up the path," Deacon told him.

There was a path?

Shit. What if he was already snow-blind? That was a thing, right? A thing that came right before death, probably.

Deacon held his hand as they trudged toward the lodge. Which wasn't just up the path at all. It was at least sixteen hundred kilometers away. Mark breathed into his scarf, and his eyes watered. What about this was he supposed to love exactly?

Fine, it was pretty. Snow was pretty. The leafless trees were stark and beautiful, the sort of thing you could write reams of poetry about if you were so inclined. Which Mark wasn't. And fine, it was kind of nice to be here with Deacon, but it was nice to be anywhere with Deacon. And fine, when they eventually reached the lodge and Mark had his cold hands wrapped around a mug of steaming hot chocolate, it might have been the best hot chocolate ever in the history of the universe. But snow, really?

They went to the rental counter at the lodge, and Mark made a face at both the idea and the price of skis. All that money to go careening down a mountain, most likely into a tree? Deacon glanced at him, and he tried quickly to school his face. "What about a sled?" Deacon asked.

"Huh?" Mark looked back at the board. A sled was cheaper. And you could sit on it, which beat going down a slope upright. Maybe.

Deacon linked his arm with Mark's. "We could go sledding. Might be easier to start with. And if you like that, we could try skiing tomorrow."

Mark nodded. "Okay."

So Deacon rented them a sled. And they dragged it to the top of Sunrise Slope. There was a family snow tubing. A few other sledders were out as well. Great. More obstacles. Also, Mark had gotten snow in his boot, and his sock was wet.

They managed to find a portion of the slope without traffic. Deacon's hand made a squeaking sound as he rubbed the back of Mark's jacket. He patted the seat of Mark's snow pants. "Get in."

Mark eyed the sled warily. It was made of blue plastic and looked like a dead fish. He climbed into the rounded front part while Deacon held the whole thing steady. "Don't let go," Mark said, a little too sharply.

"I won't," Deacon replied calmly. He climbed in behind Mark and placed his legs on either side of Mark's.

Mark gripped the edges of the sled. Deacon wound his arms around Mark. That was the moment Mark decided to stop being an arsehole. He didn't feel so cold anymore, and Deacon held him tightly enough that this no longer felt like a terrible idea. He stopped glaring at the snow and clutching the sled in a death grip and leaned back against Deacon.

"You ready?" Deacon asked.

Mark nodded. "Yeah."

Deacon shifted his hips, scooting the sled closer to the edge. Mark tried to help him. Deacon used his hands for the push-off, and for a second Mark's stomach clenched. Then they were sliding forward, and Deacon's arms were back around him.

Mark didn't have time to think. They were gaining speed, and Mark was back to using a death grip, the sled digging into his palms even through his gloves. But Deacon was laughing, and then Mark was smiling, and soon he laughed too as the world rushed by. They reached the end of the hill, and the sled skewed to the left, finally coming to a stop. Mark got up immediately. "We have to do it again."

Forty minutes later, they were ready for their last run. Mark had stopped gripping the sled, preferring to go down the hill with his arms up as high as the jacket would allow. He also liked to shift his weight as they went down, pushing the sled from side to side. Now he had Deacon in the front of the sled and was standing beside it. He planned to give it a running push, then jump in the back.

"This is gonna be the best one yet, Deke. You ready?"

"You bet."

Mark started pushing the sled. As it dipped over the edge of the hill, he darted ahead of it and tried to hop in.

And missed.

He fell on his arse, then tumbled down the hill after the sled. He heard Deacon call something, but he couldn't respond. He was too busy bouncing through the snow like this was some kind of twisted nightmare. Just before the sled gained enough momentum to escape, Mark reached out and grabbed the back of it. Deacon was jolted forward; then the sled tipped, and Deacon rolled into the snow in front of Mark.

The sled continued its riderless journey down the hill. Mark belly crawled over to where Deacon lay, laughing so hard it was difficult to breathe the cold air. "Deke? You okay?"

Deacon moved onto his back and, when Mark got close enough, lunged up and pulled Mark on top of him. He had a handful of snow ready, and he pushed it against the back of Mark's neck. Mark yelped as it slid down his coat. "Deke!" He turned over, frantically swatting at his neck, and Deacon straddled him.

"You crashed me," Deacon accused, laughing.

Mark tried to throw snow at him, but Deacon dodged.

They wrestled for a few minutes, then ended up curled in the snow, kissing.

Deacon tasted like hot chocolate. Well, cold chocolate now. And Mark could have stayed there, wrapped up in his arms forever, except for one thing.

"Deke?"

"Yeah?" Deacon bit gently at Mark's lower lip.

Mark wriggled underneath him. "I've got snow in my pants."

———

For a while, Deacon was afraid that Mark had melted in the shower. He set about building up the fire and hanging their damp clothes on the backs of the chairs, and watched half an episode of some stupid sitcom before Mark reappeared. He was pink and naked except for his towel. And his fuzzy animal hat.

"Looks like you warmed up," Deacon said, setting his phone aside. Ben had texted him that their mom was doing okay. Not only was she not worried that Deacon was wrapped around a tree on a ski slope, she'd told Ben she was looking forward to having Mark visit sometime over the Christmas break.

A stranger, in her house, carrying in all those unknown and dangerous germs. Deacon couldn't remember the last time he'd brought someone home. Back in elementary school, probably. And it wasn't just his mom's fear of germs. It was her fear of being judged for when she couldn't hide her symptoms. For when she stopped a conversation in the middle so that she could disinfect a surface their guest had touched. And now she wanted to meet Mark. Deacon could hardly believe it.

"I did," Mark said, turning around to show Deacon the redness on his hip. "Look. This is gonna be a massive bruise by tomorrow. I can't believe you people let children on sleds. It's dangerous!"

"Says the surfer," Deacon said, rolling his eyes.

"Deke," Mark explained, tucking the towel more

securely around his hips, "when you fall off a surfboard, you don't fall onto the ground. You fall into—"

"Sharks?" Deacon suggested. He pulled Mark forward into a hug.

"Water," Mark said. "Although I got some killer bruises from surfing as well. And once my board hit me in the back of the head."

"Ouch," Deacon said, lifting his hand to rub Mark's fuzzy hat.

"I don't actually remember it," Mark said. "I just remember Richo pulling me out of the water."

"Do you miss it?"

"What? The concussion?"

Deacon laughed. "Idiot."

"Sometimes I miss it." Mark nuzzled at Deacon's throat. "But America has certain advantages."

"Really?" Deacon tried not to sneeze as Mark's fuzzy hat tickled his nose.

"Well, one," Mark said. He drew back and grinned. "Are you fishing for compliments, Deke?"

Warmth rose in Deacon. "Maybe I am."

"Huh." Mark tilted his head thoughtfully. "How about this, then? You're the only guy I would ever trust to drag me into the bear-infested wilderness and push me down a hill."

Deacon raised his eyebrows. "The bears are sleeping, Mark."

"See, I'm taking your word for that. *Trust.*"

"Trust," Deacon repeated, smiling.

Mark leaned forward, hiding his face against Deacon's shoulder. When he spoke again, his voice was soft, almost shy. "And you're the only guy I'd ever trust to put his hand inside me."

Deacon exhaled. Yeah, that was real.

"Lie down," Deacon said quietly. He tugged the towel from Mark's hips. Mark was already half-hard.

Mark glanced uncertainly at the bed.

"By the fire," Deacon whispered.

Mark walked to the rug in front of the fireplace and knelt. He looked so good kneeling, the firelight flickering on his skin, that Deacon's cock stirred. He wanted Mark sucking him, Mark's hands on his ass, fingers digging in, pulling Deacon deeper down his throat.

"You all right?" Mark asked.

Deacon nodded. He went to Mark and knelt beside him. Ran his hands over Mark's damp body. Mark bowed his head. "You're gonna take my hand inside you," Deacon murmured.

Mark shivered as Deacon ran two fingernails down the ridge of his spine. The little animal ears flopped. Deacon rubbed Mark's scalp through the hat, watching Mark lower his tense shoulders and lean into Deacon's hand. Deacon slipped the hat off. Mark's hair was wet and stuck out in all directions. Deacon laughed and smoothed it.

"You feel ready to try?" Deacon asked.

Mark nodded more slowly. "Yeah."

Deacon got up and snagged two pillows from the bed. Put them on the rug. "Stretch out."

Mark arranged himself so that one pillow was under his hips, the other under his head.

Deacon's heart was pounding. Mark looked so fucking gorgeous like this. And no way was Deacon going to hurt him again. Deacon got the lube. He stripped and sat beside Mark. Stroked his back for a few minutes, gradually letting his fingers slide down Mark's crack and tease his hole. He'd take this slow. He'd take all night if he had to.

Mark pushed his face into the pillow as Deacon dipped

one finger into his ass. He used his other hand to roll Mark's balls. Mark lifted his hips so Deacon could touch his cock.

"Is that okay?"

Mark mumbled his assent into the pillow.

Deacon was hard as well. A part of him wanted to sink his cock into Mark so fast that it left them both breathless, but the part of him that needed to see how far he and Mark could take this thing was stronger. The fact that Mark trusted him to try this was still as overwhelming as it had been that first night Mark had confessed he wanted to do it.

Mark's hips jerked, and Deacon stilled his finger. Mark shifted, the muscles in his shoulders rolling, then sighed and settled back down onto the pillow. He turned his head and laid his cheek on his crossed arms. "Was close for a second there."

"I know. But we've got the whole night."

"Hmmm." Mark closed his eyes. "Should probably eat at some point."

Deacon slid the finger back inside him. "If you're thinking about your stomach, I must be doing something wrong."

Mark smiled slightly, his eyes still closed, and shifted his legs wider. "No, I think you're doing just right."

So was Mark. Adorable with the fingers of his right hand combing through the fur of his discarded fuzzy hat, like a kid with a stuffed toy, but spread wantonly at the same time.

"How did someone like you fall accidentally into my lap?"

"I think I fell accidentally onto your dick," Mark said, opening his eyes. "Accidentally repeatedly."

Deacon smiled. So much for romantic musings. Mark was so outwardly confident, but so quick to deflect anything that sounded suspiciously like a compliment. Fun and dirty and carefree, so nothing could touch him. Or angry, so it didn't matter what people thought of him. But this Mark here, this one still clinging to the last remains of his armor, was the real thing. Deacon removed his finger, drizzled more lube on his hand, and stroked Mark's crack. Loving the way Mark shifted under his touch, his hips moving again, trying to get more.

Deacon gave him two fingers, and Mark squeezed around them and sighed. His eyes drifted shut once more.

Deacon spent the next fifteen minutes slowly working four fingers inside Mark. He stretched out alongside Mark on the rug, his chin next to Mark's shoulder, and tucked his thumb against his palm. Mark was breathing deeply, though his breath caught when Deacon's thumb nudged him.

"Fuck," Deacon whispered, pressing the tip of his thumb in.

"Fuck," Mark whispered back, exhaling.

Deacon kissed his shoulder. The fire crackled, sending sparks up. Deacon felt the warmth of it on his skin, the warmth of Mark's body next to his. He pushed a little farther, and Mark didn't resist.

"Gonna be inside you," Deacon murmured.

Mark nodded. "Your whole fucking hand."

"My whole fucking hand," Deacon agreed.

Deacon moved until he found Mark's prostate. Mark's legs tensed, and he bucked his hips.

"Good?"

Mark nodded furiously, clutching the hat.

"You're squishing your kitty ears."

"Wolf," Mark murmured hoarsely.

Deacon rubbed his prostate again and slid the top part of his thumb in on the next jerk of Mark's hips. Now all he had to do was somehow get his knuckles in. He was terrified to try. He shifted so he could place his free hand between Mark's shoulders. "More?"

Mark didn't answer. Deacon stayed still and concentrated on the rest of Mark's body, stroking the smooth skin and nipping the crook of Mark's shoulder until Mark moaned. Mark buried his face in his arms and said something Deacon couldn't hear.

"What's that?" Deacon asked.

Mark's shoulders tightened. He tossed the hat aside and dug his fingers into the rug. "Make me take it," he whispered quickly. "Make me, um. Mm, please, make me?"

"Hey." Deacon leaned over Mark to retrieve the hat, spreading his fingers inside Mark as he did. He placed the hat on Mark's back. He flicked his tongue against the edge of Mark's ear. "I don't need to make you. You want this. You're opening up for me."

Deacon watched Mark press his mouth to the back of his hand, his eyes squeezed shut. "Srrd," Mark mumbled.

"Hmm?"

Mark raised his head. "Scared, a little, Deke. Sorry."

Deacon scooted up so his face was next to Mark's. Mark turned and kissed him, and Deacon worked his fingers apart and together inside Mark to the rhythm of their kiss. "Don't be sorry," Deacon whispered. "Love this. Can't believe how hot you are in there. How I can feel everything."

It was another ten minutes before Deacon squirted more lube onto his fingers and tried to work his knuckles in. He felt Mark bear down around his fingers. He pushed harder, but Mark gave a strangled groan. "Easy," Deacon soothed.

Mark closed his eyes again and worried his lower lip with his teeth. He rocked back and forth on Deacon's hand, and Deacon shifted so he could see. Each time Mark moved, Deacon's knuckles pressed against his stretched entrance.

Then Mark pushed back harder, Deacon pushed forward, and suddenly the widest part of his hand had disappeared inside Mark's body.

Mark froze, panting, his eyes flashing open. "Deke!"

The pressure around his hand was immense. It ached. He felt as though Mark's muscles might crush the bones in his hand. And if he felt like that, what the hell was Mark feeling? Fuck. Mark, stretched around his wrist. Fuck. Deacon rubbed Mark's back with his free hand. "Is it too much?"

"Fuck," Mark said, his voice wavering. "Oh fuck." He buried his face in his hands.

Deacon's heart beat faster. "You have to talk to me, Mark!"

Mark was trembling. Deacon too.

"Are you in me?"

"Yeah," Deacon whispered.

"Oh fuck," Mark moaned. He panted. "It's *big*."

Deacon twisted his wrist gently. "You want it out?"

Mark stilled. "Not yet. Gonna...gonna feel good in a minute. Almost...almost..."

Deacon stared at his forearm, at the place where it disappeared inside Mark. It didn't seem real. He'd seen pictures of this online, and that was what this had to be, another picture, because no way did Deacon actually have his entire hand in Mark's ass.

Mark let out a long, shuddering breath.

"Want me to move?" Deacon asked tentatively.

Mark shook his head. "Just a minute."

Deacon picked up the hat and swept it up and down Mark's back, letting the soft fabric soak up the tiny beads of sweat there. Put the hat aside and stroked Mark's ass and thighs, then placed his hand between Mark's legs to touch his cock. Mark arched his back and started fucking himself on Deacon's wrist. His breath caught every few seconds, and Deacon couldn't tell if the sounds he made were of pain or pleasure.

"You can move, Deke."

Deacon tried curling his fingers, and Mark's entire body went rigid. He stopped. He tried again, flexing his fingers slightly, over and over again, until Mark's breathing became rhythmic, until he rubbed his cock against Deacon's hand.

Deacon's cock strained. Mark clenched around his arm, and Deacon felt a pull through his whole body. He crooked his fingers. Mark gasped, pushing his hips up. "That's good. Fuck. That's good." Deacon did it again, and made a fist. There was still that hot, crushing pressure around his hand, but it felt good. Deacon thrust very slowly. Mark's head came up and back. There was a loud snap from the fireplace as a stick broke, and the bark curled in the flame.

They were both panting. Deacon shifted, trying to arrange himself so his cock was against Mark's hip. He didn't want to be thinking about himself right now, but his balls were so tight they hurt. His movement made Mark wince, and Deacon was about to ask him if he was okay, but then Mark shouted something unintelligible. His ass clenched so firmly around Deacon's arm that Deacon shut his eyes. His hand around Mark's cock was wet and sticky.

Mark collapsed on the rug, panting so hard Deacon thought he was sobbing. Deacon moved his hand out from under Mark and put it around his own cock. It only took a couple of strokes to bring himself off. He didn't know if it was his imagination, but Mark's ass seemed looser around his fist. The pressure and the heat were gentle now, as if Mark's body accepted Deacon inside it.

"Mark?" he whispered.

"Good," Mark whispered back. "Sorry. Couldn't help it. Didn't know... I was feeling too much, and I couldn't..."

"That was amazing."

Mark snorted weakly. "You overuse that word. What're you gonna say when they figure out teleportation, or prove string theory, or when Prescott's football team wins a national championship, and you've used up all your 'amazings' describing me coming with your fingers up my arse?"

"Did you just reference the Prescott football team?"

Mark hesitated. "Maybe."

"And anyway, this is amazing. My whole fucking hand is up your ass, Mark."

"Arse."

"Call it whatever you want; my hand is in it."

Mark grinned. "You gonna be able to get it out?"

"Why would I want to?"

"Gonna eat dinner one-handed? Are we gonna have to cut a hole in my snow pants so we can ski side by side? Am I supposed to show up at your mum's house with your hand buried in me? *Ah, yes, nice to meet you, Mrs. Holt. Your son doesn't want to take his hand out of my arse.* I'm sure that'll do wonders for her germ phobia."

Deacon swatted Mark's ass with his free hand. Smiled at the way Mark reflexively tightened around his wrist. "Enough."

Mark fell silent. They stayed like that for a while before Mark said, "You gonna keep me around awhile, Deke?"

"If you behave."

"Behave how?"

"Like a hot little slut."

Mark pretended to think. "Okay. Shouldn't be a problem." He rocked against Deacon's hand. "Think it'll get better between Phi Sig and Alpha Delt? I mean, no one died during that dance."

"You think we brought our houses together, Juliet?"

"I saw James offering Blake a snowflake biscuit at prom."

Deacon swatted Mark again. Mark stared at Deacon adoringly, face still all gold and shadows from the dwindling fire. "It's not prom."

Mark gave the slightest smile. "You're so mean, Deke."

Deacon smiled back. "Mean enough for you?"

Mark yawned and shook his head. "You can be meaner."

"I'll keep that in mind."

Deacon slowly pulled back the hand that was inside Mark. Mark sighed and closed his eyes, lines appearing on his forehead. "Ow," he murmured as Deacon tried to withdraw.

"Might hurt for a second," Deacon said.

He felt Mark bear down, the muscles of his ass pushing against Deacon's hand. It took several minutes, but then Deacon was out. He went to the bathroom to wash up, practicing flexing his fingers, trying to get rid of the cramps.

When he returned, Mark was standing by the window.

"You want to shower with me?" Deacon asked. "Then we'll go get dinner?"

Mark didn't answer.

"Mark?"

"Deke?" Mark's voice was faint. He raised a hand and pointed out the window.

"What?"

"Deke, it's a *bear*."

"Nice try."

"I'm so fucking serious right now. I've seen pictures, and that is a *bear*."

Deacon stepped up to the window and scanned the white woods outside. "I don't see anything."

"There!" Mark pointed more emphatically.

Deacon started. There among the spindly, frosted trees was a dark shape. It moved slowly and had a thick black coat that rippled as it lumbered. A black bear. "Holy shit," Deacon said.

"Deacon, you promised! You promised they were sleeping, but they're out there waiting for us."

Deacon put a hand on Mark's back. "It's beautiful."

Mark turned to him. "Beautiful? It has teeth. Sharp *teeth*."

"Don't you think it's a little cute?"

Mark hesitated. "It's small. Smaller than I thought. But maybe it's just a baby."

"If you went out there right now, it would probably run away."

Mark turned and stared at him again. "Why would I go out there?"

"I'm just saying it has no interest in eating you."

Mark threw his arms around Deacon's neck. "You'll have to carry me to the lodge. And if it comes after us, sacrifice yourself."

Deacon placed an arm under Mark's shoulders and one under his knees and lifted him. "Carry you? Like this? Naked?"

"No. I want my hat. Can wolves defeat bears?"

"Yes. But bears eat kitties."

Mark pressed his face to Deacon's shoulder. "Don't say that."

Deacon jostled Mark. "You're missing it."

"That's the *point!* I want to miss it."

Deacon watched the bear until it disappeared into the trees. Mark shifted against him. "Want down?"

Mark shook his head. "I need you to hold me forever. Or until bears are extinct."

Deacon grinned. "Sounds like a plan to me." He adjusted his grip on Mark, and Mark groaned. "You okay?"

"Sore. Gonna feel it for days."

"Maybe you can sled on your stomach. And I can lie on top of you."

"Maybe we can stay inside for the next two days. And you can lie on top of me."

"Don't be ridiculous." Deacon carried Mark to the door and threw it open.

"What are you doing?" Mark demanded as Deacon stepped out onto the cabin's small porch. Mark scrambled and kicked, but Deacon held him firmly. "We are *naked*. There's a *bear*."

Jesus, it was fucking cold. Deacon's dick shriveled immediately, and the hair on his arms stood straight up. But goddamn it, it was worth it to stand here naked holding Mark with the wind blowing soft gusts of snow around them and the whole world white and quiet. "I'm being Mark Cooper. Fearless."

"You are the opposite of Mark Cooper! Mark Cooper is properly afraid of bears and ball loss." Mark pounded Deacon's back with his fist.

"Not when I'm around, he's not."

Mark hesitated. "He's not *as* afraid."

"Because he knows I've got his back."

"He knows you'll save his arse."

"Or ream it."

"Even better." Mark shivered. "Can we please go in now?"

Deacon plucked a small icicle off the overhang and carried Mark back inside. Deposited him on the bed. Deacon put one end of the icicle in his mouth. "Kiss me," he said around it.

"You're crazy," Mark muttered. But he let Deacon push the other end of the icicle into his mouth. They both sucked on it until it melted enough that their lips met. Then they passed the last chunk of ice back and forth as they kissed.

"Get ready," Deacon whispered when they parted. He patted Mark's thigh.

"For what?" Mark asked. "My dick to turn black and fall off?"

"For dinner." Deacon smiled and planted one more kiss on Mark's forehead. "And for everything that comes next."

AFTERWORD

Thank you for reading *Mark Cooper versus America*!

If you liked what you read, consider signing up for <u>This Rebus Does Not Work</u>, a monthly Henrock newsletter where we share news, exclusive excerpts, and opportunities to win free books!

When you sign up, you'll receive a FREE collection of stories from J.A. Rock's SUBS CLUB universe.

EXCERPT FROM BRANDON MILLS VERSUS THE V-CARD

PRESCOTT COLLEGE #2

Chapter One

"An hour," Mark Cooper said. Brandon watched as Mark flopped onto Deacon's neatly made bed and stretched, rumpling the covers. "I can stay an hour, and then I need to go back to Alpha Delt. It's our mixer tonight as well, you know."

Brandon raised his brows at the open window. From the Alpha Delta Phi house next door, music was blasting and it wasn't even dark yet. Brandon already had a headache. "Oh, trust me, we know. The whole campus knows."

Deacon Holt snorted from his desk. He balled up a piece of notepaper and threw it at Mark. "Are you guys going to be the neighbors from hell again this year?"

"Shut up, nerds." Mark grinned then sat up suddenly. "I was supposed to ask if someone could come and help us with our Internet."

"What's wrong with it?" Deacon asked.

Mark shrugged. "I dunno. Blake thinks we broke it by downloading too much porn."

"Under normal circumstances I'd say that's not even possible," Deacon said. "But with you guys..."

"I know, right?" Mark's smile turned wicked.

"Okaaaay." Brandon rose. "I think it's time I leave before you two get—"

"Freaky?" Mark suggested.

"Ew." Brandon rolled his eyes. "I was going to keep it clean and say distracted. I'll catch you downstairs."

He made sure he closed the door behind him when he left. Mark and Deacon could get kind of...demonstrative, which was cool and everything. Brandon just wasn't good with PDAs.

He headed down the stairs to see if the guys needed a hand setting up. Not like Phi Sig's mixer would require much planning—board games and soda was about as rowdy as it got around here, which was how Brandon liked it. He'd pledged Alpha Delta last year, and it had been a disaster. *God.* He still hated going over there to visit Mark. Just catching a glimpse of the basement door sent something creeping under his skin.

But Bengal, last year's pledge trainer, was out of Alpha Delt now, and not in a position to be an asshole to the newbies like he had been to Brandon. The guys over there could still be douches, but they were mostly okay. Some of them were actually friendly to Brandon. A lot of that had to do with Mark.

Alpha Delta and Phi Sig had once waged a legendary rivalry, which Mark had blatantly ignored. When it had come out that he was not only gay but sleeping with a guy from Phi Sig, it kind of made the whole feud seem stupid. Like some of the guys on both sides had thought they should be angry about it, and then realized how dumb that sounded. It was the frat war that had ended with a whimper instead of a bang, and Alpha Delta Phi and Phi Sigma Kappa went from sworn enemies to uneasy neighbors in the space of an academic year. They didn't exactly have an open-door policy, but it wasn't pistols at dawn anymore either.

When Brandon dropped out of pledging Alpha Delt, he'd felt like a failure. His dad had always told him he needed to be in a fraternity. All those executives on the Fortune 500 list? Frat guys. Or 80 percent of them, or something. So Brandon had failed, which hadn't come as a great surprise to him—or to his dad—but he'd been gutted. He'd tried so hard, and just because Bengal had put him in the fucking basement that night...

Anyway, Mark had come through for Brandon in the end. And Deacon. A spot had opened up in Phi Sig, and they'd invited Brandon to join. And now it felt like home. He wasn't always on guard like he'd been when he was pledging Alpha Delt, or feeling like he had something to prove. The guys at Phi Sig didn't care about how much beer you could drink or how often you got laid. They really only cared that you didn't accidentally record over last week's *Stargate Atlantis* marathon on SyFy.

Tony and James were in the common room, tipping bags of ice into large coolers packed with sodas.

"Do you guys need a hand?" Brandon asked.

Tony wiped his hands on his jeans. "I think we're good. Pete's gone to get more chips and dip and stuff."

A nose nuzzled around the knees of Brandon's jeans. He dropped his hand and rubbed the dog's head. "Hey, Anabelle."

Her tail thumped against the arm of the sofa.

"Actually..." Tony said.

"Yeah?"

"She's pretty stinky. I guess she could do with a bath."

"I can do that." Brandon grinned. "Come on, girl!"

He slapped his thigh and headed for the back door. Anabelle waddled after him. She was getting fat too. Man, nobody was sticking to that "No leftovers for the dog" rule.

Brandon held the back door open for her, and caught her by the collar when she finally figured out what was going on.

"You're a Labrador," he reminded her and he hauled her over toward the hose. "You *like* water."

She showed him her sad eyes.

"Don't be like that," Brandon said, and she sighed. He turned on the water, and Anabelle stood there, legs stiff and snout raised, while he hosed her down. They both turned up their noses at the dog shampoo—it smelled like apples. When had dog shampoo started to smell like people shampoo? Affluenza was so widespread it was affecting pets now. Talk about a first-world problem.

He lathered Anabelle's coat, paying attention to her ears and the base of her tail. She got lots of itches there, which the apple shampoo promised to soothe.

"You gonna make friends at the party tonight?" he asked her.

She stared stoically ahead as he rinsed her.

"Probably more than me."

Brandon was not good with people. He wasn't confident enough to walk up to someone, introduce himself, and ask to hang out. Some guys could get away with that, but Brandon wasn't one of them. If he ever tried it, he knew it would smack of desperation. But tonight he was a representative of Phi Sig and had to do his best to make the rushees feel welcome. It should have been some consolation that most of them would be just as nervous as he was, but it wasn't.

"Maybe we can go and hide in my room," he suggested to Anabelle. He pulled her towel off the peg by the hose reel and began to wipe her down. Her tail thumped against his knees. "Yeah, you like this part."

The idea of hiding in his room was way too tempting. Except he knew Deacon wouldn't let him get away with it for long. Deacon was a nice guy, and he'd looked out for Brandon ever since he'd joined Phi Sig. It rankled a little, sometimes, since Brandon knew Mark must have said something to him. Slapped a flashing neon sign on his introverted back: CAUTION: SHY! Or worse, CAUTION: MENTALLY FUCKED UP! But at least Deacon didn't make a big deal out of Brandon's shyness. Sometimes Brandon even thought Deacon liked looking out for him.

Brandon hung Anabelle's towel up again and wrapped her leash around his wrist before she raced off to roll in the dirt.

"No," he told her firmly. "Tonight you can smell like apple blossoms instead of mud."

Anabelle huffed at him mournfully.

* * * *

Two hours later Brandon was hiding in his room. He'd made it through the first hour of the Phi Sig Meet and Greet before he'd run out of things to say and gotten the hell out. He sat on his bed with a book, pretending he wasn't really hiding—he was *studying*—and he didn't really need to be downstairs at all.

Next door at the Alpha Delt house, the bass was pumping and people were cheering. Brandon rolled his eyes at the noise before the disparate threads of it joined together into a chant: *"Mark! Mark! Mark! Mark!"*

Brandon crossed the floor and stuck his head out the window, but he couldn't see anything from here except the back corner of Alpha Delt. God. He hoped Mark wasn't on the roof or something stupid.

A victorious cheer rose, and Brandon sighed with relief. Whatever dumb thing Mark had done, at least he hadn't broken his neck doing it. Yet.

A few minutes later someone knocked at the door.

"Come in."

Deacon stepped inside, holding his phone. "Did you hear that?"

"Yeah. What's he doing?"

"Surfing." Deacon sat beside him and held out his phone.

There was a blurred picture of Mark. On a surfboard. In the pool.

"And…" Deacon snorted. "Yes, we have video."

They both watched, wincing, as Mark took a run up, jumped onto the surfboard, and rode it the length of the pool as the crowd cheered him on.

"He's going to kill himself," Brandon said, at the same time as Deacon said, "Crack his head open and die."

They watched the video again.

Deacon shook his head. "You'd tell me, right, if I was being paranoid? I mean, that's an incredibly stupid thing to do, isn't it? It's not just me."

"No. It's incredibly stupid."

"I am going to kick his ass," Deacon said, then corrected himself. "*Arse.*"

Brandon grinned. Mark didn't have pet peeves so much as an entire menagerie of peeves, but first and foremost was the word *ass*. He'd been training Deacon out of its use for about a year now.

"*Look,*" he'd said last night at the bar, "*I'll eat your fries instead of chips, and I'll learn what the difference is between a gallon and a liter, and how far it takes to walk a mile instead of a kilometer, but you will never take my arse away from me. Are we clear?*"

"*I wouldn't dream of taking your arse,*" Deacon had said, while Brandon had tried to pretend the conversation wasn't happening.

Mark had sucked ketchup off his finger. "*Actually, Deke, you can take my arse whenever you like, as long as you pronounce it right.*"

Brandon had blushed as bright red as the ketchup, he was sure. Mark didn't have much of a filter. He said whatever the hell he wanted and thought he could get away with it just because he had a cool accent and a wicked smile. And most of the time he was absolutely right.

Brandon sometimes envied his friend's uninhibited nature. And then he remembered it led to riding a surfboard the length of a pool with a beer in each hand, and, following that scenario to its logical conclusion, would very probably end with a visit to the emergency room and a bunch of stitches.

Mark was crazy, which worked for him but was not Brandon's thing at all.

"Sometimes I don't even know why we're friends," he said jokingly, feeling a little uncomfortable when Deacon looked at him. Heat rose in his face. God, did Deacon think he needed his self-esteem boosted or, worse, that he was fishing for compliments? He forced a laugh. "Because he is cray-zee!"

Deacon laughed, and looked at his phone again. "Yeah," he said, like he wouldn't have it any other way. "Yeah he is."

* * * *

Brandon wasn't sure how it had happened, but somehow Deacon had managed to get him downstairs again, and suddenly he was mingling.

"Just mingle," his mother used to say, waving her hand at a full room as though it was nothing to be worried about. Her smile was a little too bright though, a little too manic, as though she was afraid he'd ruin it. Milford was a small town, and everybody knew about Brandon and Mr. Fenimore. That was the worst part. In a city, maybe Brandon could have been anonymous, but not here. Even though his name was kept out of the paper, everybody knew.

After the trial, Brandon had begged his parents to move towns, or to at least let him change schools. But his dad was the town's only optometrist, and he couldn't just pack up and go. They didn't have the money for boarding school, and they couldn't send Brandon to St. Mary's. They weren't Catholic.

Brandon would have been Catholic in a fucking heartbeat if it had meant not having to walk back into his old school. He'd gone from being a reasonably popular kid to a leper, all in the space of a few months. First he wasn't invited to birthday parties and sleepovers anymore, and then kids stopped coming to his, and somehow he became *that* kid— the one with no friends, the loner, the *loser*—all the way through until he graduated from high school.

He froze as he got caught up in a crush of people. Someone walking by put a hand on Brandon's shoulder to steady himself as he squeezed past. Nothing threatening about the touch, nothing weird; the guy's hand was there and then gone. But Brandon suddenly felt too hot. He pushed through the crowd, heading for the stairs, but as soon as he started up, he saw Tony on the landing, showing a group of rushees a video on his phone.

ALSO BY J.A. ROCK

By His Rules

Wacky Wednesday (Wacky Wednesday #1)

The Brat-tastic Jayk Parker (Wacky Wednesday #2)

Calling the Show

Take the Long Way Home

The Grand Ballast

Minotaur

The Silvers

The Subs Club (The Subs Club #1)

Pain Slut (The Subs Club #2)

Manties in a Twist (The Subs Club #3)

24/7 (The Subs Club #4)

Slave Hunt (The Subs Club #5)

"Beauties" (All in Fear anthology)

"Stranger Than Stars" (Take a Chance Anthology)

Sight Unseen: A Collection of Five Anonymous Novellas

ABOUT THE AUTHORS

Lisa Henry likes to tell stories, mostly with hot guys and happily ever afters.

Lisa lives in tropical North Queensland, Australia. She doesn't know why, because she hates the heat, but she suspects she's too lazy to move. She spends half her time slaving away as a government minion, and the other half plotting her escape.

She attended university at sixteen, not because she was a child prodigy or anything, but because of a mix-up between international school systems early in life. She studied history and English, neither of them very thoroughly.

She shares her house with too many cats, a dog, a green tree frog that swims in the toilet, and as many possums as can break in every night. This is not how she imagined life as a grown-up.

Website: www.lisahenryonline.com
Blog: http://lisahenryonline.blogspot.com.au
Twitter: https://twitter.com/LisaHenryOnline
Facebook: https://www.facebook.com/lisa.henry.1441

J.A. Rock is the author of over twenty LGBTQ romance and suspense novels, as well as an occasional contributor to HuffPo Queer Voices. J.A.'s books have received Lambda Literary, INDIE, and EPIC Award nominations, and 24/7 was named one of the best books of 2016 by *Kirkus Reviews*. J.A. lives in Chicago with an extremely judgmental dog, Professor Anne Studebaker.

Website: www.jarockauthor.com

Blog: http://jarockauthor.blogspot.com

Twitter: https://twitter.com/jarockauthor

Facebook: https://www.facebook.com/ja.rock.39

Made in the USA
Middletown, DE
30 September 2023

39640757R00186